Tempted by a Rogue Prince

Felicity Heaton

ETERNAL MATES SERIES

Kissed by a Dark Prince
Claimed by a Demon King
Tempted by a Rogue Prince
Hunted by a Jaguar (Coming in 2015)

Find out more at: www.felicityheaton.co.uk

CHAPTER 1

Desolate. Depraved. Filled with violence and darkness. Dangerous.

Vail trudged onwards, dragging his feet over the harsh, rocky black terrain, no longer sure if he was describing the bleak lands surrounding him or himself. A wry smile tugged at his dry, cracked lips, splitting his lower one. The scent of blood swirled around him, an enchanting aroma that caused saliva to pool in his parched mouth. He swept his tongue over the bitter liquid spotting his lip and imagined it to be a finer type.

One not corrupted by darkness and sin.

He had lost track of his position in the seven demon realms days or possibly weeks ago. The barren environment ran past him on repeat. Never changing. Forever the same. A grim featureless realm, devoid of colour and beauty, that left him feeling as if he had been walking in circles.

Perhaps he had.

There were holes in his memories of his unending trek across this wasteland towards nowhere in particular.

Sometimes, when the strange twilight of day gave way to the pitch black of night, replays of his time under Kordula's spell bombarded him. They pressed down on him, the crushing darkness too strong to fight, battering him until his knees gave out and all he could do was scream out his rage until his voice gave out too.

After those incidents, he found himself walking again with no recollection of how he had found his feet and started moving onwards. Everything between blacking out and coming around was blank.

Horrifyingly blank.

But worse than the times when he came around to find himself stumbling onwards, were the times he woke to find himself doing so while fresh blood rolled down his tired and sore body and dripped from the black claws of his armour.

He killed without knowing about it.

Vail chuckled mirthlessly to himself.

A sure sign he had lost his mind and was no more than a monster now.

His left foot snagged on a rock and the earth welcomed him with a hard embrace.

Vail lay face down on the black ground, each hard breath stirring dust that choked him, fighting to muster the strength to push himself up and find his feet again. He pressed his hands into the sharp rocks but his muscles turned to water and his bones ached so fiercely his head swam with the pain. He squeezed his eyes shut and focused on breathing instead, but even that was a struggle now.

He tilted his head to one side and stared at his left hand as he curled his fingers into a fist, clawing at the dirt.

He couldn't stay like this. He couldn't give up. Even when he wanted to surrender and find an eternal end to his suffering. If he stayed like this, he would fall asleep and the hold the nightmares had on him would grow stronger. Those terrible memories overwhelmed him too often now, dragging him deeper into insanity, until he found it hard to distinguish between reality and the past.

He couldn't sleep.

Vail gritted his teeth and growled as he pushed himself up, his arms shaking violently with the strain, causing his entire body to tremble and his heart to race from the effort. He snarled and kept pushing, refusing to give in to the lure of sleep. His arms gave out and he hit the dirt again. The taste of blood on his tongue mocked him. He would have been strong enough to stand if he had been feeding.

He didn't want to eat.

He didn't want to sleep.

He just wanted to keep walking.

He didn't care where, as long as it was away from his past.

Vail shoved his hands against the sharp tiny rocks and grunted as he forced himself up, not relenting this time, pushing past the pain and the fatigue, and the weakness invading him. Sweat dotted his brow and trickled down his back beneath the skin-tight scales of his black armour, and white spots winked across his vision, the exertion threatening to render him unconscious and deliver him into the arms of the mad beast waiting within him. It wanted out.

It wanted blood and violence.

Retribution.

Vail managed to make it onto his knees and slumped, his breath sawing out of his lungs and his head spinning, sending the ugly world around him twirling with it.

He clawed at the ground, bloodying his fingertips, aching for the connection to the earth that this despicable land refused to give to him.

Nature hid here, buried deep, shying away from the darkness and the demons.

He longed to feel her again, to sense her warmth flowing through him and the peace that came with being connected to her.

He shifted onto his backside, crossed his legs with effort, and laid his hands in his lap. He couldn't have the link to nature that he craved right now, but he could find a sliver of peace through a different connection.

The one with his older brother, Loren.

Vail closed his eyes as they stung, the bridge of his nose burning with them and his throat tightening. He shoved aside the pain and focused on his blood, on his brother, and lifted the barrier he normally kept in place between them, shutting Loren out and making it impossible for his brother to find him.

The connection bloomed between them like warm sunshine, infusing him with peace and calm, with the constant affection his brother held for him despite all his sins and all the pain he had caused him over the past four thousand two hundred years they had been at war.

Four thousand two hundred years in which Vail had been a slave to a dark witch, forced to do her bidding against his will, whether it was massacring innocents, igniting wars between kingdoms, attacking his brother and his people, or things that were far worse. Unmentionable.

He rubbed at his arms, subconsciously scrubbing the feel of her hands from his body, the sickening lingering touches and the caresses.

And the other things.

Cold engulfed him, darkness rising from the pit of his soul as his mind travelled black paths that led him downwards into madness. He clawed at his arms and his armour covered his fingers, transforming them into sharp serrated black claws.

Vail brought his hands up and clutched at his head, digging his claws in deep and drawing blood, using the pain in the present to battle that in his past. His fangs grew longer, stabbing into his lower lip, and his pointed ears flared back against the sides of his head.

The warmth inside him increased, chasing back the icy cold, and he trembled with relief.

Loren.

His brother was aware of him.

Reaching for him.

Tears spilled down Vail's cheeks and he held the connection between them for as long as he could without risking Loren discovering his location, savouring it and using it to ground himself and anchor him to the present. The connection grew stronger, his brother reinforcing it from thousands of miles away, flooding him with love and affection, with memories of being with Loren back in their kingdom, and then even further back, to the old elf kingdom in the mortal realm, laughing like fools as they played as children in the lush colourful gardens of the castle.

Loren.

Vail severed the connection, swiftly bringing up the barrier to shut his brother out, unable to bear any more.

He clumsily stumbled onto his feet, almost falling on his face again when his knees turned to jelly beneath him, and staggered onwards, heading for the horizon.

The gods only knew where he was going. How many days had it been since he had seen his brother?

Since he had protected his brother's sweet mate?

Since he had felt magic around him again and sensed the presence of a witch?

Vail snarled, his lips peeling back off his fangs. He should have killed her. His fingers flexed at the thought of shredding her flesh, peeling it from her bones slice by slice while she screamed for mercy. He had no mercy left in him. No goodness. No kindness. No hope. A witch had made sure of that.

A witch had made him the enemy of all her kind.

They all deserved to die.

For every life that witch had forced him to take, he would kill one of her own treacherous, vile breed. He would wipe out their entire species, freeing the realms of their trickery and magic.

His thoughts flickered back to that moment on the battlefield, when Loren had stood before him, offering his hand.

Gods, Vail had wanted to take it.

He had been so close to placing his hand into his brother's one and taking the comfort he offered, the acceptance and forgiveness.

A small part of him had even dared to hope that he could return to the castle in the elf kingdom and things could be as they were before Kordula had enslaved him and he had turned on his people, making an enemy of himself in order to protect them all from her, thwarting her plan to set herself up as their queen and enslave them all.

A fool's dream.

Vail shuffled forwards, barely able to place one foot in front of the other. His ankles wobbled with each step and his muscles screamed in protest. His stomach growled, hunger riding him hard, dragging up replays of battles where he had gorged himself on blood, making himself stronger.

He denied it, too lucid right now to give in to its demands and risk awakening the beast within him, but he knew there would come a time when he blacked out again and woke with the taste of blood on his tongue. Rather things happened that way than while he was conscious. He didn't want to remember the terrible things he did. There wasn't room in his soul for any more of them. It was filled with the hideous, despicable things he had done, so black with them that not a speck of light could penetrate it.

Turning.

Vail had seen elves turn. He had seen them degenerate into monsters, tainted by darkness, craving blood and violence.

He knew that his own turning was overdue. He should have become the embodiment of darkness millennia ago, his mind warped by the things Kordula had done to him, his soul blackened by the lives he had taken, and his body contaminated by the pleasure she had wrung from it.

Bile blazed up his throat. He collapsed onto his hands and knees and vomited, dry heaving until he shook all over and his heart laboured.

He meticulously blanked his mind, killing thought after thought, memory after memory, image after sickening image, until nothing remained but cold emptiness.

His heart settled.

He stared at the black earth and his vision swam out of focus.

He needed to stop thinking about the past. He needed to stop courting the darkness, leading it on a dance as it did the same to him, luring him ever deeper into the black abyss within his soul.

He needed to think about something else.

Vail dragged himself back onto his feet and trudged onwards, staring at the ground. He recited sonnets in his head, filling it with words to keep the shadows at bay.

The terrain grew hilly, challenging his limited strength on every ascent and his ability to maintain his balance on the descents.

At some point, he crossed a border.

Vail became aware of it the moment three large bare-chested demon males teleported in front of him. Warriors. They were mostly human in appearance, but the painted black tips of the grey horns that curled from behind their ears and their vivid green eyes warned him that he had wandered into dangerous territory.

The Fifth Realm.

The three demons advanced.

Vail stood his ground. There was little point in running, and he didn't have the strength left to teleport or call his swords to him. He couldn't even muster a telekinetic blast to drive them away from him.

They eyed him suspiciously.

The largest of them, a black-haired brute with a thick scar that cut a diagonal line across his muscular bare chest, stepped forwards and curled his lip.

"Elf."

Vail bit back his desire to point out that the male was stating the obvious. No other creature in Hell shared the appearance of an elf, and none other had the black armour he wore.

His fangs itched with a need to sink into their flesh. It wouldn't appease his hunger. Demon blood tasted wretched. Toxic.

The darkness in him began to push, filling his head with visions of attacking these three males. They couldn't give him life through their blood, but they could give him something far sweeter. Something that had eluded him for so long now.

Death.

He snarled and launched himself at the leader, slamming into him and knocking him back into the other two. They immediately attacked him, pummelling him with powerful blows that only served to unleash his hunger for violence and bloodshed, giving it free rein. He turned and took on the weakest of the three, slashing across his chest with his claws and raking them down his arms, cleaving flesh and spilling blood. He laughed as the scent of it drove him onwards, pushing his fatigue to the back of his mind.

The demon blocked his next strike and delivered one of his own, a powerful punch that cracked the left side of Vail's jaw and snapped his head to his right. His vision wobbled and pain blazed a path across his face, numbing it. The demon struck him again, harder this time, and Vail's knees crumpled beneath him. Darkness encroached at the corners of his mind.

He shook it off and tried to shove to his feet, but large hands clamped down on his shoulders, two on each, and the third male grabbed his arms. Vail cried out as the leader twisted his arms behind his back, almost popping his shoulders out of their sockets with the force of his actions.

"We take him and put him with the others," the leader growled in the demon tongue behind him. "The king will be pleased we have an elf. He will want to question him about the war and the Third Realm."

They thought he was part of Loren's army that had attended the war between the Third and Fifth Realms on the side of the Third, under the banner of King Thorne.

Vail struggled but it was useless. His strength gave way before he could wrestle himself free. The darkness rose within him again, the mad beast snarling for freedom, caged by his weak body just when he would have embraced it and used it to escape and goad these demons into killing him.

A black hole appeared beneath him and he dropped into it with the demons still holding him. They teleported him into a dark stone room that smelled of fetid things, the odour so foul that it choked his lungs.

"You think we should remove his armour?" one said and Vail growled and used all of his limited strength to fight their hold.

"It needs to go. He's dangerous with it on." The leader this time.

Vail shook his head and refused to relinquish it as the three demons set to work on him, trying to slip their fingers into the neck of the black scale-like armour. He snarled and mentally commanded it to form his helm, forcing their hands off him as the scales crawled up his neck. They thickened and smoothed as they covered the back of his head and chased across his forehead, forming a point above his nose and then sweeping back over the top of his head into a series of curved spikes that flared backwards like dragon horns.

"Get it off him." The leader released his arms and pulled at his helmet, jerking his head with the force of his attempts.

Vail snapped and lashed out at him, catching him across his chest with his claws, adding more scars.

He wouldn't let them take his armour. It was his only protection right now when he was so weak. As wrecked as it was because he didn't have the strength to repair it, his claws were still intact and he needed this small connection to his people. His armour was his talisman. He had never been without it. He had always cherished it. It was his sole connection to his past.

To better days.

It kept him sane.

The leader grabbed a heavy black club and swung it at him. It connected hard with his left arm, fracturing the bone. One of the others followed his leader, picking up another of the clubs. Vail ground his teeth and desperately blocked their blows, snarling through his fangs as they beat him, stripping away the last of his strength as his tired body began to give out under the pain and damage.

The third demon, the one he had mercilessly clawed, punched him square in the face, breaking his nose. Blood streamed over his lips. His vision distorted. No. He couldn't pass out. He couldn't give in.

His mental link to his armour fragmented. He managed to muster the strength to call a pair of black trousers to encase his lower half before the scales peeled away, rapidly running over his body, and disappeared into the twin black and silver metal bands around his wrists.

Vail collapsed onto the dirty slick stone flags, a black void rising up to swallow him.

The last thing he heard was the leader ordering the others to take him to the cells and have him healed.

Healed.

He snarled, but barely squeezed the sound out from between his bloodied lips before he sank into the black void, into nightmares filled with horrific replays of Kordula and the cruelty she had inflicted upon him, a torture of mind, body and soul.

Vail swore an oath.

If this healer was a sorceress...

He would kill her.

CHAPTER 2

Rosalind stared at the unconscious male lying on the stone slab in the middle of the cell. Torchlight from the corridor beyond the thick metal bars lining one side of the dank windowless room flickered across his battered and bruised body, darkening every ugly mark and deep gash, and all the blood that stained him.

Was it his or had he hurt the bastard demons who had put him here?

She liked to think he had given them hell. Mostly because she couldn't.

He hadn't stirred in the five minutes she had been kneeling beside him, transfixed by the sight of him. He lay as if dead. Only the slight rise and fall of his chest was indication otherwise.

His hands rested on his stomach, his wrists bound by the same heavy metal cuffs that held hers. She wanted to find whoever had discovered this metal and how to impregnate it with a spell and blast them to hell. The manacles weakened her, stripping her of her powers. The only one available to her was the ability to heal, and she only had that one because the new Fifth King of the demons had given it back to her so she could heal all of the warriors who had been injured in the war with the Third King.

A war the Fifth Realm had lost when the old Fifth King had lost his head.

A war she had fought in on the side of King Thorne of the Third Realm.

A war that had changed her forever.

Since returning her ability to cast healing magic, the new Fifth King had used her whenever he had needed someone fixed, forcing her to do his bidding, and up until today, all of her patients had been demons belonging to his army.

But this man was no demon.

Her knees ached from pressing into the damp uneven stone floor but she couldn't take her eyes off him. He radiated dark energy that warned her away, telling her that he was dangerous, even as she felt drawn to him, snared by an unbreakable pull towards him.

Shuffling caught her attention and she looked across the unconscious man to the cell opposite his. A handsome man with long dark brown hair flecked with gold tied back with a thong and an unkempt beard leaned against the thick stone wall close to the bars of that cell, as bare-chested as her companion, although his skin was flawless with the exception of the fae markings that tracked up his arms and over his shoulders.

An incubus.

Rosalind muttered a protection spell beneath her breath, even though it wouldn't work. It was a habit with her. She preferred to arm herself against an incubus's charms before he could use them on her, luring her under his spell and having his way with her. Code of honour, her arse. These men pretended in public that they upheld their vow to never use their powers to seduce a woman who didn't want to be seduced, but in private they employed those powers without a flicker of regret or care about their victim. She had seen it.

The man eyed her patient, blue and gold spotting his green irises, a sign of his incubus nature as much as the markings that announced his lineage.

"Let him die," the man said, his voice a low growl of warning without a shred of compassion, and the swirls, dashes and spikes of his fae markings shimmered in hues of dark blue and burnished gold. Not anger. She knew that an incubus's markings flared crimson and obsidian when they were angry. Judging by the look in his green eyes, this was something more like apprehension.

Why?

Rosalind glared at him and flicked her knotted blonde hair over her shoulder in defiance. "It isn't in my nature to ignore the needs of another, especially if I feel I can help them, and I do feel I can help this man."

He was gaunt though, sick and not from his injuries. His skin was sallow and grey, and he was too thin, the bones visible in the backs of his dirty hands. Many of his nails were cracked, caked with grime and dried blood.

"Let him die," the incubus whispered. "This one isn't worth saving, Little Girl."

Rosalind turned her glare on him again. "Why do you say such nasty things? Do you know him?"

The incubus dropped his green gaze to the man, narrowed it, and then shifted it back to her. "Only by reputation, and if I were in your place, I would kill him and not save him. By killing him, you could be saving many lives, one this man may take if you allow him to live."

Rosalind looked at the man in question, a cold heavy feeling pulling her insides down. She knew he was dangerous, but she knew nothing else about him. She didn't know the incubus from Adam either, and for all she did know, he could be a compulsive liar or a sadistic bastard itching to get a hit of pleasure from watching her kill an innocent man.

She lifted her hand with the intent of touching her patient's arm and funnelling a spell into him to sense whether the incubus was telling the truth about him, and remembered that such spells were beyond her right now. Locked away. She had never been without her magic. It was unsettling, strange, and left her feeling vulnerable.

The man on the cold stone slab before her twitched and moaned, the sound strained and filled with agony that tore at her and compelled her to help him.

"I don't have power over this man's life," she whispered to him in reply to the incubus, her eyes fixed on his face, taking in the dark circles beneath his eyes and the hollows of his cheeks. "I don't have the right to choose whether he lives or dies."

"Because the demons told you to heal him?" the incubus said.

"No." Rosalind shook her head and looked across at him. "Because it isn't in my nature to do such a thing. I will heal him."

The man scoffed. "And you will live to regret it, Little Girl."

"I'm not a girl. I'm over one hundred years old… and do I look like a girl to you?" Rosalind stood and ran her hands down her tattered black dress, the traditional garb of a witch on duty.

The incubus's eyes followed them, the blue and gold in his irises increasing, and he muttered, "No."

He turned away, pressing his bare back against the bars of his cell and revealing the twin lines of markings where they joined between his shoulders and formed a line down his back that ended in a diamond above the waist of his low-slung black jeans.

At least he would be quiet now. She hoped. Healing always required focus, and something told her that this time it would need the highest level of concentration she could manage.

Something else told her that the incubus might be right. She might regret healing this man. If he was as dangerous as he felt, he might well kill her upon waking.

But maybe that would be what she deserved after the things she had done.

She had vowed to protect lives, to do all in her power to tend to people's needs, and she had been protecting lives in the war between the Third and Fifth Realms, but she had also been taking them.

If this man was a killer and deserved death because of it, then surely she deserved the same fate in order to maintain the balance and order of the world?

She closed her eyes against the memories that welled up, lashing at her. She hated that she now knew how to kill. She hated knowing she was capable of that darkness. It scared her.

She feared becoming like her sister, a dark witch drawing on the shadowy other side for her power—the realm of death.

But worse than that, she feared that now she knew how to kill, she could do it again if she had to, and next time it would be easier.

Rosalind opened her eyes and focused on the man in front of her, on the present rather than the past or what might lay ahead in her future.

The aura of danger clinging to him was growing stronger. He was healing himself. Was he one of the warriors from the war? If he was, what side had he fought on and what species was he?

The only way to find out the answers to those questions was to complete the task she had been sent here to do.

She blew out her breath and held her hands over his bare chest. As she lowered them, bringing them almost into contact with his skin, she channelled the only power available to her into him, seeking out his wounds and fixing them as best she could. There were so many.

Her power drained quickly and she had to take regular breaks to avoid overtaxing herself and passing out. She didn't want to lose consciousness in a cell with this dangerous stranger, not when she didn't have the power to protect herself.

The fast drain on her power confirmed something for her though. This man's injuries and wounds ran deeper than those of the flesh that she could see. He was weak for a reason, whether that was a sickness of the body or of the mind.

His eyelids fluttered and she withdrew her hands again, her breath lodging in her throat as she waited. His long black lashes lifted, revealing steel-blue eyes. His dilated pupils swiftly narrowed and his hands shot up above his head. He snarled at the cuffs and pulled his wrists apart, tugging the chain between them taut. He heaved harder, his muscles tensing and rippling beneath his bloodstained pale skin, and growled when the chain didn't break.

"They dampen our powers," she said.

His gaze darted to her and narrowed, steel blue-grey that burned into her, sending a fierce shiver of awareness through her that drew every drop of her focus to him. What species was he? Vampire? Werewolf? Both of them had a human appearance and she had met many of their kind in the past, but none had affected her as this man did.

He struggled harder against his bonds and the metal sliced into his wrists, spilling blood down his arms. It didn't stop him from fighting the restraints.

"Stop!" Rosalind snapped, her voice echoing around the stone cells.

He turned a murderous glare on her and flexed his fingers. His demeanour changed instantly, becoming distraught as his eyes went to his wrists and he flexed his fingers again. Over and over. He did it at least ten times before he began to growl and try harder, struggling against his bonds at the same time. Was something supposed to happen whenever he flexed his fingers?

He kept trying, clearly convinced that if he just kept doing it, whatever he was expecting would happen.

It wouldn't.

She could sympathise. After the demons of the Fifth Realm had captured her during the battle and she had awoken in her cell, she had tried for hours to blast the bars and every demon who had strolled along the corridor and smirked at her.

She had been convinced that she could find the trick to get around the spell embedded into the metal.

This man was too.

His eyes went glassy and he sagged against the stone bench, his cuffed wrists dropping and slamming hard into his heaving chest.

Rosalind inched closer.

The man managed to slide his gaze her way, and passed out.

She sighed, carefully moved his hands back down to his stomach, and went back to work. She held one hand over his forehead and the other above his heart, closed her eyes, and shut the world out as she channelled as much energy as she could spare into him.

"Let him die," the incubus whispered, a seductive proposition when healing the man was weakening her, leaving her more vulnerable than ever.

She lifted her head and gave the incubus a sorrowful smile. "I cannot. I must heal him. I took a vow."

His expression turned solemn. "I understand the power of a vow, but if he wakes and kills you, I will say I told you so."

She smiled properly for the first time in weeks. "I can take that."

The incubus smiled too and muttered in the fae tongue. "We're all fucked if he wakes up."

Rosalind ignored that, sure that he knew she could understand the fae tongue since most witches could speak the language as they worked closely with his kind. He was doing it on purpose to distract her from her work. One tiny mistake and she could kill her patient.

She had to maintain rigid control over her healing spell. They were dangerous, with a tendency to go awry if the controlling witch's link to it broke.

Awry being a polite way of saying inflicting crippling pain on the patient by attempting to heal anything and everything, even functioning organs and joints, before it fizzled out.

When she had no more energy to expend, she sat back on her heels and her shoulders sagged as she wiped the sweat from her brow with the back of her hand. He was looking better, but was nowhere close to being healed. She couldn't do anything more for him right now. She needed to rest until her strength returned, and then she would begin again.

She stared at him, the incubus's warning ringing in her tired mind.

Who was this dangerous and deadly male?

She willed him to wake and tell her.

She wanted to know him.

CHAPTER 3

Pain. It tore at him. Shredded his flesh. Smashed his bones. Devoured his soul. Blood. He needed it. Ached for it. Hungered. Darkness. It consumed him.

A floral scent swept around him, invading his senses, driving back the darkness and the agony. Nature. He was somewhere green and verdant, beautiful and soothing. He could see it in his buzzing mind, and could see it for himself if he could just get his eyes open.

He yearned to run his fingers through the tall meadow grass. He longed to lift the wild blooms to his nose and inhale their delicate fragrance. He needed to lay beneath the mighty oak and let the dappled sunlight play across his tired body as the melody of the branches swaying filled his mind. He wanted to breathe deep of it all and let it fill his soul with light.

Vail forced his eyes open, filled with a hunger to see the nature that brought with it such a sweet, enticing scent.

Black stone greeted his eyes. The rank odour of mould overshadowed the soft floral fragrance.

A dream?

Had he been dreaming of nature, a fantasy so real that it had crossed over into reality? He couldn't recall the last time he had dreamed. Nightmares were his constant companion. Never dreams.

But there was no nature in his dark damp cell. No sunshine. No flowers. No meadow grass.

No beauty.

"You're awake." The voice was female, edged with a quaver that spoke of fear, and a sense of familiarity.

He shifted his eyes down to her. Beauty and nature stood over him and he saw blue skies in her eyes and sunshine in the spun gold of her hair. A faint scent of wild roses clung to her. He didn't remember her, or did he? It was hazy. Her face seemed familiar.

"Remain still," she said and he complied only because he wasn't sure he could move, not even to snap her neck or tear her throat out with his fangs.

Why would he do such a thing to the delicate little wild rose?

She trembled, her shoulders shaking so violently that her matted fair hair tumbled off them and down her front.

He wanted to reach out and sweep that hair back into place.

Vail became aware of the cold heaviness of manacles around his wrists.

Hazy things started coming back to him, slowly gaining focus in his weary mind. The demons had done this to him. He was sure of that. He recalled the fight and wanting death, and waking to this female. He recalled her saying he was bound.

They had him chained and had a female in his cell.

She was a trap.

Crushing weight pressed down on his chest and his throat clogged. They had sent her in to hurt him.

To abuse him.

He snarled and fought his bonds, desperately trying to break the chain between them. He was stronger now, although he didn't know why. Power flowed through him, strength he hadn't felt in as long as he could remember. He used all of it on the restraints, bowing off the cold stone slab as he fought them.

"Please keep still." She reached out to touch him.

To lay her hands on his flesh.

Vail bared his fangs at her and rolled off the slab, hitting the floor hard enough to knock the air from his lungs. He kicked off, scrambling as he attempted to rise to his feet and placing as much distance between them as he could manage.

"Keep away," he said in English, using her tongue.

She shot to her feet and he growled at her, flashing his fangs in warning again.

"I cannot," she barked and took a step towards him. "If I don't heal you, they'll punish me!"

Fear shone in her blue eyes. Eyes that implored him to believe her as she took another hesitant step towards him. Her arms shifted, coming forwards, and metal rattled. His gaze dropped to her wrists and he blinked.

She wore the same heavy cuffs as he, and had worn them for some time judging by her scarred wrists. A foreign sensation bolted through him on seeing the pale streaks of silver and red on her delicate skin. A need that he didn't understand.

He felt compelled to take her hand in his and smooth his fingers over the scars, as if that action could erase the ugly marks of her captivity and restore her flawless skin.

He had no such power, not over flesh and bone. Not anymore. He had forsaken it long ago when he had severed his connection to his people and his powers had withered over the endless centuries since then.

And he had no reason to desire to use it on this female.

"Please?" she whispered and he lifted his gaze back to meet hers. "I have to heal you."

A healer.

What species was she? Many could heal and many of those appeared human.

Including witches.

He growled at her, unable to stop himself, a reaction to that word that would stay with him until death finally embraced him. She didn't flinch away.

She bravely stood her ground this time, although her heart missed several beats and he sensed the fear she held buried deep within her.

Not only fear of him. She feared the demons too. And something else.

Something unknown to him, but something he needed to understand. He wasn't sure why. It ran deep in his blood, a compulsion he couldn't comprehend and that made no sense to him. It tied him in knots, twisting his insides, making him feel useless and weak.

Cursed female.

He narrowed his gaze on her, studying her delicate features and the way she held herself, drinking in everything about her, searching for a clue as to the reason for his strange reactions to her. Perhaps they had drugged him. It was all a ploy to weaken him and lure him into her trap. They wanted to watch her bring him to his knees. They would laugh as he suffered at her hands.

They were attempting to play on his compassion, but that had been their mistake.

He had no compassion left.

It had been wrung out of him thousands of years ago.

"Please?" she said again and gestured to the slab. "I'm not going to hurt you. I just have to heal you."

He didn't want to lay on it and allow her to touch him. He didn't want her hands on him. Caressing. Fondling. Groping. He snarled and flashed his fangs again, and she shrank back, a little gasp escaping her.

"I would do as she asks, Mate. She isn't going to hurt you, but if she doesn't do as ordered, the demons *will* hurt her." The deep male voice was little more than a snarl and Vail cast a glance off to his left.

A male with long dark hair streaked with gold occupied the cell opposite his, casually leaning against the thick deep grey stone wall. Green eyes locked with Vail's, holding him fast. Fae markings tracked up the male's arms, flushed with blood red and ash black, a sign of aggression. He was handsome too, despite the thick dark beard. He folded his arms across his muscular bare chest, the twin cuffs he wore clanking and filling the heavy silence, but they had no chain between them.

If this male spoke the truth, then she did too, and the guards would punish her for her failure. Vail pressed his hands against the sides of his head, dug his fingers through his blue-black hair and clawed his scalp, raking his nails over it. Gods, he missed his claws. He missed his armour. He needed it back. It was the only thing that could ground him.

The male pushed away from the wall and moved to the bars. He wrapped his hands around them and his gaze slid to the female. Lingering. Possessing.

Vail bared his fangs and hissed at him, barely maintaining the human appearance of his eyes and ears. He had to hold on to his veil. He couldn't let these people know what he was. Who he was.

The man shrugged and kept staring at the female. "I warned you, Little Girl. You play with vipers and you'll get bitten."

"And I told you I will never leave someone to suffer if I can help them," she snapped and folded her arms across her chest. "Stay out of this, Incubus."

The male muttered something in the fae tongue and shoved his hands into the pockets of his dirty black jeans.

The female cast a scowl at him and bit out something in the same language.

Vail had long ago forgotten it. It had become useless to him after he and Loren had decided to save their people by moving them from the violent mortal world to the realm of Hell. No one spoke fae down here in this shadowy realm, and he had not left the elf kingdom in centuries.

No. That wasn't true. He had left it. He had turned his back on it. He had to remember that. He had gone to war with his own people.

All had forsaken him.

But not Loren.

Vail returned to the bench and sagged onto it, his heart heavy and aching behind his ribs. Loren had kept trying to save him. Why? Why hadn't his brother given up on him? Gods, he had wanted him to. He had pleaded every god of his species to make his brother leave him and forget about him. The gods hadn't listened to him. He had tried forcing his brother to end his fool's crusade to save him and save himself instead. Loren had refused.

What had he ever done to deserve such a brother?

He had murdered thousands. He had destroyed lands. He had ignited wars. He had done unspeakable things.

He didn't deserve forgiveness, so why did a sliver of his heart cling to the hope it might be his?

The female stopped in front of him and he looked up at her, caught off guard by her sudden appearance and unable to mask his pain before she saw it. Her incredible blue eyes reflected it back at him, laced it with compassion that he couldn't bear.

He closed his eyes, shutting her out, and lay back on the cold slab, no longer caring what she did to him. Loren would never give up. Vail had given up centuries ago.

His beloved brother was so much stronger than he could ever become.

The female dropped to her knees beside him and he tried not to squirm under her attention. He clenched his hands together and battled his instincts and the need to harm her. It wasn't Kordula. He opened his eyes and stared at her when his mind refused to believe that, forcing himself to see that the one tending to his wounds was someone else. Someone with compassion. Someone beautiful.

This little wild rose was nothing like the dark witch who had driven him mad by degrees, destroying every part of him and building a monster in its place.

"What species are you?" the female whispered and eyed his mouth. "Are you a vampire?"

Vail snarled at her again, exposing his fangs, and didn't answer her. He needed his strength and was using what he had to keep his veil in place while she healed him. It was difficult to maintain mortal eye colour and the human appearance of his ears while she was funnelling power into him, causing spasms in parts of his body, making him twitch and sending pain ricocheting along his nerves.

"Did you serve on King Thorne's side in the war?"

He stared blankly at her as memories swirled together in his mind, a mixed up replay of that battle. He had seen Olivia in danger and had lost his head, had slipped into a killing rage and destroyed any who had dared to come near her.

He would have killed King Thorne too if Loren hadn't appeared.

The sound of his brother's voice had grounded him together with his presence, the comforting sense of him standing nearby. Loren had brought him back from the abyss, giving him a reprieve, like a shaft of purest sunlight penetrating the blackest boiling storm clouds.

His silence didn't deter the female.

"Did you fight there and were captured like me?"

His eyes narrowed in suspicion on her. "You are no warrior."

She was too slender. Too weak and fragile. Captivity hadn't stripped her of muscle and physical strength. She had always been this way. Slender. Delicate. Not a warrior.

The effort of lifting a sword would most likely see her falling flat on her face from the weight of it.

She shook her head, her blonde locks dancing across her shoulders. "I drove the witches back. I was taking down a few demons with my spells when they grabbed me."

Witches.

Spells.

Vail batted her hands away from him and growled at her.

His head swam, the cell turning with it, and he blinked hard, trying to focus on her as pain tore through his body, her healing spell going haywire inside him without her to control it. Witches. Spells.

Witch.

"*Witch.*" He flexed his fingers, filled with a black need to wrap his hands around her throat.

The sharp sound of metal on metal shattered the thick silence and two demon males prowled into the cell. Vail fought the agony eating away at him as he lay on the stone slab and silently bared his fangs at the witch. A stay of execution. When she next crossed his path, he would kill her.

The males grabbed her and he took satisfaction from her gasp and the frightened looks she cast at the demons towering over her.

"Time is up. You did not manage your task," one male said, a grim smile tugging at his lips as he raked his gaze over her. "You must be punished."

She immediately reached for Vail, abject fear in her round blue eyes. It drove the darkness from him and something compelled him to rise from the hard slab and punish the demons who meant to harm her. He tried to move, wanted to snag her wrist and pull her to him, needed to protect her but every cell in his body screamed in agony. He was too weak.

He had been too weak to stop these vile creatures from stealing his armour and now he was too weak to protect the female. He was the vile one. Despicable. Pathetic. He had given up and now he needed to fight.

He wouldn't let them take her from him.

The two males roughly dragged her past him.

"Leave her," Vail yelled and tried to move again.

He managed to fall from the slab this time, landing on his belly, and fumbled for one of the demon's ankles. The male was too strong for him and easily broke free of his grip on his boot.

The female fought them, a wild feral creature as she clawed and kicked, and even attempted to bite them. She flailed in their grip, fear etched on her delicate features, terror that dug sharp claws into Vail's heart and tore at it. They chuckled at her futile attempts to harm them.

They would pay for that.

Vail forced himself to move, refusing to let pain cripple him and stop him from reaching her. He would fight the limits of his body and his mind and wouldn't stop until he passed out or death embraced him. He would bleed himself dry and destroy himself if only it would save her.

He crawled across the grimy damp dark flagstones towards the cell door, driven to reach her and unable to ignore the instinct to protect her that ran deep in his blood.

Little Wild Rose.

The demons slammed the cell door in his face. He tried to teleport to the other side but nothing happened. He cursed the cuffs binding him and banged them against the bars, desperate to reach her, the need so intense that it overwhelmed him and brought the darkness within him swiftly rising to the surface.

They dragged her out of sight and Vail roared his anger, eliciting whimpers from the occupants of several of the cells surrounding him.

The female shrieked in agony, the sound sending a chill skating over his arms and down his spine, and igniting his rage.

He was only vaguely aware of the world as he snapped the chain between the manacles, launched to his feet and attacked the magically reinforced bars of his cell, filled with a primal need to reach and protect the female.

His Little Wild Rose.

CHAPTER 4

Rosalind sat in the corner of her cell, staring blankly at the wall opposite her, her focus turned away from herself and her surroundings. She had fixed it on the man when the guards had dragged her back to her cell and dumped her into it, leaving her to curl up on the cold stone floor and fight the pain pulling her to pieces. Threatening to shatter her completely.

The moment she had thought about him, some of that pain had faded. He kept it at bay together with her fear. She didn't know how, or what power he had that allowed him to do such a thing, and she didn't care. All she cared about was shutting out the pain while she healed and the memories of the whip. She flinched away from thoughts of it and focused on the man again.

He was handsome, despite his gaunt appearance. His tall body was too lean, as if ravaged by hunger, leaving his bones on display beneath his dirty skin, but there was strength there still, a hint that he would outshine the incubus if he fed and put on muscle and fat again.

But he also held darkness within him that outshone the darkness in any male she had met before him, even the cruel demon king of this realm. He was violent and dangerous. A wild beast in the form of a man.

And the whole cellblock had heard it during her punishment.

The thunderous bellows of rage that had echoed around the dungeon as the guards had cut her back to ribbons with the whip had been his. He had gone into some sort of rage. Because of her?

Her last moments with him offered her little in the way of understanding him. He had snarled 'witch' at her as if it were a curse word, and the vilest one available to him.

She hadn't liked how he had looked at her either, cold and detached, yet calculating, as if he had been plotting terrible, painful things for her. Things far worse than the guards had done. There had been a wildness in his steel-blue eyes, a dark malevolence that promised pain and suffering. But all the while his expression had remained calm, placid, and unreadable. Only his eyes and his aura had given away his dark intentions. The steady current of danger he constantly radiated had reached startling heights and her magic had wanted to rise to protect her.

She had wanted to run from him and never look back.

But when the guards had come to take her, he had been a different man. He had turned all of that violence and darkness on the demons instead, and had looked at her with eyes that left her feeling he had wanted to protect her.

Mother earth, the whole affair confused the hell out of her, but she did feel certain of one thing.

He despised witches.

Rosalind hugged her knees to her chest and winced. One of the demons had busted a few ribs. Bastard. She felt them and wished she could heal them, but the demon king had made sure that she couldn't use her power on herself. She had discovered that after her first beating. If she tried to use it on herself, she only experienced agony, fire that burned her bones to ashes and left her even weaker than before.

He had also put a stop to her rather poor attempt at escaping. She had been healing one of his warriors in the infirmary when she had accidently lost her connection to the spell, leaving the demon in crippling pain. She had then touched every demon she could before they realised what was happening, unleashing a healing spell into each of them and then severing her link with it. It had been working, demons dropping like flies around her, and then she had discovered a massive flaw in her brilliant plan.

She had turned to escape through the arched doorway and found herself facing a dark witch.

The witch had gone to town on her, battering her with spells that she had no way of countering or protecting against. Before Rosalind had lost consciousness, the blonde witch had loomed over her and told her it was payback for her sisters.

Rosalind had slipped into nightmarish replays of killing the witches on the side of the Fifth King, seeing their deaths over and over again in gory detail.

She shuddered and weakly rubbed her arms, her manacles clanking with each sweep of her hands.

If the black-haired man despised witches, he wasn't going to be very happy when he discovered the Fifth King had a whole harem of them living in the castle above.

Rosalind crawled to the bars of her cell with effort, each shuffling inch forwards causing agony to ripple through her. She collapsed into the right corner and leaned her head against the cold bars, breathing hard as she stared left along the corridor towards the man's cell.

Her head swam, pain and hunger combining to turn it light and spin her thoughts together into a blur. She tried to focus on the man again, letting everything else drop away.

Why did he despise her kind so much?

Heavy footsteps sounded along the corridor at her back, coming from the direction of the dungeon's torture chamber.

The thick leather boots stopped outside her cell and she managed to tip her head back and look up the towering height of their owner. The dark-haired demon stared down at her, his emerald eyes devoid of feeling, filled with cold indifference.

"Your healing is needed," he said in a gruff, deep voice, and opened her cell door.

Who needed to be healed? One of the demons? She was too afraid to mention to this man that she was too weak from her punishment to be of use to him. She doubted she could muster the power to heal anyone right now.

The demon grabbed her roughly by her arm and hauled her onto her feet. He dragged her from her cell and along the dank corridor, moving too swiftly for her legs to keep up. She gave up trying to walk and let him pull her along, her bare toes bouncing off the gaps between the stone flags and her body hanging limp from his strong hand.

Only one guard. If she could channel her healing power into him, she could take him down. She might be able to escape. She almost laughed at that, the flicker of hope in her heart quickly dying. She couldn't walk, let alone run. She was never escaping this hell.

She wasn't powerful enough without her magic. These demons were one hundred times stronger than she was on the best of days. In a physical fight against one, she would last less than a second.

How strong would the man be when he healed?

He should be better by now. She had flooded him with all the healing spells she could manage, and the highest level ones available to her. It struck her that they were heading in the direction of his cell. She could sneak a glance at him on her way past to the infirmary at the end of the corridor.

Rosalind stared ahead, her eyes fixed on his cell to her right as they approached it.

The demon stopped outside it and her eyes widened in horror.

What had happened to him?

The man's injuries were worse than ever, and his wrists bore a new set of cuffs, heavier ones that had been bolted to the end of the stone slab where he lay. They had shackled his ankles too.

And was one of the steel bars of the cell bent?

Her demon escort opened the door to the man's cell and shoved her inside. Rosalind looked around it, unable to believe her eyes. There were deep bloodstained grooves in the stone walls beside the bars. Her eyes darted to his fingers. His nails were gone, broken off, leaving scabbed tips behind.

He had attacked the walls of his cell when they had taken her and during her punishment. Why?

A soft noise reached her ears and she stared down at him. Not unconscious as she had thought. He muttered things in an unknown tongue.

"You will stay until the moonrise. The king wants him lucid for questioning. Do not fail this time." The guard slammed the cell door and stalked away.

The moon in this realm was the weird light that emanated from the portal the elves used to bring sunshine into their kingdom. When that light shone in the seven demon realms, it meant it was daylight there, but the demons in this realm thought of it as the moon. It meant night to them.

She had most of the day to heal him.

21

Rosalind ran an assessing gaze over him. His injuries were extensive, and all self-inflicted, but she didn't think they were the reason he was in this strange state of limbo between unconsciousness and consciousness. It wasn't a physical problem. It was a mental one.

He writhed on the slab, his muttering growing darker, vicious sounding snarls that barely resembled words. What language did he speak? It wasn't the fae tongue.

She ventured a step closer to him and he lost his restlessness, growing very still. Could he sense her?

Was he lying in wait to attack her when she came close enough?

She kept some distance between them as she rounded the slab, her gaze fixed on him the whole time, monitoring him for a sign he might attack her. He began writhing again, fitful jerking movements that rattled the chains that held him pinned to the slab with his arms above his head, stretched out like a piece of meat on a butcher's block.

Bastard demons.

The male snarled low in his throat, as if he knew her thoughts and seconded them. He looked so savage coated in dried blood and dirt, and felt more dangerous than ever. She flicked a glance at the bent steel bar and the grooves in the solid stone. More dangerous than she had thought possible.

Rosalind kneeled beside him on the stone flags.

He snarled again, his eyes rolling back in his head as he sniffed, inhaling deeply. He rocked his hips and her cheeks heated. He was growing hard in his wrecked black trousers. She averted her eyes, pretending she hadn't noticed, and diligently kept her eyes away from that area of his anatomy, not wanting to ponder why he had reacted in such a way to her scent.

She reached out to touch his bloodstained hands. He growled and grew more restless, twisting on the stone slab and pulling at his restraints.

"Shh," she whispered, unsure whether he could hear her and whether speaking to him was wise when he was in this condition.

Would her presence and the sound of her voice make him better, or worse?

He hated witches. He had looked at her with murder in his eyes.

She couldn't leave him though or let him continue to suffer, and it wasn't because she was a captive in this cell with him or the orders the demon had given her. The sight of him suffering, lost in whatever strange place had hold of him, caused an ache in her chest that compelled her to help him.

"I won't hurt you. I swear it." She reached out to touch his hands and he hissed at her, flashing fangs. She barely dodged his attack, falling backwards as he launched his head forwards, his teeth clacking as they struck each other and not her flesh.

He grew wild, bucking off the slab and yanking on the manacles that bound his wrists. She wanted to reach for him but instinct held her back, warned her to let him wear himself out. He had tried to bite her. Mother earth. She covered her mouth with her hand and stared at him, her heart developing a new ache.

What dark power gripped him that he would attack her when she was only trying to help him?

He began to settle again, his movements becoming less frantic, weaker as his strength faded.

"I will not hurt you. I know you can hear me. I am only going to heal you." Rosalind moved back to her knees beside him and swallowed hard.

He slumped onto the bench, the tangled threads of his black hair sticking to the sweat on his brow.

He looked fragile, but she wasn't going to let that deceive her. This man was deranged.

What sort of male could have not only moved with her healing spell ricocheting through his body and all the injuries that had remained, but managed to find the strength to bend thick steel bars and rake deep grooves into solid stone with only his nails?

Not a sane one.

Many of the dungeon's residents had been here long enough to have gone mad and were normally noisy at night, but last night they had been silent while this man had raged.

They had feared he would escape. The guards had feared too, exchanging meaningful glances as they punished her.

She had feared too.

This male had come here insane.

What was he?

She had thought vampire before, but now she wasn't so sure.

Rosalind reached slowly towards him. His lips were bloodstained too, a dark spot of it gathered by the corner of his hard mouth. Had he tried to bite the bars, or had the guards struck him to subdue him?

His eyes flicked open and locked on her.

She tensed, her heart pounding, fear pressing her to withdraw her hand before he attacked her. She kept it hovering in the air between them, refusing to let him bully her into shrinking away from him.

"Hello again," she whispered, keeping still and giving him time to adjust to her presence. He continued to stare at her, deep into her eyes, his blue-grey ones flat and dull. Lifeless. "They brought me to heal you. It seems you, um, hurt yourself."

He exhaled softly and blinked. A good sign? Mother earth, she hoped so.

She hadn't expected him to remain calm on hearing her voice. She had expected another replay of him attempting to break free of his bonds, most likely so he could kill her.

"I need to touch you to heal you."

No response.

During her time alone in her cell after her punishment, she had mulled over their entire first encounter, and had concluded that he hated anyone touching him. She had been entertaining theories about it all day. It wasn't because she was a witch. He hadn't known that at the time.

"Can I touch you?" She wasn't willing to risk her limbs by attempting to do such a thing without his consent.

He clenched his fists and gave a curt nod.

Rosalind took it as a green light, noting that he had steeled himself, mentally preparing for her touch.

She shuffled closer, biting down on her tongue when her ribs protested and each mark on her back burned beneath her black dress.

"Harmed you?" he croaked, his voice gravelly and deep. His eyes searched hers. "Heard you... cry. You hurt?"

The stilted manner of his speech spoke to her of the incredible pain he endured, agony that she could see in his eyes, yet he was asking about her instead.

She swallowed the lump in her throat, stifling the memories of her punishment, and forced a shrug. "No worse than usual."

"Usual?" Black eyebrows dipped low, narrowing eyes rapidly gaining a dark edge and obsidian blotches amidst the stormy blue-grey of his irises. What was he? "Beat... often?"

He grated the words out from between clenched teeth and she saw his fangs were down. Maybe he was a vampire, or another form of fae. There were many in the world and a lot of them could take on a human appearance.

"It no longer bothers me." She plastered on a false smile, one she hoped would stop him from asking about it. "But... they do it often."

He growled so low that she only felt it as a rumble through her chest and then strained against his manacles, becoming so agitated that she feared he would hurt himself again. His face screwed up, his enormous fangs on display, and he threw his head back and roared as he arched off the dark stone slab.

"You need to calm down." Rosalind reached for him.

She froze when his eyes snapped open.

Purple.

Her breathing accelerated.

She shook her head.

He couldn't be.

He stared at her, vivid purple eyes flashing wildly as his lips peeled away from his fangs again. Fangs. Purple. Mother earth, she was going to hyperventilate.

His overlong black hair parted to reveal the pointed tips of his ears and she almost passed out.

Elf.

Rosalind shot backwards away from him. Pain erupted in her side, searing her ribs and stealing her breath together with him. Not a damn elf. He couldn't be a bloody elf.

She shook her head and huddled into the corner, holding her knees and staring at him as he wrestled with his manacles.

Anything but an elf. Why couldn't he be anything but an elf?

She went back seventy years, to a magical summer's day when she had been having tea in the garden with her grandmother. It had all been so peaceful and perfect. Endless blue skies. Flowers in full bloom. Butterflies and bees going about their business. A perfect moment.

Until her grandmother had turned sombre, staring at her in silence and worrying her. Rosalind had asked her what was wrong and her grandmother had looked right into her eyes with ones that swirled like a silver storm and had spoken words that had changed her forever.

In Rosalind's future would be an elven prince, and after meeting him, she would die.

When she had helped King Thorne with his war, she had specifically avoided seeing or meeting Prince Loren of the elves who had been assisting him too.

She warily eyed the elf in the cell with her. He didn't bear the markings of a royal elf, ones she had learned about during her research into the species. He didn't look much like a prince either. She tried to shake off her fear, and her rising panic with it. It was difficult. She had spent her whole life convincing herself that her grandmother had been having one of her strange episodes when she got her wires crossed and thought she was talking to someone else, and now she had the horrible feeling that it hadn't been the case at all.

She had seen Rosalind's future and had spelt it out for her.

And now Rosalind was locked in a cell with an elf.

She shook off the last clinging threads of her fear. She had met the elf Bleu without dying, and the fae history books only mentioned one elf prince. The one she had avoided. This male was not that prince. The prince had a calm aura. Not a violent one.

She blew out her breath and winced as her ribs protested.

The elf male stilled, his eyes locked on her. They were focused, but not right. He looked lost, a wild beast struggling to comprehend her and his surroundings. He drew in a deep breath.

He craned his neck, turning his head towards his right arm. What was he doing? Studying his restraints?

He sank his fangs into his forearm.

"Stop that." Rosalind raced across the room to him and stopped short of grabbing his wrist to pull his arm free of his fangs.

He released his arm and blood bloomed there. His purple eyes grew wilder and black spots formed in them like inky blotches that began to spread as he stared at her.

He growled in a commanding tone, "Drink. Female."

Rosalind's stomach turned and she shook her head. He snarled in response to her refusal and struggled against the manacles again. Blood crept down his arm, stark red against his pale skin. He spoke in his language, his voice alternating between softness and hardness, between a whisper and a growl. The thick metal restraints cut into his wrists as he frantically fought them, spilling more blood. She couldn't take it.

She grabbed his bare shoulders and used her weight to press down and restrain him, her body laying partially across his.

He stilled.

She breathed hard, every inch of her shaking, a heady mixture of fear, adrenaline, and relief sweeping through her. Mother earth, she hoped he didn't bite her or attack her. She had placed herself within easy reach of his fangs. A stupid move, but she hadn't been able to stop herself. He had been hurting himself because of her refusal. He had been losing himself to whatever came over him at times when he was under duress.

"Female. Drink. Heal."

Rosalind eyed the blood. He wanted to heal her? He was truly insane. Lacerations and wounds covered him from head to toe and he was worried not about himself but instead about her?

He urged her again, dark and commanding this time.

"Drink."

The thought made her ill but she wanted to be strong so she could escape this nightmare and didn't want him to hurt himself anymore because of her. If she could achieve one of those things, she would take his blood. Just a sip.

She knew all the fables about elf blood, including the one that said it could heal. She just wasn't sure she believed it.

Only one way to find out whether it was true.

She bent her head to his arm, poked her tongue out and tried not to think about what she was doing, sure she would retch if she did. She licked the blood, following a line of it up his arm, trying to be as gentle as she could with him so she didn't startle him.

He startled her instead.

He moaned and his hips undulated against her.

Rather than shocking her into moving away, the sound of pleasure emanating from his lips enticed her to move closer, emboldening her.

Rosalind wrapped her lips around the twin puncture marks his fangs had made and sucked, earning a dark hungry growl from him. He bucked his hips wildly, nudging against her, his actions driven by instinct rather than a conscious decision. She knew it to be true because she wanted to rock hers too, ached and burned low in her belly, possessed by a need to rub against him while she drank him down.

"Drink. Female," he uttered, his voice a bare whisper. "Ki'ara."

She instantly tore herself away from him. He called her by another female's name?

Cold engulfed her, emptiness that left her emotions reeling, clashing violently as she struggled to comprehend what had just happened and fought her instinct to bash him across his thick skull.

She spat the remaining blood in her mouth on the floor, gaining a dark glare from her companion, one that she ignored as she went to work on him. She wasn't gentle as she healed him. The bastard didn't deserve gentle after calling her by another woman's name. She would have told him to go to Hell, but since they were both already there, it hardly seemed worth the effort.

Besides, she couldn't find her voice. Her throat felt thick, squeezed so tight that she could barely breathe, let alone speak.

He passed out at some point. She didn't care enough to note when it happened, but was glad that he had left her alone in a way. She wanted to be alone.

The incubus in the cell opposite kindly remained quiet too, although he prowled his cramped quarters, his gaze constantly on her. She hated him too. She hated that he had witnessed the whole affair and could probably see the hurt on her face. She never had been good at hiding her feelings. She had never seen the point before now.

Now though, as she sat in a cell with an elf who had somehow managed to slip past her defences and get under her skin, she wished she knew how to lie and how to shield herself from others, concealing her emotions so they couldn't be used against her.

Rosalind sank back onto her heels and let her breath out on a sigh. She was done with him and still had hours before moonrise. No punishment for her.

The male's eyelids flickered and then opened.

He deserved punishment though.

Rosalind stood and towered over him with her hands on her hips. "Who's Kiara?"

He frowned, a confused edge to his steel-blue eyes. Part of her was glad they were no longer purple. When he looked like this, she could fool herself into thinking he wasn't an elf, and that she had hope of making it to her one hundred and first birthday.

"I have no ki'ara," he muttered.

She loomed over him and gave him her best glare. "That wasn't the case when you commanded me to drink from you."

His expression sharpened, darkening by degrees. "What are you talking about? I did no such thing."

She pointed a shaky finger at the marks on his arm. She wanted to see him try to deny they were his, because she wasn't in possession of a pair of fangs.

"You made me drink and then you had the bloody audacity to call me by another's name." Her heart pounded wildly, beating so fast she felt sick.

She stormed to the cell door, grabbed the bars and rattled them with all of her strength, which was considerably more than it had been prior to drinking from the bastard elf. She mentally marked the fable about elf blood having a healing ability as true.

"Guards!" Rosalind hollered, unwilling to spend another second in his company. Heavy footsteps echoed along the corridor. She looked over her shoulder at the elf, her lip curling. "The demon king will be questioning you now, and I hope the bastard gives you what you bloody deserve."

He stared blankly at her.

The guards opened the door. She huffed and strode out of it, pausing at the bars for long enough to cast him one last withering glare.

"Next time, you can damn well heal yourself."

The elf blinked, shock written across every line of his handsome face.

Rosalind ignored the bolt of heat that went through her, turned her nose up and stomped along the corridor towards her cell, shaking like a leaf in a storm and unsure whether her jelly legs would give out before she reached her quarters.

There was one thing she was sure of though.

The next time she set eyes on that elf, he was going to find out that Hell had no furies that could match a witch scorned.

CHAPTER 5

Ki'ara.

Vail refused to believe he had called the female such a thing. It was all a trick she had devised to lure him into her trap. She had heard him mutter that word, picking it out from all the others, latching onto it in the hope it would weaken him enough for her to cast a spell on him. She meant to enslave him with it, just as another had before her.

He stared at the ceiling, studying the cracks between the dark grey stones, and clawed his hair back, pulling it tight, until his scalp stung.

Had he called her ki'ara?

Beloved.

Why?

Vail laughed emptily to himself, the sound unnerving even him. The occupants of the cells on either side of his shuffled further away, evidently deciding it wise to distance themselves from his insanity.

Insanity.

Yes. That was why he had used that word for her. Kordula had driven him madder than he had thought possible, and that was the reason he had called the fair female such a name, because he had no ki'ara.

He wasn't that lucky.

The ceiling of his cell swam out of focus as his heart beat frantically against his ribs, far quicker than normal, the pace sickening him.

Filling him with dread.

It wasn't possible that it was her heart causing his to race, the product of a bond he had initiated between them by giving her blood. It wasn't. He shook his head and barked out another laugh, this one bordering on hysterical judging by the way the incubus slunk away from the bars of his cell across the corridor from Vail's and eyed him warily. She couldn't be.

The incubus.

Vail slowly tilted his head to his left to face him. "You."

The dark-haired male pointed at himself, his green eyes wide, as if he wasn't sure Vail was talking to him. Who else was there to speak with in this dreadful place? This fae was the only one he could see, and the only one who could see him where he lay, and that meant the male had witnessed everything.

He had heard everything.

Vail allowed his hands to fall away from his hair. They hung limp, his arms stretched out above his head, the length of chain securing him to the stone slab dragging across the flags.

"Did she speak the truth?" Vail said and the incubus nodded without hesitation.

Vail turned his face away to stare at the ceiling again. Ki'ara. He had called her such a thing.

"You made her drink from you," the male said in a voice laced with disgust, one that let Vail know exactly what this male thought of him. "Sick wanker."

He wasn't sure what that profanity meant but no profanity was complimentary. This male thought him wretched indeed.

"To heal her," Vail whispered to the ceiling, still unable to believe that he had done such a thing.

Yet he could feel the ties that bound them, his body to hers. He knew their hearts beat in time with each other, hers causing his to race, speaking to him of how frightened she had been when she had confronted him and the fury that lingered within her still. It would be that way until the bond was complete, something that felt impossible to him, but necessary too, as vital to him as air and blood.

Their feelings mingled and flowed from one to the other. He was weak of body and mind, hunger draining his powers, but he could sense her fear and every instinct he possessed demanded he reach her and take away the source of that fear so she would feel safe again.

Impossible. He was the source of her fear. He was the one who had upset her.

She had already removed herself from him.

When she had stopped outside his cell and looked at him, her eyes had sparked with silver fire that had danced amongst the cool blue waters. He had witnessed the power held locked within her and knew that she had longed to direct it at him. She had wanted to hit him with a spell.

Witch.

He unleashed a feral snarl and battled the sense of connection to her, refusing to believe it stemmed from anything other than his blood in her body. She was not his ki'ara. The prediction given to him as a youth had been wrong. It had all been a lie, a trick by Kordula somehow. Her ancestors had planted the seed in his head that his fated female would be a sorceress and he had foolishly believed it. They had then sent her to him and she had set her trap. He had fallen right into it.

He'd had no bond with Kordula, and he had no bond with this witch either.

Using the same power that kept his connection to Loren closed, he severed the one that linked him to her, shutting out her emotions.

His heart didn't slow though.

Demons stopped outside his cell again. Vail ignored them, focusing on his heart instead, willing it to slow and adopt a normal rhythm, one that didn't make his head spin and leave him feeling weaker.

One of the demons opened the door and held it while the other stepped inside his cell. Vail spared them a glance. They weren't the normal dungeon dwelling guards. These two wore loose black shirts with their black leather trousers, and carried a set of restraints that he didn't like.

They locked the cell door and approached him. The witch's words came back to him. He was to see the king.

The demons bent over him, clamping gleaming solid metal cuffs around his wrists and his ankles, and unlocking the ones that held him fastened to the slab. The male nearest his wrists grabbed the short chain between his new manacles, hauling him into a sitting position and then onto his feet, and he didn't fight them. He wanted to meet this king.

His knees wobbled under his sudden weight and he locked them, refusing to show any weakness around these wretches.

The other demon, slightly smaller than his companion, with a chunk of his dirty grey left horn missing, placed a thick band of metal around Vail's waist and locked it behind his back. It bit into his hips, the metal cold against his skin, but it wasn't the chill that made it crawl.

There was magic in these bonds. He could feel it sapping his strength and he growled under his breath, itching to fight it and get it off him. He clenched and unclenched his fists, battling his rising panic, trying to subdue it before it ate away at his control. He had to stay lucid. He couldn't lose control.

The demon who had secured the band around his waist placed the chain between Vail's wrists into a thick loop on the front of the band and shoved it closed, locking the chain to it and making it impossible for him to move his arms. Vail growled when the other demon placed a collar made of the same magically reinforced metal around his neck.

The larger demon opened the cell door and the smaller one shoved him forwards. The length of the chain between his ankles was only long enough for him to shuffle his bare feet over the smooth cold stones. When he reached the open door, the two males hit the band around his waist and he jerked forwards, losing his balance. A tug on his collar stopped him from falling on his face.

He glared over his shoulder at them and realised they hadn't shoved him or pulled him back. Both demons held long metal poles that were now attached to his belt and his collar, keeping him at a distance from them.

They both pushed on the ends of the poles, forcing him to move. He snarled and flashed his fangs, but had no choice but to obey. He shuffled forwards, his eyes fixed on the floor in front of his feet, shame burning through him. The chain between his ankles rattled and scraped across the stones.

He despised it.

Being restrained physically was almost as bad as being restrained by magic.

He looked at his shackled wrists. In this case, he was being restrained by both magic and a physical item. He hated that he could feel the sorcery in the bonds that held him. It crawled over his skin like an oily slick, suffocating him and making it impossible to think rationally. He hated that he could feel magic in the female too. It drove him mad.

Sent him deep into dark, twisted memories that pulled him under, tugging him away from reality and leaving him lost in a strange, deranged state that left him feeling as if he was living a nightmare—as eternal and dark as the most hellish pit in the underworld.

The demons marched him past the cells and he kept his eyes cast downwards, his thoughts turned inwards, fearing he would sense the witch and would lose his grip on reality. He struggled up the stone steps to an arched doorway and flinched as he raised his head and bright torchlight washed over his face. The guard on his left shoved with his poles and Vail silently bared his fangs in warning before trudging onwards, out into the light.

Males milled around the enormous courtyard of the black castle, some locked in mock battle and others talking in groups. Not all were demon. He spotted bear shifters and one or two dragons in their human forms.

Not all were male.

Vail growled low in his throat on sensing the presence of dark magic, his gaze instantly seeking the source of it. Two women stood off to his right, one blonde and one a redhead.

Redhead.

Vail snarled at her and launched himself in that direction, forgetting that his ankles were bound. He tripped on the short chain and stumbled, and would have fallen on his face had the two demons holding him not pulled back on the poles, jerking him upright like a marionette.

The two dark witches laughed, the high sound mocking him. He bared his fangs at them and hissed, his pointed ears flattening against the sides of his head, warning them not to laugh at him. It didn't stop them.

The warriors around them paid him no heed. They were too busy staring at the witches, hungry gazes raking over their bodies, taking in every curve put on display by their long tight black dresses.

The witches stared at Vail though, giving him their undivided attention, turning his stomach over with the force of it. Their magic was in the bonds that held him prisoner, touching him. It was all over him, that oily slick covering every inch of him now, smothering him, making him itch to wash himself and scrub it away.

All witches made him feel this way, whether male or female, dark or light, and he despised them for it.

The demons shoved him forwards, forcing him to continue his march of shame through the courtyard.

It struck him that Little Wild Rose didn't make him react in such a way. When he was around her, he wanted to fight and attack her, needed to defend himself and drive her away, as he did with these witches, but he didn't feel sickened, drowning in her magic and choking on her presence.

He shook that thought away. The cuffs she wore dampened her power so he could only feel a fragment of it, and that was the only reason she didn't repulse him.

One of the demon guards pushed him in the back. "Keep moving."

Vail came back to the world and discovered he was inside one of the towering buildings of the castle. He had lost track of his surroundings, thoughts of the witch stealing his focus, a dangerous and foolish move to have made. He should have been focused on discovering the layout of the castle and looking for weaknesses in its defences, something he could exploit in order to escape.

They entered a cavernous hall lit by torches mounted on the great gleaming obsidian pillars supporting the vaulted ceiling. Ahead of him, at the end of a long wide aisle, stood a black throne on a raised stone platform.

On that throne sat a huge demon male, his grey horns curling from beneath his jagged green helm, their painted white tips bright in the low light. They were extended, curling around themselves and flaring forwards into dangerous points, a sign of the anger that flowed from him.

His broad bare chest bore the scars of war, both recent and centuries past, and a thick braid of black hair lay down one side of it, curling over his shoulder from under his green helm. As Vail approached, his dark eyebrows drew down, narrowing his green eyes and lending a grim edge to his expression.

"King Bruan, we have brought the elf prisoner as instructed." The biggest male pushed Vail forwards with such force he almost lost his balance again and he had to fight to stop himself from turning on the inferior wretch.

He kept his focus locked on the male several metres in front of him. King Bruan.

The demon king shifted in his seat, his left arm remaining dangling over the edge of his obsidian throne.

In it was a green and black thick metal torc.

The male had lost a loved one?

Vail knew of the demon tradition of wearing a torc to signify the loss of a mate.

King Bruan lifted it, drawing Vail's gaze up with it, and stared at it with a faraway look in his eyes.

"My brother wore this," he murmured in the demon tongue, his deep voice rumbling through the room. "He lost his female centuries ago, and honoured her for all that time, upholding his vow to make the Fifth Realm the most powerful all Hell had seen."

The immense male rose fluidly to his booted feet and glared at Vail, pinning him with green eyes blazing with fury and pain.

"Frayne would have succeeded in carrying out that vow had it not been for your prince and his part in the war." The demon king lifted the torc and tightened his grip on it, his knuckles burning with the force. "Now this is all I have of him. This…"

He tossed the twisted curved piece of metal at Vail. It clattered across the stone flags, the sound loud and jarring in the cavernous room, and stopped a few inches short of his bare feet.

"And the oath I swore to my warriors when their king fell." The male prowled down the steps towards Vail, his powerful body shifting with each step, making Vail aware of the vast difference in their strength. In his current condition, he was no match for this king of demons.

Bruan stopped in front of Vail, grasped his metal collar, catching his neck with his claws at the same time, and hauled him off his feet by it, bringing Vail's face closer to his. The sweet scent of mead rolled off his breath.

"I will avenge him," Bruan snarled down at him, flashing emerging fangs. "You will tell me all you know of the locations of the elf army along their borders."

Vail held his gaze as calmly as he could manage when what he really wanted to do was claw the demon's eyes out and then dig a hole in his chest to extract his black, still-beating heart. A heart he would crush before his eyes so he could see the fear and the light of life drain out of them.

"I know nothing of troop movements," Vail stated, sure that the king wouldn't believe him even though he was speaking the truth.

Demons were thick-headed. He had learned that the moment he and his brother had set foot in Hell to build their new kingdom. Vail had wanted to take three legions of their army to teach the First and Second Realms of the demons to respect the elves. Loren had suggested a more diplomatic approach of venturing into those kingdoms and speaking directly with their kings. It had almost got him killed. His older brother had always been painfully obstinate and irritatingly diplomatic, wanting to see the good in everyone, even those who held only darkness in their hearts.

Like him.

Vail closed his eyes.

Loren.

He didn't understand why his brother fought so hard for him. Could Loren love him still, after everything he had done to his kingdom and his people?

His strength faltered, his fight leaving him for a heartbeat of time before he dragged himself back to his present location and away from the past and his brother.

Bruan was studying his face with a shrewd eye, one that Vail didn't like and that set him on edge. He had underestimated the intelligence of this particular demon and had to tread carefully if he was to convince the male he was of no use to him.

The demon king lowered him to his feet but retained his hold on Vail's collar. "You are not a soldier?"

Vail shook his head. The king eyed him closely, looking him over from head to toe and back again.

"I admit you are scrawny and weak, but you do not look like a civilian. There is a little too much pride in those eyes and a little too much courage." The demon released his collar and stepped back, as if needing to view all of him in one go in order to make a decision about his profession and whether he believed him. He eventually shook his head. "You fought well against my men. You are a soldier."

"I am no soldier, although I have done my share of fighting and killing as one of them. I left that life behind long ago. If you see pride and courage, it is born of that period of my life and nothing else. I have wandered the earth since leaving my homeland and have not set foot in it in many centuries." Vail straightened his spine, standing as tall as he could manage while the demons behind him held his neck and waist under their control. "I have no allegiance to the elves or Prince Loren."

"An elf with no allegiance to his kind, who has done his share of killing..." The king moved a step closer again, a glimmer in his eyes that Vail recognised. Madness. The loss of his brother had driven him mad, crazed by a need for vengeance. The male narrowed his green eyes on him and smirked. "I thought you a soldier we could question for intelligence on the prince and perhaps the Third King."

Bruan moved so quickly Vail wouldn't have had a chance to shift backwards to evade him even if he hadn't been held by two guards. He grabbed Vail's jaw, his fingers pressing into the left side while his thumb dug into the right, and shoved his head back. He stared down into Vail's eyes, his smile growing.

"Forgive me... your highness... I did not recognise you at first."

Vail tensed and barely bit back the growl that curled up his throat. He hadn't expected the demon to know him. He had never seen this male in his life, had never ventured this deep into the interior of the Fifth Realm, and the male was young. It wasn't possible that they had met.

The king's smile held. "You are thinking in there... calculating... you do not hide it well, Mad Elf Prince. You wonder how I know you."

Vail did growl now. The demon didn't flinch.

Vail knew of his nickname, of the things whispered about him in all the realms, the horror stories people told of him and the threats they used on their offspring. Go to bed or the mad elf prince will come for you. He knew of what they called him and he despised them all for it.

If he were mad, it was not by choice, and it was not something he wanted. He wanted... something far beyond his reach. He wanted the impossible, and that made him weak. Vulnerable. Forgiveness would never be his, and neither would salvation, but no matter how many times he had tried to purge the tiny fragment of light that remained in his soul, the small seed of hope, it had refused to die.

"You see… I got a good look at the man who helped King Thorne kill my brother," Bruan said over Vail's rumbling growl. "I was fighting Prince Loren at the time the Third King took Frayne's head… and you look too much like him to be anyone else. So your charade ends here, and I have devised a new plan. I will ransom you to your brother in exchange for the assistance of the elves in my new war."

Vail laughed at him, wiping the smile off his ugly face and replacing it with confusion. "My brother will not pay for my return… he despises me. Did you not know that I have been at war with him since long before you were born? The prince you desire to gain assistance from would sooner see me dead than align his army with yours."

Bruan's expression turned flat and unreadable, his green eyes impassive and giving nothing away.

"It is not so." The demon king bent and picked up the discarded green and black metal torc, rolling it over in his hands. "I have heard your brother is searching for you. Do you not know your brother hunts for you even now?"

"To kill me."

Bruan laughed, the booming sound echoing around the hall. "Foolish male. If I have learned anything about the older brothers of this realm, it is that they would never kill a younger sibling, one which they would have sworn to protect from the day of their birth. If your brother hunts you, then it is for no other purpose than reuniting with you."

Vail shook his head.

"You forget, we are not born of this realm." He narrowed his eyes on the demon king and smiled, gathering every ounce of his anger and pain into a tempest within him, one that the demon would see in his gaze. One that would tell this fool that his plot would end in ruin.

Vail would never play the role assigned to him. His brother would never set foot in this kingdom and he would somehow make sure of it. He would keep his brother safe, even if he had to take his own life to achieve it. Loren would feel the connection between them die. He would know what had happened to him and he would not be fooled by this mad demon king.

"Loren would see me dead, and the feeling is mutual," Vail spat at the male and snarled, flashing the tips of his fangs as his ears grew more pointed, a physical sign of the aggression surging through him, the darkness that coaxed him into goading the demon into killing him. He would ensure his brother's safety and deliver himself into death's embrace. "I would see my brother dead before he could raise a hand to harm me. I would act to defend myself and then what alliance would you have? If you even so much as send word to my brother of my location… if you interfere in our war… in my fight… I will kill every single warrior in this castle and then I will kill you."

King Bruan growled at him, his powerful body rippling as his eyes blazed green fire and his enormous black dragon-like wings burst from his bare back.

"You dare to order me? You dare to threaten me?" The huge demon male grasped Vail's collar and dragged him off his feet, leaving them dangling above the dark flagstones. He was growing, his muscles expanding as his true form emerged, turning his visage dark and demonic. "A male such as you needs to be taught humility with an iron fist. You will learn to hold your forked tongue. You will learn your place. I will have submission beaten into you and then we shall speak again."

Darkness welled up inside Vail, thick and inky, violent like a tempest swirling through his blood and igniting his fury. He snarled at the demon king, the thought of being taken back to the torture chamber shoving him over the edge into the abyss.

The beast within him rose to the fore, baring his fangs at the male who dared to threaten him, who sought to control him just as Kordula had done—with pain and punishment, stripping him of his pride and his strength. He would not let this male do such a thing to him. He would not submit to anyone.

Never again.

Vail roared and fought to lift his arms, his broken nails becoming claws as his muscles strained against the bonds that held him. The demon king dropped him and shifted back a step, signalling to the guards at the same time. One struck him across the side of his head but it didn't stop him. He arched backwards, using every drop of his strength on the cuffs, and unleashed a victorious snarl as the chain snapped free.

He turned hard, throwing one guard off balance, sending him toppling to the ground, and lashed out at the second one. The larger male struck him again, the blow coming faster than he could evade while the magic in his restraints dampened his powers.

Vail growled, baring his bloodied fangs, clasped his hands together and swung them up in a brutal diagonal arc. They smashed into the side of the male's face and he staggered sideways, towards the other demon now back on his feet.

He prepared himself to attack him.

Pain splintered across his knees, the force and speed of the thick pole slamming into them shattering his kneecaps and fracturing the joints of his femurs. An inferno blazed up his bones and he cried out his agony as he dropped to his knees on the flagstones. He bent over, his face buried in his cuffed hands as he fought the pain, struggling to catch his breath as it overwhelmed him, threatening to shut his body down and send him tumbling into unconsciousness. He had to remain awake.

He had to fight.

Not only for his sake, but for his brother's.

He needed to kill the demon king.

Vail pressed his hands into the cold stones and pushed himself up, slowly and carefully so as not to worsen the spinning in his aching mind. He had to hold it together. He would not let these wretched demons overpower him.

King Bruan loomed over him, the thick shiny silver pole hanging from his right hand and the torc still clutched in his left. Vail's legs burned, the agony numbing them but not enough for him not to sense that they were useless. In one blow, this male had defeated him. He growled, cursing himself. Hating himself.

The male laughed. "I had thought it would be more difficult to drive you into submission. Weak male."

Vail snarled and gritted his teeth so hard his fangs cut into his gums. He gathered his strength and pushed himself up, forcing himself onto his feet. His knees gave out again, slamming him back onto the unforgiving stone flags, sending more pain tearing through him, more fire that consumed every inch of him and stripped away more of his strength. He refused to give up, pushing back onto his feet and trying again. Failing again.

The demon king watched him the whole time, through every failure, laughing at him. Mocking him with his weakness.

After his sixth attempt to stand on his broken legs, the last of his strength left him and all he could do was kneel before the king, sweat pouring off him and his heart labouring. Little Wild Rose would feel it. She would know his pain, and she would know his weakness.

King Bruan hefted the silver bar in his right hand. The two demon males grabbed Vail's shoulders and he tried to fight them, wrestled with the last drops of his strength, but it was futile. His throat closed and weight pressed down on his chest, squeezing his heart and lungs. He was weak. Vulnerable. With one blow, this demon king had stripped him of his strength and his pride.

He had humiliated him.

Bruan cracked the bar across the side of Vail's head, the blow connecting hard and sending him lurching to his right. His vision swam and the sound of their laughter distorted in his ears. He growled and struggled to sit up again, but made no progress.

All he could do was bite out words in the elf tongue. "If I had my armour... if I were not enslaved... I swear by the gods I would kill you all. I would butcher you all!"

The demon guards released him and the king struck his head again, the blow splintering bone and sending him crashing to the floor. He coughed up blood and fought to remain conscious, battling the agony searing every break in his bones like lightning.

A voice within whispered to let go and allow the darkness to take him. He longed for oblivion to claim him, to steal away the pain and the world. The humiliation. He wanted to escape it.

He wanted to forget it all.

Kordula danced through his buzzing skull. She loomed over him, her crimson lips moving but her words too quiet to hear above the ringing in his ears. Her icy blue eyes slowly bled into crimson that matched the colour of her hair. She touched his face, black fingernails pressing deep into his flesh, drawing blood. Her countenance darkened, her power flowing through him and seizing control of his body, stripping away his strength. He fought her but he wasn't strong enough to stop her, and the end result was always the same.

Punishment.

Whether he did as she asked, destroying lives and spilling blood, or denied her. It always ended in punishment.

She dropped her hand to his chest and his armour peeled away, leaving him exposed. He tried to fight her hold on him, mentally begged her to stop and leave him be. He had done what she had asked. He had slaughtered an entire village. Not only the males. He had brutally killed the women and their offspring too. He had bathed his claws in blood for her. Was that not enough?

Her nails raked down his chest and he shuddered, not because she had hurt him but because of the softness of her caress. He could take her punishing him, torturing him, but he couldn't take this. He tried to raise his hands, bared his fangs at the thought of wrapping them around her throat and squeezing the life out of her. She clucked her tongue and pressed her palms against his chest, and gave him the worst form of punishment.

She kissed him.

And all he could do was let his consciousness slip away and bury himself deep, detaching himself from the situation and what was to come, and to pretend it wasn't happening again.

He wasn't strong enough to fight her.

The demon king was right.

He was weak.

He hadn't been strong in a long time. He wasn't sure he knew how to be strong anymore.

"Take him to the rack and continue our lesson in humility." Those words shattered the hold the pain and the memories had on him, dragging him back to the cold hopelessness of reality.

He wrestled with the last of his strength, desperate and crazed, driven wild by one thought as the demon guards hauled him away from the king, taking him to the torture chamber. It wasn't the knowledge of what awaited him in that room that sent him out of his mind, maddening him. They could do no worse to him than the one who had come before them.

No, it was another more disturbing and distressing thought that had him fighting even as his strength failed him, and filled him with a need to not give up and surrender to them.

They would drag him back to his cell, beaten into submission and no doubt unconscious.

He would pass the cells and Little Wild Rose would see him for what he really was.

A broken, weak and vulnerable male.

CHAPTER 6

Rosalind sat by the bars of her cell, gripping them tightly, her eyes closed and jaw clenched. The crack of the whip echoed down the corridor again, turning her stomach, and the guard dealing the blows that wetly cleaved flesh grunted with frustration once more. The elf made no sound, though she could feel his pain flow through the dungeon, held back and endured in silence.

Why?

Tears burned her eyes. There was no shame in crying out. During her captivity, she had heard the strongest of men break under the torture and the steel whips, lashed by barbs and bled until they passed out.

Her heart pounded and the whip struck again. She swore she felt each strike, each lash of the whip on her body. Pain ran through her, quiet but there, buzzing down her back and over her thighs.

The whip cracked again. She heard flesh give but no cry, no other sign that it had struck its target and rent another gash in the elf's body.

Rosalind tightened her grip on the thick steel bars, clinging to them so fiercely that her knuckles blazed white and her bones ached. Anger boiled within her, a seething need to do something even when she was powerless to act on her rage. Her magic was bound. The only thing she could do was endure, just as he did, and hope.

Hope that they would bring her to heal him.

She had cursed him, hated him with a force that had shocked her, when he had called her by another's name, but when they had led him past her, she had known only pity for him.

He had walked with his head bent, his eyes cast downwards, and she had seen his shame in them. They had stripped him of his pride.

Silence finally fell, the strange sensation of pain in her fading as her heart settled at last. Had they stopped?

She craned her neck, needing to see along the corridor to her right, but couldn't find an angle that would permit her to see all the way to the end of it.

What seemed like hours later, the same two guards who had marched him from his cell appeared again, not holding the elf by his arms but dragging him by his ankles. They had stripped him bare, leaving not a stitch on him and no shred of dignity, and they had done it on purpose. They meant to degrade him completely.

The tears stinging her eyes wobbled on her lashes, hot and fierce, as they dragged him past her. His arms stretched out above his head, the manacles holding his wrists clanking on the flagstones and his head jogging around as it hit the gaps between each stone. A river of blood, red and stark, followed in his wake.

Her gaze widened and she covered her mouth, stifling a wave of sickness when she saw the deep lacerations criss-crossing his bare chest and arms, and cutting deep grooves in his thighs. His head bounced off another gap and lolled towards her, his firm bloodied lips parting. She stared at his mouth in horror.

His fangs.

Mother earth.

They had ripped out his fangs.

Rosalind reacted on instinct, stretching her arms between the bars towards him, her fingers barely brushing his before he slipped beyond her reach.

She sagged against the steel bars, her right temple pressing into them and her arms laying on the floor of the corridor, one in a smear of his blood that also coated the chain between her cuffs. She would make the demons pay for their cruelty. He had done nothing to deserve such punishment. Mother earth, she would make them pay.

One day.

But for now, all she could do was sit and wait, and plot.

She shuffled back into the corner, as far from the bars of her cell as she could get, and huddled into it. She smoothed her tattered black dress over her knees, hugged them to her chest with the chain between her cuffs dangling across them, and rested her chin on them. The guards would come for her. They would bring her to heal him. Until then, she would wait in silence, saving her energy, the strength he had given her with his gift of blood.

She would bestow that same gift upon him.

She wasn't strong enough to fight these demons without her magic, but he was strong enough to fight them without his psychic powers. She would make him strong.

Her eyes slipped shut and she forced them open again, unwilling to succumb to the lure of sleep. Sleep didn't bring her the rest she needed. It only brought her pain, a horrific replay of the war and a parade of the souls she had destroyed in that single dark night.

Rosalind held her knees tighter and rocked, trying to focus on other things. Her garden would be overgrown by now. She would have her work cut out for her when she returned to her cottage. Many of her clients would be angry with her too. They were waiting for the potions they had ordered. She would have to apologise to them all.

Perhaps the demon king Thorne had been kind enough to somehow tell them what had happened to her, if he didn't think her dead that was. So many had died in the war. So many lives snuffed out. Rivers of blood had run across the black ground.

Her eyes slipped shut again and the nightmare swallowed her, devoured her with sharp teeth that tore at her flesh and crunched her bones. Broken hands grasped her, missing flesh in places, and she fought them as they pulled at her clothes, tearing them from her body and leaving her exposed. They clawed at her, lacerating her flesh, leaving long red marks criss-crossing her body.

They grabbed her wrists and pulled her down into the endless darkness, into a vivid replay of the battle that had left a terrible scar on her soul. She saw herself killing, saw the faces of her victims this time, witnessed how her magic tore them to pieces and shattered their bodies, killing them in the most painful ways imaginable. She clawed at her hair and screamed for it to stop, but no sound passed her lips. With every death she dealt, her heart grew blacker, the darkness in it spreading.

Until she called on all that death and darkness, reaching beyond the grave to the other side.

Rosalind shot awake, her heart racing and breath sawing from her lungs. She ran trembling hands over her matted blonde hair, pulling it back from her face, and forced herself to take in her surroundings. Tears blurred her vision and she blinked them away. She was in her cell. It shouldn't have been a comfort to her, but it had become one. She was in her cell and her power was locked inside her, beyond her reach.

She couldn't kill anyone without it.

She couldn't destroy another life.

She couldn't take another step closer to the darkness.

She rocked back and forth, slowly purging the effects of the nightmare. How long had she been unconscious, trapped inside a twisted replay of her past?

There were five clay bowls outside her cell. Five feedings of disgusting and questionable slop meant two and a half days.

It had been two and a half days and the demons hadn't come for her. Because she had threatened that the elf could heal himself next time?

No. The demons didn't care about such things. If they had wanted him healed, they would have forced her to do it.

A dark-haired demon stopped outside her cell and curled a lip at the five bowls and then at her as he preened his dusky grey horns, stroking their curved lengths from the root behind the top of his ear to the tip near the lobe. His emerald eyes shifted to her, he rolled his bare shoulders, and then unlocked the door.

"Out," he grunted.

Rosalind dug her fingers into the gaps between the thick stone blocks of the wall beside her and slowly pulled herself onto her feet. She straightened and did her best to walk confidently across her cell to the door, unwilling to show weakness in front of the huge demon male glaring at her. She wobbled at times, the drain of her nightmares combining with her lack of sustenance to make her weak. She felt sure that without the elf's blood in her body, she wouldn't have managed to walk at all. She would have been crawling to the demon.

He grabbed her arm in a bruising grip the second she was within reach, scooped up one of the bowls and shoved it at her.

"Eat."

She eyed the unappetising slop that matched the colour of his horns and considered refusing it, her stomach rebelling at the thought of eating it when she wasn't sure whether it was food that was two days old or freshly delivered today. The demon's grip on her arm tightened. She took the hint and the bowl, closed her eyes and grimaced as she swallowed the thick lumpy liquid, choking on it.

The demon snatched the bowl away and tossed it onto the floor, knocking over the others and spilling their contents across the flagstones.

"Come." He dragged her with him along the corridor, mercifully away from the torture room.

Following the dark crimson stain that formed a trail towards the elf.

Was she to heal him? She didn't dare ask the demon. They didn't like it when she questioned them. It normally earned her a trip to the rack and she wanted to see the elf. He would be healing by now, but she didn't have the heart to carry out her threat and leave him to suffer. She would heal whatever injuries remained.

The demon stopped outside his cell and Rosalind stared in horror.

The elf hadn't healed at all.

He lay on the stone slab, as nude as the day he was born, left there for everyone to see. His eyes darted around behind their closed lids and he muttered things beneath his breath in the elf language. He was in that strange state again, trapped inside himself just as before.

"Heal him. King Bruan wishes to speak with him." The demon shoved her into the cell and locked the door behind her.

The king wanted to see him again, after he had subjected him to such vicious torture? Why?

Rosalind walked to the elf where he lay chained to the stone slab, bent and tore a strip of material off the bottom of her black dress, bringing the hem up to above her knees. The chain between her manacles swayed and clinked as she draped the piece of material over his hips, covering him with it and giving him back some of the dignity the bastard demons had stolen from him.

He growled.

"It's okay. It's just me," she whispered but the sound of her voice only made him worse. He struggled against his restraints, rattling the chains that fastened him in place, splitting open several of the gashes across his chest and arms.

"Out," he snapped. "Leave. *Witch*."

Her heart sank. She hadn't been very nice to him during their last encounter and hadn't expected him to be thrilled to see her, but for some reason it hurt that he was back to wanting her away from him.

She drew in a deep, fortifying breath. "I hate to remind you, but I don't exactly have a choice here. Either I heal you, or they do to me what they have done to you."

He stilled, tensed and then growled again, darker this time, a rumbling sound that sent a ripple of danger through the air and rang her internal alarm bells. He was gearing up for a fight.

The question of the day was did he want to fight her or the demons?

He had tried to protect her before. Was it that same desire that made him growl now? Was it the thought of her being tortured that upset him?

"I'm healing you, whether you like it or not." She moved around the other side of him, allowing the light from the corridor to wash over his body and help her with her task.

She began with a visual inspection, not wanting to risk enraging him by laying her hands on his body until it was necessary.

The incubus prowled around his cell across from her, his bare feet silent on the stone floor but his movements still a distraction, together with the unsettling feeling of his intense green gaze fixed on her.

"Bloody annoying git," she muttered in the fae tongue, knowing he was listening, and brought all of her focus onto the elf.

Her visual check came to an abrupt stop when she hit his knees. A soft gasp escaped her and she covered her mouth.

His knees were bruised and swollen, spotted with red beneath his tight skin. The demons had broken them. She bent and hovered her free hand above them, her heart going out to him. Her healing power warned her that it wasn't only his kneecaps they had broken. There were several fractures in the ends of his femur bones too. She couldn't imagine how painful it had been for him at the time it had happened, or even now.

The demons hadn't stopped there though. They had brutally broken his feet and his hands too. She leaned over and ghosted her fingers over the left side of his head, down from his temple to the thick layer of dark stubble coating his jaw. Black bruising mottled his swollen cheek and eye. Someone had dealt terrible blows to his head.

Rage burned through her and she clenched her fists. The bastards. What had he done to deserve such punishment?

What would the king do to him this time when his men dragged the elf before him?

Death would have been a mercy.

Rosalind sank to her knees beside him, staring blankly at his face as his lips moved, his voice growing quieter as he settled. Her heart ached with a need to help him, and with something far more dangerous.

A hunger to avenge him.

She sucked down a breath and held it, searching for solid ground again. She couldn't allow herself to feel anything for him, not when she wasn't sure who he was or the specifics of her fated future. She had to act professionally. She was here to do a job, and she would do it to the best of her abilities.

Rosalind reached for his mouth to check on his fangs.

He snapped and snarled at her, the feral sound startling in the silent dungeon. She withdrew her hand to a safe distance, giving him time to settle again. His fangs were growing back but she had expected them, and his wounds, to have healed more than this in almost three days. He was an elf. He had the ability to heal rapidly when healthy.

He fought his restraints again, uttering dark-sounding things to himself, or possibly her, his wild behaviour reminding her that he wasn't healthy. Not in mind at least. What had happened to him to drive him towards a madness so deep that it could grip him like this?

She continued checking him over, pondering her patient and considering asking the incubus what he knew of him. She never had liked learning about people from someone else though. When she had healed the elf, and he was calm, she would ask him about himself. It was dangerous, might only increase the sense of connection and care she felt towards him, but she wanted to know. She wanted his name at the least, and his story at most.

If he told her his, then she would tell him hers.

Rosalind ran a final assessing gaze over him. He was still too thin. When had he last fed? He needed blood to heal wounds and keep his strength up, and she hadn't smelt blood in any of the bowls the guards carried on the trays at feeding time. It was a scent she would never forget now. One that would always stand out to her, even over the foul odour of the slop they fed her.

The elf had given her blood to heal her though, weakening himself.

Her gaze darted to her wrist and away again. No way that was going to happen. Feeding him from the vein was the swiftest way of increasing the care she already felt for him. She would give him blood, but without directly feeding him. Perhaps she could pour it into his mouth from a bowl, but she didn't have one. She would get one somehow, and feed him later.

She focused on healing him with her power, working on the worst of his wounds first. His knees were slow to heal, the bones refusing to mend beneath his battered flesh. She willed them to do as her spell asked, to knit back together and become strong again. Her spell fizzled out before even the smallest fracture had closed. She called another one and channelled it into him, chanting this time to maintain a strong focus and aid the spell.

Rosalind managed to get one femur healed before her head spun and she had to stop. She peeled her eyes open and looked at his face. What was wrong with him? Why wasn't he healing? His body should have assisted her magic, his natural healing ability using the spell as a burst of power to rapidly heal him.

Something was wrong with him.

He needed more than sorcery to get him healed and was too weak to heal himself naturally. The dark arcs beneath his eyes were worse now too, his sunken cheeks alarming her. He had looked ill when she had first met him, but now he looked close to death.

She was weak herself, but she might still have what he needed and the power to save him. Finding a bowl was no longer an option. She didn't have time.

He didn't have time.

Rosalind swallowed hard and before she could reconsider what she was doing, she used one of his remaining claws to cut a line across her wrist.

He sniffed.

Stirred.

Muttered, "Ki'ara."

That woman's name again. She silently cursed him for calling her by another's name and had to force herself to remain in place and not give in to the urge to slap him and make his injuries worse.

Or strike him and leave.

It would certainly be more satisfying than helping him and letting him think another had done it. This woman. This Kiara.

His fingers curled into fists and clenched, and his body tensed and bowed off the dark stone slab. "*Ki'ara.*"

"That's not my name, dammit." Before she could stop herself, she slapped him hard enough to rattle his brain in his thick skull, and the chain between her wrists followed her swing, battering him too.

He snarled, lunged and had his mouth latched around her uncut wrist before she could begin to pull it out of his reach, his whiskers scraping her skin. He bit down, blunt teeth bruising her flesh below the manacle, and growled in frustration. Rather than releasing her, he bit harder, clearly not grasping that his fangs were missing.

Rosalind cried out and finally managed to wrestle free of him. Her wrist throbbed, sending white-hot pain ricocheting up and down her arm.

"Shh, Ki'ara," he murmured softly.

She grunted darkly, stood and kicked the slab he was laying on. Her foot ached from the blow and she hopped, clutching her buzzing toes.

When he groaned, the sound pained, she stopped and stared down at him. He writhed on the stone, his face screwed up and his agony flowing over her. Why wasn't he healing as he had before?

Was he weakening?

It worried her. She didn't want to admit it, didn't want to feel anything for this man, but it worried her. She could feel his pain still, running through her like an undercurrent, all focused in the places where she could see injuries on him. His knees. His hands and feet. The side of his head. How? Why could she sense those injuries as if they were in a way her own?

Because he had given his blood to her to make her stronger? Had it formed a connection between them?

"Female... come," he husked and she almost did until he tacked on, "Ki'ara."

"No." Rosalind stood her ground, holding her bruised and throbbing arm to her chest while blood trickled down her other one. From a wound she had made for him. And then the bastard had started calling her that name again.

He opened his eyes with great effort and struggled to focus them on her. They kept rolling back into his skull but it didn't deter him. When they finally settled on her, they were purple again, hazy with pain and bloodshot.

He tried to lick his lips but only made it as far as touching his tongue to them, and his throat worked on a hard swallow. He was thirsty. Hungry. She swore she could feel it in him, and she could definitely see it in his eyes and the way they fixed on her, implored her as if only she could end his suffering.

She would be a fool to go near him.

But then she always had been a healer first and foremost, had never been able to see anything in pain without helping it, and this elf was in agony.

She kneeled beside him again and held back, giving herself a moment to reconsider the lunatic move she was about to make. For all she knew, he would drain her dry and kill her. His purple eyes tracked her. How lucid was he? Conscious enough to answer some questions before she placed her life in his hands?

She needed a reason to do it. She needed to understand what was wrong with him.

Maybe then she would know how to heal him with her magic.

She lowered her gaze to his mouth and stared at it, fixing all of her focus on it and ignoring the heat that curled through her as he stared right back at her, his purple eyes locked on her face with such force that it rocked her.

"Your fangs are gone," she whispered, cleared her throat to dislodge the tremble from her voice, and added, "They're regenerating, although slowly. Why slowly?"

"Blood."

A reasonable request and one she would get around to after he had answered her question.

She nodded. "I will give you some."

His black eyebrows dipped low and he managed to shake his head. Had she misunderstood?

"Gave you," he croaked, his voice thick and hoarse.

Rosalind frowned now. "The blood you gave to me? But why would that affect your healing ability?"

His eyes slipped closed and lines bracketed his mouth as his body heaved off the slab, shuddering and tensing. Blood trickled from a deep gash across his chest, sliding down his ribs. He groaned.

"You," he whispered. "Ki'ara."

She didn't understand. He thought she was this woman he always spoke of with a deep husky rumble in his voice and that meant he was healing less quickly, because he gave her blood? It didn't make sense at all.

His eyes opened again, glassy now. Whatever grip on his sanity he had mustered, he was losing it and was beginning to slip back away from her.

"Blood. Ki'ara. Give. To. Me." He laboured over each strained word, pain etched in his eyes and on his face.

"My name isn't Kiara," she snapped. "It's Rosalind!"

"Not. Kiara. Ki'ara." His eyes rolled closed and then flicked open again, sharper now. "Not. Name. Ki'ara."

"Not a name?" She risked it when he shuddered again, thrashing against his bonds, and placed her left hand on his forehead, leaving her right one on the slab beside him. He instantly stilled and she swept her fingers over his dirty skin, stroking the sweat-slicked black hair back and waiting for him to attempt to bite her again. He didn't. She stared down into his eyes. "What is it then?"

He husked, "You."

Something flickered amongst the pain in the depths of his purple eyes, something hot and fiery.

Dark and possessive.

It spoke of hunger and desire, of passion that caused heat to flare in her veins and burn through her, turning her blood to flame and scalding her cheeks.

"Me? I'm ki'ara?" Rosalind sat back, needing a moment to take that in and get her body back under control. She placed her hands in her lap and toyed with the chain between her cuffs, more confused than ever.

Whatever a ki'ara was, the term obviously had a special meaning, and he used it for her, said it with dark desire in his eyes each time. A term of endearment? She eyed him. He only used it when he was lost in whatever darkness haunted him, maddened by it. When he was sane, she was a witch with a capital B, judging by the way he said it. He despised her then.

But he needed her now.

She had never met a man who made as little sense, and confused her as much, as he did.

"Blood." He sounded strained again, weaker than before.

He had answered her question and she had promised him blood, and if he thought her to be this special-whatever-it-was then maybe he wouldn't kill her after all.

She lifted her cut wrist and placed it to his mouth. His firm lips brushed her skin, sending an achy hot shiver coursing through her entire body, and then he closed them around the wound and sucked greedily, yet softly.

There was reverence in his gentleness and it almost knocked her on her backside. She hadn't expected him to be so careful and gentle when he was hungry. It shocked her and stripped away another layer of her defences, leaving her more vulnerable than ever to this mysterious elf.

He grunted and his huge body lurched off the stone slab. It healed before her eyes, every wound closing and bruise disappearing, far quicker than she ever could have accomplished with her magic.

Mother earth. How was that possible? Just who was he?

Her answer came in a fashion that did knock her on her backside.

Colourful markings flashed into existence, lines of symbols that curled from his nipples around the square slabs of his pectoral muscles and across his collarbones to swirl around his deltoids. They chased over his hipbones and down beneath the black material she had placed over him too.

Rosalind realised with dread that he was no ordinary mysterious elf.

He was an elf prince.

She snatched her wrist away from his mouth, her heart slamming against her ribs as she clutched the chain between her restraints and told herself that she was seeing things. He wasn't a prince. He couldn't be.

The incubus in the cell across from her grunted, "You should have let him die. You should have kept far away from him, Little Girl. You know who he is, don't you?"

Not a prince. Not a prince. Not a prince. She looked at the incubus, willing him to say anything other than the inevitable.

The man smirked, his placid cool grey markings giving nothing about his feelings away. "I warned you, but no… you just had to go healing the mad elf prince. He's killed thousands. He's warred with his brother for millennia. You'll be lucky if he doesn't kill you now you've given him what he needs to restore his strength."

Rosalind shot to her feet. "You bloody well did not warn me. You said he was dangerous. You didn't say he was a damn prince!"

If he had, she probably would have kept her distance from him. She would have blindfolded herself to work on him. She would have done something to stop her fated future from playing out and ending in her death. Her throat closed and she breathed hard and fast, fighting her rising panic.

Blood. She had given him blood. What if the demons hadn't fed him for a reason? What if they had been keeping him weak to stop him from breaking free and slaughtering them all?

Her gaze fell back to the elf prince and widened. He was already looking better. There was colour to his skin beneath the blood and dirt, and she could no longer see his ribs or his bones. The man was putting on muscle right before her eyes.

Mother earth.

She backed away from him and shook her head. What had she done?

The incubus's words rang in her mind.

This elf prince had killed thousands.

It didn't frighten her, not as the incubus had intended. Perhaps she was mad too, but all she could think about was whether this elf prince could tell her how to cope with what she had done and the nightmares that plagued her, showing her killing those witches and demons, tormenting her until she felt she was losing her mind.

She couldn't judge him as the incubus did. She had taken lives too now. Each life haunted her. Each soul tormented her.

The elf snarled and thrashed against his bonds, his actions growing in their violence and causing the manacles to cut into his wrists and spill blood. The chain holding his ankles burst free of the stone and she took another step back, fear pounding through her. He was growing stronger. If he broke the chain holding his wrists, nothing was stopping him from killing her.

He suddenly stilled.

She breathed hard in the silence, staring at him, amazed by how quickly he had regenerated. He was perfect now. From the slight points of his nails to his honed, powerful body. Every part of him had healed.

All from a few drops of her blood.

His eyes snapped open and he snarled through his regrown fangs, "What did you do to me, Witch?"

He didn't remember.

"I gave you my blood," she said and his expression darkened dangerously.

"No... why... why would you do that to me?" The wildness that had been in his purple eyes when he had been lost in whatever madness gripped him was coming back again and her magic wanted to rise and protect her.

Rosalind held her cut wrist to her chest and kept her distance, ignoring the sting in her heart. "You asked."

He hissed at her, his pointed ears flaring back against the sides of his head through his overlong blue-black hair.

"What have you done?" he snarled and flexed his fingers, his claws growing into deadly points. His fangs lengthened. "What have you done?"

Rosalind had had quite enough of him. She stomped across the cell, towered over him and shoved her hands against her hips. "I did exactly what *you* asked of me."

He panted hard, his muscular chest heaving, and looked as if he was going to lose control or pass out. Rosalind hoped it was the latter.

"You told me I was this ki'ara thing and asked for blood." She jiggled her left foot, a nervous trait she had never quite gotten under control, and waited for him to explode.

"Would not... never... curse your sorcery... I will not let you bewitch me too!" He bucked off the stone slab, holding the chain of his restraints in both of his hands and pulling on it. The thick metal cuffs bit into his wrists as he tugged, rubbing them with each attempt he made to break the chain holding him to the slab. A red line formed and then blood bloomed.

"Stop it. You're hurting yourself." She was damned if he was going to damage himself and undo her hard work. The demons would demand that she heal him again and she really wasn't in the mood. She would probably tell them to go to Hell and then she would have to take a trip to the rack for her insolence.

Rosalind reached for his wrists.

He sucked in a sharp breath and instantly stilled, his purple eyes locking on her cut wrist and his colourful markings flaring over his body. "You are bleeding."

"Duh!" she snapped. "You asked for blood. I supplied. Remember?"

He stared at her wrist, a pained look entering his eyes, and jerked his chin, his voice distant as he murmured, "My female bleeds. I will heal her."

Rosalind froze. "*Your* female?"

His eyes shifted to meet hers, dark and possessive, filled with fire that scorched her. "*Ki'ara.*"

Hers widened as it dawned on her that he hadn't been calling her a sweet name to get her to comply with his requests, or even because somewhere beneath his witch-hating exterior he liked her.

No. Not at all.

He had been calling her by a special word, one reserved for a person who was one in around seven billion.

His fated female.

Rosalind suddenly had an urge to see what all the fuss was about fainting fits.

Her legs buckled beneath her.

"Oh. Dear."

CHAPTER 7

Vail stared at the witch, filled with conflicting feelings that threatened to tear his slender grip on sanity away from him and struggling to process the urges running through him. A wild need to reject what had happened, and her at the same time, combined with whispers that warned she was out to harm him, but the strength of that need to shove her away was nothing in comparison to the power of the other urge he felt as he gazed at her cut wrist.

A potent, commanding and controlling need, one darker and more powerful than his desire to distance and protect himself, ruled him.

A need to protect the female he instinctively felt belonged to him.

Had been made for him.

He laughed at that, a short bark that drove the witch further away and had her tucking her wrist to her chest and looking at him with blue eyes that announced she thought him insane.

She was right about that. He was mad. Mad because of a witch. Mad because he had vowed to kill all her kind. Mad because of her and his desire to protect her.

The sweet, soft scent of her blood drove him mad too. He stared at her wrist, his regenerated fangs itching to tear into her flesh and bring her pain, to make her suffer as he had, even as he ached with a need to seal the wound and heal her.

He couldn't get to her though, and she seemed reluctant to bring her wrist to him so he could satisfy that dark urge to steal her pain away.

Her dishevelled ash-blonde hair bounced against her slender shoulders as she began to pace. The chain of her restraints jangled with each frantic step that carried her across the width of his cell. He could feel her unease, could sense her confusion and doubt, and her fear.

He knew he was the source of all those feelings within her, and that he was powerless to take them away. She had every right to doubt him, to believe him insane, to not trust him. He vaguely recalled attempting to bite her. The sound of her pained cry had driven into the twisted mess of his mind like a spear, shattering the madness's hold on him and dragging him back to the present.

To her.

Gods. Why?

Was she his?

Or was this all some ploy by her, a trick or a spell, something she had cast upon him while he had been vulnerable, just as Kordula had?

He snarled at that, his fangs dropping and his ears flaring back against the sides of his head. No sorceress would ever bewitch him again. He would kill any who tried.

The witch stopped and eyed him, her fair eyebrows dipping low above those crystalline cool blue eyes. They held him transfixed, entranced him before he could look away, and a strange calm flowed through him, carrying away his agitation and his pain, leaving only peace behind. He hadn't felt such a thing in millennia. He had forgotten what it felt like to be at peace.

It shattered the second silver stars sparkled in her irises, dancing among the blue, reminding him what she was.

"*Witch,*" he growled.

She huffed, turned her nose up at him, and resumed her pacing. "A witch who just healed your arse, and don't you forget it."

How could he forget it? Her blood ran in his body, a heady wine that intoxicated him. No doubt it was working a spell on him for her, luring him deeper under her influence, placing chains on him that would bind him to her and hold him faster than the ones that bound him to the slab.

His gaze flickered to her wrist. Although, he might have bound her to him. He could hear her heartbeat and it no longer matched his.

Vail flexed his fingers, unable to stop the restless twitching as his thoughts turned troubled and his mask of sanity threatened to slip again.

The witch stopped.

Stared at him.

He pinned his gaze onto the ceiling, focusing on it and trying to shut her out together with his driving need to heal her.

To keep himself from asking her again to approach him, he began a mental assessment of his body, detaching himself from the world at the same time so the memories of his injuries and how he had sustained them remained at bay.

His feet were no longer broken. His hands were strong. His bones were mended. His flesh healed.

His knees. He shifted his legs, bringing his knees up, and his eyes widened when cool air washed across his backside.

Vail quickly lowered them, opened his eyes and craned his neck. A strip of black material lay across his hips. Other than that, he was naked.

He glanced at the witch's knees. Pale, a little knobbly from kneeling on the hard stone, and very exposed. The hem of her black dress was ragged. She had torn the strip that covered him from it, and deep inside, he felt grateful for her kindness.

He didn't know how to process that either.

He forced his gaze back to the ceiling, trying to let it all flow into him and not fighting it. If he fought it, he would lose his grip again. The darkness would surge within him, and gods help him, he didn't want her to feel that in him.

Vail closed his eyes.

The witch risked a step closer. Rather than triggering an attack, her proximity soothed him.

Gods help him.

The scent of nature swirled around him, adding to her calming effect, and flowed through him, chasing back the darkness. He wanted to embrace it, but couldn't when it all stemmed from her. His Little Wild Rose.

She was a witch though. A fickle, deceiving, sorceress. He would never forget that.

No matter how deep he fell under her spell, he would always remember that she was a witch and he would never forget the cruelty her kind were capable of.

He squeezed his eyes shut and distanced himself from her, shutting down every physical response and every emotional reaction to her proximity, each betrayal by his own body and heart.

He refused to crave the touch of a female capable of controlling him, of hurting him and using him as another had. He would guard his heart to protect what little sanity he had clawed back over his months of wandering Hell and cleansing himself by killing her kind.

He didn't want to be mad. He chuckled to himself, the mirthless and hopeless sound loud in the heavy silence. He didn't want to be ruled by rage and a desire to deal pain and death and destruction.

He didn't want to feel driven to seek his own end.

Not anymore.

Now, he wanted to get word to his brother and warn him of the Fifth King's plans.

To do that, he needed to escape this place.

The witch's blood that he could still taste on his tongue, could sense flowing through him and repairing his damaged body, had gifted him with the strength he needed. The hunger that had ravaged him, depleting his strength and making it easier for the madness to grip him, was gone.

But the blood she had given him had also strengthened his connection to her. Lost to his madness, he had not only instigated the bond between them but he had completed it in a way. They had exchanged blood now.

That troubled him, but his broken mind didn't react to it in the way he expected. The beast didn't rise. The darkness didn't swell within him. The memories of her giving blood to him didn't merge with those of Kordula forcing hers upon him.

His heart remained calm.

That troubled Vail most of all.

The witch began to move around his cell again, shuffling steps that spoke of the fatigue he had seen in her eyes and in her drawn expression whenever her strength slipped and her anger at him faded. Whenever she drew near to him, warmth flowed over his tired body, offering comfort that threatened to unsettle him.

But it was the smell of her blood that tugged hardest at his darker emotions. The constant subtle scent stirred memories, a swirling tempest of violence blended with something more terrible. Something more dangerous.

Pleasure.

He curled his fingers into fists and clenched them, battling the surging tide of memories, of hands that stroked and lips that caressed. Those memories became ghostly sensations before he could find the way to stop them, the brush of fingers and tongues across his flesh, and he squirmed under their attention, tried to shift his body away from them. Hands grasped his shoulders, pinning him in place, claws digging into his skin. Hot breath skated across his cheek and tickled his ear. Whispered words that were more a threat than a sensual promise, alarming him.

No. He shook his head, frantic as fear rose to clog his throat and his lungs constricted. He writhed, uttered a silent plea to leave him alone, to use another for pleasure and give him peace. The phantom hands and lips danced lower, caressing his stomach. The breath washed over his navel, a purr of approval now. A hot palm closed over his groin.

"No?" The female voice dripped with confusion but it speared the darkness like a bolt of lightning, shocking him to his core.

Vail's eyes shot open and he stared at the blonde witch, his chest heaving as he struggled to breathe normally.

"You said no. You talking to me?" She looked around the cell. "Or a ghost?"

His breath left him in a rush, he tipped his head back and sagged against the cold stone. "A ghost."

Her gaze intensified, boring into him. He refused to look at her and wouldn't answer her if she dared to ask him what had been happening in his head.

She resumed her pacing, moving closer this time, and the scent of her blood yanked the whole of his focus to her. He flicked his gaze down to her. She clutched her arm to her chest still.

"Come," he said, his tone hard and commanding, and she arched an eyebrow at him. He didn't care if she thought him rude. Her blood scent was pushing him too hard, shoving him towards the brink, and he couldn't afford to lose himself to the darkness right now. He needed to plot, and that meant he needed her healed, and preferably out of his cell. "I will heal you."

She shook her head. "I would rather take my chances with septicaemia. It's less likely to kill me."

Vail growled at her, grasped the chain that fixed his arms to the stone block above his head, and pulled on it with every ounce of his strength. He needed to heal her and he would heal her, whether she liked it or not. He had to do it. He had no choice in the matter. The need to heal his female ran deep, drove him mad and demanded he comply. It didn't care that he couldn't reach her. He didn't care. He had to reach her somehow, or convince her to come to him.

He had to heal her or he would lose his mind.

He arched his back and grunted as he pulled harder, straining against the thick steel chain and the cuffs that held him.

He would heal her.

His female bled because of him. She bled for him. She had given her strength to him and now he would take care of her.

The metal cuffs bit into his wrists but it didn't stop him. Nothing would. If he couldn't break the chain, then he would claw at the stone until it gave way.

He went to turn onto his stomach.

"Stop that." The witch rushed to him, her hands flying towards his shoulders, and abruptly halted with her palms only millimetres from his skin. The chain between her restraints swung back and forth, close to touching him. She hesitated, fear making her eyes sparkle, and went to pull back.

"My female bleeds," Vail whispered, transfixed by the red line across her wrist. It was ragged and still seeped blood. The need to lick that blood away, to seal the wound and heal her, tore at him. He jerked his chin, lost in the scent of her and his need to heal her. "Come, Ki'ara. I will not hurt you."

She hesitated still.

A strange sensation, one forgotten so long ago that it felt new to him, stabbed straight through his heart.

Hurt.

Not a physical pain but an emotional one born of her rejection and her evident lack of trust where he was concerned.

Vail withdrew, settling on his back. He could understand why she refused to place her trust in him. He had done nothing to earn it and he didn't deserve anyone's trust, least of all hers.

The witch surprised him by moving her wrist closer to him.

He eyed her hand, a wild feeling growing within him and unsettling him with insidious whispered words. She was going to touch him. He couldn't let her touch him. His throat tightened. His lungs squeezed.

He couldn't let her touch him. He had to drive her back and keep her away from him. His fangs lengthened. A snarl crawled up his throat.

Vail used all of his will to swallow it back down and forced his fangs away. She meant him no harm. He needed to heal her.

She meant him no harm.

She would not touch him.

His eyes flickered to hers and they echoed his fear back at him. His female feared him. He would give her reason to believe him capable of good as well as evil, of kindness as well as cruelty.

He drew in a deep breath, savoured her scent, and held back the darkness as he swept his tongue over the wound on her wrist. The rich taste of her blood bloomed on his tongue, a thousand flowers that exploded into a meadow and instantly constructed a vision of nature so perfect and peaceful that he warmed right down to his marrow, as if the sun caressed his skin and not her pure azure gaze.

But the darkness would not be denied. As the taste of her faded, it swept across the land, wilting the flowers and blackening their stems, stealing all beauty, colour and life from his perfect vision of nature.

Vail bit back a growl and turned his face away from her, fearing he would tear into her flesh with his fangs if he remained near her.

"Leave me," he snarled and sensed her withdraw.

The distance that opened between them ripped at him, causing a fierce ache behind his ribs and a yearning for her to come closer again, to ignore him and sit with him. He needed the warmth she brought with her. He needed the calm that she awakened in him.

He needed her away.

Cursed witch.

She had cast her spell on him somehow and already he was falling deeper into it, snared in her trap but not incapable of escape. He could still break free of her charms. No witch would control him, never again. He knew how to break their spells now. He knew how to free himself.

He would kill her.

No. Vail squeezed his eyes shut and his heart throbbed. Little Wild Rose was his ki'ara. She had healed him. She had shown him tenderness, compassion, and care. She belonged to him.

He belonged to her.

He clawed his hair back and growled as his fangs lengthened.

A witch had told him such a thing before. The words taunted him, echoing around his mind in her wretched voice. He belonged to her now. He would do all she bid.

He had shown her tenderness, compassion and care. He had healed her. He had thought that she had belonged to him.

He had ended up belonging to her. A slave. A sword. A whore.

Little Wild Rose would do the same to him if he gave her the chance. She had cast her spell, had taken the first step by tricking him into believing her to be his ki'ara.

Just as Kordula had done.

He dug his claws into his scalp and the sting of pain gave him something to focus on while he untangled the threads of past and present, slowly regaining his sanity.

Two huge demon males stopped outside his cell. The same two who had taken him before the king. The same two who had taken pleasure in stripping and beating him, teaching him a lesson in humility he had refused to learn.

He bared his fangs at them and hissed.

They eyed him with surprise, frowned at the witch where she stood behind him, still holding her wrist to her chest, and then exchanged a glance.

Vail schooled his features, unwilling to give anything away. They would know from his condition what had transpired, but he couldn't allow them to suspect it went beyond an offering of blood to heal him. He would never allow them to know that Little Wild Rose was his fated one.

"She gave him blood," the smaller of the two said in the demon tongue. "Should she be punished?"

Vail barely suppressed the growl that rumbled through his chest at the thought of these demons harming Little Wild Rose purely because she had sought to help him. The king had clearly ordered him healed and by her hand, and she had done just that. Only she had chosen a more merciful method of healing him, one that hadn't provoked a violent response or pushed him deeper into madness.

The larger demon seemed to consider the other one's question and Vail almost lost his grip on his temper. He wasn't sure he could retain it, or his grip on his sanity, if they punished her. He didn't think he was strong enough to bear feeling her pain and knowing he was the cause. He wanted nothing to do with a witch, but the instinct that said she was his mate and under his protection ran deep, controlling him and overriding the need to keep her away, replacing it with a desperate desire to pull her closer and shield her from the world.

Judging by how calm she was, unafraid of these demons as they considered punishing her, she didn't speak their language and knew not what they were discussing. He was glad of it. If she had feared, he might have lost his head and threatened them. He couldn't allow them to think he had any feelings for her, because he knew they would report it to their king, and their king would use it against him.

The big male grunted. "King Bruan said for the witch to heal him. I say she has done just that. I do not think we mention her methods to him though. He might punish us for not watching her."

The smaller demon opened the cell door and beckoned to her. She cast a glance down at Vail before gathering the chain between her cuffs into her hands, walking past him and out into the corridor. The larger male took hold of her arm and Vail had to clench his jaw in order to silence himself and stop himself from warning them not to take her from him, and not to lay a hand on her.

The two demons spared him one last glance before locking the cell door and leading the witch away.

CHAPTER 8

Vail closed his eyes, locked his senses onto the witch and tracked her through the dungeon. The squeak of a metal door opening and closing brought him relief. They had taken her to her cell. She would be safe there for now.

He pulled his focus away from her and pinned it back on everything that had happened, able to look at things more clearly now that the witch was no longer present.

His mind ran in circles, leaping from one moment to the next, patching together the snippets he could recall from the times when the darkness had gripped him. With each pass, things grew clearer, but his focus began to slip back to the witch. He couldn't smell her anymore. He could only feel her, and her emotions were as turbulent as his own. Fear stood out amongst them, potent and powerful. Why was she afraid?

He needed to know.

The bond between them was quiet, but it fascinated him. He had never felt anything like it. It was as if a part of him that had always been missing was suddenly there, filling a void in his soul and completing him, even though he knew he was far from whole. If this was a trick, it was a powerful spell behind it. He felt physically altered by the exchange of blood, could strengthen the link by nurturing it, coaxing it closer to the surface of his skin, until he swore he could feel her near him and smell her sweet scent of nature again.

"Little Wild Rose," Vail whispered and reached for her without thinking, needing to sense that she was there at the other end of the bond and that this confused and concerned her as much as it did him.

"The demons said the king wanted you healed again so he could speak with you." The male voice intruded into his thoughts and shattered the link he had fostered between him and the witch.

Vail looked off to his left, across the corridor to the incubus. The male rubbed at the thick dark beard coating his jaw and his green eyes gained a wary edge. The swirls, dashes and spikes that formed the lines of his markings along his forearms flared in hues of dark blue and dirty gold. The male feared him.

He recalled the incubus speaking with the witch, saying things about him. He narrowed his gaze on the male. An incubus was no match for an elf. It would have been wise of the male to hold his tongue rather than dare speaking to him.

The incubus sat beside the bars of his cell, leaned his bare back against the thick grey stone wall and rested his arms on his knees, his skin pale against the black jeans he wore. Vail noted that he wore the same cuffs as he and the witch, but was given more freedom than both of them. There was no chain holding the two cuffs together.

Vail stared at him, assessing his build and his physical appearance. Judging by the male's long, shaggy dark hair drawn back into a thong and his unkempt beard, he had been a prisoner for some months, if not years.

"Don't even consider hurting Rosalind." The incubus's markings began to change, obsidian and crimson chasing back the other hues, alerting Vail of his anger.

Vail snarled at him, flashing his fangs and warning him that telling him what to do with his ki'ara would end in his death. No doubt the incubus wanted her for himself. She belonged to Vail now though, and he would allow no male to touch her.

He paused.

Rosalind?

Was that her name? It was familiar. He searched his memories of their times together, caught a fragment of a moment when she had shouted at him that her name was Rosalind.

It was pretty. A fair name for a fair witch.

Vail caught himself and growled. Even the most black hearted of witches had fair sounding names. It was all another trick, a method of luring him into believing her weak and vulnerable, in need of his protection.

"Chill," the male said in a flippant tone, one that drew another growl from him. "I'm not interested in the witch."

Vail didn't believe that for a second. He glared at the male. The incubus held up his left hand, revealing a gold band around the ring finger. The male was mated?

"I figure that since we're stuck across from each other, maybe we should get to know each other... because you look like a man with somewhere to be and I have somewhere I need to be too." The incubus lowered his hand onto his knee and twisted the gold band around his finger with his thumb, a distant look in his eyes. "The name is Fenix. I don't suppose you like being called Mad Elf Prince so your name would be?"

"Vail," he said, surprised that the male knew of him yet didn't know his true name. Had history forgotten it? Was that all he was to the world now—the mad elf prince? Vail shook those questions away and focused on the male across from him. Incubi were strong and possessed an ability to teleport. The male could be useful in an escape. "You are mated?"

"Yes... and like your little bond with the witch... it's complicated."

Vail wanted to deny that he had bound himself to the witch, but failed to see the point. Incubi also had the ability to sense emotions in people, to influence desire and manipulate feelings. That ability and his position in the dungeon, directly opposite Vail's cell, had given the incubus enough clues to piece together what had happened between him and the witch. If the incubus felt protective of the witch, perhaps Vail could use that to his advantage, playing on his feelings to convince him to be of service during an escape.

Fenix heaved a sigh and idly ran the fingers of his left hand down the bars of his cell, his ring scraping the metal.

Vail twisted his arms, lowering his left one and allowing the chain to slide through the ring holding it to the slab so he could bring his right hand to his face. He scrubbed the several days' worth of stubble on his jaw and longed for his armour and his claws. With them, he would be able to scrape the irritating stubble away. He had no desire to end up looking as the incubus did, with a thick mass of hair covering the lower half of his face.

"Is your mate here too?" Vail said.

The male looked across at him and shook his head.

"Not anymore. She was here but the bastard Frayne killed her right in front of me… and now I do not know where she is."

That didn't make any sense to Vail. If the female was dead, then she was gone and this male knew exactly where she was. Had the male lost his mind on losing his female, or was there more to his bond than he was telling Vail?

"Frayne is dead, slain on the battlefield by King Thorne of the Third Realm. I witnessed it myself." Vail inched himself up onto his elbows and studied the incubus for a reaction.

His fae markings remained deepest red and black.

"I knew of that, but it hasn't assuaged my hunger for vengeance in her name. She had called herself Evelyn this time."

"This time?" Vail couldn't hold that question back. "You speak of her as if she comes back from the dead."

A solemn smile touched the incubus's lips beneath his beard. "She does. We are cursed. She more so than I, but I have the worst side of it. I have to bear being driven to find her, and then seeing her living out her life without knowing of me, and I know if I dare to make her love me again, she will die."

Fenix closed his eyes and buried his face in his hands and Vail gave him a moment of silence, sensing his need to battle the surge of powerful emotions that had crossed his face and had coloured his voice, and his fae markings too. They shone in hues of black, purple and blue now, giving them a solemn appearance, one that spoke of suffering.

Seeing his female living without him tormented this incubus, drove him mad with a need for her, even when he knew that if she fell in love with him, she was cursed to die.

"She is reborn upon her death, stripped of her memories, and placed back into the world. I have to find her… or the one who did this to us. Yes… I need to find him. I cannot bear it anymore. I must lift the curse before she ends up dead again." Fenix pushed trembling fingers through his hair, dragging the long lengths back from his face, and looked up at Vail. The sombre hues of his markings changed again, black and red sweeping over them as his green eyes narrowed on Vail. "You want out of this place, and so do I. I have to get out of here."

Vail wondered if he looked as crazy as this male, driven wild by the things that tormented him, and by his captivity.

The steady echo of footsteps warned him that now was not the time to discuss escape plans. Two guards approached, the same males who had taken Little Wild Rose from him.

They stopped outside his cell, both of them dressed formally now, wearing loose black shirts tucked into their black leather trousers. Vail assumed they had fixed their attire to make themselves more suitable for their task of bringing him before their king.

The smaller male grinned and held up a pair of black trousers, reminding Vail that he was nude beneath the strip of material Rosalind had kindly bestowed upon him.

"Perhaps we should make him walk naked." The larger demon snatched the trousers from his companion, bunched one leg in each of his fists, and threatened to tear them in half.

Vail's heart jerked in his chest and he pulled on his restraints, battling the sudden desperate need to ask these demons for mercy. He stifled that desire, schooling his features into an expression of indifference even when his insides were twisting in knots, tightening at the thought of having to walk naked through the entire castle, forced to endure another form of humiliation.

The warriors in the courtyard would see him, and no doubt mock him.

The bear and dragon shifters too.

The dark witches.

He clenched his fists, grasping the chain as his heart pounded wildly, driven to a thunderous beat by the thought of those witches seeing him nude and exposed.

Vulnerable.

Before he could stop himself, he looked at the largest demon and whispered, "Do not."

Those words felt like an admission of weakness, as if he had just revealed a chink in his armour through which these two demons could hurt him, but he hadn't been able to hold them back. He had clung to the tattered remains of his pride, had endured every lash of their whips and every taunt in silence, giving them nothing and not allowing them to see how they humiliated him, but he wouldn't be able to cope with such complete degradation in front of others—in front of witches.

The demons seemed to consider his request and then the larger one smirked and waved the trousers at him, teasing him with them.

"I do not think he learned the lesson our king wished for him. Maybe a walk through the castle naked would help him learn his place and that humility." The smaller demon went to take the trousers from his comrade.

Vail growled at him from between clenched teeth, on the verge of begging the males to let him have the trousers and a shred of his pride, and promising he would behave with more civility towards their king.

"Leave him alone, you bloody bastards!" The female voice rang through the dungeon at startling volume and with so much venom that many of the occupants of the other cells became restless.

Fenix chuckled.

The two demons looked shocked and the smaller one lowered his hands to his sides.

"King Bruan probably wouldn't be pleased with us if we did make him walk naked," the larger one muttered and gestured to the cell door.

His companion opened it, entered the cell and walked straight around Vail to the cuffs and the chain attached to the stone slab. He unlocked the ring that held Vail's chain, grabbed one of his restraints, and hauled him into a sitting position. The larger male unlocked the cuffs around his ankles and tossed the trousers at him.

"Dress. The king wishes to discuss his plans with you."

Vail did so without hesitation, quickly slipping the black cotton trousers on and pulling them up. They were too large, but the waist was small enough that they didn't fall down, but rather hung low on his hips. The larger demon fastened the ankle restraints back in place and then the other one pulled him onto his feet.

Neither male spoke as they led him from the cell and along the corridor, but Vail wouldn't have paid them much attention even if they had. His thoughts collided, flitting between the witch and the king, and his current location.

He couldn't fail to notice that they hadn't restrained him in the same manner as before. The chain between his ankles was long enough for him to stride with purpose without the risk of tripping, and the chain between his wrists hung free, swinging with each determined step he made. They had given him more freedom, and were allowing him to walk sandwiched between them. Why? Was it on the king's orders?

Instinct told Vail that it wasn't a good thing. The king had treated him roughly before, had resorted to torture in an attempt to break him and convince him to comply with his orders and play a part in his plan. Now, that same vicious, cruel and manipulative male was having him escorted in a more comfortable fashion, given clothes and more freedom, and Vail suspected it was an attempt to lure him over to the king's side.

The male had a new plan and Vail had a feeling he wasn't going to like it.

He catalogued everything as he walked, making notes of all the details and the route the demons took. He scanned all the occupants of the cells too, but none of the males they contained were of any use to him. Only the incubus seemed healthy enough in mind and body, and had powers that could assist him in an escape.

And escape he would.

He would find a way to leave this place behind him and warn his brother, and he would use the incubus to help him make it happen.

Little Wild Rose. Her scent rushed over him like cherry blossoms caught in a breeze and his step faltered. He glanced her way, catching a brief glimpse of her huddled in the corner of her dank cell before she raised her head and he averted his gaze so she didn't see him looking at her.

He couldn't leave her behind.

Violence and darkness surged within him whenever he thought about her, barely tempered by softer foreign emotions, and part of him knew that taking her with him was too dangerous. She was liable to drive him mad, to steal away his sanity with her presence, but he couldn't leave her behind.

He glanced back at her, locking eyes with her in the split second before the wall of her cell stole her from view, and his heart thudded hard against his ribs.

Darkness warred with light inside his soul, the swirling black swamping more of it, driving back the slender glow of good as he drifted further away from her.

He used his limited powers to close the connection between them as much as he could now that they were bonded. The compulsion to keep himself closed off to her was strong, overwhelming, and he did it without hesitation.

Not because she was a witch.

But because he didn't want her to know him. He knew how dark and ugly he was inside, how twisted and broken. He had become aware of it the moment Kordula's spell had broken with her death.

Her death had freed him from her rule, but not from what he had done. Four thousand years of killing, four thousand years of memories, and four thousand years of destroying lives, kingdoms and those he loved. All of it had remained after her death and lived on in his blackened soul. Everything he had done now rested on his shoulders, a weight that was too much to bear and was slowly driving him to his knees.

Loren had thought taking Kordula's life would free him, Vail knew that and knew his brother had done it out of kindness, believing he would be restored and saved by his actions.

Loren had condemned him.

Vail had tried to come to terms with everything. He had fought the dark memories and attempted to convince himself that responsibility for all that death and destruction rested on Kordula's shoulders and was hers to bear.

But it had been his hand that had taken those lives. His powers that had brought kingdoms to their knees.

His pleasure on seeing them fall and the lands run red with blood.

Kordula had only given him the orders and compelled him to obey.

It was the darkness inside him, the beast she had awakened in him, that had taken pleasure from rending flesh with his claws and smashing bones to ashes. It still took pleasure from it now.

He took pleasure from it.

When he had gone into a killing rage in order to protect Olivia during the battle, he had retained awareness of his actions. He had been the one in control. No one had compelled him to brutally slay all those demons, dragon shifters, and vampires. No one had controlled him.

He had been free, the master of his own body, and yet rather than fight with honour and a sword, he had chosen to savage his opponents with claw and fang.

Like an animal.

Kordula had awakened the beast.

But Vail had embraced it.

And now it was one with him, growing stronger each day as the weight of his sins filled his soul with darkness, dragging him down into the black abyss.

He knew that if Little Wild Rose felt that in him, she would leave him the second she could. The greater part of him wanted that, and welcomed it.

There was a strange fragment of him though, a tiny corner of his soul that had somehow survived four thousand years of torment and hell, that feared her doing such a thing to him because it knew that she was already becoming his anchor to this world.

His everything.

No matter how hard he fought it.

If she turned her back on him, that part of him would die and his fall would be complete.

He would become the darkness all elves feared and the world would know his wrath.

Light flickered over his skin and he squinted against it, his eyes quickly adjusting to the brightness as he strode through the arched doorway and into the courtyard. Huge braziers burned at intervals, illuminating the wide area.

His gaze scanned his surroundings, documenting everything, from the routes the guards took as they moved from building to building along the high wall, to the number of non-demons he could see. He focused on the arched doors and windows of the dark stone buildings dotted around the wall of the courtyard, trying to discern what their purpose was as the guards led him across the expansive open area towards the towering main castle ahead of him.

Vail noted that the witches were not present tonight.

His two demon escorts quickened their pace and he kept up with them, his chin raised and back straight as he eyed the warriors around him. They paused at their work to watch him pass, darkness in their emerald eyes but a touch of wariness too. No doubt they were seeing a very different male from the one who had passed through this same courtyard only days ago.

One who commanded more respect and inspired more fear.

The smaller demon in front of him shoved the twin black wooden doors of the main castle entrance open. Vail followed him into the darkness, continuing to catalogue everything he could see, including the corridors that ran off from the hallway. The one on his right appeared to go into a stairwell that led upwards, while the one to his left ran into the walls.

"Prince Vail." The deep male voice boomed through the great hall as they entered, echoing around the high vaulted ceiling and the enormous obsidian columns that supported it.

King Bruan rose from his black throne and stepped down from the raised platform at the end of the aisle.

A very civil and friendly greeting from the demon male who had ordered him tortured into submission. He had suspected the king thought to charm him over to his side, and now he knew the male planned to do just that.

Vail tamped down his urge to snarl and bare his fangs at the manipulative demon king.

No one controlled him. Not anymore.

The two guards dropped back and Vail approached him, keeping his posture relaxed even as he calculated his chances of successfully launching an attack on the burly demon king.

The larger male strolled along the aisle towards him, his long black leather-clad legs easily eating up the distance between them. Obsidian dragon-like wings rested furled against his bare back.

The king wore no crown. Another attempt to appear friendly, as if they were of equal standing.

Vail failed to see how that was possible. This male was far beneath him, a youngling demon playing at being a king. Even if this man ruled for millennia and conquered every demon realm, Vail would still refuse to view him as an equal.

He tipped his chin up and looked down his nose at the male who stood at the same height as him. King Bruan's six-feet-six frame was far broader than Vail's, and thickly muscled, but his physical strength wouldn't be the determining factor in a fight between them. Vail was strong now with Rosalind's blood flowing through him, and with the restoration of his physical strength came the restoration of his psychic powers.

Vail could crush King Bruan like a bug with his telekinesis alone.

Only the infernal magic-laced cuffs were stopping him from doing so right now.

"You wished to talk?" Vail said in the demon tongue and swept his gaze over the demon king from head to toe and back again, searching for any physical weaknesses he could use against him.

The king seemed in prime condition, and with Vail's powers bound by his restraints and two demons watching his every move, he wouldn't win against him if he attacked him. Not yet.

For now, he would have to settle for seeing what the king wanted with him and using the inevitable walk back to his cell to continue searching out weak spots in the fortress and possible escape routes.

"I have considered what you said and perhaps you are right and blackmailing your brother into an alliance is not the path to take." King Bruan's green eyes flashed brightly, a twisted edge to his smile that Vail didn't like. The male flicked his long black braid over his muscled shoulder and moved a step closer. His voice dropped to a whisper. "I want to kill your brother for his part in the war and deal a blow to the elves."

Vail gave no reaction to that announcement. He schooled his features and waited, knowing Bruan wasn't done. The king wanted him to react, to ask what he intended to do. He was playing Vail and testing his allegiance, and if he questioned Bruan, the king would know he had lied about wanting Loren dead.

As much as he despised the vile demon, he had to play along and gain the king's trust. Eventually, the king would give him more freedom, and with it would come an opportunity to escape.

And then, Vail would kill him.

King Bruan flared his wings and then furled them against his back. He signalled to one of the guards.

Not one of the guards, Vail realised as an oily slick slithered over his skin. Magic. The sudden increase announced a witch had entered the great hall. The magic smothered him, growing stronger as she approached, threatening to strip him of his sanity. He clung to it, unwilling to lose it now when he needed it most. He had to remain lucid. He couldn't allow the king to see his weakness. The male would exploit it.

He would use the witch against him.

Make her touch him.

The oily slick on his skin became twin patches that moved over his body, roamed it like hands caressing him, and shifted to form fingers that stroked and danced lower. He shuddered and closed his eyes, forced his mind away from the magic and reached for something to steady him.

Little Wild Rose danced into his mind, all of nature in her wake, green and colourful and beautiful.

Her eyes met his, the colour of clear morning skies spotted with stars, and warmth flowed over his skin, burning away the dark stains of black magic that marred it.

Vail opened his eyes and fixed them on King Bruan, shutting out the blonde witch as she handed the demon a clay mug. The male lifted the vessel to his lips, took a great gulp of the sweet smelling liquid, and lowered it again. He rubbed his other hand across the back of his mouth and held the mug out to Vail.

"We will have a bargain, you and I. You will help me defeat your own flesh and blood, or I will use you to lure him out and take his head in front of you, as the demon king did to my brother."

Vail raised his cuffed wrists and snatched the mug of mead from King Bruan's grip. He knocked back the contents, the potent alcohol rushing straight to his head and threatening to send him to his knees, and tossed the mug. It smashed on the stone flags near the witch and she scowled at him, her dark eyes becoming spotted with bright crimson.

He bared his fangs at her.

King Bruan could go to the very bottom of the fiery pit of Hell where all dark souls went after death and Vail would personally escort him there.

The demon male had made two mistakes.

One, Vail refused to be an instrument of revenge against his brother. He had vowed never to hurt Loren again, and would do all in his power to keep that promise and keep him and his people safe.

Two, he would never carry out orders against his will again. No one could command him now. He would never subject himself to the rule of others. He was free, the master of himself again, and King Bruan would realise that when he carried out the plan that had just come to him.

He would play the loyal mad elf prince to this wretched demon, vowing to kill his brother, and when he had gained the king's trust and more freedom, he would escape and send word to Loren. Once he had warned his beloved brother, he would kill Bruan and turn the wrath of the demons of this realm upon him, drawing it away from Loren and the elves.

He would sacrifice himself for the sake of his brother and his people.

It was the least he could do to make amends for his sins.

There was only one flaw in his plan. One complication.

Little Wild Rose.

He would have to find a way to get her to safety and away from the demons before he could carry out his plan to kill their king. He would have to know that she was safe or he wouldn't have the strength to face death and embrace it. He would feel compelled to remain with her and protect her.

Loren.

He would beg his brother to show her mercy and give her shelter, protecting her in his stead. Loren was more capable of protecting her than he was. His brother would take care of her, would treat her well and ensure her happiness.

Vail couldn't do such a thing.

If she remained near him, he would eventually hurt her, or worse. The thought of coming out of a black rage to find his claws dripping with her blood stopped him cold and froze his heart.

"You accept my terms?" King Bruan said, pulling him away from thoughts of his fated female and back to reality, to the presence of a dark witch.

The blonde watched him closely, suspicion colouring her dark eyes.

"Do as you please," Vail said in the demon tongue. "As long as Loren finally dies by my hand."

Bruan's expression darkened. "And why should you have that honour?"

Vail snarled, the feral sound rumbling through the cavernous room. The witch took a step back, placing King Bruan between her and Vail, and it was hard to stop himself from attacking her, even when he was at a disadvantage. He forced his focus back to Bruan.

"Because I have been waiting to kill my brother for forty-two centuries so I can seize the throne," Vail bit out and advanced a step, closing the distance between him and the king, and flashed his fangs as he grinned. "If you allow me to be the one to kill Loren, you will have a powerful ally in the elves when I take the throne back."

Bruan stared at him in silence. It pressed down on Vail and doubts surfaced. He held his expression and the king's green gaze, unwilling to allow the male to see beyond his veil of fury and hunger for power to the unsettled feeling growing inside him. He would succeed in his plan. He would convince this wretched demon to give him more freedom and then he would bring the kingdom down on his head.

"I will need time to consider your request." Bruan signalled the two guards and they marched forwards, coming to flank Vail. "Take him back to his cell."

Vail held the king's gaze, silently challenging him and refusing to back down. Demons respected strength, both physical and mental. He would give the king reason to respect him.

"I will be the one to kill my brother. Only then can I claim the throne and no one will stop me from achieving that which I desire. I have not fought Loren for four thousand years for a demon to snatch this victory from my grasp." Vail moved another step closer and stared down at the king. "Give me my victory and I give you an army of elves, and the power to take any demon kingdom you desire."

He turned away before Bruan could form a response and strode down the aisle, heading straight for the arched door at the end. The two guards hurried to catch up with him and Vail breathed slowly, steadying his heart to stop it from racing. Either he had just earned himself another brutal round of torture at their hands, or he had earned the respect of their king.

The game was afoot and the next move belonged to Bruan.

CHAPTER 9

Nature swirled around him, pushing back the darkness and the nightmares, drawing him into the light. Vail breathed deep of the floral scent, taking the sweet elixir down into his lungs, desperate to use it to ward off the memories that had swamped him the moment he had closed his eyes.

A soft melody enchanted him, the sound of her voice giving him comfort the likes of which he hadn't felt in over four thousand years.

Little Wild Rose.

She was close to him, her proximity offering him peace and respite from his nightmares, keeping the memories at bay.

A male voice joined hers.

The incubus.

Anger curled through him, a possessive rage that swiftly claimed control and urged him to tear Rosalind away from the bars of his cell and kill the male.

Vail tried to rise from where he slept and snarled as chains held him in place. Shackles meant to weaken him. He growled and fought his bonds, uncaring of the fact that the thick metal cuffs sliced into his wrists and pain seared his bones. All that mattered was reaching his female and keeping the male away from her.

He needed to get her away from the incubus.

He needed to kill him.

He hissed and bared his fangs as they punched long from his gums. His ears flared back against the sides of his head.

His eyes opened and locked on the male.

Vail growled at him and fought his bonds, pulling hard on the chains that held him. His blood flowed over his hands, making his grip slick, but it wouldn't stop him. He would break free and destroy the incubus. He dug his fingertips into the links of the thick chain and roared as he arched his back and threw all of his strength into his next pull.

"Keep away from him," the male said and Vail lost it.

He wrestled with his bonds, using every last drop of his strength to fight them, determined to break free. The cursed male meant to lure Little Wild Rose away from him.

He meant to take her from him.

Darkness loomed inside him, eating away the light, destroying it as it rampaged through his body and unleashed the part of him he didn't want her to see. The part of him he needed in order to escape his wretched bonds and kill the male.

Vail embraced it, snarled as he lost himself in it, and laughed as he yanked harder on the chain.

The incubus would pay for his attempt to steal what was his. Little Wild Rose belong to him now. He would destroy the male, would bathe his claws in the wretch's blood and tear him limb from limb with his bare hands, and then he would claim the female.

She belonged to him now.

All would know it.

Vail arched off the stone slab again and roared as he grasped the chain and pulled on it, felt it start to give even as his body did the same, pain ripping through his every muscle and searing his bones.

He dimly heard her soft voice through the rush of blood in his ears and the fierce drumming of his heart.

She spoke with the male.

Vail fought harder, yanking on the restraints. He would kill the male and then he would claim his Little Wild Rose and she would know she belonged to him. She would never betray him again.

Never.

Her voice came again.

His muscles twanged and pain shot through him, tearing him apart and turning his limbs rubbery. He collapsed onto the slab, breathing hard and shaking all over, the chain falling from his weakening grip. He snarled under his breath and tried to grasp the chain and keep fighting, but he could barely shift his wrists and couldn't move enough to pull the chain tight.

Her light soft voice came once more, and it was clearer this time. She was close.

"Vail." His name fell from her lips and he sensed her warmth near his forehead.

Not touching him, but hovering close.

He cracked his eyes open and unclenched his aching jaw.

"Vail?" she whispered again and he blinked slowly, lost in her glittering blue eyes. "Why did you hurt yourself? Was it another bad dream?"

"Why?" he croaked, frowning at her, the answer eluding him. Why had he hurt himself? He had fought the bonds because he had wanted to reach her. He had wanted to protect her. From what? His jaw clenched again and he turned his face away from her, to his left and the male in the cell there. He bared his fangs at him.

The witch looked at him too.

Vail turned his growl on her.

"I thought we went through this?" Fenix said. "I'm mated. I'm not interested in your female."

Little Wild Rose gasped and looked down at Vail.

He averted his gaze, staring at the dirty stone floor of his cell, not wanting her to see in his eyes the reason he had lost his head.

Jealousy.

What was wrong with him? He didn't want the female. She was a witch. Witches were cruel, manipulative, and traitorous. She would use the spell she had cast on him against him, forcing him to do her bidding. She would betray him.

Hurt him.

"I'm not attracted to the incubus," she whispered and those words didn't bring him pain. They brought him pleasure.

They chased away the darker feelings that had gripped him and controlled him, but those feelings lingered in the background, lurking and waiting to make themselves known again.

Like his memories did.

Fenix looked at Little Wild Rose.

Vail hissed and flashed his fangs, and tried to wrench his arms free of the cuffs so he could reach the male and teach him not to look upon his female.

"Settle down." A large demon male stopped outside his cell. "Or we'll take you away and teach you a lesson until you learn to be quiet."

Vail paid him no heed. He growled at the incubus and kept wrestling with his bonds, attempting to break free so he could claw Fenix's eyes out. That way, the male wouldn't be able to look upon his female.

A second demon appeared outside of his cell, followed by a third. The first demon opened the door and the three of them entered.

"Leave him alone." The witch launched to her feet, rounded him and blocked the demons' paths to him. "He hasn't done anything."

She was defending him?

He stared at the back of her head, unable to process what he was witnessing. The witch was protecting him.

His shock only increased when she shoved one of the guards in his bare chest, making him stumble backwards a few steps. The male turned on her with a snarl and his dusky grey horns curled, growing larger until they twisted over and around themselves and flared forwards into twin deadly points.

"Leave her alone," Vail snapped and resumed his fight against the bonds, putting all of his strength into it this time. Little Wild Rose was in danger. He had to protect her.

He would protect her.

The demon backhanded her and she grunted as she collapsed into a heap on the stone floor.

Darkness swallowed Vail and he growled at the three demon males as her pain blazed across the side of his face and his knees.

"Punishment time for you," the second demon said in English and roughly took hold of her and dragged her onto her feet.

Vail cursed him in the elf tongue and pulled harder on the chain, thrashing against it. Little Wild Rose looked over her shoulder at him and shook her head, her blue eyes imploring him to settle. He refused. He wouldn't let her sacrifice herself for him. He was her male. He could bear the punishment for her. It was his duty.

"Get your filthy hands off her," Vail snarled in the demon tongue and kicked out at the second male, knocking his knees together. "Harm her and I will have your head."

The third male grabbed hold of Vail's head and slammed it hard against the stone slab. Pain spider-webbed through his skull, sending his senses reeling and his ears ringing. By the time he had his faculties back, the three demons were gone, and so was Little Wild Rose.

No. He tugged at the chains, his strength failing him as a vision of her being taken to that room, that den of torture, filled his mind. He weakly grasped the chain and shook his head, his senses reaching for her.

She had done nothing wrong.

She had only sought to protect him.

He flinched with the first echo of a strike on his back and snarled with the second and her first cry of pain. It rang through the dungeon, shrill and filled with the agony he could feel in her.

Pain that was his fault.

He snarled with each cry, with every strike, swearing he would make amends somehow. He would make the bastard demons pay for hurting her. He would pay too for his part in her punishment. It was his fault. She suffered because of him.

Every blow and every whimper tore at him, driving him madder and pushing him towards the brink of losing control. He clung to awareness of her and to his sanity, refusing to let the darkness seize him while she suffered. He had to remain steady for her, even when he wanted to rage and lose himself to the darkness living within him. She could sense him as he could sense her, and he could feel her reaching for him.

Vail opened the connection to her, allowing her pain to flood him, holding no part of him away from her. He closed his eyes and mentally wrapped her in his embrace, cocooning her in the only way he could, sharing her pain to lessen her burden.

In the midst of her physical pain and the connection between them, he discovered something that rocked him.

Little Wild Rose held pain inside her, pain that was tearing her apart. He couldn't discern the source or the reason for it. He could only feel it was there, a constant presence. It was something she lived with and tried to bear, just as he lived with and tried to bear his sins.

Vail pulled her closer, used their connection to calm her and give her strength, and steal what pain he could away. He would bear it all for her if he could, and the revelation shocked him and awakened the part of him that had been waiting for his defences to slip.

Inky darkness swirled around him, curling up his legs to pull him down into the abyss. It whispered insidious words, ones that struck deep, embedding themselves in his heart and threatening to tear it to pieces.

She was a witch. Witches deserved pain. They deserved to suffer. He had vowed to destroy them all.

He would destroy her.

He knew it. He could see it playing out in his mind. She would turn on him. She would use his weakness against him, the soft feelings he had dared to have for her and the shred of hope that his future held something good, not eternal darkness and death.

She would take it all and she would destroy him, and in turn, he would destroy her.

Vail growled as she slipped from his grasp, oblivion swallowing her.

He clenched his fists, bowed off the slab and roared until his throat burned, his anger pouring through his veins like acid.

He had lost himself and knew she had felt it. He had been wide open to her, no part of him remaining hidden, and he had thought of her death at his hands.

No.

He flexed his fingers, clenching and unclenching his fists, shaking his head the whole time. She couldn't see that part of him. She couldn't see how dark he was inside. Ugly. Wretched. A vile animal.

She couldn't.

Someone stopped outside his cell.

The scent of her sweet blood hit him with the force of a tidal wave, knocking him so hard he half growled and half whimpered as his gaze sought her.

She hung limp between the two large demon males, her upper arms held by them. Her knees almost touched the floor and her head lolled forwards, her fall of blonde hair obscuring her face. Red coloured it in places and stained her fair skin too.

Rosalind.

Vail snarled and tried to launch himself at the bars, filled with a need to pull her away from the two males and into his arms where she would be safe.

The demon males laughed and one grasped her hair, yanking her head up. Vail's stomach turned, rebelling at the sight of her face. Her right eye had swollen shut and her lip had split. Blood trailed down her chin to her jaw and still trickled from her nose.

Little Wild Rose.

"Bastards," Vail growled and again tried to shove off the slab and reach her. His left arm twisted behind him, his shoulder socket popping as his arm snapped free of it. He growled through his pain and kept trying to reach her, his heart burning at the sight of her and the knowledge it was his fault.

He hadn't needed to kill her with his own hands. He had condemned her to death at the hands of these men by trying to protect her.

74

"Leave her be," he snarled and wrenched on his left arm, twisting it in the cuff, on the verge of gnawing his hand off to free himself so he could reach her. "Give her to me."

The demons laughed again and dragged her away.

Black inky spots dotted his vision and he roared, the sound dark and feral, a growl more beast than elf. His fangs lengthened further and he twisted on the slab, and unleashed a snarl as he grabbed his left arm and shoved his shoulder back into place. The dark spots began to swamp his vision, obscuring it as he gave himself over to the mad beast eating him from the inside out.

His remaining sliver of consciousness tracked Rosalind, clinging to her. The demons didn't take her to her cell, or the torture room. They dragged her beyond the sphere of his senses.

Vail stared at the ceiling, as still as a statue, and just as cold and void of emotion.

The demons would pay for hurting her.

He would take his Little Wild Rose from this place and no one would hurt her, never again. She would be free of the demons.

He would kill them all for her.

Starting with the king.

The incubus spoke, dragging Vail back from the brink of insanity and making him realise he had been speaking aloud.

"Sounds like a plan."

CHAPTER 10

Rosalind woke surrounded by darkness and the scent of damp and dead things. She blinked but the darkness remained, inky black and so thick that no light penetrated it. She felt over herself. Physically checking her body had become a habit in this place, a process that gave her something to focus on. She reached her shoulders and head, and frowned.

No injuries.

There was only one way that was possible. The king had used one of his dark witches to heal her. Why?

She wrapped her arms around herself to keep the chill off her skin and pondered the answer to that question, and the other one that had plagued her before the guards had come and taken her from the elf's cell.

Why had they taken her to his cell in the first place?

When they had pulled her from her cell, she had expected to find him injured and in need of her healing spells. He had been asleep and unharmed, but the demons had pushed her into his cell and had ignored her questions. The incubus across from him, a man named Fenix, had told her a little more about her companion.

Vail.

Apparently, he had returned unharmed from his meeting with the king, and the two of them had talked before Vail had suffered one of his episodes and had passed out.

Had they brought her to him as another perverse form of torture?

Her presence disturbed him, awakening whatever dark things haunted his soul and were his reason for despising her kind. If they had used her as a method of hurting him, driving him mad and sending him sinking into his wild state, then she wished pain upon them. He was broken and tormented enough as it was, without their perverse cruelty adding to it. Having her brought to him just to make him lose his mind was sick and twisted.

It was bad enough that they had teased him with the threat of walking naked through the castle. Their threat had sent him dangerously close to losing his grip on his sanity again and she hadn't been able to bear the feel of him suffering and sensing his desperate urge to fight or beg for the clothes, to retain a tiny scrap of pride as they tried to strip him of it. She had shouted at them before she could consider the consequences. No man deserved that sort of treatment.

Tonight she had reacted to their tormenting him again, hurling herself between him and three demons. She had wanted to protect him.

Madness.

He wanted to kill her. She had felt it in him before she had passed out from the pain of her torture. She had sensed him with her, knew that it had been the bond between them and that for some strange reason he had wanted to comfort her and take her pain.

To torment her?

Was he torturing her just as the demons tortured him, teasing her with something she desired only to take it away and watch her crumple?

In the wake of his kindness had come cruelty.

A colourful, explicit vision of her death at his hands.

She laughed to herself. Perhaps that death was what her grandmother had seen. It was the mad elf prince who would kill her.

Rosalind shook her head and buried her face in her knees. No. She couldn't allow herself to believe such a thing. She wasn't going to die. He wasn't going to kill her.

She couldn't deny that he wanted to hurt her, to make her suffer for some reason. She could see it in his eyes at times, and could feel it in him through their bond. He fought those desires, but they were there, and they frightened her. Something haunted him and drove him to want to harm her, and whatever it was, it had something to do with sorcery and witches.

Fenix had been about to tell her when Vail had awoken and had tried to break his bonds.

Because he had been jealous.

She clawed her hair back and shook her head again, her mind and heart going in circles. She lost track of time, getting nowhere as she tried to unravel the mystery of Vail and decide what she should do.

There was only one thing she could do. She had to protect herself and that meant she had to distance herself from Vail. Down here, Vail and the demons posed the biggest threat to her. If she could just keep her distance from Vail, and could be on her best behaviour for the demons, then she stood a chance of escaping one day and returning to her life.

She wasn't sure she knew how to live that life anymore, but she wanted to go back to it and leave this madness behind her.

She wanted to live.

She would do whatever it took in order to make that happen.

Even trick Vail into thinking she was his mate so he would help her escape, and then leave him at the first opportunity.

Footsteps sounded in the corridor outside her cell and a sliver of light cut through the darkness. She stared at the glowing line across the bottom of the solid door, her breath hitching in her throat. A shadow caused the line to stutter. A key grated. The door creaked open.

A towering demon male snorted down at her. "Prince Vail has demanded to see you."

Demanded? She stared at the demon. Since when had the demons been obeying Vail?

The demon grabbed her by her left arm, digging his claws in, and dragged her from the cell. She stumbled along behind him, her head reeling as she tried to figure out where the demon was taking her. He wasn't taking her to the elf's cell, or her own. He was taking her up.

He shoved a door open with the flat of his hand and stomped along a corridor. Stone arches cut into the wall on her left revealed the courtyard of the castle. Her heart pounded and she looked ahead, towards the main towering dark building. Vail was there now?

Mother earth. What had happened while she had been unconscious?

The demon led her up to the first floor and pushed her ahead of him into a large richly decorated room.

Her heart stopped dead.

Vail lounged before her on a huge day bed covered in colourful velvets and furs, conversing with the demon king, as if they were best friends. He leaned against a mound of pillows, his hands still cuffed but the chain between them gone, allowing him to prop his left elbow on the richly coloured cushions while his right hand rested on his black leather-clad thigh. Gone too was his overlong blue-black hair, shorn into a neater length around the sides and back but left in tousled wild strands on top, and the beard that had been growing in. The sight of him clean-shaven and bathed left her speechless.

Mother earth, he was gorgeous.

And he looked every bit the dark prince as he lounged before her in a Devil may care sexy slump, his honed bare torso on display for her eyes to devour and his long legs clad in tight black leather that accentuated their lean muscular form.

Sin on a stick and she wanted to lick him from head to toe.

His appearance also made her acutely aware of the state of herself—dirty, unshaven, and in need of a good hot bath. Maybe they could bathe together and he could scrub her back for her, among other things.

Rosalind caught herself and shut down her dangerous feelings, forcing herself to look at Vail with clear eyes and at those who surrounded him.

The women draped all over the king twittered at something he said, lavishing the demon with their attention, all of them naked and beautiful.

Vail's cool purple gaze slowly drifted away from his companions and settled on her.

Rosalind's blood began a slow boil as she took in the scene.

The women fawning over the king were close to Vail on the day bed, their legs brushing his at times, and he showed no adverse reaction to them, not as he always did to her. Her heart ached and she squashed it, refusing to let the sight of him with several nude beauties affect her.

The demon guard dragged Rosalind forwards and dumped her on the dark stone floor in front of Vail, as if she was a piece of garbage.

"You have seen her now. Satisfied?" the king said in English, tossed her a bored and uninterested look, and went back to palming one of the women's breasts.

"No." Vail raked cold eyes over her. "I have need of the female."

The demon king lifted his head from the brunette's neck. "What need?"

Vail smirked at him. "I need to fuck her."

Rosalind's cheeks burned and she spluttered, torn between finding her feet and punching him, and swearing at him from where she knelt like a servant before him. She didn't have a damn clue what had gotten into him but the man before her was nothing like the one she had left in the cell.

The one she had protected.

Swearing won.

"You bloody son of a bitch." Rosalind shot to her feet.

The demon guard backhanded her so hard she flew several feet across the room and hit the flagstones with enough force that it knocked the wind from her. Pain burned in her right elbow and spread up her arm.

"Strike her again, and I will kill you," Vail said in a thick, dark growl and the aura of danger he always emanated grew stronger, pulling her magic to the fore to protect her.

Rosalind pressed her hands into the floor and breathed slowly as she pushed herself onto her knees. The world spun and rocked around her, but the pain in her arm began to fade as her senses stopped reeling.

The demon king laughed. "Have your female."

The male waved Vail away as one of the women kissed down his bare chest towards his stomach.

Vail stood in a graceful and effortless move, stormed across the room to Rosalind and grabbed her arm, hauling her onto her feet.

Her heart pounded wildly as she met his gaze. Desire darkened it, the black abyss of his pupils devouring the purple of his irises as he stared down into her eyes, holding her immobile.

Mother earth. Fear beat through her veins, making her head spin violently. He wouldn't. She swallowed her heart down from her throat and tried to back away from him, afraid he would take her right here in front of the demon, as the king wanted and expected.

Vail growled. "None other than me can see my female. I will take her to a private room."

King Bruan's face fell and he eyed her, and then Vail.

Her heart quickened and she tried to twist her arm free of Vail's grip. What the hell was wrong with him? She wasn't going to sleep with him, not here and not in private. She was done with him and if he tried anything, she was hitting him with the biggest healing spell she had and letting it tear him apart.

"We have a deal," Vail said in a low, dangerous tone. "I have offered my assistance, but I will not be of much use to you if I am not at full strength. You have surely noticed the effect a drop of this female's blood has had on me?"

The king nodded.

"In order to defeat my brother, I need what this female will give to me. I need her blood and her body." Vail pulled her with him, towards the demon king, and she ignored the hot shivery ache that coursed through her in response to his words. He didn't need her. He was up to something. He was using her. He bloody well wouldn't get the chance. "Now, do you desire my assistance or not?"

Rosalind couldn't believe him. Fenix had told her that he had been at war with his brother, his own flesh and blood, for forever but she had been foolish enough to think that perhaps that was over now. She hadn't realised that he still desired to kill the other elf prince.

She couldn't allow it.

She knew Loren in a way. He had helped King Thorne in the war against these demons. She had met the prince's woman, Olivia, and had formed the beginnings of a friendship with her and her friend Sable. She wouldn't let Vail snatch Olivia's man from her or help these demons in their fight against Thorne.

Rosalind twisted her arm in Vail's grip and came close to breaking free. His fingers tightened against her, his short claws pressing into her bare flesh, and he turned cold eyes on her.

"Do not fight me unless you want to do this the hard way... with an audience."

She froze, heart going wild and throat closing. He wouldn't. He hated being touched.

He had let those women brush against him though. He only hated her touching him.

Was he really going to do this?

She stared up into his eyes, trying to see the answer in them and feel it in him. She couldn't sense anything. It was as if he had closed the connection between them or had severed the bond. His eyes remained blank and unreadable, giving her no answer.

Was this all an act or was he working for the king now?

"Very well," the demon king said as one of the women nibbled his throat and rubbed herself against his thigh. He palmed her backside and grinned at Vail. "You may have the cell she occupied, and a guard will be outside the door at all times."

Vail nodded and dragged her with him towards the door, following the demon guard. She clawed at Vail's hand, trying to prise it off her, a weight crushing her chest and her knees wobbling with each swift step he forced her to take.

She had to get away.

She had to escape this madness.

The journey back to the cell passed quickly and was over before she could get Vail's hand off her arm. He pushed her into the black cell and the door closed behind him, leaving only a chink of light until the guard slid a panel on the door open, revealing a small barred section, throwing light across Vail.

Rosalind couldn't breathe.

She backed away as he advanced on her, unsure what to expect.

Was he really going to take her blood and use her?

The hungry, dark edge to his eyes said he might.

CHAPTER 11

Rosalind wasn't sure whether to back away or stand her ground as Vail advanced on her. Towering at least a foot taller than her and with the honed, powerful muscles of his torso on show, he was a sight to behold but it wasn't his impressive physique or the knowledge that he was stronger than she was and could easily overpower her that frightened her.

It was how she reacted to him. It was the desire that flickered within her like an eternal flame, small right now but growing, steadily becoming a wildfire that she feared would consumed her.

She told herself on repeat that she couldn't succumb to him, no matter how tempting this dark elf prince was to her.

She didn't know all the details of her prediction and giving herself to him or falling for him might be the instrument of her downfall and death.

Vail closed the gap between them, his powerful presence commanding all of her focus, luring every shred of her attention to him even as she fought to retain some distance between them. Her skin hummed from his proximity, begging for the feel of his caress despite her best efforts to clamp a lid on the arousal spiralling to dazzling heights inside her.

He stood over her, his intense violet eyes locked on hers, holding her under their spell.

She breathed hard, her chest heaving against the confines of her black dress, anticipation stripping her strength as she trembled before him, awaiting his next move.

He inched closer, until she swore she felt his heat and his power engulfing her, drugging her into a haze that she was powerless to resist.

His lips parted, revealing a hint of fangs, and her knees threatened to buckle.

"Do you have a good level of healing power right now?" he whispered and it took her a moment to take in what he had said.

He wanted to talk about her power? He wanted her to use it around him?

What had happened to the man who had threatened to kill her because she was a witch and had tried to attack her whenever she used her power near him?

She stared blankly at him, wondering if she had lost her mind during her punishment and this was all some twisted fantasy. It would explain why she had found herself fully healed on coming around and why her eyes kept betraying her and falling to his firm lips, silently begging them for a kiss she felt sure would spell her doom.

"Well?" he husked, his deep voice doing strange things to her insides, scrambling them until she found it hard to think and even harder to drag her gaze away from his sinful mouth.

Mother earth, he was beautiful.

Breathtaking.

She looked up at him, drowning in his dark beauty, in the allure of her grim reaper.

His left eyebrow arched. His rich violet eyes turned dark with impatience.

Rosalind looked him over, cursed herself for taking her time about it, studying every lithe and seductive inch of his body. She had to snap out of it. He wanted to kill his brother and she wouldn't allow that to happen.

"You don't look hurt, so why do you need to know?" she snapped in a low voice, not wanting to alert the guard but not willing to let Vail order her around either.

His other eyebrow shot up. "Because we are going to escape."

She would have laughed at that suggestion had her heart not leaped into her throat and her hope not soared. He couldn't be joking. Mother earth, he just couldn't be. She had ached for escape ever since she had awoken in her cell all those weeks ago. She searched his eyes, trying to see the truth in them. They showed her only darkness and desire, hunger that sent a shiver racing through her body and stoked her temperature up another notch or five.

She glanced beyond him to the door, aware of the demon waiting there.

"There's no way to break these dampening bonds and we need them off in order to escape," she hissed at Vail and his expression didn't alter from one of desire mixed with determination.

"I can handle that," he whispered and she frowned at him.

He truly had lost his mind.

"How?" She jerked her chin towards his solid metal cuffs. "Yours are the strongest. I've seen you give them hell, with all of your strength, and you haven't made a bloody dent in them so I don't see how you think you're going to open them."

"I do not plan to open them." He eyed her warily and hesitated, and her stomach plummeted into her feet. He was up to something and she had a terrible feeling she wasn't going to like it. "Do not watch."

The sinking feeling grew worse and she automatically reached out to grab his arm, but stopped short when he flicked a glare at her hand.

"I don't like the sound of that," she whispered. "What do you intend to do?"

He hesitated again, his arm near her hand twitched forwards, as if he wanted the contact between them, and then he backed off a step.

"Do you have a good level of healing power right now?" he asked again, his tone firmer this time.

Her eyes widened as it dawned on her. "No. No, you are not going to do that. You're bloody insane... you know what happens if you hurt yourself."

She reached for him and he backed off another step and shook his head, his eyes darkening dangerously. She stood her ground, needing to spell things out for him because he had to be crazy to be considering this course of action.

"No. I mean it. It's too dangerous. The pain and me using my powers will send you to that dark place and you'll kill me."

She expected him to placate her by lying and saying he wouldn't kill her.

He didn't. He just turned his back on her.

"Very well," he said in a low voice. "If you cannot heal what I intend to do, it will not stop me. I am stronger now and will eventually heal it."

Rosalind did grab his arm now. She snagged his wrist and pulled him back to face her, expecting him to snarl and swat her hand away. He didn't. He stared down at her hand on his arm, emotions she couldn't decipher crossing his face, and then raised his eyes to meet hers. The elf was full of surprises today and she didn't like any of them.

"Eventually." She couldn't help pointing out the critical word in what he had said. "Until then, you'll be in tremendous pain and you'll need blood, and that will make you dangerous too. You'll probably still kill me. Mother earth, I really am doomed to die."

He cocked an eyebrow at that.

She didn't give him a chance to ask about it, or let her down by not asking.

"Better to take the quicker route and hope you can control yourself, than allow you to hurt yourself and draw out your pain. I won't let you do it. I won't let you suffer like that." She planted her hands on her hips and ignored the flicker of surprise that lit his purple eyes. "So yes, I have power."

Before she could turn away, he clutched his right hand and viciously twisted it. Pain screamed through her hand in response, every finger burning violently, the agony almost blinding her. She held it to her chest, gritting her teeth to stop herself from crying out. She hadn't realised that she would experience an echo of his pain.

Vail made no sound as he shattered his bones in strategic places, each crack and snap forcing bile up her throat and tearing a grunt from her. When he squeezed his broken hand and pushed it through the steel cuff, she clutched the wall and barely stopped herself from vomiting from the pain.

How could he do such a thing without making a single sound, without showing a flicker of the agony he had to be experiencing? She only felt a shadow of what he was going through, and it was enough to have her breaking out in a sweat and on the verge of passing out.

He looked down at her and his violet eyes glimmered with the agony he was holding inside.

Rosalind pulled herself together and rushed forwards to help him.

His demeanour changed in an instant, his expression twisting into a dark snarl as he flashed his long fangs at her. His ears flattened against the sides of his head, his warning hiss sending her magic spiking and wanting to protect her. She squashed that desire and focused on him instead. She had to help him right now or she was going to pass out from the pain.

"I need to heal you," she whispered and held her throbbing right hand to her chest. "Please. It hurts so much."

His gaze dropped to her hand and softened. He swallowed hard and she risked reaching out to him, sure he would allow her to heal his hand now that he knew she felt his pain and was suffering too.

The moment her fingers connected with his broken right hand, he snarled at her.

"*Witch.*"

The manacle hitting the floor was the only warning she had before his left hand shot out and his fingers closed around her throat. Light flashed over his body. Cold darkness engulfed her, sending her head spinning, and she cried out as her back slammed into the stone wall metres behind her. His bare chest heaved from the exertion of using his partially bound powers and she prayed to mother earth that he didn't teleport her again. She didn't think she would remain conscious if he did and she needed to heal him.

Healing him suddenly became a non-issue when his fingers tightened against her throat and he shoved her harder against the rough stones, pinning her off the floor by her neck. She struggled to breathe as the force of his grip crushed her windpipe. Cold weight pressed down on her chest, squeezing her heart as tightly as his grip squeezed her throat.

"Vail. Release me," she wheezed but he only tightened his grip, pressing his short claws into either side of her neck.

The demon looked in on them and she tossed him a hopeless but pleading look. He quirked an eyebrow but didn't make a move to help her. The bastard probably thought it was sex play. He turned away again.

Rosalind mustered all of her strength as black spots winked across her vision and grasped Vail's left arm with both of her hands. Big mistake.

He flashed fangs at her and growled in her face, and squeezed her throat so hard that she almost blacked out.

Her gaze dropped to his broken right hand, her own aching in response, each bone on fire. She let her hands fall from his arm and hung from his grip, slowly gathering her strength as she fought the black wave threatening to pull her under. Speaking to him wasn't going to get her anywhere. She had to heal him. If she could just heal him, she might be able to bring him back from the dark place he had gone.

She inched her left hand forwards and used her remaining strength to call up a healing spell, the strongest one she could manage in her current condition.

Darkness swept through her, bringing a chilling cold in its wake, and she paused and stared into Vail's eyes. Black spots coloured his purple irises, darkness that she could feel within him. It spread through her, a vile hunger for violence and blood, a terrible desire to tear into flesh with her teeth and snap bones.

A burning need to destroy.

All of it aimed at her.

Because she was a witch.

He was going to kill her.

The second her fingers made contact with his wrist, she grabbed his hand and unleashed the spell, channelling it into him so quickly that all of her strength rushed out of her, leaving her with only enough to cling to his hand and keep the spell working. Her heart laboured and the darkness encroached, swallowing the edges of her vision.

Vail growled at her, flashing dangerous daggers, but she kept going, refusing to die here and clinging to the hope that he would come back to her when he was healed and his pain no longer rode him, driving him into the dark embrace of his sickness.

His grip on her neck loosened and air scraped over her sore throat and burned her lungs.

His violet eyes widened, fixed on his hand where it still grasped her throat, his claws pressing into her flesh. He shook his head and stumbled backwards, blinking hard as he released her.

Rosalind hit the ground in a heap and coughed as she tried to breathe normally. She looked up at Vail and he stared down at her, his eyes locked on her throat. She lifted her hand and touched it, feeling the bruises he had caused.

He squatted in front of her and reached out towards her throat.

She flinched away.

Vail snatched his hand back and withdrew again, shuffling backwards, placing some distance between them.

He still wasn't quite with her. She could see it in his glassy eyes. Over the time she had known him, she had come to recognise that the black spots discolouring his violet irises were a visible sign that he wasn't fully in control.

He threw her a pained look that conveyed every feeling she could sense in him through their link and turned his face away.

She rubbed her throat, fighting to breathe normally and subdue the fear that filled every inch of her, driving her magic to the fore to protect her. It wasn't the thought of that magic provoking Vail into another attack that made her battle her fear with everything she had.

It was the pain she could feel in him. Not a physical hurt, but an emotional one.

He sat balanced on his toes, his nails idly scraping the stones between his bare feet and his eyes averted. Tears glittered on his long dark lashes and she could sense every drop of the pain that tore at him, together with the darkness and the shadows that haunted him, tainting his heart and his soul.

Corrupting and weakening him.

She could sense it all through their link, experienced it as she had his dark hunger to kill her because she bore magic.

Just as she could also feel his distress and horror, and knew in her heart that it was because she had faced the monster within him.

He hadn't wanted her to see those things. The link between them faded and she knew he had the power to control it and was closing it and shutting her out again.

Rosalind sank onto her backside and stared at him in silence, unsure what to say and what to do. He continued to scrape his nails over the stone, the action methodical, a set length and interval. It seemed to calm him and she didn't want to interrupt, felt he needed a moment to pull himself back together and pretend she wasn't there, bearing witness to this side of him.

He was fractured, in mind, body and spirit. Before her was a broken and dangerous male, and his hold on his sanity seemed even more tentative and fragile than she had thought.

Why?

Who had broken him?

Her heart said it had been a witch. He hated her kind for a reason, and she had a feeling she didn't want to know, even as she needed the answers.

He murmured softly in the elf tongue, the words lyrical and beautiful, and his violet gaze darted towards her and away again. He inched closer, remaining on his haunches, his bare feet shuffling on the stone. He flicked her another glance, scraped his claws over the stones again, and whispered in his language. She caught a 'ki'ara' in there and the edge of pain in his eyes as they met hers before leaping away again. He shuffled a little closer.

She kept still, waiting to see what he would do.

With his eyes remaining averted and his face turned away from her, he reached out and gently laid his left hand on her throat. Her pain faded and her eyes widened as bruises appeared on his neck.

He was taking her injuries.

Incredible.

The bruises disappeared quickly, the remnants of her healing spell taking care of them for him.

He lowered his hand and his head, the longer strands of his blue-black hair falling forwards, and clawed the stone floor.

She was about to speak and shatter the silence when he blinked, lifted his head and raised his right hand.

"It worked." He turned his arm this way and that, staring at it as if it was a miracle.

Completely unaware of what had happened.

His purple gaze swung her way and the beginnings of a smile tugged at the corners of his mouth. It faded and he frowned, reached for her but withdrew his hand before it could make contact with her cheek.

"You have been crying. Why?"

Rosalind didn't have the heart to tell him that he had attacked her and had come close to killing her, not when all the pain and suffering that had been in his eyes just seconds ago was gone.

She rubbed her cheeks, hiding the evidence of her pain, afraid he would keep asking about it and would realise he had hurt her. She never had been very good at lying, but it was better than telling him the truth.

"Don't break your other hand," she whispered and looked down at it, hiding her eyes from him and sending a prayer that he wouldn't detect her coming lie. "Healing your right one drained me."

She waited for his response, holding her breath and hoping he would do as she asked. She didn't want him to go through that madness again. Not because it frightened her or because he might kill her this time. She didn't want it to happen because she felt sure that if his mind eventually healed enough for him to remember it, for him to recall the things he did when lost to the darkness, he would hate himself.

She wanted to spare him that pain.

"Try teleporting," she said but couldn't bring herself to look at him.

Pale blue-purple light burst across her eyes and when her vision returned, he was gone.

The sounds of bones crunching and the muffled cry of the guard outside the door turned her stomach. The scent of blood reached her nose, acrid and sharp, stirring memories of her own that she would rather forget. She stared at the slick patch creeping under the door, her breathing accelerating as her heart began to pound.

Blood.

She had spilled so much blood.

She had killed.

Rosalind backed away from the wet pool of dark liquid, unable to take her eyes off it as a horrific replay of the battle flashed through her mind. The agonised cries of her victims rang in her ears and bright bursts of colourful magical spells detonated across her eyes. She had taken so many lives. She had murdered them all.

She shook her head. She had done it to help the others, to protect Thorne's men and those of Prince Loren, and to keep Olivia and Sable safe for them. It had been the warriors of the Fifth Realm or her and her comrades.

She couldn't have saved both of them.

She'd had to choose.

Screams shrieked in her ears and she covered them with her hands, trying to block out the sound. Bloodied hands reached for her, flesh peeling away to reveal bone and tendon, and she squeezed her eyes shut and backed away, her heart beating wildly as she desperately tried to evade their grasp.

Her back hit something solid.

And warm.

"Witch." Vail's snarl shattered the illusion engulfing her and she swiftly turned to face him. The dark edge to his expression melted away in an instant as he looked down at her, right into her eyes.

She should have shut down her fear and hidden it before turning towards him, but she had been gripped by a powerful need to see him and know she was no longer on the battlefield, going against everything she had once stood for and taking lives instead of saving them.

Now he had seen it in her, the same darkness he feared her seeing in him. They were both murderers. They had both done terrible things. And she feared she would lose her mind as he had lost his, and the darkness would consume her.

He cocked his head, studying her, and she looked away from him, unable to hold his gaze while he was scrutinising her, attempting to see in her eyes what she hid in her heart. He couldn't know. Regardless of how she had felt a few days ago, when she had thought he could tell her how to cope with the pain of having taken lives, she could never tell him. It was her burden to bear. Her sin. He had enough of his own.

Besides, she wasn't even sure he would care or give her the ridiculous comfort she needed if she did tell him.

The urge still pressed down on her though, making her squirm. She held it back, convinced it would pass if she ignored it for long enough and telling herself that Vail wouldn't give her the comfort she desired. He wouldn't care that she had taken a few lives and it haunted her, so why did she wish that he would?

Mother earth help her but it was becoming impossible to keep her distance from him, to pretend that he wasn't the most gorgeous man she had ever met despite the darkness he held within him and his madness, and that she hadn't found herself fantasising about kissing him on more than one occasion. She was doomed. If not to death, then perhaps to a broken heart. Vail would sooner kill her than love her, and she was a fool if she thought he was capable of anything but hate for her.

He stared at her for what seemed like hours, the thick heavy silence pressing down on her, and then metal scraped on metal.

Rosalind risked a swift glance his way to see what he was doing.

Unlocking his remaining cuff. It clattered to the ground, and he placed two thin silver and black bands around his wrists. She gasped as black scales swarmed from them, rippling over his skin and covering him in skin-tight armour that left nothing to the imagination as it hugged his powerful body. She had heard that elf armour responded to the owner's mental commands, and that only weapons forged of the same metal could penetrate it. It was magic. There had to be some latent form of magic in the ore that allowed it to reshape itself and shrink into a tiny space, or grow to cover an entire six-feet-six of toned, handsome elf.

She shook her head and mentally deleted the last part of that thought.

Vail pulled a short silver sword out of thin air and held it out to her.

Rosalind instantly backed away, shaking her head. She couldn't lay hands on anything designed for killing when death cries still haunted her. She couldn't trust herself with a weapon. Not anymore. Never again.

The elf raised an eyebrow at her and the sword disappeared.

He flexed his fingers and his black armour covered them, transforming them into serrated sharp claws. That was what he had expected to happen that day when they had first met in his cell, when he had flexed his fingers all those times. He had been distraught because of the loss of his armour. He held his hand out to her.

"Come. Female."

She hesitated, wary of touching him. Could he bear her touch without ill effect when wearing his armour? It provided a protective layer between them, preventing skin contact, but it wouldn't stop him from sensing her magic.

He flexed his fingers again.

Rosalind placed her hand into his and gasped as pale blue-purple light swept over his body, down his arm and up hers, and the cold dark swallowed her again.

They landed in the corridor outside the cell and Rosalind's eyes widened as they fell on the dead demon guard, bile scorching her throat before she turned her back on the gruesome sight. Vail released her and moved around her. The strange light flashed again and she sensed Vail on the other side of the door. Ditching the dead demon in the cell to cover their tracks?

Rosalind supposed that covert tactics were probably Vail's forte having spent several thousand years evading Loren and everyone out to capture him.

He reappeared in front of her and she stumbled back a step, her heart leaping into her throat. It was going to take her some time to get used to him unexpectedly popping into existence.

He hesitated and then grabbed her hand again, and teleported.

Her head spun this time, mind whirling as they reappeared in the corridor outside his old cell in the dungeon.

Fenix got to his feet and casually strode to the bars of his cell. "All went to plan then?"

Vail nodded. Rosalind frowned. The two men had conspired with each other, forming a plan to get her out of solitary and back with them so they could all escape together?

She was surprised, but glad that Fenix was coming with them. It would help her maintain some distance between her and Vail, and she needed that right now.

Vail released her, teleported into Fenix's cell and unlocked his cuffs for him. The incubus tossed them away and stretched his arms above his head, causing the muscles of his bare chest to flex. Rosalind muttered a spell to protect against his charms, even though she knew it wouldn't work while her wrists were still bound. Fenix winked at her.

Vail tossed a snarl over his shoulder at her and then quickly looked away, but not before she caught the conflict in his purple eyes.

It seemed this bond had him as confused and torn as she was about it. She wanted to ask if there was a way to break it, but failed to see the point in wasting her breath. Elves had one fated female they could bond with and that reeked of a forever commitment to her.

Forever.

Her eyes widened.

"Mother earth…"

She was immortal.

As a witch, she aged slower than humans, but she wasn't immortal. She had reached her hundredth year in this world, and had another fifteen or so before she went through her second transition. That transition would have made her ageless, her appearance fixed in what mortals perceived as mid-thirties, but it wouldn't have made her immortal.

Would she even go through that second transition now?

Vail had already fixed her appearance for her, changing her biology with his blood and the bond.

What if she didn't go through it? She was powerful and had mastered many high level spells years before others in her family had been able to, but her second transition would unlock her powers to a greater extent.

She needed to go through that transition if she was to reach her full potential as a witch.

Fenix teleported out of the cell and into the corridor beside her, and said in the fae tongue, "Five quid says I can guess what you're thinking."

Rosalind scowled up at him. "I wouldn't even give you a penny. Bloody bastard elf."

Fenix chuckled. "That would be your bloody bastard elf prince husband."

Husband.

A shiver snaked down her spine and she stared into the cell at Vail. He glanced her way, light traced over the contours of his skin-tight black armour, and he disappeared. She braced herself a second before he reappeared next to Fenix.

Not next to her.

Was he going to use Fenix as a sort of blocker now?

She couldn't blame him if he did. She had been planning to do the same thing, using Fenix as a physical wall to keep her distance from Vail.

Vail made a silver sword appear in his hand and held it out to Fenix. The incubus took it without hesitation and executed a few jabs and twirls with it.

"Nice." He practically purred in approval of the weapon and she envied him a little, wishing she'd had the courage to take the blade for herself.

Rosalind looked down at her cuffs, unsure whether she wanted them removed. With them dampening her power, she couldn't kill anyone. All she could do was heal. All she could do was good. She was safe with them on, and the thought of giving them up twisted her insides into knots and had her heart beginning to race.

She would be useless in a fight with the cuffs on though, restricting her movements, and there was no way they were going to get out of the castle and away without encountering trouble. She had incapacitating spells at her command. She could use them to freeze anyone who dared to attack them. She could get them out without them resorting to killing.

Rosalind sucked down a steadying breath and held her hands out to Vail, the length of thick chain between them rattling as it swung.

Vail stepped towards her, the key in his hand, and then stopped.

A chill went through her.

"Get on with it. Remove them." Her heart started to pound as her gaze darted between his and the keys. Something flickered in his violet eyes. She shook her head and lurched towards him, making a grab for the keys.

They disappeared from his hand.

Her thoughts rattled at a million miles per hour, leaping between two conclusions, neither of which she liked.

Either he intended to leave her bound or he intended to leave her here.

"Don't you dare leave me," she whispered, fear getting the better of her. She didn't want to be trapped here anymore, and the guards would kill her when they discovered Vail and Fenix were gone. They would punish her for their actions and escape.

The hard angles of his face softened a touch, just enough that she noticed it, and relief crashed over her, bringing with it startling warmth as she stared up into his eyes, catching a glimmer of what might have been concern or compassion.

It lasted barely a heartbeat, a faint flicker of something good and sweet, before darkness consumed it.

"I will not, but I cannot release you. Your power." His face twisted and he buried his clawed fingers in his black hair, clutching his head. "I can sense it now. Pushing. Evil. Wretched witch."

Rosalind took a step back and he jerked his head up, his eyebrows furrowed and purple eyes imploring her, as if he feared her taking another step away. But why?

The inky spots were back in his irises, infesting the beautiful clear amethyst, and they multiplied as she stared into his eyes. With his dampening restraints gone, and all his powers returned, he could feel the magic in her clearer than before and it was playing havoc with him. There was something else in his eyes too, a deeper fear, one that controlled him to a degree.

Fear for himself or for her?

"Vail?" she whispered and his grip on his head tightened, he looked away and then back at her. "Tell me why you won't remove them."

She was pushing him too hard but she needed to know. Having her powers bound would stop her from being able to hurt him, and others, and she wanted that, but she also hated feeling her magic trapped inside her. The chain between the cuffs was short too and restrictive. It would be easy for her to fall and be unable to save herself, and she would be useless in a fight. She wouldn't be able to defend herself.

She would have to rely on him and he had given her no reason to believe that he would protect her.

Rosalind looked down at the cuffs clamped around her wrists. If they stayed on, she felt certain she would meet her doom just as her grandmother predicted. If she had a date with death, she at least wanted it to be on her terms. She wanted a shot at surviving and that meant having her powers available. But if they were available, she wasn't sure she would be able to stop herself from killing again. If they came under attack, she would defend herself and Fenix, and Vail, and she felt certain that she would kill in order to save them. She would do it without thinking and without hesitation, and she wasn't sure she was strong enough to bear knowing that she was capable of such a thing.

"I do not wish to hurt you," Vail whispered and she looked up into his eyes, catching the truth behind his words in them.

That soft confession swayed her and she was grateful for it. It had taken him courage and strength to voice those words.

Rosalind nodded. "Promise me you will release me when you're ready though."

Vail stared down into her eyes and the air around them grew thicker, the world falling away as she lost herself in the clear amethyst depths of his irises.

He raised his left hand, his claws flexing, bringing it close to her face but not touching her, and his eyes searched hers as he whispered, "I might never be ready to release you."

Her heart pounded hard, heat chasing through her veins and desire flaring unbidden, stronger than she could fight it.

His veiled confession rocked her to her soul and shook her, stripping away her strength and her resolve as it revealed a side of him that left her more confused than ever.

He had meant more than releasing her from the bonds.

He had meant from him.

He might never let her go.

Mother earth help her, but the crazy part of her she kept trying to pretend didn't exist wanted him to hold on to her with both hands, even when she knew fate had other plans.

He might not get to keep her for long.

Death was waiting for her, the grim end of a prediction she had spent her whole life hiding from, trapped by it and afraid to live and do all the things she wanted to do in case she ran into an elf prince.

Now she had met that handsome, damaged elf male, and she was damned if she was going to keep hiding from her fate and holding back from doing the things she wanted to do.

She stared up into Vail's beautiful eyes, seeing a man she could easily love, one who had already placed a claim on her affection. She was falling hard and she was falling fast, and she was going to stop running from her feelings for him. She was going to embrace them instead and risk everything. She was going to crack his armour and mend his heart, and then she was going to claim it as hers and him as her mate.

If she was destined to die, then she was going to live and love first.

CHAPTER 12

Little Wild Rose muttered under her breath in the fae tongue, her blue eyes focused on her work as she used a healing spell on Fenix. No doubt, the witch cursed Vail's name. She had been unimpressed when she had discovered that the plan was to teleport short distances through the castle and that neither he nor Fenix possessed the power to teleport two with them. He had agreed a destination within the castle with Fenix, a point they both knew, and had teleported Rosalind there. It had been his first mistake.

The more powerful the person he was teleporting with him, the bigger the drain on his power. Little Wild Rose was infinitely more powerful than he had suspected and the accumulated drain on his strength from teleporting with her several times in close succession had weakened him dramatically.

His control had slipped.

The feel of a witch close to him, her body against his, had sent him down a dark and terrible path and he had hurled Rosalind away from him before blacking out.

When he had come around, Fenix had been restraining him, bending his arms behind his back while shoving his face and chest into one of the stone walls of the corridor.

The witch had wisely kept her distance, her delicate features set in a wary expression.

Vail had made his second mistake.

He had suggested Fenix be the one to teleport her to their next destination—the courtyard.

The second Fenix had slipped his arm around Little Wild Rose's waist, Vail had seen red.

He had attacked Fenix, barrelling into him and taking him down, wrestling with the incubus so he had ended up on top. He had pinned the wretched male to the grimy damp stone floor and had hammered him with blows, and the male had deserved every single one.

He had touched Vail's mate. He had placed his dirty paws on Vail's female.

And the gold and blue that had flickered in his eyes had said he had been enjoying the feel of her curves beneath his fingers and her body tucked close to his.

Vail narrowed his purple gaze on the male, his dark hungers renewing, rising again to whisper dangerous words in his ears.

The male wanted her still.

Fenix watched her hands as she moved them over his face but his green eyes kept flickering to meet her blues, studying them and her face.

Vail growled low in his throat and advanced a step, rising to his full height to intimidate the inferior male.

The incubus glanced at him and then returned his gaze to the witch.

His witch.

His female.

His ki'ara.

Vail snarled and teleported in a flash, appearing between the incubus and his Little Wild Rose. He pressed his hand into her hip, guiding her behind him, keeping her hidden from Fenix's gaze. The male would not take what was his.

The female belonged to him.

He bared his fangs again and hissed, warning the male away.

Fenix stood his ground, palming the hilt of the sword he held point down at his side.

A soft huff broke the tense silence.

Vail looked over his left shoulder at the witch. She pulled his hand away from her hip, tossed it aside and moved out from behind him, pinning him with a black look.

"Really?" she snapped and shoved her hands onto her hips.

Hips he had touched.

Hips he wanted to touch again.

Witch.

Vail shook his head, spurning his desire to lay his hands on her, to feel her soft flesh give beneath his fingers again and have her warmth seep into his skin.

He did not desire to touch the witch.

Vile. Evil. Vicious little rose. She would likely prick him with her thorns and make him bleed.

He would not fall under her spell.

"And now we're back to hating me. Great. Has anyone ever told you that you're mercurial?" She turned her nose up at him before he could respond and looked at Fenix. "Or maybe he is just mad."

Vail grabbed her roughly by the arm and spun her to face him, dragging her closer at the same time so she had to tilt her head back to hold his gaze, hers filled with fire.

"I am not mad, but if I am, then it was one of your kind who made me so. Never call me such a thing. Never judge someone when you know nothing about them, *Witch*... it may save your life." He threw her arm aside and stalked past her, heading towards the end of the corridor that led up to the courtyard.

He didn't care if they followed him or not. He didn't care if a thousand men awaited him in the area ahead.

He would welcome it.

He wanted to fight. He wanted the taste of blood on his tongue and the feel of bones shattering beneath his blows. He needed the pain and the rage, and the release.

He tossed a vicious snarl back down the corridor at Fenix and Rosalind and teleported. If Little Wild Rose believed him mercurial, then he would show her just how mercurial her mate could be and just what he did to witches who annoyed him.

Vail reappeared in the middle of the courtyard facing the immense dark castle that rose up at one end of it. Several demon warriors immediately turned his way but he paid them no heed as he scoured the occupants of the courtyard for the females he had seen in the times he had passed through it.

Darkness slithered over his skin, igniting his rage, and he swung his gaze to his right, towards the source of it.

Witch.

With a hiss and a flash of fangs, he disappeared. The redhead was unprepared for him. He appeared above her, dropping out of the air and taking her down, his booted feet pressing into her shoulders. His weight drove her hard into the flagstones and he grinned as the back of her head smacked off the black ground and she unleashed a pain-drenched cry.

Two black ribbons swirled around her left palm and Vail shook his head at her. He shot his hand out, snatched hold of her left wrist, and viciously twisted it, snapping the bone. She cried out again, the agony in it sending pleasure flooding him, a high that drove him to hurt her again.

To make her suffer as he had.

He drew in a deep breath and fought to control the hunger for violence, the dark need to inflict pain and steal pleasure from it. It pushed at him, stronger than he could resist, and more powerful than he could ever hope to control. It drove him to punish her, to take his time over it and ensure she knew first-hand the depth of the pain he had survived, and the torment he had endured. He wanted to condense four thousand two hundred years of agony, of hope-destroying torture, into four extremely painful minutes.

The same as he did to every witch he came across.

Warmth swept over him from behind, carrying the scent of nature that drove back the darkness pulling him under.

Little Wild Rose.

The sound of battle reached his ears and he realised with horror that the dark witch beneath him was calling out to her brethren.

Vail ran his black claws across her throat, so her cry for Alyssum ended in a gurgle as blood gushed from the deep wounds and poured into the punctures.

He pushed off the dead witch and called his twin black blades to him at the same time, preparing to hurl himself at the blonde witch she had called.

The sight of Rosalind trying to evade the blows of the demon warriors froze his heart in his chest. Ice crawled across his skin.

Little Wild Rose.

His ki'ara ducked and rolled, leaped backwards to avoid the six-feet-long blades the huge males swung at her. The chain between her manacles swayed and rattled with each desperate move she made and Vail snarled at himself.

He had left his ki'ara defenceless.

He teleported and reappeared behind two large males who were attacking her. Her eyes widened as they flitted to him and she threw herself to one side, rolling under a strike aimed at her neck. Vail growled and slashed down the bare back of the biggest demon, ripping a cry from the male. He thrust his other sword at the smaller male, but the demon unfurled his black leathery wings and kicked off, beating them hard as he took flight.

The larger demon turned on Vail, bringing his sword around in a diagonal arc. Vail ducked under the blade and teleported, dropping out of the air above the male. He twisted in the air, twirled both of his black swords so they pointed downwards in his grip, and snarled as he drove them deep into the demon's shoulders, slicing clean through tendon and bone. The male roared and fell to his knees. Vail landed behind him, pulled both of his swords out of the demon's back, and swept his left one in a fast arc, severing his head.

Rosalind gasped and Vail paused only long enough to satisfy his need to see she was unharmed before teleporting after the smaller demon. The male was about to touch down on the high dark stone wall surrounding the courtyard when Vail appeared above him, landed on his back and knocked him out of the air. He shoved with his feet as they neared the pavement, slamming the male into the slabs with such force that they cracked and the male spewed blood from his mouth.

Vail grinned, stepped off the male's back and brought his swords down in two swift strikes, cutting straight through his wings. He raised his swords to finish him.

A female cry caught his attention and pain swept through his side, blazing fiercely.

Little Wild Rose.

He turned and growled when he spotted her using her thick metal cuffs to block the sword coming down at her.

Wielded by the blonde witch.

Alyssum threw her free hand forwards and a dark purple orb flew from it, hitting Rosalind in the chest and sending her flying across the courtyard. Vail teleported in an instant, sent his swords away and snatched her out of the air, landing in a crouch on one knee with her tucked against his chest. He drew back to check on her.

She remained curled up in a ball, her ash blonde hair strewn across her face and her eyes screwed shut.

"Witch?" Vail said and she let out her breath, her blue eyes slowly opening and rising to meet his. The warmth in them, the relief that shone so clearly, stole his breath from his lungs and he found himself staring down into them, picking out every dazzling fleck of silver that floated on azure seas.

Bewitched. She had truly cast a spell upon him, but it wasn't like any he had experienced before. It ran deeper, held him fast and refused to let him go, and part of him liked it. "You are unharmed?"

She blinked slowly, looking as lost as he felt.

The battle raged around them, Fenix fighting the demons back unknown to Vail. He knew only Little Wild Rose as she lay tucked safely in his arms, pressed against his chest, her backside resting on his right thigh and her back supported by his bent left knee.

What spell had she cast upon him that had enslaved him so completely that he felt driven to protect her, felt warmed inside whenever she looked at him as she was now, and felt he would go mad without her?

"Look out!" She grabbed his shoulders and pulled him down on top of her, so their chests pressed together and he could feel her heart hammering against his.

He stared down at her mouth, so very close to his, so perfect and soft, her rosy lips parted in sweet invitation.

The oily slick of magic crawled over his skin, detonated above him and showered him with pain.

Witch.

He shoved off Rosalind, twisting to face Alyssum at the same time. The dark witch smirked at him, her long black dress fluttering and whipping around her ankles as her eyes filled with crimson fire and she called another spell. Her gaze dropped to Rosalind where she remained on the ground and darkened with intent.

Vail hissed, his pointed ears flattening against the sides of his head, and mentally completed his armour, forming his spiked black helmet. The slats of the mask flowed down to conceal and protect the lower half of his face, and he kicked off, launching himself at the witch. She hurled the spell at him instead of Little Wild Rose.

The twisting black orb slammed into his left shoulder and sent him into a spin. He growled behind his mask and teleported, using the shift to right himself and appearing behind her. He lashed out, raking his black claws down her back, and grinned as she cried out and arched forwards to evade him. He stepped into her, hooked his right leg around both of hers, and shoved her in the back, sending her toppling to the ground. He pinned her with his right knee and poised himself to strike.

She grunted and stretched her right hand out, her focus fixed on Rosalind where she was finding her feet with the help of Fenix.

Vail snarled as Rosalind turned wide blue eyes on the witch and defensively brought her hands up. Her face twisted, her panic drumming in his veins. She wanted to call her magic and he had callously left it bound, had been too weak to give her the freedom he now used to his advantage. He growled at himself, disgusted by how weak he was, and how cruel.

His Little Wild Rose could have defended herself had he been stronger.

The quiet voice locked deep within him battled with his darker side, the one that said she could have defended herself had she taken the weapon he had offered. He had no need to release her magic.

When had he become so weak and despicable?

Fenix grabbed her and teleported them just as Vail shoved his claws into the back of Alyssum's hand, pinning it to the stone flags beneath her. She cried out and he silenced her by running the claws of his other hand across her throat. Blood flowed across the flagstones as she choked, her life seeping out of her, and he held her down with his right knee, waiting for her heart to stop before he flipped her onto her back and called his black blades to him.

He drove one through her heart and severed her head with the other, and then teleported to the other dead witch and gave her the same treatment, ensuring neither of them would come back.

He scanned the warriors in the courtyard. All of the large demon males stared at him. None were fighting.

Where had Fenix taken his female?

Vail shut his eyes, unconcerned by the demons closing in on him, and focused on her. He frowned when he located her some distance away, beyond the boundaries of the fortress. The wretched male was attempting to steal his ki'ara.

He would pay for his insolence.

Pale blue-purple light traced over Vail's body and the darkness swallowed him, its cool embrace a comfort. He couldn't recall the last time he had been strong enough to teleport a long distance, or had the power to heal his armour. It felt good to have it complete again, without any weak points, and to be able to travel great distances in mere seconds.

He appeared a few metres ahead of Fenix and Rosalind, facing them and the great black fortress beyond them. The male drew to a halt but the witch kept walking, her eyes fixed on him and her hands slowly coming up in front of her.

"Are you hurt?" she said in a soft voice that spoke of concern.

He wanted to bare his fangs at her in warning to make her stop too, but managed to force a shake of his head instead.

Relief joined the concern in her blue eyes, but it quickly melted into a darker emotion, one he was more familiar with.

Anger.

She stopped her approach, planted her hands on her hips so the chain between her manacles rested across her stomach and scowled at him. "What the bloody hell did you think you were doing?"

"Rosalind." Fenix flexed his fingers around the hilt of his sword.

The witch didn't heed the male's warning.

Vail flicked him a glare, daring him to attempt to attack him, and then locked his eyes on the little witch, giving her all of his attention. She shrank back.

Towards the incubus.

Vail mentally commanded his helmet to return to the rest of his armour, revealing his face, and his top lip curled back off his fangs.

"Come. Female." He held his hand out to her.

She eyed it with reproach.

"I have a name. Until you use it, I see no reason for me to do anything you ask." She folded her arms across her chest. "And I'm most certainly not following orders from you."

She walked towards him, her gaze fixed on his, and he expected her to take his hand and do as he had requested, falling into line with him and keeping her distance from the incubus.

She stomped straight past him instead, and he followed her with his gaze, turning so he could keep track of her, a frown forming.

Fenix chuckled and muttered under his breath as he passed him, "You have a lot to learn about women, my friend."

Vail curled his lip at the incubus and at the witch's behaviour.

"I vote we teleport *there*," Fenix said and pointed with his blade to black hills that rose in the distance and sharply dropped away on one side.

"That would take us towards the Seventh Realm." Vail had no problem with that, since it would also take them further from the elf kingdom and had been the realm he had originally meant to head towards.

Beyond the Seventh Realm lay the black lands of the Devil's domain.

Hell proper.

Vail wanted to go there.

His gaze drifted to the witch where she had stopped several feet ahead of Fenix and stood staring in the direction he pointed. The thought of taking her towards the Devil's domain sat in his stomach like a lead weight, dragging his insides down to his boots. She didn't belong in such a dangerous, dark place.

Fenix nodded. "I have allies in the Seventh Realm. They could help us find a portal to the mortal world."

Vail arched an eyebrow at that, taking a moment to recall that fae couldn't teleport between the realms without a portal, and then frowned at the way the witch's eyes lit up. Her relief and happiness flowed into him through their bond. She desired to return to the world above.

A fiercely possessive instinct demanded he not allow it. He didn't belong in that world, and that meant he couldn't let her reach it. He needed to keep her with him, even when the sane part of him said to let her go there, where she would be safe, so he could seek out his brother and warn him of the Fifth King's dark intentions. He growled at that part of himself, shunning the suggestion. She belonged with him now, not in that place of fae, mortals and witches.

No doubt she desired to return to a fae town, where the witches had covens and peddled spells and potions.

Towns that contained hundreds of her kind.

Vail silently bared his fangs at that.

He would kill them all.

All would pay for what Kordula had done to him.

A slender hand brushed his arm, the touch driving him into the darkness as magic crept outwards from it, curling around and holding him.

He looked down and saw black nails, cut like claws and stark against the pale fingers that held him in their unrelenting grip. Those fingers loosened, stroked, began a slow sweep up his arm towards his elbow. The magic strengthened, seizing control of him and holding him in place, trapping him within his own body. He tried to shake his head, tried to find his voice to ask her to release him, but he could neither move nor speak. All he could do was watch, his stomach churning and heart beating erratically, knowing what would come next.

"Vail?" A soft voice like a playful breeze through the leaves of a mighty ancient oak chased the darkness back and long black nails transformed into short clear broken ones, the perfect white skin becoming mottled with dirt and scratches.

He lifted his eyes to their owner, caught between darkness and light, lost for a moment.

She looked up at him with beautiful blue eyes filled with understanding, with warmth and no trace of dark intent.

"Shall we go?" she said and he recalled they had been discussing teleporting further away from the castle. "Before those demons reach us?"

She looked beyond him and he sensed the males approaching, caught her wrist in a firm grip, and teleported with her, cutting off her gasp.

They reappeared near the black hills the incubus had mentioned and Vail pointed out their next destination, a valley below the cragged cliffs just beyond them where the ground plummeted hundreds of feet.

"The fissure, near the S bend." Fenix pointed and Vail nodded. The incubus teleported.

Vail pulled Rosalind closer, fearing losing her in the leap, and disappeared. He appeared a short distance from the canyon and looked around for Fenix.

The incubus appeared after him, out of breath and looking paler than before.

"You're not well." The witch broke free of Vail's grasp and went to the male, taking his arm and helping him to a boulder.

Fenix settled himself on it, set his sword down beside him and shooed her away. He preened his long hair, untying the thong that held it back from his face, raking his fingers through the tawny lengths, and then retying it. If the incubus thought it would deter the witch, or make him suddenly appear less as if he was about to pass out from the exertion of teleporting, then he was very much mistaken.

Little Wild Rose assumed what Vail was coming to think of as her take-no-prisoners stance, placing her hands on her hips and tipping her chin up.

"You need to rest. You're weak from captivity." Her words fell on deaf ears.

Fenix tried to stand.

Rosalind shoved him back down onto the rock.

They repeated it two more times, during which Vail wondered how many attempts it would take for one of them to give up. Fenix tried once more before surrendering to the indomitable will of Little Wild Rose.

"We cannot afford to rest." Fenix's green eyes scanned the featureless black valley. "We are exposed here."

The male was right. The demons would easily spot them if they remained where they were. They had the advantage of higher ground.

"Darkness will fall soon. We will keep moving on foot to conserve our strength. The valley mouth cannot be further than a few miles." Vail gestured over the fissure to his right, towards where the two sides of the valley converged into another slim canyon. "We may rest there."

"I need to feed," Fenix muttered to himself.

Vail growled and the male held his hands up.

"Don't worry, Mate. She isn't on the menu." Fenix carefully pushed himself up, his bare chest rippling with the effort. The fae markings that curled around his biceps and over his shoulders flared black, purple and deep blue with accents of bright gold and cerulean.

Vail didn't know what they meant, but the witch backed away from him, whispering something beneath her breath.

She understood the colours and didn't like them, and that was enough for him. He placed himself between her and Fenix, holding his hands out on either side of him to shield her.

Fenix sighed. "I did say she isn't on my menu. I meant it. The downside to this horrible fucking place you call Hell is a startling lack of women, but that doesn't mean I have a hard-on for a bloody gruesome end. I would sooner starve than get on your bad side."

Vail had a feeling the male had desired to tack on 'Mad Elf Prince' to the end of his somewhat noble, and extremely sensible, observation and decision, and it made him want to slam the male into the ground and sever his hands anyway.

That way, he would think twice about offending Vail and would have no hands to touch his female with.

"Maybe we should get walking?" the witch said and he had to bite his tongue to stop himself from snarling at her and her attempt to control him.

She turned her back before he could respond and started walking, following the edge of the fissure. Fenix drew in a deep breath and disappeared, reappearing on the other side of the abyss and stumbling a few steps before finding his balance and a steady stride. Vail caught up with the witch in a few paces, clamped his hand around her wrist and quickly teleported her across to the other side, landing with her behind Fenix and releasing her.

"Thanks," she muttered to her hands and kept walking, her head bent now and gaze locked on her shackled wrists.

Vail refused to look at them. If he did, he would be reminded of the reason he needed her to wear them, of his weakness, and of the danger he had placed her in because of that weakness.

He had lost his mind when he had sensed her power though. The moment his hand had slipped free of the cuff in that dark cell, the dampening spell had faded and his senses had become stronger and sharper again. He had felt the magic in her and sensed it all around him. His broken hand had been agony, the pain so strong that every instinct he possessed had demanded he protect himself while it weakened him.

Made him vulnerable.

Gods, he knew she had lied to him in that cell. He just didn't know why. To protect herself? Any sane person would have done the same thing she had, stopping him from breaking his other hand. He had blacked out enough times only to come around with blood on his hands to know that he had done something terrible in those mindless moments when the beast had been in control and it had frightened her.

He stared down at his own hands as they walked, his focus split between the thoughts that clouded his mind and his surroundings, monitoring them to ensure that no demon could sneak up on them.

He flexed his serrated black claws, seeing them dripping with blood. Whose blood?

How many times had he wondered that?

How many times had he come out of the darkness to find he had killed and not knowing whose life he had taken?

When Kordula had controlled him, he had been aware of every life he had ended. He had fought as a warrior, keeping to his code, and had catalogued the faces of his fallen foes, wishing them a good afterlife. He had been honourable in that small respect and it had allowed him to feel that a part of the man he had once been still remained.

Now even that small piece was gone, taken from him by Kordula from beyond the grave, so his downfall was complete. No part of the man he had been once remained.

She had destroyed him completely, rebuilding him in a weaker image, a pathetic male with no honour, no pride, no conscience and no feelings whatsoever.

A male who knew only fear and allowed it to control his actions, even to the extent of placing the life of a female at risk.

A female who deserved her freedom.

A female who deserved a male better than he could ever dream of becoming.

A female he was beginning to believe truly was his ki'ara.

CHAPTER 13

Vail tried to keep his focus on their surroundings as he brought up the rear of their small group, but it kept slipping to the witch where she walked ahead of him. Her pain echoed on his body as they trekked towards the mouth of the canyon at the end of the grim black valley, each pebble that bit into her bare feet causing him both a physical ache and one that ran deeper.

He fought the urge to glance down at her feet and failed. His eyes drifted down her shapely form, slowing as they reached the hem of her tattered black dress. A layer of dust from the harsh terrain covered her lower legs, thinner on her calves but growing thicker until it formed a black soot over her ankles and feet.

That black dust didn't stop him from noticing the crimson patches on the soles of her feet.

He swallowed hard and looked away, averting his gaze far off to his left and pinning it there.

What kind of male allowed such a delicate little female to endure such pain and discomfort?

He clenched his fists until his black claws sliced through his own armour and bit into his palms.

A weak male, one unworthy of a female with the strength to endure that pain and discomfort without complaint and without slowing her pace.

Perhaps he could elevate himself from such a position and offer her some comfort and relief at the same time.

"Witch," he said and she kept walking. Her earlier words echoed around his mind. She would not respond to such names for her, but he couldn't bring himself to use her true name, not when the last witch he had called by name had forced him to do it. Vail ground his teeth, fighting back the rising darkness, and bit out, "Little Wild Rose."

She stopped and cast a confused look back at him.

At least he had managed his task, although it had left him feeling exposed, vulnerable in a way, more so than if he had used her given name.

He halted before her, bent down on one knee and called all of his focus, ignoring her curious gaze. The barrier between him and his brother fell away, leaving him feeling more exposed than ever, and he pushed beyond Loren before he could detect him to his rooms within the castle.

Loren had kept them for him, allowing him to retain the ability to call objects from them to him, his only possessions, and he had never been as grateful to his brother for that kindness than he was now.

He held his hands out and teleported a pair of elven boots to him. They were millennia old, but sturdy still, made of blue dragon hide with wrought silver scrollwork on the sides and back of the heel. He set them down in front of Rosalind, the ancient white oak soles bright against the black rock, and looked up at her. She stared down at them, her delicate features etched in lines of surprise that he found he liked on her, especially when her eyes shifted to his, a touch of warmth in them.

Something akin to affection.

Something that reminded him painfully of Loren.

His brother had looked at him in such a way many times. He recalled each time vividly, and the pride that had burst to life within him, especially when he had been but a boy and Loren had been the centre of his universe.

Tears rose unbidden as the connection between him and Loren strengthened, his brother reinforcing it, reaching for him across the vast distance. Fair Little Wild Rose's expression altered, becoming one touched with concern, and her pale eyebrows dipped above her beautiful clear blue eyes.

Blue eyes that now looked similar to Loren's whenever they had been in the mortal world as youths, moving unnoticed among the humans and the other fae.

Gods, how those eyes had laughed, had shown him love, had shone with fear, and had relayed everything his brother had been feeling. None of it hidden. Everything on show for him to see.

Gods, how those same eyes had shown him pain too, had revealed the staggering depths of his distress and his fear, and had cut at Vail throughout the millennia, dealing blows more deadly than any physical wound, leaving him scarred deep in his soul.

Vail lowered his head, dropped to both knees and snarled as he shoved his claws deep into the earth. He dug at it, raking up the black dirt and bunching it into his fists.

He had never wanted to hurt his brother.

He had fought so hard to resist and Kordula had punished him viciously for it each time he had succeeded in refraining from dealing the killing blow.

He had tried to break her spell, not for his own sake but for his brother's.

And when that failed, he had done all in his power to ensure his brother would never be alone.

He had moved Heaven, Hell and the mortal realm to find his brother's fated female, the one who would be worthy of his brother's compassion and devotion, and would draw his love away from Vail.

So he could end his miserable existence without hurting his brother.

But his brother's love for him hadn't faded when Vail had gifted him with Olivia.

Gods help him, but it had only grown stronger.

Vail dug his claws through his black hair and pulled it back. He pressed the tips into his scalp, trying to focus on the pain in order to ground himself enough to allow him to bring the barriers back up. He couldn't take it. The feel of Loren reaching for him, encompassing him in love he didn't deserve, was too much.

He threw his head back, arching his chest towards the black vault of Hell, and unleashed every drop of his fury, his pain and his despair in a growl that sounded more beast than elf. His lips drew back from his fangs in a grimace and tears cut down his temples, racing into his hairline.

His chest heaved, his heart labouring as the memories came crashing down on him from all sides, sweeping in to batter him and carry him away.

The scent of nature swirled around him, soft and enchanting, a meadow in full bloom, transporting him back to his vision of wild flowers and tall grass, and lazing under an oak. He could almost see the sunlight playing through the leaves, each magical shaft of light catching his attention and bringing him peace.

Magical.

"Breathe, Vail," she whispered and rather than push her away as every dark instinct screamed at him to do, he focused on her and pulled her closer instead. "Just breathe through it."

He sensed her hands hovering close to his elbows, felt her heat wrapping around him with her scent and the constant quiet hum of magic she emanated.

His heart settled as he did as she instructed, slowing his breathing to match hers and then bringing it down further, to a normal rhythm for him. The connection between him and his brother cleared, and he swore he felt surprise through it, laced with fear.

Vail opened his eyes, his palms trembling against the sides of his head, holding it with crushing force that made his skull ache.

Little Wild Rose stood over him, hands just above his elbows, the chain between her manacles pulled tight. She ghosted her palms back and forth along his arms but didn't touch him, and he was grateful for it. He was barely holding it together, her voice and presence the only thing keeping him grounded. That would change if she dared to lay her hands on him, even when part of him wished it wouldn't—ached to be able to bear her touch just this once because he needed the comfort.

He needed to know he wasn't lost beyond hope, too maddened by his history to ever come back.

"Breathe," she whispered with a half smile. "Let go of your head now. Come back to me."

To her?

His hands fell away from the sides of his head, dropping into his lap, and he stared up at her, searching her blue eyes for the truth and shocked when he found it there among other things he couldn't decipher. All of it on show for him. None of it hidden.

Gods, he ached with a fierce need to pull her into his arms and hold her, to see if she was truly real and that she truly was his ki'ara, and it wasn't all another trick to strip him of power and enslave him.

But he couldn't trust himself.

The bond between him and his brother rippled with emotion, giving him the comfort he could never allow himself to receive from Rosalind.

Fair Rosalind.

His Little Wild Rose.

She stood before him, a slender sylph-like creature who had witnessed the worst in him but somehow found the strength to bravely step within his reach and risk everything in order to bring him light in his darkest moments. She seemed more fantasy than reality, too good and pure of heart to be anything other than a figment of his demented mind, something dreamed up in a fit of madness for him to cling onto and hold to his chest.

A beautiful shadow of the hope that had long ago died in him.

"You going to kneel there all night giving her moon eyes or are we good to get moving again?" Fenix's deep voice boomed around the valley, reminding Vail that they weren't alone.

He wasn't sure what the term 'moon eyes' meant but he presumed it was not a good thing.

Or perhaps it was something unsettling judging by Rosalind's reaction.

Her cheeks turned dark pink and she busied herself with the boots he had given to her, slipping her cut bare feet into them and diligently keeping her eyes away from him.

Vail scrubbed away all sign of his tears and held the connection between him and his brother open for a few seconds more, cherishing the deep bond between them, before he closed it.

He rose to his feet and waited for the witch. She shuffled around in his boots, testing them out.

His boots.

Vail growled low in his throat at that, the sight of her wearing one of his few possessions awakening a startling reaction in him. He liked it.

When she lifted her head and flashed him a brilliant smile, one that relayed her gratitude and said his thoughtfulness had touched her, he experienced an even more startling reaction.

His gaze dropped to her rosy lips and he felt a low tug in his belly, a yank in her direction together with a sudden urge to do something horrific.

He wanted to kiss her.

He flashed his fangs and hissed at her instead. *"Witch."*

She backed off a step, hurt flickering across her face, causing her smile to fall away. She opened her mouth, snapped it shut again and spun on her heel, giving him her back. He kept his boots firmly planted to the black earth until she was over two metres away and then he started after her, keeping the distance between them steady as he slowly, piece by piece, destroyed the dark need she had somehow placed inside him.

Magic.

Her restraints weren't working and she had cast a spell on him to force him into wanting her, just as Kordula had done before her.

The remaining sensible part of him whispered that it wasn't magic. Her powers were still at a low level just within range of his sharp senses. They hadn't grown stronger.

It was the bond then.

She had wanted to kiss him and the bond had wanted to force his compliance in order to satisfy his female's needs.

Vail settled on that as the reason behind his need to kiss her and closed in on her as they drew near to the end of the valley.

"You will rest ahead. I will stand guard while you and Fenix sleep." He fell into step beside her, but kept some distance between them, so the constant level of magic she radiated didn't push him over the edge.

He couldn't afford such a thing when he was still fighting the effects of opening his bond with Loren in order to bypass the barrier he had placed on the elf kingdom millennia ago, shutting Kordula out.

Now, he used that same barrier to keep him from returning whenever he was weak and wanted to see his homeland again. As much as he desired it, longed for it, the elf kingdom was no longer his home. None there would welcome him after the terrible things he had done to his people and to his brother.

Little Wild Rose looked across at him and shook her head, causing her blonde tangled waves to bounce against her shoulders. "I don't sleep."

Vail frowned. She didn't sleep? All creatures required sleep, even witches. He looked deep into her eyes, trying to detect whether it was the result of a spell, or she had a reason she didn't want to sleep.

Was it because of the dark things he had felt in her back in the solitary cell? She had been gripped by a sort of madness, a hallucination that had shaken her and had made him feel she shared something in common with him.

Something haunted her.

Did it haunt her sleep too?

If it did and she refused to sleep because of it, then whatever awaited her in her dreams had to terrify her.

It was on the tip of his tongue to ask her, the words all lined up and all very civil, when she turned her cheek to him and sped up.

Vail bit back a growl of frustration. Was he this frustrating to her? Whenever he thought he could speak civilly to her and might learn something about her and come to understand how she affected him so deeply and was able to bring him out of the darkness, she distanced herself.

She turned quiet and thoughtful, drawing into herself and away from him. Whatever she was thinking, it troubled her. He felt the weight of it on his heart, a steady ache laced with fear.

They entered the canyon, the steep cragged black sides rising to over one hundred feet above them. He had to drop behind her again, the winding rocky corridor too narrow for them to walk side by side. The vertical walls stole all light, plunging the path ahead into darkness. Fenix led the way, scrambling up an incline before disappearing over the brow, his fae sight most likely as clear as Vail's was despite the darkness.

"Bugger." Rosalind slammed face first into the path, her pain echoing in his right knee and palms. "Bloody sod it. This is stupid. I can't see a damned thing!"

Vail cursed himself. He hadn't even thought about the fact that she wouldn't be able to see in the dark without a spell to aid her.

She huffed and ground out a few things in the fae tongue that he didn't understand, but that drew a chuckle from Fenix. Vail's name came up.

They were speaking of him to each other, knowing he couldn't understand them.

He snarled at her and then Fenix, and the incubus wisely turned away and kept walking, swinging his blade up to rest on his bare shoulder.

"Why do you not sleep?" Vail refused to be civil now she had resorted to speaking about him behind his back but right in front of him, no doubt saying nasty things about him. Things he probably deserved. "You require rest."

She didn't respond. She didn't even look at him. She dusted herself off and started walking again, bending forwards and using her hands to feel the path ahead.

The chain between her manacles jangled on the black rocks.

Vail grimaced. "Are you upset because I refused to release you?"

She shook her head but he wasn't convinced.

He ventured closer and glanced down at her wrists. They were bloodied where the thick metal cuffs clamped tightly around her slender arms, new scars forming on her dirty skin. He dragged his gaze away, shame spiralling through him and leaving him feeling wretched that his fear of her hurting him was causing him to hurt her.

"What are your powers?" he whispered, afraid she might answer and he might not like it. He had met light witches in his time, those devoted to good and helping others. Was she one of their kind?

"I would never use them on you, Vail. We're allies." The glance she gave him said that she thought about them as more than allies.

She desired him.

The darkness within him was swift to rise, surging up like an unstoppable tide to sweep him away. A growl rumbled through him, his fangs lengthening in response to the threat she posed, and he backed off a step to stop himself from shoving her away.

She meant to deceive him. She wanted to lure him into her web and place him under her spell. She was vile and treacherous.

She would enslave him the moment he let down his guard.

No. Vail clawed himself back from the brink, refusing to surrender to the darkness and the need for violence stirring within him. He gritted his teeth and battled his urge to lash out at her, to hurt her before she could do the same to him.

She stared at him, her blue eyes enormous, sparkling with silver stars. Vail bared his fangs at her.

She withdrew another step, her hands rising to her chest, the action cutting at him together with the hurt and fear that flickered in her eyes. An overwhelming need to reach out and comfort her surged through him, a desire to apologise and make amends, even as the darker part of him whispered that this was his chance to strike without her seeing it coming.

Vail tunnelled his black claws into his hair, pressing their sharp tips into his scalp, and focused on the pain, using it to drive that compelling voice out of his head.

He chuckled under his breath as his heart twisted, torn by conflicting desires, and the voice grew stronger, mocking him.

No female in her right mind would ever desire a male like him.

He had never been good like Loren, not even before the sorceress had driven him mad, pushing him over the brink with glee and sending him plummeting into insanity. His behaviour around the witch was a clear indication of how bad he was inside—how evil—and how weak he was too. He couldn't shake his instinct to protect himself whenever she used a trace of her power around him, or drew too close to him. That instinct made him twitchy and snappish, and filled him with a violent need to harm her in order to save himself.

What kind of female could ever desire a male such as that?

A ki'ara deserved love and respect. She deserved to be cherished and protected, kept safe by her devoted mate, pampered and given all she desired.

He could never do such a thing for her. He couldn't give her the life she deserved as an eternal mate. His fated female.

He would forever be a danger to her, more likely to harm her than protect her, to put her through hell than give her a life filled with comfort and love. She would never feel secure around him, would always doubt his actions and his feelings, believing on some level that he despised her because of what she was, and that would constantly play on his mind, keeping him on edge and the darkness a relentless presence at the back of his mind, waiting to strike.

He closed his eyes, shutting out the witch and the world around him, searching deep within himself for a glimmer of good, for something that would make him worthy of any female or anyone's affection.

Four thousand years ago, before he had met Kordula at the borders of his kingdom, he might have been worthy of the love of a good female.

Finding his fated one had been everything to him back then, and even his prediction about her hadn't swayed him from his mission to locate her.

His female would be a sorceress and when they met, he would be maddened.

All the centuries after that prediction had been given to him, Vail had thought it to mean he would go crazy over her, not be insane when he met her.

When Kordula had used that prediction to spring her trap, he had lost all faith in it. He had spent millennia believing it had all been a trick devised by her kin to lure him to her so she could enslave him and attempt to steal control of his kingdom.

Vail cracked his eyes open and stared at Rosalind, deep into her eyes. Heat stirred behind his breast, warmth that eased his tired body and calmed his turbulent mind as it spread through his limbs. Peace.

Now, he believed in his prediction again, because she was standing before him, her dazzling blue eyes locked with his and filled with tender concern that triumphed over her fear, driving it back into the shadows of her heart.

He was insane, knew that without a doubt even though he despised admitting it and couldn't bear to hear others say it about him, and now he had met a sorceress he recognised as his mate.

Perhaps everything he had been through and endured was so he could reach this moment, and had happened in order to bring them together in this dark place, but he wasn't sure whether it had all been worth it.

He didn't trust her, and he could never trust himself.

He didn't understand her either.

She seemed troubled and refused to sleep. Why? He wanted to command her to tell him so he could do all in his power to help her, but she wouldn't speak about it with him. He didn't know what to do. He didn't know what someone should do in this situation.

He might have once, but not now, not when everything that had once been normal for him and was normal for others was now alien and confusing, beyond his grasp.

He didn't know how to be kind, or affectionate. He wasn't sure how to encourage her to speak.

His only point of reference was Loren. He had watched over his brother whenever he was in the mortal realm with his ki'ara, Olivia. He had seen how they interacted with each other, a series of gentle touches constantly reaffirming their bond without them even knowing it. He had seen his brother's love for his female, and his devotion, and his happiness.

He was glad Loren was happy, but that emotion felt foreign to Vail too. Unknown. It was something he was no longer capable of feeling.

He only knew the darker side of emotions. He knew pain and rage, fury and hatred. They filled him and ruled him, made him who he was now.

If everything he had suffered had been to bring him to this place at this exact time, to deliver him into the presence of his fated female, then perhaps it had also been for another reason too.

To bring Loren to his ki'ara.

It had taken a decades long hunt to find his brother's fated female, and in that time Vail had secretly visited many male witches, seeking their knowledge to point him towards Loren's future mate. Every visit had threatened to push him over the edge, had filled him with hatred as he had waited in their presence while they had used their magic to scry for Olivia.

Every visit had ended the same way, with him going out and killing in order to purge himself of his fury and his dark hungers. He had gorged himself on blood until he had come close to passing out, swallowed by his lust for it. It had awakened an addiction that he fought to this day, a terrible thirst for blood that would send him into the arms of the darkness that lived within him if he gave into it.

That addiction had been the sign that had opened his eyes to how close he was to becoming one of the tainted and he fought it as best he could, a part of him unwilling to surrender to it and the fate that awaited him.

He would become a savage beast, his powers fading with each life he stole during his rages, with every soul he consumed as he drank its host dry. He would become something worse than a vampire—one of the very creatures who had fathered that species.

One of the tainted his brother and he had left behind in the mortal world when they had withdrawn the elves to this realm to save them all from such a dark and terrible fate.

No elf desired such a thing.

Not even him.

So he fought the beast within him that bayed for blood and hungered for the kill, clinging to his pathetic existence and a shred of hope that he might somehow save himself or find death before the darkness consumed him forever.

His fangs itched at the thought of blood and he glanced at Rosalind's neck.

His markings flared into existence, a hot prickly flush that chased across his skin and illuminated the darkness as they shone through the scales of his armour, throwing colours across her face.

He hungered for another taste of her. The thought of biting her stirred more than his hunger though. It stirred desire in his veins, a powerful need to place his hands on her hips and draw her slender body against his, until he could feel her breasts pressing against his chest and could capture her mouth with his. His blood caught fire, the intense heat rising rapidly and blazing through him, an inferno only she could quell.

The dark beast within him snarled and railed against that dangerous desire, and Vail staggered back a step, horrified by what he had wanted to do.

He could not touch the witch.

He felt the ghostly press of her hands on his flesh, saw the cell around him again and her above him, her blue eyes roaming his body as she touched him.

Laid her hands on his body.

Her bare flesh against his.

Vail turned his back on her and struggled to focus on something else, anything other than the press of her warm hands on his skin.

He reached for the bond with his brother, needing the calm that flowed through him whenever he opened it, washing him clean of his sins for an all too brief span of time.

The tiny remnant of the man he had once been, a man who felt more like a ghost to him now or an illusion of a life he never had, turned against him and whispered that he didn't deserve Rosalind.

She was too bright to look at, too beautiful and pure, and he was ugly and tainted, darkness made flesh.

On the verge of a descent into a black abyss from which he could never return.

She had felt that inside him through their bond. She knew how wretched he was and how close to the edge, that he was holding on with just the tips of his claws, in danger of becoming little more than an animal, like so many elves before him.

"Vail?" she whispered and he snarled over his shoulder at her, needing her away from him.

"Leave me." He staggered forwards a few steps and his right shoulder hit the jagged black wall of the canyon.

He wanted her to leave, hoped she would never turn back and would slip out of his wretched life, safe away from him, even though she was more vital to him than air and he would die without her.

He could bear the pain of his memories and the weight of his sins, but he couldn't bear her being gone. He couldn't bear knowing he would never see her again, would never bathe in her light and sense her sweet emotions, or be blessed by her smile. It stole the breath from his lungs and squeezed his heart in his chest.

He growled and clutched at the obsidian stones, pressing his claws in deep, the pain in his heart eclipsing that in his fingertips as he fought the fierce need to grab her wrist and pull her into his arms, to hold her and press her close, and refuse to let her go.

She had bewitched him completely, but he feared this wasn't a spell. This was something infinitely more dangerous.

Something that drove him mad with a need to spurn her at the same time as he needed to hold on to her.

Her magic swirled around him, stronger now, warning of her proximity and that she had ignored his request to leave him alone. Joy battled despair, a sliver of affection fought the overwhelming force of hatred, and all combined to claw at his limbs and pull him deeper into the darkness.

He clung to the cliff face, fearing he would harm her if he loosened his grip. He tried to fight the darkness back but it was too strong. He had refused to fight it, had wanted it to consume him and end his existence, and now that he wanted to overcome it, it was too late.

He chanted a protective charm beneath his breath as images crashed together in the black of his mind, a mash of Kordula and Rosalind, blending together until his memories became warped and he couldn't distinguish between what had really happened and what was a lie constructed by the madness infesting him.

Little Wild Rose had never punished him, but a vision of her looming over him, black claws poised to strike and cleave his bare flesh, played out in his mind. She laughed, the mocking sound grating on his pride, tearing it to pieces, as he cried out his agony. Each searing laceration stole his breath, the pain so intense that black spots winked across his vision and she distorted, wobbling above him. She flicked her blonde hair over her shoulder and it turned red like blood, dripping over her bare breasts.

She leaned over him, her blue eyes holding jagged patches of ice and crimson, and her red lips parted as she pressed her hands into his chest, pushing him onto his back.

He tried to growl at her, tried to fight and shove her away, but he couldn't move. Her hands roamed over him and she dipped her head and swept her lips in a trail across his skin that made it crawl. She lowered one hand, cupped and fondled him, purred as her magic poured over him, stealing command of his body.

Violating him.

A hand shackled his wrist and his claws scraped over stone, a black wall that loomed before him. Bile blazed up his throat and he bent over, emptying the pitiful contents of his stomach on the rocks. Rocks. Sharp as knives. Not a feathered mattress. What torture did she have in mind now?

His stomach rebelled again, the feel of a hand on his wrist sending him deeper into twisted memories that overlaid onto the present.

He managed to look at the delicate hand holding him. Not tipped with black nails. Dirty and small, and fair.

But it was touching him.

Spreading vile magic over his flesh together with heat that scorched him.

And her scent spoke of hunger and need.

Hunger that rose within him too.

He looked up at her and she laughed, a flash of white teeth between red lips, and twisted his arm, pinning his back to the jagged black wall so the sharp rocks bit into his naked flesh. She writhed against him, her power too strong for him to overcome, and then pressed the full length of her bare body into his and kissed him. Her taste flooded his mouth, a sickly sweet poison that drugged him into complying and shattered the last of his will.

Shudders wracked him and his throat burned until he gagged and shoved her away. He bent over and vomited again, his whole body heaving as he tried to expel her toxic taste. Cold sweat trickled over his skin, no longer bare but covered with his armour. Armour that felt too tight and confining. He clawed at it, his throat burning and tightening, desperate to get it off him. His knees shook, muscles turning to water as he retched again and again, bringing nothing up.

His legs gave out and he collapsed onto the black ground.

What had she done to him?

He had commanded legions. He had run a kingdom. He had scored countless victories on the battlefield. He had been strong and powerful. A prince.

She had stripped all of that from him, leaving him weak, scarred and broken. A pathetic creature. He lost his mind when he needed it most and retained it when it only offered him pain, a terrifying replay of four thousand years of that woman's touch, of claws scraping, teeth nipping, palms kneading and fingers stroking.

A hand encircled his wrist.

Restraining him.

Vail yanked his arm away from her, rising at the same time and stumbling onto his feet. He turned on her and snarled when he saw Kordula before him.

"Vail." Her sweet sing-song voice cranked his fury up to startling heights.

He wouldn't let her cast a spell on him. He would kill her. He would put an end to her and she would never be able to hurt him again.

He laughed and launched himself at her, his claws ready to sink into her flesh. A male appeared between them, a handsome fae who pulled her out of the path of his blow, leaving him clawing at thin air. The fae brandished a sword, pointing it at him.

Vail would kill the male too.

He turned on them and bared his fangs.

"Rosalind, keep back," the male said.

Vail staggered backwards, those words hitting him like a physical blow, and fell against the rocky cliff face.

He stared wide-eyed at the witch.

Not Kordula.

Rosalind stared back at him, her eyes enormous and her fear flooding the link between them.

Vail looked down at his hands where they clutched the cragged stones behind him, at the black serrated claws that covered his fingers, weapons he had come dangerously close to using on her. He lifted his gaze back to her, and then shifted it to her right, to the incubus male who was still touching her, grasping her upper arm.

Laying his fingers on her bare flesh.

Darkness descended again, filling him with a fierce need to tear the male away from her and gut him.

A flicker of understanding crossed the witch's face and she pulled free of the male's grip, and advanced a step towards Vail.

"Vail?" she said softly, her gentle voice calming one part of him while it enraged another, his dual natures tearing him between giving his female what she desired by stepping towards her and slashing his claws across her throat before she could utter a spell to pull him back under her command.

He pressed back against the wall, despair rushing through him as his heart pounded hard against his ribs, driven by the fear that he would harm his Little Wild Rose.

He did the only thing he could to spare himself, and her.

He teleported.

CHAPTER 14

Rosalind stared at the place where Vail had been and was now gone, disappeared out of her life. She didn't know what to do, or how to combat the sudden emptiness inside her, a space that he had filled in her heart. He had shut her out again.

His behaviour had frightened her and she knew that he had sensed it through their bond, and she had tried to fight her fear for that reason, not wanting him to believe that she was afraid of him or she thought him a monster. He had caught her off guard though, his demeanour changing abruptly and his eyes gaining a crazed and dangerous edge as his power had risen.

Hers had warned her away from him, but she hadn't needed it to alert her to the danger. She had seen it.

The madness had gripped him again, snaring him and stopping him in his tracks, stealing him away from her. It had been more powerful this time, a dark malevolent force that had left him clawing at himself and snarling in the elf tongue, not hearing her as she had spoken to him and tried to break its hold on him.

And then she had felt the darkness in him.

The agony.

The fear.

The despair.

The sickness.

She had wanted to help him and had needed to shake the hold the madness had had on him. She knew better than to show him pity and knew he wouldn't appreciate her making him feel weak when he already felt weak and vulnerable because of everything that had happened to him. Because of a witch.

It had pounded in her mind, in time with her racing heart. A witch had driven him mad and she had wanted to help him. She hadn't been able to stop herself. She had reached out to him before considering the consequences and he had turned on her.

Foolish witch.

She had driven him away.

She had known better than to lay her hands on him, knew that he didn't like witches touching him, and she had still done it. The moment she had and he had turned on her with murder shining in his eyes that had been closer to black than violet, she had realised something dreadful.

Vail had suffered greatly and he still suffered now, tormented by the things that had happened to him—by the things a witch had done to him.

One of her kind.

"We have to find him," she whispered, more to herself than Fenix.

The incubus prowled closer, a wary aura around him. "He'll be long gone and impossible to trace."

She raised her gaze to meet his but it was hard to see him in the low light. Vail's markings had constantly glowed throughout his episode, shining through his armour where the scales overlapped, chasing back the darkness and allowing her to see him. Now he was gone, and that beautiful light was gone with him.

Rosalind closed her eyes, pressed her shackled hands to her chest, and focused on her connection to Vail. It wasn't gone. It was weak, but still there, giving her hope.

She smiled. "Not impossible. I can feel him, but I can't use my magic to enhance it. It will take me some time with the connection this weak, but I will find him."

Fenix sighed, the huff heavy with an unspoken desire to question her sanity.

"Is he really worth the effort?" he said in a low voice, one that had a sharp edge to it that she didn't like. He wanted to leave Vail behind. "He tried to hurt you. He attacked you."

Her smile turned solemn and she opened her eyes and stared down at the ground, unable to distinguish it from all the other black around her. Fenix was right, but he was wrong too.

"That wasn't Vail," she whispered and wished those words had come out firmer, more confident and certain. "Something is wrong with him."

"Something is wrong with you," Fenix snorted and shuffled a step closer, so she could feel him nearby, his aura mingling with hers. "Wanting to go after him when you should be making a break for freedom."

She frowned in his general direction and folded her arms across her chest as best she could, the chain between her cuffs jangling and filling the tense silence. "I take it you're not going to help then?"

Her heart clenched at the thought he might be serious and might leave her if she chose to find Vail. With her wrists bound and powers restrained, she was a sitting duck. The demons would find her in no time and would take her back to the castle, or worse.

Fenix sighed again. "I can't leave a woman alone in a place like this. Besides, the mad bastard might find out I left you and come after me."

A chuckle slipped from her lips. "He probably would."

Because Vail was the biggest and most confusing contradiction she had ever met. One moment, he didn't want her and he looked ready to kill her, and the next he looked as if he would die without her. She didn't understand him at all, but she wanted to. She needed to know what had happened to him so she could help him move past it, if that was even possible.

She had to believe it was though, if only so she kept believing there was a chance for her too, a shot at her coming to terms with what she had done and moving on with her life.

However much life she had left anyway.

"So, we look for him, and hope he doesn't kill us when we find him," Rosalind said and trudged onwards, her sore feet slipping around in her oversized boots.

Boots that Vail had given to her and she couldn't recall ever receiving a more wonderful, thoughtful and welcome gift.

They had been the last thing she had expected when he had knelt before her, and so had his reaction.

What had made him cry?

What had brought such a strong, powerful man to tears?

She focused on him and the slight link between them, needing to feel him and know she was drawing closer to him again. She scrambled up another incline, groping around in the darkness. Fenix remained behind her, occasionally steadying her when she tripped or correcting her course when she veered towards one of the walls.

A replay of her every moment with Vail in this valley ran through her head, distracting her at times. She couldn't understand him at all. He flitted from cruel to kind, from withdrawn to open, from malicious to affectionate so quickly that she couldn't keep up. He tied her head, and her heart, in knots that felt impossible to unravel.

Her boot snagged on a rock and she tripped over several more and landed flat on her face.

"Bloody Hell." She shoved herself up, dusted her knees off and swore she could feel Fenix smirking at her.

"I can try teleporting us."

Rosalind shook her head, knowing he could see her because of his heightened vision. "It's not worth the risk and I don't want to put you in danger."

He laughed. "Look around you, Sweetheart. Danger is everywhere."

She huffed. "You know what I meant. You need to eat... or feed... or whatever it is you do to replenish your strength."

Her stomach growled, reminding her that she needed to eat too. She rubbed it through her dress, doubting she was going to get her hands on some food anytime soon. A warm breeze blew down the mouth of the canyon, carrying the scent of fire and ash. They had to be close to the plateau she had seen above the valley and she wasn't sure she was glad of it. A plateau just meant a huge expanse of more dark, one that she could easily get lost in and possibly fall into another canyon and kill herself.

Mother earth, she hoped that wasn't the way she was destined to go. She at least wanted to go out fighting or with some honour or something. If she had to die, she wanted it to be for a cause, not because she couldn't see a damned thing in the inky dark of Hell.

Fenix squeezed her shoulder, his hand warm on her bare skin. "Buck up. My mate in the Seventh Realm will feed you."

She smiled at the fact he didn't say 'feed us' and was tempted to act shocked that he didn't swing that way.

A shriek pierced the darkness.

Fenix instantly grabbed her arm in a bruising grip and teleported. The swirling sensation brought what little she did in her stomach up her throat and she almost threw up when they landed. The breeze was stronger, carrying an acrid stench of brimstone, and a blazing fissure lit the land ahead of her. Flames belched up from it, punctuating the darkness and driving it back.

Another scream came, the agonised cry sending a shiver down her spine. Fenix readied his sword.

Rosalind cursed her restraints and started to wish she had taken the weapon Vail had offered.

A demon came charging towards them from a small ramshackle set of buildings in the distance, silhouetted by the flames that burst from the lava canyon, shooting high into the air. Rosalind prepared herself, her heart starting a steady pound against her ribs and her mouth going dry.

The demon wasn't slowing. He sprinted straight at them, a wild look on his bloodstained face as he tossed a glance behind him and then another, stumbling with his second and barely keeping himself upright. She had the startling feeling he hadn't even noticed they were ahead of him.

He was going to mow them down. He wasn't out to fight them at all. He was fleeing.

He was running from something, and running for his life.

A black shadow dropped out of the air and landed on his back, sending him crashing into the dirt just metres from Rosalind and Fenix. Fire blazed up behind the dark figure, silhouetting his lithe form, from the tips of his claws that dripped with blood to the sharp points of the dragon-like horns that formed a spiked crown atop his head.

She felt the wraith's eyes on her, burning in their intensity, scorching her. Vail.

He didn't take his eyes off her as he ripped into the demon.

Before the war between the Third Realm and the Fifth Realm, she had never seen someone die. The brutality and gruesome face of death in war had shocked her when she had witnessed it, but what she saw before her now made it pale in comparison.

Vail was savage and brutal as he snarled and tore his foe apart just feet ahead of her, clawing at the male's flesh and spilling his blood on the black earth. The flames that shot up behind him were a fitting backdrop for his violence and darkness as he rose to his feet, turned his profile to her and stared off into the distance towards the small group of buildings.

Five demons appeared in swirls of black.

Vail drew his twin obsidian swords out of the air, teleported and attacked them, a one-man army as he took them all on at once. He threw his hand towards one, sending him flying through the air with a blast of telekinesis, as he struck at another, slashing a diagonal line across the demon's bare chest with his sword. He spun, ducked beneath the blow the demon aimed at him, and crossed his swords across the male's throat.

Rosalind looked away, covering her mouth as he decapitated the demon.

He tackled the remaining four, his swords nothing more than shadowy blurs as he lashed out with them, stabbing and slashing, giving his enemies no quarter as he pressed them backwards, away from her and Fenix.

One of the larger males landed a blow on Vail's jaw, the force of it sending him down onto one knee.

Rosalind reacted on instinct, rushing forwards to help him.

Vail's hand shot out towards her, his claws spread and palm facing her, and he looked over his shoulder at her. His near-black eyes held hers and she stopped dead as she read their silent command. He shot to his feet and attacked the demon, using each slash of his swords to drive the male back.

Away from her.

He was protecting her.

Rosalind didn't even notice Fenix joining the fight, assisting Vail and taking two of the demons off his hands. She stared at Vail, more confused than ever.

The scent of blood cut through the stench of the lava canyon and she looked down at her feet and realised with horror that she stood over the corpse of the decapitated demon.

Thick shiny liquid oozed around her boots, turning the soles dark. Her breathing accelerated and her eyes widened, her throat closing as she backed away and shook her head. The death cries of the demon's companions rang in her ears.

How many of his kind had she killed?

How many friends had she taken from him?

Loved ones?

She stumbled backwards, tears filling her eyes. She had done it to protect her friends.

She looked down at her hands and saw the blood of all the souls she had taken on them.

So much blood.

So many lives.

Heat swept through her, a sense that she wasn't alone filling the void in her chest and comforting her, and she turned her face towards the source of that feeling.

Vail stood before her, his chest heaving and his black armour slick with blood. Crimson splattered across his face too, an arch of red spots and slashes that darted from the right side of his jaw across his nose. The spikes of his helmet shrank and disappeared, the scales drifting down and back into the rest of his armour, allowing the warm breeze to tousle his hair.

His near-black eyes were wild, filled with dark hungers she could sense within him.

He needed more enemies to kill.

These six demons, and however many he had slaughtered at the village, hadn't been enough to satisfy the hunger for violence that rode him.

"Keep your distance," Fenix whispered close by her elbow and flexed his fingers around the grip of his sword.

Vail snarled and bared his fangs, his pointed ears flaring back and flattening against the sides of his head as his eyes narrowed on Fenix.

"Vail won't hurt me," she said with all the confidence she could muster, not taking her eyes off him, giving him all of her focus because she knew deep in her heart it was what he needed and desired. He needed her to see only him, to face him as he was and not flinch away and seek the protection of another male. He needed to know that she didn't fear him, even when the need for violence gripped him. "You did this to protect me. Didn't you?"

She believed that. The canyon would have brought them to this plain, and into the presence of these demon warriors who lay dead at her feet because of Vail. She would have had to fight them with her wrists and powers bound, so Vail had fought them for her, just as he had taken on her foes in the castle courtyard.

She braved a step towards him, bringing all of his attention to her.

"You fought to protect me."

He looked off to the left of his feet, his claws curled into fists and he closed his eyes, his nostrils flaring as he drew in a deep breath.

"More will come," he muttered beneath his breath and she glanced beyond him to the gathering of buildings near the fissure. "Too many."

That sent a cold shiver tripping through her. If Vail thought there were too many for him to handle, then she wanted to get away before they showed up. Having seen him fight, she could easily imagine that too many for him meant numbers in serious double figures.

She scanned what she could see of their surroundings, searching for an alternate route, one that would keep them away from the demons for long enough that they could escape and lose them.

"We need to split up," Fenix said and her focus shot to him.

"What?" She had to have heard him wrong. "Split up?"

He nodded. "It will make it harder for the demons to track us."

She looked at Vail and he nodded too. He might be on board with the insane suggestion of splitting up but she certainly wasn't.

"There's safety in numbers." She tried to squash the note of panic in her voice, not wanting to sound as if she was about to blow a gasket at the thought of being left alone in a demon realm without her powers.

Fenix nodded. "That's why you're going with him."

He pointed to Vail. Vail stared at her, the intensity of his gaze sending a hot achy shiver through her bones.

"We should stick together." She refused to give up and wasn't going to allow either male to bully her into changing her mind. "That's final. We're not splitting up. I won't allow it."

Fenix smiled. "That's what I like about you, Rosalind. You're opinionated, bossy and stubborn as Hell, but… you have a flaw."

"I do?" Her eyebrows shot up and his smile widened, blue and gold swirling in his eyes.

He stepped towards her, brushed his fingers across her cheek, earning a low growl from Vail, and shook his head.

"You tend to see the good and overlook the bad… and that's why you would never have seen this coming." He kept his gaze fixed on hers, the blue and gold in his irises brightening and swirling together, compelling her to keep looking at him, pulling her under his spell. She cursed him for using his charms on her, making her hazy and compliant, unable to hate him or fight him, and she wanted to do both as she dimly realised what he was going to do. He leaned in, his heat surrounding her, spreading through her veins, and whispered, "Be careful, Little Girl, because I knew one just like you once and that flaw you share got her killed, eight times over. It's time I tried not to make it nine. See you around."

He pressed a kiss to her forehead and disappeared.

The warm haze that had suffused every inch of her dissipated, leaving her cold. Anger curled through her veins. Awareness crept in, of her surroundings, of Vail watching her closely, and of the fact that the incubus had lured her into a stupor so she couldn't fight him and had teleported.

"Bloody son of a bitch." She stamped her foot and growled in frustration. Vail arched an eyebrow. "We need to teleport after him or something."

His eyebrow didn't fall. If anything, it crept higher.

"No," he said, his deep voice low and husky, stirring heat in her veins as easily as the incubus had with his charms. "We do not know where he went, and Fenix is right. We will travel faster separately, and the demons will find it harder to track us."

She cursed him in the fae tongue. She never had liked the fact that men had a tendency to stick together and form allied fronts against women, and it really grated on her nerves right now, when they had just lost one of their fighters because the men had refused to listen to reason.

Teleporting around the land would have given them ample chance of losing the demons. Splitting up seemed like a terrible idea, and not only because they had lost a good warrior and she might be forced to fight.

It had left her alone with Vail.

She muttered a protection spell beneath her breath, wishing she had her powers so she could use her strongest wards to keep the growing attraction, the intense pull, she felt towards Vail at bay.

Maybe Fenix was right and she had lost her mind. The dark elf prince standing before her, his black armour slick with the blood of his enemies and a touch of madness in his sharp gaze, was the last person in this universe a sane woman would find alluring and attractive.

But if she had lost her mind, then she couldn't bring herself to care that it was gone.

Because the damaged man standing before her wore armour splattered with blood because he had risked his life in order to protect hers, and the madness that touched his eyes was because another man had dared to lay his hands on her and place a kiss on her forehead.

And she found that beautiful.

She forced herself to turn on the spot, needing her eyes off Vail so she could build up some resistance to the urges flowing through her, the intense desire to cross the short span of earth between them and thank him with a kiss that would probably be the death of her.

But what a way to go.

She shoved that thought away and looked in every direction, but it all appeared the same to her. Flat plains. Lava rivers. The occasional silhouette of mountains.

Where in this desolate, dangerous land was safe?

"So where do we go now?" She glanced back at Vail, catching him staring at her with hungry eyes that echoed the growing need inside her.

Vail pointed far off to his right, beyond the edge of the valley they had walked through, in the opposite direction to the one they had been heading towards.

"And what's over there?" She squinted but couldn't make out anything in the pitch black.

Vail stood in silence, a battle raging within him that obliterated the subtler sensation of the desire she had detected through their link and vibrated within her. Whatever laid in that direction, he was reluctant to take her there. Why?

His clear purple gaze drifted back to her.

"The Third Realm."

Rosalind's heart leaped in her chest. He was going to take her back to the Third Realm? The thought of seeing everyone again lifted her spirits and she took a step towards Vail. His eyes narrowed on her, focused and searching, and she realised he had been waiting to see her reaction to his decision and he wasn't pleased. Why?

The answer to that question came to her as he turned his back and stared off into the distance, the belching flames casting a golden outline down his noble profile as they leaped from the gorge beyond him.

She hadn't hidden her excitement over returning to that kingdom, a place where he no doubt felt he didn't belong because of whatever dark things haunted him and his relationship with his brother.

A place she had no doubt he would leave after depositing her there, assured that she was safe and with people she knew and trusted.

She didn't want him to leave, but right now, she could see no way of making him stay. He had been pleased when Fenix had suggested they head towards the Seventh Realm, in the opposite direction to the Third Realm. Her eyes widened as something dawned on her.

In that direction lay the elf kingdom too. Vail had been moving away from it, distancing himself from his homeland, and now he was going to head back towards it for her sake.

She wanted to tell him that they could go another way, but the words slipped away as he turned back to face her and held out his hand.

Rosalind swallowed her heart and the pain growing in it, stirred by the thought he meant to leave her for real this time. In a matter of seconds, she would be in the Third Realm and Vail would teleport out of her life forever.

She searched his dark eyes, part of her desperate to see something akin to hurt in them, a flicker of pain that would let her know that the thought of parting from her hurt him as much as it hurt her. They revealed nothing to her, his schooled features hiding whatever he was feeling and the link their bond created stone cold and empty.

Bastard.

She turned her face away from him, closed her eyes and placed her hand into his, bracing herself for the teleport and the inevitable separation that would occur after it.

Vail's clawed fingers closed over hers, his armour cold against her skin.

She waited, her breath lodged in her lungs, refusing to leave them.

Nothing happened.

Rosalind opened her eyes and frowned. Vail growled, the sound born of the frustration she sensed rippling through their link.

"What's wrong?" she said and he snatched his hand back and paced a short distance away. Her stupid heart leaped as her mind supplied he didn't want to take her to the Third Realm after all. He couldn't bring himself to part from her.

"I cannot teleport out of this realm. They have sealed the borders with a powerful binding spell. All of the portal pathways between this realm and the others are closed to me."

Those words were a bucket of icy water on the fire burning in her heart.

She bit back her desire to snipe at him and tamped down her ridiculous hurt over the fact that he still wanted to ditch her. Who was she kidding? They were a match made in Hell. No matter how fiercely she desired him, how much she fell for him, he despised witches and she couldn't see him overcoming that hatred, not even for her.

Rosalind rubbed her arms and tried to keep the bite out of her voice. "So we cross the realm to the border and if we can't walk across it, I'll unlock it with a spell."

She felt Vail's gaze on her, boring into the side of her face, spreading wildfire heat through her veins.

"During the war between the Third and Fifth Realm, the Fifth sealed the Third, stopping Thorne from teleporting back into it with Bleu and Sable." She ignored Vail's growl.

Was it because she spoke familiarly of the demon king of the Third Realm or another elf? Bleu had been handsome. A little moody and distant, but far less mercurial than Vail, and far nicer to her. She couldn't resist embellishing the truth to find out whether Vail was suffering another jealous episode. Sure he knew that Thorne was mated, she amended events to focus on the unmated elf instead.

She smiled sweetly at Vail. "Bleu was a great help. He teleported me to the First Realm and from there we travelled to the border with the Third Realm and I used a spell to unlock it. Well, actually I reversed the spells, which was tricky because it was several layers deep, so we could teleport into the kingdom but no one could teleport out. Bleu was so impressed with me that he—"

Vail disappeared in a flash of pale blue-purple light and reappeared right in front of her, his fangs bared on a snarl and his eyes flashing bright violet as his pointed ears flared back against the sides of his head. He lifted his hand to her face as if to touch it, his palm hovering close to her cheek, and stared down into her eyes, his nostrils flaring with each hard breath.

"Speak not of the male," he growled in a low voice, one that sent a hot shiver bolting through her, igniting her blood in her veins, and bared his fangs again. He shoved away from her and clawed his blue-black hair back from his face, burying his fingers in it and pressing his palms to the sides of his head. "Despises me. Cannot blame him… will not let him take the witch… from me. My ki'ara… my female… my witch."

He cast a dark look her way and paused.

His eyes blackened.

Narrowed.

"Will kill the male."

Rosalind shot forwards, holding her hands out in front of her, afraid Vail would attempt to teleport and find success this time, leaving her behind and going hell-bent on a mission to kill a man who was innocent. She would never be able to live with herself if he killed Bleu because of her attempt to make him jealous, and part of her knew he would never be able to live with what he had done either.

"Vail," she whispered and he froze, a flicker of violet breaking through the black in his irises. "Believe me when I say Bleu only had eyes for Sable. He sort of lucked out there since she's now Thorne's mate, but that's his problem."

Vail stared at her, intense and focused, setting her nerve endings alight.

"My ki'ara." Those two words spoken in a deep husky growl cranked her temperature higher, until she was burning inside, part of her wishing he meant the possessive snarl and passion behind them.

The desire that shone in his eyes.

His hand shot out and snagged her wrist, and he yanked her against him. She stumbled, landing with the full length of her body pressed against his, and her heart launched into her throat, fear that he would react negatively making her take a step back so they were no longer in contact.

Vail growled the moment she did, tugged her back against him and stared down into her eyes, a dark possessive edge to his that thrilled her. She had wanted him jealous, but she hadn't been prepared for the force of the feelings it would stir in her, the startling depth of her desire and her need for him.

"My female," he murmured, a sexy rumble to his deep voice that melted her insides.

He wrapped his arm around her waist, pinning her to his side and leaving her speechless, and teleported.

Rosalind stared up at him as the darkness swallowed them, filled with a sudden wish that it would take weeks to reach the Third Realm, because she felt on the verge of a breakthrough with her mysterious, beautiful elf prince.

CHAPTER 15

Vail sat with his back against the wall of the small ground-level cave, his right arm resting on his bent knee and his gaze on Rosalind. She lay on her side opposite him where he had placed her, curled up and sleeping fitfully, her ash blonde hair cascading like spun gold across the black rocky ground.

She had passed out shortly after they had escaped a vicious pack of Hell beasts. The seven gigantic canines had pursued him and Rosalind for miles, tracking their scents across the terrain, no matter how many valleys, fissures or mountains they crossed.

Vail had been aware of them the whole time but had kept their hunters from her, unable to bring himself to frighten her with the knowledge that they had a pack on their heels. She had been flagging since leaving the spot where Fenix had split up with them. Her hunger was a constant echo in his belly, the rumbling of her stomach so loud at times that he felt convinced that the Hell beasts had tracked them by that sound rather than their scents.

She needed to feed.

He dug the bare fingers of his left hand into the dirt, grounding himself with the feel of it and giving him something calming to focus on as he tried to devise a way of giving his mate the sustenance she required. Without it, she would perish.

He snarled under his breath at that, his fangs lengthening at the thought he might lose her. He had hunted his whole life. He could provide for her.

He would provide for her.

She was his now and he had a duty to ensure she was well fed, safe and happy.

She moaned in her sleep, her hands shoving at thin air, fitful movements edged with desperation that he could feel in her.

Nightmares haunted her.

He blinked and leaned towards her, reaching with his bare left hand, and paused with his fingers close to her forehead. What was he doing?

He stared at his dirty fingers, so close to brushing her fair skin, to what? Soothe her? Chase her nightmares away?

He was probably the cause of them.

He had caught the way she looked at him whenever he killed. She thought him a monster.

He forced himself to lean back again, the action taking effort, his body refusing to comply with his mind's commands.

Or perhaps it was the part of him that longed to gently lay his fingers on her and stroke her cheek, to ease her while she slept and give her good dreams.

That longing was both foreign and familiar, as if the capability for good and kindness had always remained within him and hadn't been purged as he had thought.

Had he not sought his brother's ki'ara as an act of kindness to him?

Had he not fought Kordula's commands to kill Loren and had disobeyed her to protect him?

Was there good within him still?

He cast his eyes away from Rosalind and picked at the dirt again, focusing on it and seeking nature. She was still buried deep, held far away from him, but she felt closer now.

His gaze roamed back to the witch and studied her, absorbing her beauty and fairness. She twitched again, thrashing against an invisible foe. Her right arm shot up, smacked off the wall as she rolled onto her back, and jerked her left with it as the chain between them snapped tight.

She lashed out with her legs, whimpering as she clawed at thin air.

A tear cut down the side of her face.

Vail was across the cave in an instant, kneeling beside her and clutching her restraints, his heart pounding wildly against his chest. He held her manacles, ridiculous fear clawing at him again, stopping him from doing as he wanted and holding her wrists instead. She fought him, her struggle increasing along with the fear he sensed in her.

"Little Wild Rose," he said and held her tighter, stopping her from hitting him. "Wake now."

She didn't. Tears streamed down her temples and she gasped for air, sending him into a spin, a whirlwind of emotions he wasn't equipped to deal with.

Concern. Compassion. Fear. Anxiety.

He leaned closer, locked her hands to his chest with one of his arms and lowered his free hand towards her. It trembled, the shaking growing violent as it neared her cheek. Her warmth seeped into his palm and her legs thrashed against his side. She kneed him in the ribs and cried out, her fear a sharp pain in his heart.

Vail sucked down a breath and pressed his bare palm against her cheek.

A shiver bolted up his arm, a thousand volts that jolted him and left his mind reeling.

She was warm and soft beneath his calloused fingers.

"Little Wild Rose... wake up," he murmured softly, lost in the feel of touching her and fascinated by it.

Her eyelids fluttered and he snatched his hand back, afraid of how she would react if she found him touching her.

She would punish him.

He dropped her hands and shuffled backwards, his heart clenching. When her eyes opened and fell to him, he averted his and bowed his head.

He waited for her to berate him.

Punish him.

He shouldn't have touched her. He didn't have permission to touch. He had to behave himself or bad things happened. *Bad things*. She would punish him because he had been insolent and unruly. He had dared to touch her.

"What happened?" she whispered, her voice hoarse and thick. "Are we in a cave?"

He nodded but kept his eyes averted. He couldn't speak. He wasn't allowed to speak. If he spoke, she punished him.

He flexed his fingers, forming his black serrated claws from his armour, and raked them across the black stone floor of the cave on either side of his knees, etching lines in the hard basalt.

"I fell asleep?" She sat up and rubbed her eyes.

He nodded again, but remembered what she did to him whenever he lied to her, and quickly shook his head instead.

"I did fall asleep or didn't?" She brushed her hair back, working on some of the knots with her fingers.

He wasn't sure how he could answer that without speaking. She didn't like it when he spoke. She didn't like that he would snarl things at her in a voice that dripped with venom and deadly intent.

He stared at the worn smooth ground in front of his knees and reached for it. His hand shook but he couldn't stop it from trembling. She might punish him for this. She had punished him when he had done such a thing before, breaking her command not to communicate with Loren's ki'ara.

He scratched two words into the rock with his claws.

"Passed out?" she said and he felt her eyes on him.

He flinched away, quickly withdrawing his hand and curled up. Waiting. She would strike him for sure. Or worse. Not worse. He shook his head and flexed his claws. He didn't want worse.

"Vail? What's wrong?" She reached for him and he flinched again, jerking his head backwards. "Did something happen while I was out?"

He shook his head, and then nodded. Couldn't lie to her. She always knew when he lied.

"Look at me."

He had to obey. If he didn't, she would do bad things. He lifted his head and looked across at her, the pace of his heart sickening him together with the memories that collided in his head.

Blue eyes held his, soft and sparkling with stars. Blonde hair swayed across her chest as she leaned forwards, planting one hand on the black ground for support, drawing closer to him.

"What's wrong?" she said, her voice a sweet melody, filled with warmth and light.

Little Wild Rose.

His Little Wild Rose.

"Tell me."

That was right. He could speak to her. He had spoken to her and she had seemed to enjoy it at times, but hated it at others. She didn't like it when he cursed at her or threatened her, or ordered her around, but she had never punished him for it.

"Nightmare." He pushed that word out, testing the waters.

Her shoulders slumped and she rubbed the back of her neck. "I hate them."

He frowned and edged closer, compelled to offer her comfort. "Woke you."

She smiled. "Thanks. Did something happen while I was asleep?"

He hesitated, icy claws gripping and squeezing his heart, knowing she was asking what had happened to him to make him like this, a weak male, twisted by his past and controlled by it.

"Vail?" She spoke his name so softly that warmth curled through him.

He had never known his mother, she had died giving birth to him, but knew if he had met her that she would have said his name with as much love and tenderness.

"Woke you," he said to his knees and exhaled a hard breath before adding, "Touched you."

Her shock rippled through their link.

"Oh. Did you shake me awake?" she said and he shook his head, cursing her for presuming he would use a violent touch to rouse her. "How then?"

Vail kept his eyes pinned on the floor, lifted his left hand and mentally commanded his armour to recede from it. He drew in a steadying breath and brought his hand close to her cheek. Her warm breath skated across it, making his skin tingle and his whole body ache with a need to press his palm against her cheek again.

He wanted to feel her softness and her warmth.

"I see." She ghosted her right hand over the back of his, the action causing her hair to shift towards him and sweep across his skin.

A shiver went through him, heightening every need that consumed him and drove him to touch her. Even her hair was as soft and smooth as silk against his skin.

His breathing quickened, his chest heaving with each one, and he risked looking at her. She met his gaze the moment he did, her delicate features set in a placid expression but one that held warmth and understanding.

"You can touch again… if you want." Those words were tempting, a spell without magic that bewitched him into complying with her suggestion.

Gods, he wanted to.

She pressed her hand closer to his, so they almost touched.

His stomach squirmed and he snatched his hand back.

Her face fell, a hint of sorrow darkening her eyes and turning them stormy, and she lowered her hand into her lap. "At least you didn't bare your fangs at me this time. I guess that's progress."

He ignored that remark and shuffled back to his side of the cave.

Her stomach growled, the grumbling noise loud in the tense silence.

Her cheeks blazed and she dropped her eyes to her stomach, idly rubbing it through her black dress and causing the fabric to tighten across her breasts.

Vail tried not to stare.

His mouth turned dry, he swallowed hard, and dragged his gaze away. It fell on his right forearm and he frowned. There was a form of sustenance he could offer her.

His black armour peeled back from his forearm, he raised it to his mouth and sank his fangs into his flesh close to the marks he had made for her before.

Rosalind gasped. "What are you doing?"

He released his arm and offered it to her. "Drink."

She shook her head.

Vail growled. "Drink. Female."

"You need it. If I take that, it will make me stronger but it will weaken you. You need to feed too. What will you eat?"

His eyes betrayed a direct order and slid down the smooth column of her throat, lingering on the curve he could see through her tangled blonde hair.

Her throat worked overtime on a hard swallow, cranking up his hunger, making his mouth water and his fangs itch. She tasted like sunshine and flowers, and everything good. Her hand shot up to cover the spot his gaze bore into and she gasped, and he realised he had growled.

"See, this really isn't a good idea."

"Drink." He shoved his bleeding arm towards her.

She hesitated, her cheeks darkening. "Well… there's sort of another reason this might be a bad idea… last time… you, um… liked it."

He frowned, not following her.

She swallowed again and waggled a finger towards his groin. "*Liked* it, liked it."

His eyes widened.

Blood dripped from his arm and fell in slow motion to the black ground.

He had grown hard for her?

That part of his anatomy seemed to recall it and twitched in response beneath his skin-tight black armour. He crossed his legs so she wouldn't notice it and stared at his bleeding arm.

His need to provide for her and keep her strong warred with a need to shove her away and force her to keep her distance. He growled under his breath and battled his body at the same time as his mind kept conjuring images of her taking his blood, her hands on his flesh, clutching him to her mouth as she fed from his vein. His cock twitched again.

"Still want me to drink?" she said, sounding seductive in his addled mind.

Gods, did he. He couldn't recall the last time he had grown hard of his own volition. It threatened to dredge up his dark and twisted memories, but something held them back. Desire for her. Need of her. It should have repulsed him, yet he found himself aching for it and for her.

"I guess we're doing this then," she muttered and got onto all fours, and his body jerked hard in response, sending a shiver straight down his shaft to his balls.

He focused to shut out his memories and hold them at bay, used all of his willpower to ignore the ache in his groin, and offered his arm to her.

The second her lips made contact with his flesh, he hissed and tipped his chin up, pressing the back of his head hard into the cragged wall of the cave. His fangs lengthened, aching with a need to pierce her flesh. She suckled softly, each pull like a shot of the most potent drug—liquid Heaven. Shivers, hot and fierce and electrifying, rushed in a constant stream from the point where her flesh met his, heating every inch of him and leaving him boneless, too addled by the pleasure to move and make her stop.

He couldn't recall the last time he had felt pleasure either.

Never with the witch.

Witch.

He stared at Little Wild Rose, seeing a witch and feeling a need to push her away. His body didn't respond, his limbs too heavy to move. Only when she released him, giving one last flick of her tongue that shot down his hard cock too, did he find the strength to draw his arm away.

He leaned back into the wall, breathing hard, hazy with pleasure and feeling as if he was floating.

"Did I hurt you?" she whispered and he shook his head. The darkness commanded him to snarl and take her blood now, to make her pay for laying her hands on him, but he didn't have the energy.

The pleasure and blood loss combined beautifully to mercifully leave him powerless to act on those dark hungers.

All he could manage was to lift his arm to his mouth and lick the puncture wounds. His skin tasted like her. He savoured it, taking her into him, satisfied that he had fed his ki'ara and she would be safe for now, until he could hunt for her and find her something nutritious to eat.

Her gaze bore into him and slowly lowered, drifting down his chest and then his stomach, and falling lower still. He flicked a glance at her and she quickly looked away, a rosy hue climbing her cheeks. He shifted his legs, keeping his erection concealed from her, knowing she had wanted to see whether she had affected him this time as she had the first time she had taken his blood.

Vail felt certain she would affect him like this every time.

"Come," he said and she eyed him, a wary edge to her expression. He held his right hand out and called an object to it.

Keys.

Rather than coming to him, she shrank back against the black wall of the cave. "Are you sure?"

He wasn't, but he nodded anyway, hoping that he could handle feeling her powers and knowing now was probably the best time for them to do this, while he was too hazy to muster the strength to harm her.

He had forced her to trek across dangerous lands because of his fear of her powers, and she had shown great courage to do so without complaint and without asking him to release her. It was time he showed courage too, and treated his female the way she deserved to be treated.

He held the keys out to her.

Besides, even with her cuffs on, he could still sense her magic and it still caused him to lose control at times. He had come to doubt that the effect the presence of magic in her had on him could be any worse if he gave her the freedom she desired and deserved.

She held her wrists out to him.

Vail shifted to kneel before her, took hold of her left manacle, careful to avoid touching her skin, and focused on his task as he unlocked it, not on the magic he could sense emanating from her. Her first cuff fell away and swung from the chain, the weight tugging her other hand down, causing it to brush his bare arm.

Her magic grew stronger, flowing over his skin, but it felt different to Kordula's.

Not an oily slick, like dark witches possessed.

He released her other wrist and she jumped to her feet, stretched and grinned, her happiness trickling through their bond.

She looked tempted to use her powers until she glanced his way and caught his scowl. She lowered her hands to her sides.

"Allies, remember... but I won't use it around you. Promise." She held her hand out to him and he refused to take it, rising to his feet without her aid.

He stooped, picked up her discarded manacles, and teleported them back to his rooms in the castle, together with the keys.

She frowned at him and muttered something about trust issues.

Evidently, she was upset he had chosen to keep the manacles. He refused to apologise for his behaviour. She would thank him for keeping them should her magic prove too much for him to handle and he ended up attempting to kill her. He was sure she would prefer to be shackled again over being dead.

"Where to now?" She approached the mouth of the cave.

Pale light washed over her as she scanned their surroundings and drew him to her. He was powerless to resist her, his feet carrying him to her side as his eyes remained locked on her face. Power hummed around her, not much stronger than it had felt before. She was keeping it in check for him and he appreciated her thoughtfulness.

"Are we closer to the Third Realm now?" She looked over her shoulder at him.

"In a way."

Her fair eyebrows dipped above her blue eyes. "We are heading there, aren't we?"

He looked off into the distance and focused there, feeling the tug inside him that had manifested shortly after he had arrived at the cave with Rosalind.

"In a roundabout fashion." He started walking, the pebbly black ground crunching beneath his boots.

The witch hurried to catch up and fell into step beside him, but wisely maintained some distance between them. He found himself focusing on her power and the link between them as he walked, intrigued by it and the differences between Rosalind and Kordula.

"Roundabout?" She frowned at him again and rubbed her wrists, brushing the dirt and dried blood off them.

Vail nodded. "I used much of my power battling the demons and teleporting us through this kingdom. I must rest."

Her frown hardened, causing her lips to purse. "Didn't you rest at the cave?"

He kept his eyes fixed ahead, towards the distance, following the pull inside him and letting it guide him.

"No. I cannot rest here." He nurtured the feeling within him, savouring it and how it made him feel. Relieved. Calmer. Home again at last. "We will head for the forest."

"Forest?" The witch stopped in her tracks and looked around them. "I hate to tell you this… but there is no forest here. This is Hell… it's black as far as the eye can see."

She looked so certain of herself that he was almost loath to correct her.

He hesitated, a quiet voice stating that he didn't have to explain himself or allow her to see that part of him. He didn't have to let her in. He could tell her it was so and that was that, and she wouldn't argue with him. Much. He could hold her away from him and not give her power over him.

He shifted his gaze back to the distance, feeling the pull coming stronger now, and sensed Rosalind close to him, her eyes on his face, the link between them filled with confusion and a deep need that he found he couldn't ignore.

She wanted to know him.

Gods, he hoped she didn't regret it or do anything that would leave him feeling exposed and make him turn on her.

"I can feel it in my bones," he whispered, more to himself than to her, part of him hoping she might not hear him and the tiny piece of information about himself that he offered to her like a ridiculous olive branch, wanting to construct a sort of peace and understanding between them. He kept his eyes on the distance, trying to ignore how her gaze bore into him, focused and intense, giving him all of her attention. "It feels pure and clean, alive and thriving amidst all the darkness and death. We can rest there. It will do us both good."

He kept walking before she could say anything, striding ahead of her as if he could run away from what he had just done and pretend it had never happened. He hadn't let her in. He hadn't just opened his chest and given her a clear shot at his heart and destroying him.

He couldn't remember the last time he had spoken about himself to anyone, or the last time anyone had wanted to know about him. Everyone he met fled his presence or fought him. None wanted to spend a second with him, but Rosalind had spent hours in his company, and had only looked as if she had wanted to fight him for a few of those.

But never flee.

Little Wild Rose didn't run from him.

She ran to him.

She pressed him, pushed him, coaxed and comforted him, and all because she wanted to know him.

He didn't understand why.

There was so much about her that he didn't understand and didn't think he ever would. She held mysteries within her, locked deep in her heart—the heart that was still closed to him and fiercely protected.

If he confessed his foolish desire to know her too, would she open to him as he had to her?

"You have a connection." She bounded up beside him and he flicked a glance at her. Her blue eyes shone with the curiosity he could sense in her. "You do, don't you? You're connected to nature and that's why you can feel it miles away in the middle of this bloody horrible place."

He couldn't recall seeing her this happy before, not even when they had decided to head towards the Seventh Realm to find a portal that would take her back to the mortal world, or when he had announced he was taking her to the Third Realm. Was it because he had freed her or because she had discovered something about him?

He had his answer when she leaped in front of him, causing him to jerk to a halt to avoid colliding with her.

"I'm in touch with nature too, being that sort of—" She cut herself off.

Vail finished for her on a growl. "*Witch*."

She backed off a step but stood her ground. Not fleeing. Never fleeing. Little Wild Rose was a brave one.

He focused on her power, feeling the threads of it around him, examining it to see if what she had just told him without actually voicing the words was true.

There was a reason she felt different to Kordula and the other witches, one he had suspected and now knew to be true.

She was of the light, not the dark.

Light witches were connected to nature and drew on her power.

"What I feel is nothing compared with what you must... would you... I mean, I don't want to pry, but I read that elves have a varying level of a connection with nature but I never realised it was strong. I thought it was like what I felt."

He nodded to let her know he would tell her more about the connection he possessed and continued walking, moving around her and leading the way across the featureless black terrain, following his instincts.

She came up beside him again and smoothed her hands over her hair, pushing it back from her face, revealing it to him. Her beauty struck him hard when she smiled up at him, her stunning blue eyes shining with it and a flicker of excitement.

His mate was beautiful.

Light and full of goodness.

A female far beyond what he deserved.

He looked away from her, unable to bear how brightly she shone when he was so dark inside and underserving. She sighed, the quiet sound drawing his attention back to her, and kept pace with him.

"My connection to nature is strong, far stronger than most other elves, but all elves would be able to sense the forest ahead of us if they focused hard enough."

She glanced up at him again, her gaze lingering for a few heartbeats, before she stared off into the distance and squinted. He held back his smile. Little Wild Rose could try with all of her might and she wouldn't be able to sense the forest as he could.

"Is it stronger because you're old or because you're a prince?"

Vail's step faltered but he masked it so she didn't notice how deeply her use of his status affected him. It had been a long time since someone had referred to him as a prince. Not a mad elf prince. Just a prince.

"I have not been a prince in a long time. Almost as long as I have been in this world." He picked up the pace and she had to alternate between walking and jogging to keep up.

"I just meant you come from a powerful family," she said and fell behind. Stopped.

He halted and looked back at her, unable to take another step without assuring himself that she was well.

She bent over, rubbing the sole of her bare right foot while holding her boot upside down in the other hand. She shook it, grumbling about pebbles.

"Are you injured?" he said and she shook her head.

"You going to answer my question now?" She shoved her foot back into her blue dragon hide boot and stomped towards him, a tiny female on a mission.

He huffed and kept walking, getting the distinct impression that refusing was pointless. She would only press him until he answered.

"I have a strong connection because of my lineage. I inherited it from my mother."

Rosalind's feelings shifted, becoming laced with warmth as they flowed around him. "What was she like?"

He swallowed the lump in his throat. "I would not know. She was the first life I took upon entering this world."

And he wished she had been the last, but part of him feared that position would belong to Rosalind.

And he would die shortly after her.

He didn't think he could continue existing in a world without her in it and without her light to hold back the darkness inside him.

"Vail, I… I'm sorry," she whispered and he shook his head, dismissing her apology. "What of your father?"

"He passed when I was very young. My brother raised me."

She walked a few more steps and then quietly said, "I sort of met him… in the Third Realm. He seemed nice."

Vail smiled at that. "Then you know who is the better brother, and that it is not me."

"I think I will ignore that pity ditty… does he have a connection to nature like you do?" she said and he cast her a glare, catching her wicked smile, before looking ahead of him again.

Confusing female. He wasn't sure whether she was teasing him. He wasn't sure he had ever been teased to know it when it happened.

He nodded. "He does, but mine was always stronger."

Another smile curved his lips as he thought about all the times he had made his brother jealous with the things he could do.

"Happy memories?" Her soft voice lured him back from them and he looked down into her eyes, and nodded again. "It's nice seeing you smile."

It fell away and he wondered just when he had found the ability to smile again.

He had a feeling that Rosalind had given it back to him, together with emotions he had thought were dead and gone, and he would never feel again.

"So what can you do?" She placed her arms behind her back, linking her hands across her bottom.

"I can sense her feelings. My brother can do such a thing too. We can feel her joy and her anger. However… I can heal nature too."

Her eyes lit up and she stopped again, turning to face him. "Seriously?"

He wasn't sure why she felt he would lie about such a thing. "Yes."

"Can you heal people?" Her eyes searched his, darting between them, bright and luminous, and full of the curiosity he could feel in her.

Vail frowned, stifling the pain that pricked his heart.

"Perhaps once, but not now, and not for a long time if I were ever capable of it. I can only heal nature. I can reverse the damage done to it, but my powers… they are weak and corrupted." Because he was weak and corrupted, filled with darkness that nature didn't like, and so the connection between them was dying, fading more with each step closer he took to the black abyss and becoming one of the tainted. "I can only heal small things now."

"I wish I had such a connection," she said and walked with him, her soft voice edged with the envy in her words. "What I can feel must be the smallest fraction of what you can."

"Come." Vail held his hand out to her. "Let us reach the forest and rest."

She shifted her gaze from his hand to meet his. "And would you show me your abilities? I think if you use them, I might be able to sense your connection through our one."

She looked as if she would like that and he found himself nodding, willing to reveal another part of himself in order to please his female.

His ki'ara.

Her hand edged towards his and he braced himself, mentally preparing for the feel of her skin on his and resisting the urge to cover his hand with his armour, the small part of him that wanted to feel her flesh-to-flesh with him again overpowering the darkness that snarled at him to shove her away.

Her fingers brushed his palm, a little gasp escaping her at the same time as a hot bolt of lightning leaped through his bones, and she pressed her hand to his.

Vail stared at their joined hands, his heart pounding in his chest, and absorbed how warm and soft she was, how delicate she felt beneath his fingers as he closed them around hers. Her power grew in strength, their physical connection making it easier for him to feel it as it twined around his arm, and he battled the dark need to tear at his own skin to get it off him.

He drew in a deep breath. She would never use her power to harm him.

Little Wild Rose had said they were allies.

But she had looked at him with eyes that had asked if they could be more than that.

Those same eyes held his now, dark with desire, with need that he could feel in her because it lived within him too.

He pulled his hand towards him, luring her with it, holding her gaze the whole time.

He wanted her.

He closed his eyes.

But he could never trust himself not to hurt her.

He tightened his grip on her hand and teleported.

CHAPTER 16

The darkness around Rosalind evaporated and her eyes widened as she took in the sight before her. Vail had been right. There was a forest in the middle of Hell, a leafy oasis that sprawled over a range of hills, stretching as far as the eye could see in front of her and to her left and right, a stark contrast to the forbidding black lands at her back. She couldn't quite believe it.

Vail's hand slipped from her wrist and he collapsed to his knees. He leaned over, clutching at the ground, and breathed hard, the tousled strands of his blue-black hair hanging across his brow, revealing the pointed tips of his ears.

"Vail?" She crouched beside him and resisted the desire to touch his shoulder.

He had explained to her that teleporting her drained his powers. Apparently, an elf could easily transport two people with him, if they were mortals or other weak species, but because she was powerful, he found it taxing to teleport with just her in tow.

He shook his head, silently warning her away, and she backed off, giving him a moment and not wanting to provoke his darker side, the one that constantly lurked beneath the surface, waiting for his strength of will to give out so it could seize control.

She rose to her feet and looked down at him, again wondering what a witch had done to him to drive him towards madness.

He lifted his head, his firm lips parting to reveal the tips of his short fangs, and stared at the thick forest with a glimmer in his violet eyes that spoke of the relief she could sense in him through their link.

Vail pushed himself up onto his feet, wobbled as he rose to his full impressive height, and took an unsteady step towards the trees. Rosalind remained close to him, on hand to help him if he collapsed again. His gaze narrowed, lips pressing together to form a hard determined line, and he took another step. He wanted to reach the forest, and mother earth, she wished she could help him achieve that desire. He looked like a man whose life depended on reaching it, or perhaps his sanity depended on it.

His hands twitched at his sides, claws flexing, as if he wanted to reach out to the oasis of nature and draw it to him.

She had tried to stop him from constantly teleporting them across the black lands of the Fifth Realm in order to reach this slice of paradise, worried that he would end up like this or would pass out from the exertion. That had earned her a few rounds of snarling and flashing of fangs whenever she dared to suggest they walked, and at least one instance of him saying he needed to get her to the forest so they could rest and he could hunt for her.

That touched her, but she didn't want to rest.

The nightmare still haunted her, a colourful and hideous twisted replay of the battle. She tried not to think about it but it was constantly there at the back of her mind, ready to leap to the fore and play out again whenever her guard slipped. She couldn't take it. Every replay tore at her soul and left her bleeding inside, close to collapse.

Every replay left her feeling she was stepping closer to the darkness, treading a path that would inevitably lead to her embracing the evil side of magic, drawing on powers from beyond the grave and dealing in death.

She wrapped her arms around herself and rubbed her bare arms, trying to keep the sudden chill off them.

Vail paused and looked back at her, a flicker of what she wanted to believe was concern in his purple eyes. She shifted her gaze to the trees only metres from them now, trying to focus on better things, ones that might give her a moment's peace amidst the black maelstrom threatening to tear her apart and destroy everything that she was, reconstructing her in the image of her sister.

Tall rich green grasses fringed the forest and brushed her legs as they entered its boundary. Her eyes delighted in taking everything in as they walked deeper into the trees. Vail's step gained strength and steadiness with each metre farther they moved towards the centre of the forest and away from the black demon lands.

Colourful flowers spotted the green blanket sweeping around her and she had a strong desire to pick some and gather them to her, to cherish the beauty of nature. Towering trees provided shelter and light too, their branches dotted with glowing white flowers.

"Incredible," she whispered and reached up to brush her fingers over the flowers on a low-hanging branch. The petals closed in response, the light dying, and she withdrew her hand, afraid she had killed it with her careless touch. Before her eyes, the flower bloomed again, reopening and sparkling like starlight.

"We have them in the elf realm." Vail's deep voice sent a shiver tumbling down her spine, the gravelly edge to it and the feel of his gaze on her combining to thrill her.

He sounded better, and different.

She looked across at him and found he looked different too. He stood a little taller, his eyes a little brighter and clearer as he took in the forest, and a smile played on his firm kissable lips.

He looked like a man who had just stepped into a glorious dream and was loving every moment of it.

Or perhaps one who had just stepped into a moment in his past, one from long ago and long before a witch had done something to change him and leave him scarred.

She touched another flower, smiling as it closed and waited for her to withdraw her hand before opening again and shining brighter, illuminating her fingers.

Vail looked around them, his chest expanding beneath his skin-tight dragon-scale black armour as he drew in a deep breath and exhaled it in a long sigh.

Rosalind couldn't help smiling at him. She had never believed him capable of appearing so happy.

Filled with joy.

He brushed his fingers over a patch of long grass mottled with what looked like blue cornflowers, a flicker of a smile on his lips.

"I read that the elf realm is like a paradise." She moved a step closer to him and he frowned, all of the light leaving his eyes and his expression turning solemn.

He swallowed hard, curled his fingers into fists and lifted his eyes to meet hers. "It is."

The husky edge to his deep voice and the feelings she could sense in him said that he didn't want to talk about his homeland and she had hurt him by mentioning it, ruining his momentary happiness. Her stomach twisted, a heavy weight settled on her chest, and an apology rose to the tip of her tongue.

He turned away from her before she could put voice to it and continued walking, his shoulders a little lower than they had been before she had brought up the elf kingdom.

She hadn't meant to upset him, or take away the joy this place brought to him, and she felt wretched as she trailed behind him, searching for a way to bring back his smile.

The distance between them grew as she slowed, her eyes drawn to a small clearing off to her left. Mushrooms. There were herbs in the bushes too. She hurried to them and began gathering the ones she recognised, using the skirt of her black dress as a basket. She was short a few ingredients, but what she had would be effective.

She waited until Vail was further ahead and then used her magic to enhance what she had and transform it into a sort of round cake. It came out looking more like an unappetising brown blob, but beggars couldn't be choosers.

Rosalind nibbled one edge of it as she caught up with Vail. The effect was instant, a buzz tripping along her nerve endings like an intense sugar rush that left her a little high, filled with energy, and also a little numb, as if she had just done shots with a whole bottle of tequila.

She welcomed that numbness and the respite it granted her, leaving her mercifully free of her guilt and all the things she had been dwelling on. She didn't care about them anymore. She didn't really care about anything other than somehow finding a place she could bathe, getting some tasty food in her stomach, having fun and leaving the past few horrible months behind her.

And staring at Vail's fine backside as he walked.

Mother earth, the man had the bottom of a god.

It dimpled beneath his black armour as he strode ahead of her, delicious and tempting. Not wanting to make the rest of him feel jealous because she was paying more attention to his bottom, she took in the rest of him, inch by hot inch.

He had beautiful shoulders. She liked the way they moved as he walked, and how the powerful muscles of the top of his shoulders bunched as he stretched an arm above him to brush his fingers across the leaves of the trees, as if he needed that brief contact with nature to heal him.

He had strong hands too. How had she failed to notice that? They were big, powerful, and looked very wicked whenever he lowered them and his black armour covered them again, transforming them into claws.

Rosalind nibbled on the brown cake.

Her eyes drifted down the shifting symphony of his back to his bottom again.

He looked over his shoulder at her, a slight frown pinching his eyebrows, and she quickly looked away, hoping he hadn't caught her. He turned away again.

She snuck a glance at him.

Mother earth, she wanted to climb his tall frame and lick his ears from lobe to pointed tip.

She looked down at the brown cake. Perhaps she needed to lay off it.

She shrugged and took another small bite.

She was supposed to be living before she died.

Vail disappeared through a thicket and she raced to catch up with him. The branches clawed at her, snagging her hair and scratching her arms. She fought them back and broke through.

Into a stunning glade.

Trees formed a circle around it, their thick trunks holding back the shrubs and the long grass, leaving a lush green blanket spotted with little white flowers in the centre. Tiny insects floated around in the air, shining like glow worms, so that when she looked up through the opening in the trees, they looked like stars glittering in the night sky.

She turned on the spot in the middle of the glade, amazed by it. She wanted to feel it.

She pocketed her brown cake and kicked off her blue boots. The short grass was blissfully cool on the soles of her aching feet. She scrunched it between her toes and laughed.

Vail arched an eyebrow at her and strode past, heading away from the glade.

"Can't we rest here?" She didn't want to leave this place. Ever. She wanted to live here, surrounded by magical nature.

With Vail.

He nodded and pointed in the direction he was heading. "There is water this way. I can smell it."

Water.

"Mother earth!" She raced forwards, drawing a growl from him when she bumped him on the way past, and darted through the trees.

She ran for what seemed like forever without finding the water.

Liar. Liar. Pants on fire. There wasn't any water.

She broke through the trees and stumbled to a halt. "Bloody hell."

A massive lake stretched before her. Trees surrounded most of it but on one side, off to her right, rose a black cliff. A waterfall thundered down it and more of the twinkling insects danced just above the mist at its base where it plunged into the lake. Above it, loomed a great mountain. Green swathed the base of it but the top third was bare black rock.

"Do not run off like that again," Vail said as he strode out of the forest behind her and she looked over her shoulder at him.

And cursed.

He wore a pair of black trousers held closed by lacing over his groin, his twin black and silver bands containing his armour around his wrists, and nothing else.

Rosalind snapped her jaw up and her mouth shut.

He stopped at the edge of the water, stooped and scooped up some in his hands, and drank it just as she lunged at him to stop him.

He looked back at her and frowned, clearly catching her horrified expression. "It is safe. Everything here is. I know it."

Because of his connection to nature, a bond that she was growing more envious of by the second.

"I will hunt and you may bathe. We shall meet back at the glade." He walked away before she could say anything and she wanted to be angry with him for ordering her around, but found herself admiring his bare back instead.

His colourful markings flashed over his arms and down his back, and mother earth, they curled over his hips too and beneath his trousers.

He flicked a glare at her. "I can feel you staring, *Witch*."

"Rosalind," she said and he paused, an incredulous look on his handsome face. "My name is Rosalind. Stop calling me witch. It's rude."

He stared at her a few seconds longer, during which her heart thundered, adrenaline making it race. She really had to lay off the brown cake. Her darling mate was obviously affected by all the nature, but the calming effect it had on him wouldn't stop him from lashing out at her if she kept pressing his buttons.

"*Witch*." Vail snorted and walked away.

Rosalind huffed and followed the shoreline in the opposite direction to him. She dipped her toe in the water and shivered. It was chilly. She didn't fancy bathing in the open either, where Vail might see her.

Or maybe she did.

She glanced back in the direction he had gone and grinned as she imagined him sneaking a peek at her. Her smile fell. He would probably feel compelled to kill her for it shortly afterwards, blaming her for his own wickedness because she was a witch.

She really needed to know what the deal was with him and witches.

There was no way she could help him move past what one had done to him until she knew exactly what that one had done.

She doubted he would ever tell her though. He would probably kill her just to shut her up.

She sighed and followed the lake towards the waterfall. Maybe she could bathe behind it. That would give her some privacy.

A stream cut across her path.

It was small and she swore it was steaming.

Rosalind dipped her foot in the water and smiled. It was warm. She banked right, following the stream into the forest. It babbled over rocks and down a slope, flowing from one of the hills towards the lake. Her heart flipped in her chest when she reached the top of an incline and spotted a large pool ahead in amidst the glowing trees, with a small waterfall cascading into it.

She bent at the rocky edge and waved her hand through the crystal clear water. It was deliciously warm, reminding her of the spa she had once visited with her sister before her sister had decided to join the family business as a dark witch.

Rosalind stripped off her black dress and her black underwear and slipped into the hot water, a sigh escaping her as it swept up her body to her stomach. She stepped down into the deeper water and sat on the rock. The sparkling water reached her shoulders, lapping at her chest. She sighed again and leaned to her left, reaching for her clothes on the bank. She pulled the brown cake from the pocket of her black dress, nibbled it, and set it down on a dry rock. She took her dress and underwear, and dunked them in the water, washing them as she soaked.

It felt wonderful.

All of her stress and her aches melted away.

She picked up a smooth stone from the ones scattered along the rocky bank she sat on and used it to scrub her dress. It would have been easier to make a new one using magic, but she was wary of upsetting Vail and undoing the progress she felt she had made with him over the past few days.

He had touched her several times without hissing or showing any adverse effects, and she had realised that if she let him be the one in control, and let it be his choice, that he was a much nicer, and saner, man to be around.

She hadn't expected him to touch her cheek to wake her in the cave though.

That had been a monumental leap for him and it had taken its toll, sending him to whatever dark things haunted him.

She set her dress aside and used the stone on herself, scrubbing her body with it. Stones couldn't help her with some tasks though. She had to resort to a low-level spell to shave her legs and other areas that badly needed some attention after months in captivity.

After scrubbing herself from head to toe, she pushed forwards, ducked under the water and swam to the deeper area in the centre of the pool. She dived down and kicked off the bottom to launch herself out of it, spraying water everywhere. She laughed and did a lap of the pool, relishing the heat and being clean again, and then set about washing and untangling her hair.

When every inch of her was clean and rid of all signs of her captivity, she lay on her back in the pool, floating close to the surface, her gaze on the glowing insects as they played above her.

She lost track of time as she lay there with only the noise of the waterfall tumbling into the pool in her ears and the insects for company.

It was incredible how changed she felt by something as basic as a bath.

She felt human again, or a witch at least, more like her old self than she had done since leaving the mortal world to help Thorne.

It felt good.

Rosalind raised her right hand and stared at the pads of her fingers. Prunes.

She sighed and reluctantly rolled over and swam to the edge of the pool. She didn't want to leave it, but Vail was probably wondering where she was and she didn't want to worry him.

Back in the castle, she wouldn't have believed him capable of worrying about someone, but he had proven her wrong about that. He had been right and she needed to know someone before forming an opinion of them. He had shown concern for her several times after their escape. She pulled herself out of the pool and let the water run off her.

He had shown her other emotions too.

The cooler air chilled her skin and her nipples puckered.

It wasn't only the cool air turning them into hard peaks though. It was thoughts of Vail and the way he had looked at her at times with dark eyes filled with desire, with hunger that thrilled her and made her crave the feel of his hands on her body.

She coughed to clear her throat and shoo that thought away and focused on dressing instead. She dried her underwear with another low-level spell, and then her dress, and put them on. Wearing clean clothes felt like a gift from mother nature herself.

She smoothed her hands down the black dress, stooped and picked up her brown cake, and took a little bite before starting back towards the camp, following the stream that would lead her to the lake.

Thoughts crowded her head and she was feeling honest enough with herself to admit Vail was the focus of most of them. Had he managed to find them something to eat? It was all a little medieval but romantic of him to hunt for her, doing the man's work while she bathed and washed her clothes.

She reached the lake and started along the bank. Her steps slowed as she spotted a figure in the lake. The water was only dimly lit by the trees surrounding it but there was no mistaking that it was Vail standing hip deep in the water.

Naked.

Rosalind ducked into the trees, fearing he would spot her and somehow make out she had forced him to bathe naked for her viewing pleasure.

She told herself she should cut through the trees to reach the camp, but her feet refused to move. She hid behind a thick trunk, clutching it and sneaking a peek of him, not missing the irony that she was doing exactly what she had fantasised he would if she bathed in the lake.

She couldn't take her eyes off him as he washed, no matter how many times she told herself that she was prying and taking away his privacy, and taking advantage of him in a way. She had hated those demons when they had brought him to his cell naked, and now she was spying on him while he was nude. She had to go.

She pushed herself away from the tree and then leaned back in again, cursing herself for not being strong enough to walk away and give him some time alone to bathe.

He scooped water up and let it run down his shoulders and back, and then slicked his wet hair back, revealing the pointed tips of his ears.

Rosalind's gaze drifted down the strong contours of his back to his bottom. Delectable.

She became aware of something as she watched him. He was methodical and detached from what he was doing, washing in a sort of order, working down from top to bottom in a right to left fashion. His gaze was distant, locked on the waterfall and never straying from it, but it was sharp too. He was focused on his surroundings and not on himself, and it struck her that he rarely focused on himself.

Because he feared doing so?

He turned in the water, so he was side on to her, and her eyes shot wide.

Not just naked. Naked and hard.

His impressive length rose from the water, slick with it, drawing her gaze no matter how fiercely she tried not to look at it. Her heart raced and her mouth dried out, her eyes glued on his length. A low throb started in her belly and heat curled through it.

He didn't seem to notice he was rock hard, or he was ignoring it. He didn't touch there as he washed himself.

Most men she knew would have been doing something about it, not waiting for it to go away.

He lowered his hands and cleaned his lower back, arching forwards to reach it and causing his hips to thrust out of the water and his stomach and chest to tense.

Rosalind's face heated and she shoved away from the tree and hurried back to the camp, cursing herself for spying on him.

She busied herself with preparing the glade, trying to keep her mind off Vail and get her raging desire back under control. She gathered firewood, stacking it in the centre of the glade, and only stopped when it was the size of a bonfire. She really had to get her mind off Vail.

Gloriously naked.

Deliciously hard.

Vail.

She shouldn't have peeked.

She took half the firewood and stacked it in a spot between two trees, and stared at it. Vail flickered through her mind again, a vivid replay of how he had looked in the lake, rubbing his glistening naked body. Sin on a stick, and mother earth, she wanted to lick that stick.

Rosalind shook herself and went back to the clearing. Vail was probably hunting by now. Maybe she could find a way to get the fire started so it was ready when he returned.

Returned from bathing naked.

And hard.

A thought rose unbidden, causing the blush on her cheeks to darken.

Had he been thinking about when she had taken his blood?

In the cave, he had tried to hide it from her, but that had only confirmed that he had grown hard from the feel of her drinking from him, taking his potent blood into her body.

Every inch of her ached in response to the memory of that moment and how good it had felt to her too, setting her on fire inside and leaving her burning for him long after they had started their trek to the forest.

She rested her back against a tree and slid down it to her bottom, and stared at the stack of twigs she had built in the middle of the clearing.

The memory of drinking from him swirled together with the one of him washing in the lake, playing havoc with her and setting light to her desire. She ached with need, hot and shivery all over, so sensitive that even the brush of the short grass on her calves was too much for her to bear.

She had to get her mind off him and the temptation he represented before he returned. She still didn't know the exact details of her prediction and acting on her desires with him might be the thing that triggered her death.

There was one way she could dampen her desire for him, so she didn't act on it.

Rosalind glanced around. Stopped herself. Glanced again. She shouldn't. Couldn't resist. She wasn't like Vail. She couldn't ignore the ache. The hunger. Either she did something about it before he returned or she would end up pouncing on him.

She cast another glance around and bit her lip as she slipped her hand beneath her black dress. Her cheeks heated but they weren't flushed from desire and arousal. She felt stupid. She couldn't do this.

Her fingers touched her black knickers. She was damp though. So lustful she might burst.

She would do it quickly and then get the fire started, and Vail would never know.

Rosalind took a deep breath and dipped her hand into her underwear. Her eyes slipped shut and she sank against the tree trunk. The first touch of her fingers on her slick nub was bliss, sending a thousand volts blazing through her.

She stroked the hard bud, shivering each time, imagining it was Vail's fingers on her, teasing her towards climax.

She shoved him out of her mind. She couldn't fantasise about him. It was too dangerous.

Her lust-addled mind drew him back again, making her picture him standing across the glade, his purple gaze hooded and dark with hunger as he watched her. He was hard in his black trousers, straining against the lacing, the tip of his cock almost on show above the waistband. Bare-chested too. Droplets of water cascaded over tensed, honed muscles. Delicious.

Dangerous.

She tipped her head back and breathed harder, lost in the fantasy and barely resisting the need to dip her hand lower.

A twig snapped.

Her eyes shot open.

Her fantasy stood on the other side of the bundle of firewood, his bare chest glistening with water, heaving with each laboured breath. His erection was visible in his trousers, thick and long, straining against the black material.

Rosalind moaned.

Just as she had imagined.

He scrubbed his left hand over his mouth, staring at her, his purple eyes boring through the layers of her dress to her hand where it still intimately touched her. He frowned and absently palmed his length, his jaw flexing as he rubbed the heel of his hand down it. It seemed he couldn't ignore it now or deny the need burning through him.

Blazing through her.

"Vail," she whispered. Breathless. Nervous.

His eyes darkened.

She withdrew her hand from her underwear, accidentally flashing it at him.

His nostrils flared and he growled, dark and menacing. Thrilling.

"My female hungers."

Mother earth. She shivered, those words growled with hunger, possessiveness and a promise of passion electrifying her.

Light traced over his body and he was before her in a flash, his hand clamped around her wrist and pulling her onto her feet. Her heart beat wildly. Her mouth went dry.

He stared at her damp fingers, a war raging in his eyes.

She trembled.

"Vail?"

CHAPTER 17

Vail raked his eyes over Little Wild Rose. Gods, he wanted her. He wanted to satisfy his female. It beat within him, a fierce demand, forcing him to obey every male instinct he had regardless of how it made him feel.

How he feared.

She was beautiful as she stared up into his eyes, a tremor of nerves echoing through their link, speaking to him of the fear she held inside her too. The pure light from the flowers on the trees bathed her clear fair skin in hues of white and blue, making the sensual soft bow of her lips appear even more lush and red, tempting him into claiming the kiss that had been on his mind for days now. He wanted to kiss her.

He wanted to claim her.

Her dazzling blue eyes held his and he picked out every fleck of silver as he wrestled with his desires, his overwhelming need for her, struggling to come to terms with it and keep it under control. It drove him to touch her, to lay his hand on her fair skin again and brush his fingers across her flesh to feel her silkiness. Her warmth.

Little Wild Rose.

His ki'ara.

His breath lodged in his throat, trapped there by her beauty and brightness. She was too bright. Too pure. Too good for him.

But he couldn't stop himself from wanting her.

He couldn't hold himself back any longer.

He reached out to lay his trembling hand on her shoulder and she reached for him too, her left palm aimed at his bare chest. He stared at it, his chest cranking tighter with each millimetre closer she came to touching his flesh.

He couldn't take it, no matter how fiercely he desired it.

He growled, spun her to face the tree and shoved her dress up to her shoulders, exposing her bottom. He raked his gaze down the line of her back to her black cotton underwear. He wanted to touch her where she had been. The sight of her pleasuring herself, a look of unadulterated bliss on her pretty face, had frozen him in his tracks and had him hard in an instant.

Wanting her.

She tried to touch him again, her hand fumbling behind her and he growled. She froze, her heart pounding in his ears, her scent laced with the heady aroma of her arousal.

His female hungered and he would give her what she desired. He would pleasure her and satisfy her.

"Vail?" she whispered and tried to turn towards him.

He grabbed her shoulder and forced her back towards the tree, unwilling to let her face him while they did this and uncertain whether he could retain his grip on his sanity if she did. He wouldn't let her be in control. He couldn't. She whimpered, the erotic sound sending a bolt of hot lust through him, making his aching hard length throb against the tight confines of his black trousers.

Gods, he wanted her.

She needed him so fiercely that it rocked him and drugged him to a degree, addling his mind until all he could think about was satisfying his dark need to be inside her, filling her and taking her.

Her hips swayed, thighs rubbing together, and the scent of her arousal increased, swamping his senses and sending his need soaring.

Vail held her shoulder with one hand and pulled at her black underwear, exposing her bottom. He growled at the lush twin peachy globes and released her shoulder so he could shove her underwear down to her knees. He rose behind her again, length pulsing with need, so hard that he hurt. He ghosted his hands over her bottom, his gaze falling lower, to the point where she had been touching when he had come upon her.

Pale curls covered her, hiding her from view. He bit back a growl, grabbed her hips and pulled them backwards, forcing her hands to slide down the trunk she grasped for support. She stood bent over before him, all of her exposed to his hungry eyes. A feral need replaced his desire, a consuming hunger to take her.

His gaze flickered to her face, catching her watching him, her wet blonde hair strewn over her shoulders. Her cheeks blazed and she rocked her bottom upwards, the dark hunger in her eyes calling to him. His female needed him. She desired him.

Wanted him as fiercely as he wanted her.

He snarled and tore at his trousers, freeing his steel-hard length, grasped it tightly in his fist and entered her in one stroke.

She cried out as he drove himself to the hilt, her wet heat gloving him as tightly as his fist had.

He withdrew and thrust back in, her whimper of pleasure encouraging him to do it again and again. He couldn't remember the last time he had been the one to do this, the one to initiate and be in control. It was intoxicating. Drugging. He liked that he was in command. He could do as he pleased and she was at his mercy. His slave.

He was the master now.

Vail pumped her deep and hard, withdrawing almost all the way from her before plunging back inside her tight channel. Her heat scalded him, her wet walls gripping at him, coaxing him deeper as she moaned. He drank down her cries of pleasure, savouring each one, desiring to elicit more.

His own pleasure blasted through him, so intense that his knees trembled and shook, weakening beneath him, and his breath stuttered. It overwhelmed him, fiery bliss that poured through his veins, setting every inch of him alight and making him burn for more.

He had never felt like this before, knew that with a certainty that sent him reeling. Nothing he had ever experienced had felt this good, this intoxicating. This heavenly and perfect. No one had even come close to making him feel as Rosalind did. His mate. His female. She truly had been made for him.

She reached back with one hand again, attempting to touch him.

He growled at her, darkness rising swiftly to obliterate the softer emotions flooding him. She wasn't allowed to touch. He was in control now. He needed to be in control.

He grabbed the back of her neck with one hand and her hip with the other, holding her immobile as he increased the pace of his thrusts, filling her deeply with each fast stroke. He grunted and growled, his balls drawing up as each thrust sent pleasure shooting through him. He pounded into her, out of his head with need for her and a slave to his thirst for her, to the hunger that had been building within him since the moment he had set eyes on her.

His thighs brushed hers and he snarled as he sensed her magic, couldn't stop himself from gripping her tighter and being rougher with her. Witch. He tried to shut his mind to the flashbacks that began to fill it, a thousand moments of Kordula restraining him with her power and riding him against his will. She had stolen all control from him.

He would be in control this time.

Little Wild Rose was his now.

CHAPTER 18

Rosalind gripped the tree trunk, torn between the pleasure ricocheting through her body with each deep plunge Vail made and the pain in her heart. She cursed him in her mind, hating how he had changed and now refused to let her participate. She hated how he rutted her and that she was too lost to the pleasure to take back control, too drugged by the feel of him inside her, filling and stretching her, intoxicating her.

His grip on her neck jerked tighter and he grunted. His cock throbbed and pulsed, spilling his seed within her, and he went rigid and still. His hands trembled against her.

She reached for the link between them and the glimmer of emotions she could feel said that his orgasm had shocked him, but she couldn't bring herself to believe it.

She dug her fingers into the bark to steady herself. As soon as he had pulled himself back together, he would pull out of her and leave her wound tight. She knew it. This had been a terrible mistake.

His grip on her hip and neck loosened and she braced herself for the inevitable rejection, preparing to feel used and hating him for it.

Vail tensed and released her neck, but didn't pull out of her. He trailed his fingers down her bare back, his touch surprisingly soft and shocking her. He murmured quiet things in the elf tongue as he swept the pads of his fingers down the line of her spine.

She kept still, breathing hard as he gently caressed her, exploring her with a tentative touch while still lodged inside her. He was nervous. Afraid. Unsure. She could feel it and she wanted to take away his fear, to find the source of it and vanquish it for him. She didn't have that power so she relaxed and allowed him to take the lead, letting him do as he pleased and hoping it would bring them back to a more intimate level and ease his nerves. And hers too.

He stroked lower and she arched her back into his caress, unable to stop herself as the pleasure of it consumed her and seized control of her body. He shocked her again.

He groaned.

The sound of pleasure emanating from his lips sent a shiver through her, keeping her arousal at a low boil in her belly together with the feel of him still inside her, intimately connected to her.

Rosalind closed her eyes and clutched the tree, the bark rough beneath her fingers. She forced herself to relax again and didn't move as he explored her. He would bolt if she startled him. She could feel it. He was on the edge, torn between touching her softly and clawing her and pushing her away. Punishing her.

Why?

What had happened to him to make him like this?

Heat rushed through her veins when he shifted and she felt his warm breath on her bare back. Anticipation curled through her, a hunger to feel his lips trailing over her skin, as softly as his fingers had, stirring her desire and sending trembles of pleasure through her. He halted above her, his breathing coming quicker, and she could sense his panic rising.

"Vail," she murmured, hoping to encourage and soothe him.

He snarled and grabbed her hips.

He shoved into her, his length hard again, and she cried out in pain.

He stilled.

"My ki'ara hurts," he whispered, his lips so close to her back that they brushed her skin with each word, making her quiver and heat wherever he touched and where their bodies joined.

She barely bit back her moan as ecstasy tripped through her, taking her higher, leaving her at the mercy of her desire. She wanted to rock on him, needed him to touch her again and give her release. He swept his lips across her skin, the light touch too much for her, making her shake all over and whimper.

He murmured softly, "I will make her feel better."

She bit back a moan when he moved again, thrusting gentler this time, slow and deep at a steady pace that threatened to send her out of her mind.

She held on to the tree and loosed a moan when he placed his hands on her hips and shifted his left one lower, over her belly. He dipped it into her folds and fumbled with her sensitive nub, his actions a little clumsy, telling her that somehow this incredibly gorgeous elf prince was new to touching a female there.

He curled his hips, each plunge of his cock into her and flick of her bud tearing another moan from her and sending heat shooting through her, fire that pooled in her belly and made her want to beg him for more.

Desire got the better of her and she shifted back against him.

He snarled and gripped her hips so she couldn't move, his claws pressing into her flesh. He thrust into her, rougher again, wild and fierce, grunting each time their hips met. It bordered on painful.

She looked over her shoulder at him.

He was lost again, black blotches marring his beautiful eyes. Crazed. Dangerous.

She did the only thing she could think of to bring him back from that dark place he went to often.

She whimpered.

He instantly stilled again, his purple eyes softening and clearing, and moved more gently, rocking into her with steady strokes. He touched her again and held her gaze as he slowly pumped her. It was so erotic and arousing that she moaned low in her throat, her blood heating to a thousand degrees and body shivering in response.

No man had ever looked at her as he did, and certainly not while making love to her, his gaze devouring hers, commanding her attention as he took her. It was powerful and intense, and divinely masculine, and it left her trembling.

She kept still, giving control over to him. He needed it. She knew that. He hated it when she touched him. He hated it when she rocked onto him. He hated it when she participated, rather than letting him be in command.

Someone had done a real number on him.

He stroked her sensitive bud in time with his thrusts, mastering her body, lifting her higher and higher until she felt she was floating, giddy and on the edge of a freefall into bliss.

He withdrew and plunged back in, as deep as she could take him, and she cried out as hot sparks exploded through her and she quivered around him, her body milking his. He looked as if he wanted to pull out of her, clenched his teeth as she throbbed and pulsed, her body bursting with heat and pleasure that left her hazy and a little braver.

Rosalind pressed back against him and flexed her body around his rigid length.

He grunted and his cock jerked, hot release pumping into her with every hard pulse.

His expression turned horrified.

He staggered backwards, pulling free of her, and cast her a tortured glance before light traced over his body and he disappeared.

Rosalind turned and leaned her back against the tree. Her trembling legs gave out and her backside hit a root. She shouldn't have pushed him, but the incredible pleasure of her climax had overwhelmed her, destroying every fragment of common sense and crushing her inhibitions.

She couldn't remember a time when she had experienced such an intense, full-body release. She had definitely never felt unable to stand after sex before. She had always laughed when the incubi in the fae towns had offered to leave her legs useless, telling them it was all a fallacy made up by men who thought they were gifts of the gods.

She stared at her shaking knees, feeling boneless and sure she would find it difficult to walk for an hour or two.

Not such a fallacy after all. She just hadn't met a man capable of giving her that sort of pleasure.

It left her feeling that the whole affair with her dark elf prince was more complicated and confusing than ever. One itch for him scratched, and subsequently replaced with a startling insatiable itch for more.

She sagged back and used her sorcery to find him, a small spell to enhance the connection between them. It was easy when he was still inside her, mingling with her.

He hadn't gone far.

Relief swept through her and on its heels came a desire to go to him in the hope she could learn why he was the way he was and had what happened to him. He would lash out at her if she did pursue him. He needed a moment, and she would give it to him, and hope that he would return to her.

She kept tabs on him as she cleaned herself up, trying to ignore the fact that she was still achy and hot, hungry for him. She blamed it on her returning power. It was playing havoc with her as much as Vail did.

When she had managed to tamp down her rising desire and felt a little more presentable, all evidence of what had happened gone, she got to her feet and leaned against the tree trunk, waiting for them to steady.

Rosalind sighed up at the twinkling bugs hovering in the dark opening between the leafy canopies of the trees around the glade. She wriggled her toes and bent her knees, finding her legs stable at last.

She tramped around, keeping herself busy by tossing a few more sticks onto the pile in the middle of the clearing, arranging it into a neat pyramid, and using a spell to light it. Flames burst from the centre and quickly spread, blue at first but turning orange as her spell settled.

She sat by the fire, mesmerised by the flames, drew her knees up to her chest and waited.

The sky had grown infinitely darker, and the woods far colder and more forbidding, by the time Vail finally returned.

He refused to look at her as he entered the glade, keeping his gaze downcast. He was wet and the skin of his arms and bare chest was red in places. He had gone to the lake and washed himself, rubbing himself raw right after being inside her.

Rosalind returned her gaze to the fire, her heart stinging, and ignored him as she struggled to erase the hurt that caused in her.

He loomed on the other side of the fire and held a black bird-like creature out to her.

Rosalind cast a scowl at the feathered thing, unsure what she was meant to do with it and not in the mood to talk to him. She looked back at the fire, hugged her knees tighter, and rested her chin on them.

Vail sat on the other side of the flames and plucked the bird in silence, his gaze locked on his work. He was using the task to hide from her. He wanted to be near her, but didn't at the same time, and she didn't understand why.

She couldn't take it anymore.

She hated the oppressive atmosphere that hung over the camp and the tension between them. It wasn't how things should have been after what they had done together. It wasn't how she had foolishly hoped they would be.

She glanced at his face. He looked as troubled as she felt but it didn't offer her any comfort.

"Why did you leave?" she whispered to the fire.

He stilled, his fingers paused at their work and his eyes on the shiny black feathers scattered around his feet.

"I had to," he said in a distant voice. "It was for your sake…"

She lifted her head, anger rising like an unstoppable force within her, driving her to confront him. She was tired of not understanding him. She was sick of him holding her at a distance and drawing her closer whenever it pleased him before driving her away again.

"I wanted you to stay," she snapped and a shower of blue sparks exploded from the fire, dancing high into the air between them. Vail scowled at them. She scowled at him. "You hurt me by leaving."

His gaze shot to meet hers, he blinked, and then looked away again, off to his left. "I would have hurt you had I stayed."

That sent ice through her that instantly quenched the flames of her anger. She could see that he meant it.

She bravely whispered, "Why?"

He didn't answer. He shoved the plucked dead thing on a pointed stick and held it over the flames.

Feathers blew around the short grass. She picked one up and twirled it in her fingers, her gaze locked on it.

"Didn't you like what we did?" she quietly said.

His purple gaze snapped to her, intense and fierce, burning into her and demanding she look at him. She could sense his rising fury and his pain, but it wouldn't stop her this time.

She kept her eyes on the black feather, hiding in staring at it just as he had hidden when plucking it from the creature, and swallowed her fear.

"Who made you hate me?" The feather shone in iridescent colours in the firelight, but it didn't fascinate her. She felt nothing as she stared at it, heart in her throat, feeling as if she balanced on the brink of a fall that would kill her.

"I do not hate you," he muttered and turned the creature over above the fire. "You are my ki'ara. I could never hate you."

But he could never love her.

She fell quiet, letting the feather fall from her fingers, and buried her face in her knees, hiding from him and the pain beating in her heart.

Foolish witch.

She should have known better. She should have been stronger and resisted the temptation to give in to her desire. There was only one way giving herself to him would have ended, no matter what she had done, and she had been an idiot to think otherwise.

Vail muttered things in the elf tongue. All she caught was an occasional 'ki'ara'.

She was stronger than this. She wouldn't let a madman rule her life and she was done with his games. She was damned if she was going to spend her last days in this world letting someone dictate what she could or couldn't do. She had taken care of herself since leaving her family decades ago, before her first transition, and she certainly didn't need anyone to take care of her now that she had her powers back.

She lifted her head, resolve flowing through her and strengthening her heart, giving her the courage to do what she had to in order to save herself, even though it was going to hurt her too.

But it probably wouldn't hurt him.

And that only made her hurt worse.

He offered the charred creature to her.

Rosalind stood, brushed her bottom down, and looked him straight in the eye, fighting the part of her that wanted to crumble and go back on the plan.

She took a deep breath and tipped her chin up.

"I think it's best we part ways now." She stormed off before he could respond, leaving him in the glade.

She sped up as she entered the trees, until she was running flat out, biting back the tears that burned her eyes and berating herself. She was such a bloody fool. She should have been stronger. She shouldn't have given herself to him.

She should have known it would end this way, with her heart torn to pieces.

She ran along the lakeshore, the stones cutting into her bare feet.

She didn't need him now that she was free.

She could find her own way home. She had never needed a man to look after her and she wasn't going to begin now, and definitely not with someone as messed up as Vail. He would be the death of her.

Probably already was.

She wished she had never met him.

Her heart reproached her, saying it wasn't true. She was glad she had met him, didn't regret her feelings for him and the time she had spent with him, but that didn't mean she was going to stick around now that he had made his feelings clear. He didn't feel the same way as she did.

He couldn't hate her because she was his mate.

The bond had made him want her, it had made him want to be with her, and it made him unable to hate her.

That told her everything.

Without the bond, Vail would have killed her for being a witch back when she had first met him.

Everything he had done, every kindness he had shown her, had been because of a stupid bond.

She hated him for it.

She barked out a laugh. It seemed the bond didn't work the same way on her. She hated him with a vengeance and she was done with him.

There had to be a portal somewhere in the forest. If she could find it, she might be able to cast a spell to allow her passage through it.

The waterfall thundered ahead of her.

A distant roar shattered the stillness of the forest and creatures fled their roosts.

The air ahead of her shimmered like a heat haze.

Vail appeared in the midst of it in full armour, the black skin-tight scales covering him from razor-sharp claws to the tips of his horned helmet. His near-black eyes narrowed on her.

Rosalind skidded to a halt and back-peddled but he advanced quickly and was on her before she could turn to run the other way. He grabbed her, twisted her in his arms, and clutched her, pinning her against his body.

She muttered a spell, not wanting to hurt him but unwilling to let him hurt her. Before she could finish it, he teleported.

The moment they appeared out of the darkness in the middle of the glade, she finished the spell, blasting him away from her.

The tree he hit wrapped branches around him, binding him to it as the spell stole his ability to teleport. He growled and fought the branches, a wild edge to his purple eyes but pain in them too. Her heart ached and she silently apologised to him, hating herself for not only using magic on him to stop him from pursuing her but forcing him to harm his beloved nature too in order to protect himself.

She ran again, crashing through the forest in the other direction this time, away from the lake.

Branches whipped at her and scratched her bare arms and calves, but she didn't slow. She couldn't slow. She had to keep running.

Tears blinded her and she dashed them away, her strength fading as she stumbled from tree to tree, forcing herself to continue even when she desperately wanted to turn back. He would free himself eventually, or her spell would wear off and return his ability to teleport free of his restraints. She didn't need to go back. She had to keep going forwards.

"Rosalind!"

That roar stopped her dead and she looked back the way she had come, her heart lodged in her throat and beating there at a sickening pace. Her legs shook and she blinked back her tears.

He had never said her name before.

She gripped the tree beside her, torn between running away from him and running back to him.

"Rosalind," he roared her name again, little more than an anguished cry filled with the agony she could feel in him, incredible pain that drove her to return to him because he needed her.

He was calling for her.

For all his faults, even though he had snarled and clawed and said spiteful things that had hurt her, she couldn't bring herself to leave him. But she couldn't bring herself to believe he felt anything for her either, beyond what the bond made him feel, and she wouldn't go another step with him until she knew why he hated witches.

He owed her that much.

CHAPTER 19

The moment Rosalind emerged from the forest and entered the glade again, Vail's gaze snapped to her and the anguish she could feel in him through their bond faded, some of the black in his eyes dissipating with it. His expression softened and he stopped his struggle against the branches that wound around him, pinning him to the thick tree trunk behind him.

He looked down at the branches restraining him and then back at her, an expectant edge to his eyes that was going to switch to darkness when she spoke.

"Oh, I'm not here to release you," she said and rather than the darkness she expected to rise within him, he sagged in his bonds and exhaled on a sigh that reeked of resignation. His gaze held hers as she moved out into the open, towards the fire, a touch of relief in it that echoed through their link. She huffed. "I feel you're glad to see I'm back, but I guess that's just a product of the bond... right? You don't really care if I'm here or if I'm gone. You only think you do because this irritating bond makes you feel that way about me."

She stopped directly in front of him, with the fire between them, and tried to stop her leg from jiggling as she battled a bout of nerves that threatened to have her knees buckling beneath her. Vail stared at her, the intensity of his gaze only increasing the speed of her twitching.

She needed to get a grip. She jerked her leg to a halt and decided to make herself more comfortable. She was done with playing nice after all, pandering to his madness. He couldn't harm her now.

Rosalind waved a hand over her dress, using a spell to create a new one, ignoring Vail's warning growl and how he struggled against the branches that bound him again.

The top half of the black dress hugged her stomach and chest, the front dipping low as the two diagonal pieces of material crossed over her breasts, leaving modest cleavage on show. It covered her arms too, from shoulder to wrist, concealing the ugly scars of her containment. The skirt flared out from her hips, loose and wild, reaching only midway down her thighs, leaving their slender forms exposed. She switched her modest underwear for a push-up black lace bra and a pair of shorts edged with lace, and formed a chunky pair of black leather ankle boots suited for trekking through Hell on her feet.

A sweep of her hand over her hair and it dried and settled in subtle waves that curled playfully around her shoulders and down her back.

She used a final spell to create a comfortable green velvet armchair behind her and sat down on it, placing her arms on the rests and staring across the fire at Vail.

He snarled at her, flashing fangs, a dangerous and wild edge to his eyes again.

"Not so relieved about my being back now, are we?" she said and his gaze focused on her, filled with dark intent. "Glare all you want. It's all you can do until I decide to release you."

For some reason, that sent him plunging into madness.

He roared and bucked against the branches, tried to bite them as he used all of his strength in an attempt to break free. Pain tore through her, agony that cut her to the bone and had her on her feet, crossing the glade to him. She hadn't meant to hurt him, and he was hurting.

Not physical pain, but an emotional one so deep that it left her shaking and sick, on the verge of vomiting.

"Vail," she whispered and risked his wrath by reaching up and placing both hands on his cheeks, cupping them and gently restraining him.

He stilled, his chest heaving against the branches with the force of his rapid breaths, his eyes wild and locked on her. They gradually cleared, the black in his irises receding, leaving only inky spots behind, and his breathing slowed as he looked down at her.

"I said something wrong, didn't I? This wouldn't happen if you would just let me in and tell me what happened to you."

The pain flowing through her ebbed away, but didn't disappear. It remained at a low level, a constant ache in her heart.

She brushed his cheeks with her thumbs before withdrawing her hands and lowering them to her sides. She looked down at her boots and heaved a sigh.

"I'm not buying into this bond, because I can't, and you only feel something for me because of it. But—"

He growled at her, cutting her off, and she raised her head again. Pain swam in his eyes and he tried to move his left arm, his jaw clenching as he struggled against the branch that held it.

"You want it free so you can lash out at me?"

He shook his head, an edge to his emotions that warned he didn't like her saying that he wanted to hurt her, and tried again to get his arm free.

"It's not happening. Deal with it. I've been nice. I've tried to understand… but you hurt me. You hurt me and I won't let that happen again. I have enough to deal with without you adding to it." She went back to her comfy chair and sat on it, waiting to see how he would respond.

His face fell, his eyes falling with it, locking on the fire rather than her. Shame crossed his handsome features and he closed his eyes.

"Do not want to." Those words came out strained and hoarse, laced with anger and pain. "Did not mean to hurt my ki'ara."

She huffed.

"That says it all really, doesn't it? You don't want to hurt your ki'ara. Not me… it's not me you don't want to hurt. It's your mate. It's genetically imprinted on you. Be honest with me, Vail." She folded her arms across her chest and he raised his gaze back to her face, hurt shimmering in it. "If I wasn't your mate, you would have killed me the day we met."

He growled at her, the pain in his eyes flaring, darkening the rich purple of his irises. "No."

Mother earth, she wanted to believe that, but she was done being a fool.

"Was any of this real?" she whispered, her throat thick and tight, making it hard to speak. Tears rose against her will, stinging her eyes, and she drew in a deep breath to hold them back so he wouldn't see how much he had hurt her.

The pained look on his face said he didn't need to see it. He could feel it.

"You want to comfort me now? Because your mate hurts. Not because Rosalind the witch hurts. None of this was real... and I was stupid to believe it might be, and now I will probably pay the ultimate price. Maybe that will be a good thing. Maybe leaving this world will end this hurt I have inside me that grows every day." She laughed at how melancholy and melodramatic she sounded. She had never been one for theatrics or pitying herself, but she seemed stuck in a vicious cycle of it these days. "I just wish one moment had been real. One look or touch. Just something, anything, so I don't leave this world feeling I threw it all away and died for nothing."

The black slashes of his eyebrows met hard above steely purple eyes. "Die? No death for Little Wild Rose."

She laughed at him now. "I don't think you get a say in it. Even I don't get a say in it. I don't want to die... but I don't get a choice. Meeting you took it from me."

"Why?"

Rosalind shifted her shoulders. "I'm not saying. You have your secrets and I have mine, and they're none of your business really."

He growled and struggled again. The branches creaked as they tightened around him in response.

"Real," he ground out and she waved her hand to stop the branches from squeezing the life out of him so he could speak.

"What was real?"

He looked away from her. "It."

It?

"I need a little more than that," she said.

He flashed fangs her way and then lowered his gaze again, slumping in his restraints at the same time. "Wanted you."

Her cheeks flushed but she refused to let him win her over with pretty words designed to make her believe him capable of feeling anything for her.

"You wanted your mate. I was horny and you felt the need to take care of it. Don't deny it."

He shook his head. Not denying it? Or she was wrong?

His eyes met hers, clear purple and steady with intent.

"Wanted you before that." Pain tightened the lines of his handsome face and he growled and tipped his head back, and banged it against the trunk of the tree. "Little Wild Rose thinks me a monster. Would never want a monster."

"Mother earth, no!" She shot to her feet, raced around the fire to him and caught his cheeks again, stopping him from pounding a hole in the back of his skull. She dragged his head away from the trunk and tipped it down so he was facing her again. "I don't think you're a monster, Vail. You're a bloody annoying bastard at times and you have issues, but you're not a monster."

"Made me a monster," he whispered, his eyes unfocused and lined with tears. Pain rose within her again, agony so intense it left her breathless. If it consumed her like this, tore her apart inside, and she felt only a shadow of it through the bond, what was it doing to him? He shook his head, the wild strands of his black hair falling down to brush his forehead, and his eyebrows furrowed. "She made me a monster."

Tears dotted his black lashes, threatening to fall, and she couldn't take the pain that echoed within her, the fierce agony that burned her soul to ashes and ignited fury in her veins.

"Who, Vail?" she whispered, struggling to keep her voice steady so she didn't rouse him from his current state, losing the chance to understand him at last.

"Kordula." He ground his teeth and shook his head, and then laughed, the sound chilling and mirthless. "They said my mate was a witch... they said my mate was a witch... lies... tricked me... *enslaved me*."

A chill went through her. "This witch... enslaved you."

He threw his head back and laughed, tears cutting down the sides of his face. "Four thousand two hundred and twenty eight years... one hundred and fifty seven days and three hours under her spell... four thousand two—"

She placed her hand over his mouth, unable to bear hearing him repeat that.

Only one type of witch could live that long and do that sort of terrible sorcery. A dark witch.

A dark witch had enslaved Vail and held him captive for four millennia. She covered her own mouth with her other hand and stumbled away from him, her spell instantly shattering as tears filled her eyes. She hadn't known.

She never would have bound him with her magic if she had known.

The tree released him and he collapsed into a heap on the ground. His armour peeled away from his hands and torso, and he tugged the grass into his fists, holding on to it as if it was his only lifeline and the only thing keeping him sane.

"Vail, I... I didn't know. I never would have... you have to believe me." She crouched beside him, fighting her desire to touch his bare back, knowing if she did so now when he was free, there was a risk he would turn on her. "Why did she do this to you?"

He looked up at her through the tousled strands of his blue-black hair, his purple eyes shining with hurt and anger.

"Wanted my kingdom. Had to protect my people… attacked them and made them hate me… only way to warn them. I had to do it, Little Wild Rose. I had to… I had to… she punished me for it. Always punished me when I was bad."

Mother earth, she wanted to hunt down the bloody bitch who had done this to him and tear her to pieces.

Vail clawed at the earth, dirtying his fingers.

"Never want me back… made me try to kill Loren… made me kill others… innocents." He shook his head and closed his eyes, his jaw clenching. "Punished me if I disobeyed."

She didn't want to ask how. She didn't think she could bear it. No wonder he hadn't cried out when the demons had tortured him. He had probably grown immune to such violence and pain. No wonder he lost his mind when fighting, becoming savage and cruel, an unstoppable force.

Four thousand years of being held against his will, forced to kill and forced to fight his brother, and punished whenever he found the strength and courage to go against his orders and attempt to save rather than slaughter.

"Vail," she whispered and reached for his shoulder.

He teleported away from her and snarled, flashing his fangs. "Do not touch. No touching. Please. I was good. I did what you wanted. I was good. No punishment today."

He clawed at his chest, leaving red lines across his pale skin, and growled through his teeth.

"Bad things. Always does bad things… no matter what I do. Says it's a reward. Reward." He laughed and it ended in another pained growl. He called his armour back and dug his claws into his scalp, squeezing his head with his palms, and dropped to his knees, breathing hard. "I do not want it. I do not want her touching me."

He rocked back and forth and Rosalind stared blankly at him, struggling to take in what he was saying and the gravity of it.

He threw her a pained look. "No reward. No bad things. I did what you wanted. Please? Do not… hands… touching… not a reward. Fondling… hate her… want to kill her. Will kill the witch. Somehow. Will stop her… and she will not control me anymore… and I can die."

"Vail, no." Rosalind pushed to her feet and crossed the glade to him. She reached out to touch his face and he flinched away.

"Do not touch."

She nodded and kneeled before him instead, aching with a need to comfort him, horrified by what he had said and what she placed in the blanks he had left for her to fill.

He had been told that a witch would be his mate, and this one called Kordula had used that to trick him into thinking he had found his fated one. She had enslaved him with a spell, seizing control of him so she could seize control of his kingdom.

He had done the only thing he could to spare his people from her reign of terror. He had turned on them, making an enemy of himself, severing the bond and trust that existed between them.

She couldn't imagine how hard that had been on him. He had turned on those he loved, his people and his brother, in order to save them, and even that act of sacrifice hadn't truly spared them. Kordula had turned Vail against them, forcing him to attack his own people and murder them, and attack others too, and forcing him to fight his own flesh and blood—the brother he clearly loved.

Her heart ached fiercely for him. He had done terrible things, and had been used terribly too.

Her mind went back to the cells at the castle and how he had acted, how maddened he had been by his captivity, and how he had reacted whenever the guards had left him nude, exposed and vulnerable. She ached to erase those memories for him, knew how much they pained him now she knew about his past. She had hated what they had done to him at the time, but now she really despised them for it.

She still couldn't comprehend the full horror of what he had been through, how his life had been for the past four thousand years, a span of time that seemed like an eternity to her, or how deeply it had all affected him. She wanted to ask him things, but it would only hurt him and dredge up more bad memories that might bring out the darkness in him, and he had suffered enough. He needed to rest, to find a sense of peace and calm again, and she wanted to help him do that.

He looked up into her eyes and clawed at his scalp, drawing blood. His words rang in her ears and his demeanour told her everything. She could see it all in his eyes, how Kordula had abused him, fracturing his mind and shattering his heart and his soul.

She understood the reasons behind his behaviour too, and no longer resented him for anything he had done. She only wished that she had talked with him before their earlier moment.

Not to spare herself the pain, but to spare him the anguish and make the whole experience a better one for him, one that might have erased a fragment of his suffering and placed him on a path towards a better future, towards as normal a life as he could expect to have now.

She wanted to help him overcome his past and how it had coloured his perception of certain things, especially the ones that should have been beautiful experiences.

Ones he now viewed as a violation.

"Vail," she whispered and he blinked but didn't stop clawing his scalp.

She bravely moved her hands towards him. His gaze followed them as she brought them up his arms and held them poised over his.

"Let it go now." She smiled at him and tried to feel good things, knowing he could sense them in her. "No one is going to punish you... or touch you if you don't want to be touched. I'm sorry I used a spell on you. I never wanted to hurt you."

His shoulders lowered and he looked down at his knees. "Never wanted to hurt you... Little Wild Rose."

She smiled sadly, her heart hurting. "Because of the bond—"

"No." He jerked his head up. "Not the bond. Because you... you're... you smell like nature... like roses and rain... more pretty than the most beautiful bloom."

He looked away again and she swore he blushed.

She definitely was.

"Little Wild Rose bloomed for me," he husked in a thick, gravelly voice filled with hunger and her cheeks scalded.

She wanted to mention that she wasn't the one who had experienced two climaxes but held her tongue, not wanting to provoke the darkness within him. Now she understood why they had shocked him though, and that he grew hard for her.

"It was the bond," she muttered.

The tiniest tilt of the corners of his lips warmed her heart.

"Not the bond. Little Wild Rose wants me... as I want her." His smile faded and he looked up at her, searching her eyes, his violet ones darting between them. "Not the bond."

She shook her head, giving up her fight to be mad at him and make him pay for what he had done, because she could see in his eyes and feel in him that it had been real. He felt something for her, and she was crazy enough to feel something for him, something that ran deep in her blood and consumed her.

"Bad mate," he growled beneath his breath. "Frightened Little Wild Rose. Thinks me a monster."

She sighed. She couldn't take it anymore. She couldn't deny the need to comfort him and make him see that she didn't think he was a monster, and he wasn't really a bad mate either. Just one who had a lot to overcome. Four thousand years of being abused by one of her kind.

"I hope she's dead," Rosalind bit out.

Vail looked confused.

And then startled when she placed her hands over his, drew them away from the sides of his head, and clutched them together by her heart.

He stared wide-eyed at his hands and swallowed hard, his pupils gobbling up his irises. Perhaps placing his hands right against her breasts hadn't been her wisest move.

She lifted them and toyed with his black claws, her fingers coming away stained with his blood. He frowned and his claws disappeared, his armour receding into the twin bands around his wrists, leaving his chest bare and his lower half clad in black trousers.

"Rosalind shouldn't have to touch my claws."

She smiled at the use of her name and the sincerity in his gaze as he looked at her.

"Did you kill the bitch?" she said and his demeanour changed abruptly, darkening dangerously.

"No."

She cursed. How the bloody hell had he broken the witch's spell on him?

"My... brother... killed her."

That explained a lot. "I'll have to thank him if I ever meet him again. No one deserves to go through what you did, Vail. No one."

He didn't flinch away when she risked brushing the backs of her fingers across his cheek.

"You should rest," she murmured, lost in his eyes as they held hers, intense and focused, with a hungry edge that threatened to stir her desire again.

Now really wasn't the time for that sort of thing. Both of them needed to process what had happened.

"Little Wild Rose must rest too," he said as she drew her hand back to her chest and released his.

She nodded, hating lying to him but knowing he would grow upset if she told him she didn't intend to sleep. She couldn't. The nightmares were waiting and she wasn't strong enough to face them right now.

She would spend the night watching over him instead, as he had watched over her in the cave, taking care of her.

He stretched and then curled up on his side on the grass before rolling onto his back. She cursed him for looking so tempting stretched out like that, his honed torso on display, and shuffled further away, closer to the fire.

She sat with it warming her side while she watched him drifting off to sleep, his hands resting on his stomach, fingers stained with earth and blood.

Part of her wanted to cling to her anger, but the rest said to let it go. Tomorrow was a new day and now she knew more about her mysterious dark elf prince. She was finally beginning to understand him.

The trouble was, it had only made her fall harder for him and deeper under his spell.

She didn't want to love him.

She didn't want to fall for him when she would only end up torn away from him.

It frightened her.

But she wasn't alone. She had seen it in his eyes and felt it through their bond. Far beneath his scarred exterior, somewhere in the depths of his heart, he felt something for her too, something that wasn't the product of the bond between them or born of his instinct to be a good mate.

And it frightened him too.

She sighed, prayed to mother earth for guidance as she realised it was already too late for her, and watched over her mate as he slept, wishing him good dreams.

She didn't want to love him.
But she did.

CHAPTER 20

Vail came awake to the feel of Rosalind watching him and a deep sensation of peace, as if a terrible weight had been lifted from his soul and he had slept for days. He felt rested, more so than he had in as far back as he could remember. He lay on his back with his eyes closed, breathing in the scent of nature and the feel of it surrounding him, a tranquil oasis that Rosalind added to, perfecting it.

He remembered speaking with her after she had bravely returned to him, easing his anguish and his fear that she had left him forever and he would never see his ki'ara again. He recalled how upset and hurt she had been because of him and the notion that he only desired her because of their bond and the fact she was his fated female.

That notion would have made sense to him once, no more than days ago when they had been in the cells of the castle. He would have agreed with her, unable to believe that he could feel anything for a witch without it being forced on him, whether it was by sorcery or the instincts the presence of his mate awakened in him.

Now that notion seemed ridiculous to him.

He feared examining his feelings too closely, worried that the darkness he held within him would rage to the fore if he did because they were feelings for a witch, but he knew in the sliver of his heart that had remained good that he felt something for her.

Not because of a bond. Not because of a spell.

But because she was beautiful, and pure, and good, and she had shown him so much compassion and care, had sought to understand him and had weathered his mercurial moods.

She had stood by his side when he had been calm and rational, had bravely faced him when he had been little more than a beast and wanted her blood, and had knelt with him when he had been crushed by the pain he held locked deep within him.

And she had come back to him when he had needed her and had been gripped by fear that he had lost her forever because of all the mistakes he had made with her.

She had worked her way into his heart and because of her, the sliver of good in it was growing, beginning to drive back the darkness.

His mind drifted further back, to what they had done prior to him upsetting her and her almost leaving him.

His body flushed with heat at the memory of being inside her, feeling her clenching him, and hearing her breathless moans as she gave herself to him. His markings sparked to life in response, sweeping across his skin, making him shiver as their fire scalded him. He shuddered and bit back the growl that rumbled up his throat, a hungry snarl born of his desire to do it all over again, the pressing need to bend her over and be inside her once more, spending himself in a mutual release of passion.

That shocked him.

He had expected the darkness to seize him, twisting his memory of what he had done with Rosalind together with his memories of Kordula, turning them into a waking nightmare that would strip him of control and unleash the beast held locked within him.

He didn't understand it but decided it had to be because he had been in control for a brief moment. A moment of sheer madness. As much as he desired to do it again, it was too great a risk to allow it to happen or to indulge in daydreams about it. He wasn't sure he would be able to retain control next time, pulled back from the brink of hurting Rosalind by his deeper instinct to protect and please his mate.

Vail focused and shut down his body, used to mastering it after millennia of doing everything in his power to refuse Kordula.

He slowly opened his eyes and tilted his head towards Rosalind.

She sat on the green armchair she had created in the centre of the glade, her feet tucked near her bottom, with a lot of long pale toned leg on show. He knew she had transformed her clothes into ones that were more revealing to test him, and to spite him perhaps. He tried to move his eyes away from her legs, and his thoughts away from his desire to stroke them and slowly ease them apart, but it was impossible.

Only her lifting something to her mouth gave him to strength to stop staring at her legs.

He raised his eyes to her face and frowned as she nibbled on the lump of something she had made, her striking blue eyes fixed on the dying fire between them. The carcass he had cooked for her had been picked clean, only bones remaining, and he was glad that she had fed well, but it left him wondering why she needed the brown lump.

She lifted her eyes, settled them on him, and smiled softly. It didn't chase the fatigue from her eyes that he could also sense in her through their link. She hadn't rested. Why? Because of the nightmares? He wanted to ask her about them, and also about something she had said that troubled him.

She had mentioned dying several times now.

He didn't like it. He didn't want her to die and he would do all in his power to ensure it never happened. She belonged to him now and he wasn't letting her go when he had only just found her. He needed her. She would tell him why she spoke of death as if it was coming for her and he would find a way to save her. First, she would tell him what she ate.

"What is that?" he said, his voice gravelly with sleep.

A flush of guilt crossed her face and she looked away. He frowned and narrowed his eyes on the brown cake, growing suspicious of it. He focused harder on her and their link, attempting to sense everything about her, pushing past the fatigue he could feel to deeper things.

At the deepest level he could reach, he sensed a flicker of something that disturbed him.

Intoxication.

He turned his frown on her and bit out, "What is it?"

She shifted it in her hands, her gaze locked on it now. Avoiding him. Whatever it was, she felt she shouldn't be eating it and feared what he would think.

"Tell me." He wouldn't let her get away with her silence and wouldn't stop pressing until she told him what she ate so he could put his fears to rest.

She sighed and flicked a glance at him, and rattled off a list of herbs and mushrooms.

Many of which rang warning bells in his head.

The mixture was not meant to nourish her.

It was meant to numb her.

Why?

She stood before he could ask, brushed down the back of her black dress, and hurried towards the path to the lake.

"I'm going to wash." She tossed the words over her shoulder and disappeared into the woods.

Vail tipped his head back and stared at the black sky, resisting the need to follow her and press her to tell him why she desired to numb herself and why she refused to sleep. What haunted her in the nightmares that she hated?

He sat up, pushed onto his feet and stretched, clasping his hands together and raising them above his head. He yawned and called his armour to him, sending his black trousers away as the black scales swept over his skin, covering him from boots to wrists.

Vail lowered his hands and looked around the glade, breathing in the beauty and the scent of nature, and absorbing the calming effect it had on him. As much as he desired to stay in this sanctuary forever, they needed to continue their trek now that they had rested. He had rested anyway. He didn't think Rosalind would rest, no matter how many days they remained here. It was better they continued their journey. He doubted the Fifth King had given up his pursuit and if they lingered then the male's warriors would find them.

His gaze roamed towards the path to the lake and his thoughts to Rosalind.

Why did Little Wild Rose use herbs and mushrooms to give herself relief?

He didn't like it. He wanted to be the one to give her relief and give her peace of mind, even though he felt sure he lacked the qualifications to do that. What peace could he offer her when he could find none for himself?

He sighed, picked up his blue elven boots that Rosalind had worn, and focused to send them back to his rooms in the elf castle. Once they were gone from his hands, he set about disposing of the firewood and the evidence of their stay, trying to keep his mind away from thoughts that only troubled him.

He attempted to fix them on their next move, planning their journey. He couldn't teleport through the woods when he couldn't clearly see a landing site and he wasn't willing to risk ending up in a tree or worse, not while Rosalind was with him. They would have to walk.

The trek through the woods towards the Third Realm would be long but being surrounded by nature would do him good, and her good too. Perhaps he could show her the things he could do, as she had asked, and that might distract her from whatever ailed her and build trust between them.

Once he had gained that trust, she might unburden her heart to him just as he had unburdened his to her.

Rosalind returned from the lake, the ends of her blonde hair damp and curling, wrecking his concentration as his mind immediately leaped to picturing her in the water, bare and beautiful.

He growled in response to his markings flaring and this time the darkness within him did rise, pushing him to bare his fangs at her. She meant to tempt him. She wanted to lure him under her spell again, bewitching him with desire, until he surrendered to it. It was the reason she had dressed so provocatively. It was all part of her plan. During their trek, he would be drawn to looking at her, studying her curves and remembering what they had done. Eventually, his need for her would overwhelm him and she would seize control of him then and attempt to touch him.

Once she had skin contact with him, she would enslave him.

Kordula had done such a thing.

She had used his desire against him.

Rosalind frowned at him, a flicker of hurt in her blue eyes. He turned away from her and began walking, needing to place some distance between them. He sensed her following and was thankful that she kept her distance, giving him time to master his darkness and drive it back into submission.

Little Wild Rose had no intention of enslaving him. He had seen her horror and felt her anger when he had told her the things that Kordula had done to him, and her guilt too. He had sensed something else in her as well, a powerful tenderness and affection, and a need to comfort him. She desired to help him, not enslave him.

He brushed his bare fingers over the grass that grew tall between the trees as he walked through it, following his deepest instincts, the ones that connected him to nature. The forest was vast, at least three days trek to the edge closest to the Third Realm. The thought of being surrounded by so much beauty for three days soothed him, giving him more control over his darker nature.

Rosalind walked a short distance behind him and he found it increasingly difficult to keep his focus away from her as they trekked, heading deep into the heart of the forest.

Her power was growing.

It was no longer a low-level hum of magic around him.

He felt it constantly now, surrounding him and smothering his connection with nature, stealing it away from him. He glanced back at her over his shoulder, scowling at how oblivious to his pain she seemed, her eyes dancing over the trees and flowers, fascination shining in them.

Vail focused harder on his bond to nature, using it to shut out the sense of magic in the air and his connection to Rosalind.

It became more difficult four hours into their trek, when the path widened and she moved forwards to walk beside him. His focus on nature shattered when she brushed against him and he turned on her, snarling and flashing his fangs as her magic spread over his armour and seeped down to his skin.

She immediately backed away. "Sorry."

He rubbed his arm and glared at her.

She turned her profile to him and ate more of her infernal concoction.

Now she was numbing herself to him.

Vail snatched the brown lump from her.

"Give it back." She reached for it and he held it high above his head. She huffed and planted her hands on her hips. "That's just childish. Give it back, Vail."

"No." He shook his head, ignoring the fiery shiver that went through him on hearing his name leaving her sweet lips.

She scowled and jumped on the spot, attempting to reach it. Her magic grew stronger. If she used it on him, she would pay the price for it. She was lucky that the thought of losing her had dulled his temper and his fury about her using magic to bind him to the tree, but she wouldn't be so lucky again.

"Give it back," she said, a note of pleading in her voice.

"No." He wouldn't surrender his prize because he couldn't bear seeing her using it to numb herself. He couldn't bear seeing her slowly falling apart as he was slowly getting better.

He didn't want the darkness to take her. He was doing this for her own good. Just as she had pressed him to tell her why he had lost his mind and why he hated witches because she had wanted to understand him so she could help him, he would press her to tell him why she refused to rest and took an intoxicating substance.

"I am no fool, Little Wild Rose. I know of nature's remedies and I want to know why you take herbs and mushrooms that numb you. Is it for the same reason you refuse to sleep?"

She stopped her attempts to reach the brown lump by jumping for it and glared at him, the silver in her eyes sparking.

"Just give it back. I need it and that's all you need to know."

He shook his head. "I cannot. I will not stand by and let you do this to yourself."

She folded her arms across her chest, squeezing her breasts together. He refused to let them distract him. Her rosy lips settled in a mulish line that warned she wasn't going to speak and she wasn't going to stop being angry with him until he surrendered the concoction to her.

Vail scowled down at her. She would speak, and he would not return her precious mixture.

"You said you desired to understand me, Rosalind," he said and her expression softened. Because he had used her given name? She had come back to him when he had done so last night, fear driving him to call for her and make her return, no matter how much using her given name had pained him. It had been sheer instinct that had pressed him to use it then. Perhaps he could bring her back to him with it again now. "Please, Rosalind. I only desire to understand you. You speak of nightmares and death, and take a mixture that leaves you intoxicated and numbs your feelings. I must know why."

Her face softened further, a glimmer of something in her blue eyes that felt like resignation and perhaps relief, but then her expression hardened again. She attempted to reach the brown lump, jumping higher this time, but still nowhere near to taking it from him.

"Little Wild Rose," he snapped and flashed his fangs as he spoke. "You will tell me why you take this concoction or I will send it away forever."

Her eyes widened and she stopped jumping, her gaze locked on him. She stared at him for long seconds, a myriad of indecipherable emotions swirling through her and their link. She would not tell him. He sighed and focused, preparing to teleport her herbal mixture to his rooms in the elf castle and to endure her wrath for his actions.

She lowered her head, casting her gaze down to her feet.

"How do you do it?" she whispered, so quietly he almost didn't catch it.

He bent lower, trying to see her face and regain her attention so he could see her eyes and see if they shone with the pain he could feel in her, rising above her other feelings and consuming her.

She closed her eyes, shutting him out.

"How do I do what?" Vail lowered his hand and looked at the brown lump in it, and then back at her.

"Kill without feeling anything."

He frowned now, unable to follow her or make sense of what she was asking.

What did his past and abilities as a warrior have to do with her nightmares and the concoction? Was she attempting to divert his attention away from her, rousing his memories so they overwhelmed him, driving him mad so he left her in peace?

He refused to let it happen and battled the darkness that threatened to rise within him, unwilling to give it control when he had an important mission in progress.

The health of his mate came before his own, and he wouldn't allow it to stand between him and discovering what ailed her.

She sighed, her slight shoulders shifting with it, making her golden waves dance across her chest.

"I've taken lives too now," she whispered and his frown hardened, his fear that she was attempting to distract him melting away as all of his focus came to rest on her and her wellbeing. She rubbed her arms with her hands and sighed again, the sound strained this time, speaking of the hurt he could feel in her. "In the war. I killed people. Each life haunts me. Each soul torments me. I know it isn't the same for you. Fenix told me that you've killed thousands of people. You must have somehow shut yourself off to the reality of the things you have done... or you have killed so many that it made you numb to it... I envy you for that, Vail. You can take lives so easily, without a flicker of remorse, if you feel threatened."

He could do no such thing, but she seemed convinced that he did.

She turned her cheek to him and opened her eyes, looking off into the woods.

"I fear I'm going to become like my sister... a dark witch. I'll become the darkness that is growing within me. I can feel it."

Vail stepped closer to her, drawn to comforting her and unable to remain at a distance, even when her magic pushed at him and smothered him. He would endure it for her, in order to offer her comfort. His beautiful female hurt and he couldn't bear feeling it. He had to soothe her pain and ease her heavy heart.

"Rosalind," he whispered and she refused to look at him.

He raised his free hand, pretending it wasn't shaking as he edged it towards her and that his chest wasn't growing tight, squeezing his heart and his lungs. He breathed through it, reaching for her cheek, and tamped down his desire to tense when they made contact. Her skin was soft like silk on his palm and warm like sunshine. He turned her head towards him, forcing her to look at him, because she needed to see in his eyes that he meant every word he was about to say.

"I see only light in you, Little Wild Rose. Purity. Goodness. You are nothing like me. You are looking at darkness," he said and her eyes softened, a hint of compassion warming their blue depths. "Fenix is right and I have killed thousands, and perhaps there was a time when I felt debilitating guilt over my actions, but I learned to cope with it and to manage it. Eventually, I became used to what I had to do in battle. I was raised a warrior, trained to cope with every action and the reaction it caused in me. I am hardened to it now, but that does not mean I do not feel remorse at times. Even when under the control of Kordula, I fought with honour and wished my adversaries a good journey to the afterlife, but I still knew that in battle it is a case of you or them, and I did not wish to die."

She shook her head, pressing her cheek against his palm. "I didn't want to die either... I didn't want my friends to die."

"A true warrior then. A warrior fights to protect those around them. You fought to protect your friends. It was war, Rosalind. I fought there too in order to protect someone."

"You did?" Her pale eyebrows dipped low above her rich azure eyes. "Who?"

"My brother's ki'ara."

"Olivia... oh, Vail... I'm so sorry. It was my fault that she was out there. She wasn't meant to be on the battlefield and neither was I, but I had to do something to help them. They were being driven back by the dark witches and I just had to help them. Olivia insisted on coming with me." She pressed her hands to his, pinning it to her face, her eyebrows furrowing. "I'm sorry that you had to fight because of me."

Strange little ki'ara. She always worried about him more than she worried about herself.

"Now I feel more guilty," she whispered and went to lower her head, but he held her fast, pressing his fingertips along her jaw.

"That you feel guilt is a good thing," he said.

She sighed. "It doesn't feel good."

Vail managed to smile. He could remember his first battles, when he had been a youth and had wanted to lead their armies into victories. Loren had tried to tell him the benefits of peace over war, but he had been too headstrong. He had been too intoxicated by the thought of gaining them more land and respect within Hell.

His first kills had left him wracked with guilt, just as Rosalind felt. Those days felt like an eternity ago because he only felt guilt when killing for one reason now.

"It is better than taking a life and taking pleasure from it."

She stared at him, her eyes wide, but not judging him.

He closed his eyes to conceal the darkness rising within him, no doubt tainting his irises, and said, "I feel pleasure when killing. That is the mark of a monster, Rosalind. That is true darkness."

It tormented him together with the things he had done, and the things that had been done to him. Graphic replays of fighting and taking sick pleasure from it tortured him in his darkest hours along with hurting his people and his brother, and all the things Kordula had made him do with her. Rosalind wasn't darkness. She was light to his darkness.

"You were under a spell," she said in a low, gentle voice that soothed him, a soft melody that wrapped him in warm comforting arms.

He wished that were true, if only because she believed it so fiercely and he didn't want to disappoint her. He couldn't lie to her though. She needed to know what true darkness was so she would understand that she was nothing like him.

"It was not just when Kordula was controlling me, Rosalind. It happened even after Loren had killed her and set me free from her spell. It happened in

the battle between the Third and Fifth Realm when I was defending Olivia."
He looked her in the eye, holding her gaze, not allowing her to hide from the
ugly truth about him. "It happened when I fought those demons just days ago."

When his memories rose and induced his madness, unleashing the darkness
within him and turning him into little more than a beast, he found pleasure in
killing. He experienced a sort of ecstasy, an addictive and intoxicating release,
and he was bone-deep afraid that he would harm Rosalind, or kill her, in
pursuit of that high.

Whenever the madness seized him in its relentless grip, he hated her. He
saw no difference between her and Kordula, even though he could see a vast
difference right now.

"Will it ever go away?" she whispered.

"The guilt?" he said and she nodded, her eyes imploring him to say that it
would. He wouldn't lie to her. "It will fade in time, as you come to terms with
what you have done and come to realise that it has not made you dark or evil.
It has changed you, but only in part, and the rest of you remains the same good
and noble female who desires to help others even at the risk of her own life.
We are light and darkness, you and I... and perhaps one cannot survive
without the other... perhaps fate brought us together because of that."

She smiled at that, and he was glad to see it again. It coloured her eyes,
brightening the blue and making the silver twinkle at him.

"Light and darkness," she repeated and he sensed a flicker of relief within
her.

It warmed him. He hadn't expected to feel deeply affected by what she
would confess when he had asked her about her reasons for refusing to rest,
but it felt as if it had changed him and it had changed her, and had somehow
brought them closer together. Is this how she had felt when he had told her
about his past?

"We have walked far, and you feel tired. You must rest, Rosalind." He
hesitated, uncertain of how she would react to what he would say next. "I will
watch over you."

Her expression softened, a glimmer of warmth lighting her delicate
features.

He offered the brown lump to her.

She stared at it for the longest time and then shook her head. "I don't need
it anymore. Thank you, Vail. You see the good in me just as I see it in you,
and I can't thank you enough for showing it to me and making me see it
again."

He felt his cheeks heat and busied himself with using telekinesis to hurl the
concoction far into the forest in order to avoid her inquisitive gaze and get his
blush under control.

Rosalind didn't help matters.

She slipped her hand into his free one, linking their fingers together.

A hot current bolted up his arm, sizzling his nerve endings and setting them alight.

He stared down at her, lost in her blue eyes and the fact she was holding his hand, reeling from the one-two blow.

She hit him with another one that shook him to his core and awakened every male instinct he possessed.

She smiled and said, "We can rest together."

CHAPTER 21

Vail led Rosalind deeper into the woods, his sharp purple gaze constantly scouring the area ahead of them and his hand still tightly grasping hers. She had expected him to turn on her when she had foolishly slipped her hand into his, risking her neck in order to have some physical contact with him and show him that what he had done meant a lot to her. It had surprised him, and his reaction had surprised her. Rather than pushing her away, he had held her tighter, his fingertips pressing into the back of her hand.

They walked through the low grasses, winding between the towering trees, and she stared down at their joined hands, fascinated by the sight of them and trying to remember the last time she had held a man's hand, and the last time a man had held hers with such possessive force.

Force that said that now he had overcome this small hurdle and was able to bring himself to hold her hand without his darker memories pushing to the fore and sending him out of his mind with a need to protect himself from her, he wasn't going to relinquish it.

She didn't mind.

She liked the way he held her, as if he would never let her go. She liked it almost as much as she liked what he had said to her, speaking of them as if they were meant to be together. As if they were the balance the other needed and completed each other.

Foolish of her, but she couldn't seem to convince herself to keep some distance between them. Not anymore. Now all she wanted was to move closer to him. She wanted to have all she could of him before the fate he spoke of that had brought them together tore them apart.

Confessing everything to him had relieved the weight on her heart but she still didn't want to sleep and she felt certain he wouldn't be happy when he discovered that. Guilt still wracked her and she knew that if she closed her eyes and let sleep take her, the nightmares would be waiting. No amount of Vail watching over her could change that.

Her gaze roamed up his strong arm, taking in all the small black scales that covered it, reminding her of the dragons she had seen in the battle, and settled on his profile. The white flowers on the trees bathed his face in pure pale light, highlighting his sculpted cheekbones and the straight line of his nose, and making his violet eyes bright and intense. His male beauty captured every ounce of her attention, stealing her focus away from herself and their surroundings.

He had tried to make her see him as a monster, but she still couldn't view him as one. He held darkness within him, a terrible violent need born of everything that had happened to him, but he held good within him too. He had a sliver of light in his heart, and she had a sliver of darkness. She smiled at that. Maybe that made them perfect for each other.

Vail stopped near a thick tall shrub that curled around the trunk of a towering leafy tree with a gap between them on one side that formed a cosy cave. He glanced down at her hand and frowned, his nostrils flaring and his eyes darkening. She reached for the link between them, desiring to know his feelings and whether he was suffering a delayed reaction to touching her. She could sense no darkness rising within him and the aura of danger he emitted remained constant.

He released her hand with a flicker of what might have been reluctance in his eyes, ducked into the cave between the shrub and the tree, and settled himself with his back against the trunk.

Rosalind wasn't sure where she was meant to sit. There was only one tree to lean against and very little space inside the small hollow in the bush. If she sat next to Vail, they would be close to each other. Perhaps a little too close for his comfort. He was twitchy today and it was her fault. She had been giving her magic free rein, allowing it to rise back to her normal levels that flowed through her, and she knew he could sense it and he didn't like it.

Since confessing everything to him and unburdening her heart, she had pushed her magic back within her, keeping it at bay to give him some respite from it. She couldn't make it disappear completely though, and sitting so close to him would subject him to it and push at his control. She didn't want to upset him. She didn't want him to hate her. She wanted things to remain calm and peaceful between them for a while. She wanted to feel what it would be like if her magic wasn't a constant issue between them and death didn't wait around the corner for her.

She wanted to know what loving and being loved by Vail felt like.

He busied himself, carefully clearing a spot beside him with his telekinesis, tossing leaves and twigs aside with flicks of his fingers to expose the soft grass the covered the tree's roots.

When he had finished, he looked up at her, his purple gaze locking on hers and holding her captive.

He crooked his finger.

Rosalind swallowed hard and hesitated, earning a frown from him.

"Maybe this isn't a—" She didn't get a chance to finish that sentence and tell him it wasn't a good idea.

Vail used his telekinesis to pull her close to him and the second she was within reach, he grasped her wrist and tugged her down into his arms. They wrapped around her like steel bands, holding her a little too tightly.

Rosalind didn't want to mention that. She lay against him, stiff as a board and startled, her heart thundering as quickly as his was against her ear, and held her tongue. This was new to him and it was clear he didn't know what to do, and that he would withdraw again if she made him feel stupid or that he was doing things wrong.

He was trying to be nice, to be gentle and comforting, after he had spent thousands of years having every shred of kindness beaten out of him.

It touched her deeply, warming her heart and melting it, leaving her even more in love with him than she wanted to admit.

Rosalind listened to the fierce drumming of his heart. It was strong but unsteady and she could sense the fear that caused it to race. He remained stiff as she began to relax, rigid and guarded. Afraid.

He clumsily petted her hair, his fingers trembling, making her heart ache for him. His motions were as stiff as the rest of him. Unnatural. She wanted to wrap her arms around him and hold him, needed to tell him that it was alright and he didn't have to push himself, because the ache in her heart grew so fierce that it brought tears to her eyes as she realised something.

He didn't know how to do this anymore.

He didn't know how to be affectionate.

It tore at her and she was too tired to fight and hold back the tears. They tumbled down her cheeks as she pressed her cheek harder against his chest, offering him comfort in the only way she could as emotions clogged her throat.

She laid her right hand on his chest.

He tensed.

Rosalind kept still, not wanting to scare him into reacting or bring back any terrible memories. She held her nerve though, keeping her hand resting lightly on his armoured left pectoral and feeling his gaze on it. This was a huge step for him and one wrong move could spell disaster. She didn't want to push him over the edge. He hated himself when the memories took him. He hated how the darkness born of his terrible past and the abuse he had endured seized control of him and made him do things, and she knew it was because it reminded him of Kordula controlling him.

He needed to feel in command, the master of his own body and mind.

She didn't want his past and the darkness within him marring this moment with her. She wanted this to be a good memory, maybe one that could help him in the fight against his bad ones.

Her heart pounded against her ribs, out of rhythm with the thunderous beat of his against her ear.

She slowly relaxed into him, expelling her breath on a sigh and resting more heavily against his chest and side.

He remained tensed for a few strained minutes and then finally began to relax too, his heart settling at the same time hers did.

Rosalind waited a few minutes more before she moved her right hand, slowly so as not to startle him, and softly stroked his chest. His black armour was cool to the touch, the scales bumpy beneath her fingertips, but it warmed wherever she had been. Colourful light shone through the scales that edged the hard square slab of his left pectoral. His markings. He reacted to her touch and it fascinated her, luring her into touching him in other places. She held that desire back, not willing to risk destroying the peaceful moment they shared.

"You feel healthier now. Because of my blood?" she whispered and ran two fingers across his chest, watching the markings flare and shine through the points where each scale of his armour met. "You healed so quickly."

He didn't respond.

She tilted her head back, looking through her lashes at him.

He stared down at her hand, his violet eyes wide and tracking her every move. She smiled and slowly swirled it over the top of his left pectoral and then down, skimming her fingers just beneath it. When she settled her palm on his chest, he swallowed hard.

She knew she shouldn't, but she couldn't stop herself from whispering, "Your armour can't be comfortable. Wouldn't you prefer to feel my hand on your skin?"

His eyes rapidly darkened. "No."

She tensed, waiting for him to shove her away.

His breathing quickened and he muttered things in the elf language. She sensed his panic rising, sweeping through him and their link.

"Vail," she murmured softly, hoping to capture his attention and steal it away from the dark thoughts that were causing him distress. "I'm not going to hurt you. You're in control here. You're holding me."

His breath hitched. His gaze snapped to her.

He stared into her eyes, every inch of him tensed.

She swallowed her fear and dragged up her courage, and muttered a quiet prayer that he wouldn't kill her.

"It's your choice, Vail. Your decision. You're in control."

He swallowed again and looked down. She gasped when she was suddenly touching bare warm skin, her head reeling from the breakthrough and desire pushing her to stroke his delicious body.

She checked that urge and settled against him again, feeling him breathing and listening to his heartbeat as it finally settled into a normal rhythm for him, much slower than her own. He began to relax too, his muscles going slack.

He gently placed his arms around her and murmured things in the elf language, his beautiful deep voice making it sound musical like a lullaby. She caught the odd 'ki'ara' but didn't press him to tell her what he was saying.

It was private things.

Things that he wasn't ready to allow her to know yet and feared her knowing too. She had a few of those sorts of things herself, and she wasn't ready for him to know them yet either, and she definitely feared him finding out about them.

He stroked her hair with his right hand, brushing his fingers through it, the steady slow action soothing her together with his melodic voice, luring her into sleeping.

Rosalind fought the urge coming over her, struggling to drive the heaviness out of her head and stifling a yawn. She wanted to stay awake and ask him things about his powers, his armour, and how her blood had healed him so quickly.

The words wouldn't line up on her tongue though, her foggy mind unable to provide the necessary questions. She closed her eyes and blinked them back open, only for them to fall shut again, her eyelids too heavy to hold open any longer.

Being in Vail's arms was too comforting and she couldn't remember the last time a man had held her like this, with so much care and tenderness.

She couldn't remember ever being this close to someone.

She couldn't remember ever feeling this way about someone either.

She had never loved someone as deeply as she loved Vail.

He had claimed her heart completely.

CHAPTER 22

Rosalind flicked a glance back at Vail, a smile playing on her rosy lips and dancing in her beautiful blue eyes. The golden strands of her silken hair bounced across her shoulders with each step she took and fluttered in the warm breeze. She lifted her hand and curled her hair behind her ear, hooking it away from her face.

She was radiant today, full of light and smiles as they trekked through the forest, and he couldn't take his eyes off her. The beauty of the nature that surrounded him paled in comparison with her. She was a goddess.

She turned away and ran her right hand over the ridged trunk of a tree she passed, caressing it in a way that took him back to when he had held her while she slept.

How it had felt to have her hand on his chest.

It had felt good, the physical connection between them filling him with heat but soothing him at the same time. She had stroked his chest through his armour, but that caress had been nothing compared with how good it had felt to have her palm on his bare chest, branding his flesh with her imprint.

He stroked the place she had touched, feeling a ghost of her palm on his flesh beneath his armour.

Cold slowly crept in, crawling over his skin to that place, outlining where her hand had been. She had touched him. His step faltered and shadows formed at the corners of his vision, turning the forest there dark. Those shadows advanced as he slowed and the hand he pressed against his chest became the touch of another.

Always fondling and stroking, whispering words in his ear of how she would reward him. His breathing quickened, his heart labouring as he felt her hands all over him, leaving no part untouched and unsullied by her quest for pleasure. He tried to swat them away, snarled at them and clawed at his armour, but they wouldn't cease. Every hand, each of what felt like thousands, swarmed towards one point—the place on his chest where he touched—and then drifted lower, coming to cup him. To squeeze him.

He closed his eyes and growled at the touch, fought the memories that surged up and crashed over him, bringing Kordula to life again in his mind. He ground his teeth, his fangs cutting into his gums, as she caressed him, pouring magic through his veins to restrain him so she could violate him.

Pleasure herself on him.

He dug his claws into his scalp and squeezed the sides of his head as he saw her stripping him and touching him, stroking him as she used her magic to force his compliance and held him with it, stopping him from stopping her.

A hand touched his where it clasped his head.

Vail smacked it away. "Do not touch me."

He stumbled backwards, hitting a tree and tripping over the roots, almost landing on his backside as he fought to remain upright. He snarled and flashed his fangs, seeing Kordula before him.

Advancing on him.

"Vail?" she said and he cursed her for using his name. She had no right to use his name. She was not worthy of speaking it.

"Vile witch," he snarled and launched forwards, seizing her throat in his clawed left hand. "Do not speak my name."

"Vail, please?" she whispered, red lips drawing back into a strained line as he tightened his grip and her icy blue eyes imploring him even as they began to sparkle with crimson fire. "Come back to me."

"Never!" He threw her aside, watched her smack into a tree and land in a heap. She had grown weak. Now was his chance to end her and free himself of her forever. "Now you die."

"Vail, don't." She lifted her head and looked up at him with crimson eyes through her long red hair. The colour in it rolled down towards the tips like blood, leaving fairest gold behind. Her crimson eyes flickered blue and filled with starlight. "See me, Vail. See your Little Wild Rose."

He stumbled backwards, her words a physical blow that knocked him, and had to dig the claws of his left hand into the nearest tree to stop himself from collapsing to his knees as he realised what he had done.

He had struck his fated female.

He had threatened to kill her.

He shoved himself away from the tree and paced to a safer distance, needing a moment to gather himself and suppress the darker urges threatening to seize control of him.

"Vail." His name trembled on her lips.

He cursed under his breath in the elf tongue and shook his head. "Stay away."

She didn't heed him. He felt her approach, felt her magic sliding over his skin and seeping into his flesh. He clawed his scalp, focusing on the pain, desperately trying to hold himself together and stop the darkness from taking him. He shut out the whispered words that demanded he make the witch pay for what she had done. She meant to enslave and violate him too. She had no right to touch him or to use his name, and he had to teach her that in a lesson she would never forget.

She lightly stroked his back.

Vail turned on her with a snarl. "Do not touch me!"

Because the softest caress felt like the hardest strike and he couldn't take it.

He raked his claws down his chest, slicing through his armour and backed away from her.

His stomach squirmed, her tenderness twisting it into painful knots that made the dark voice in his head demand she pay. He couldn't take it. He pressed the points of his claws into his chest and growled through his clenched teeth. The softness of her caress sickened him. He hated her for it. He despised her gentleness.

He would rather she grabbed him roughly than touched him softly.

"Leave me," he barked and she flinched away but quickly recovered, standing her ground and tipping her chin up in a defiant way that tore a warning growl from him.

Now was not the time for her to be stubborn and brave.

Now was the time for her to run.

"You can overcome it," she said, her voice steady and calm, radiating foolish confidence.

She looked so innocent and trusting. He must have looked that way once, millennia ago, when he had first met Kordula.

"Fight it. Remember the good things." She shifted her foot as if meaning to step towards him and he hissed at her through his fangs.

She backed off a step instead, her blue gaze wary and her magic growing stronger.

It crawled over his skin, sending him closer to the edge, skirting the fall into oblivion and the mindless rage that awaited him there.

"Remember the good things, Vail."

He stared at her, breathing hard and trying to battle the dark hungers growing within him. They were too strong.

He was too weak.

"I cannot." He took a step backwards, fear gripping his heart in icy claws. Fear for her safety. He didn't want to hurt her. He didn't want her to see the true face of the monster he had become. She wouldn't understand it. She would leave him.

"You can, Vail. I know you can. Fight it. You're stronger than this. I know you are."

He spat a curse at her.

"I hate that you are so understanding." He teleported, appeared right in front of her and grabbed her shoulders, dragging her against him. He bared his fangs and his pointed ears flared back through his black hair, flattening against the sides of his head. "Perhaps I do not want to remember the good things. Perhaps I do not wish to fight something insubstantial."

A glimmer of fear broke through the hope in her eyes, obliterating it.

He stared down into them and snarled at her.

"Perhaps I just wish to fight."

Her eyes widened and she shook her head as the colour drained from her face.

"No, Vail. You do not want to fight."

He growled and tightened his grip on her, pressing the very tips of his black claws into her flesh through the sleeves of her black dress.

"I do. I want to fight… Witch. You will pay for what your brethren have done to me. I will show you what I have done to your kin… and you will know the pain I have suffered." He pressed his claws in harder, giving himself over to the darkness so she would feel it within him and her magic would react in order to protect her.

It rose as if on cue, coming to sweep around him, becoming a physical thing as it grew in strength. It whipped her blonde hair around, causing it to flutter across her face, but she didn't take her eyes away from his.

"I will not fight you, Vail."

He smirked. "Then you will die."

"Maybe I will. Maybe I'm okay with that. But will you be? Fight it, Vail," she whispered, her eyebrows furrowing. "Fight it because I will not fight you."

He squeezed her arms so tightly that she gasped and her pain shot through him. He growled, turned with her and kicked off, slamming her back against a tree and pinning her there. His back echoed with her hurt. Pain he had caused in her.

She would fight him now.

She would do it to punish him for hurting her.

He deserved it.

"You can have your freedom if you fight me for it, Witch."

She stilled, her eyes enormous and her shock flowing over him. Her magic instantly subsided.

"Why would you want such a thing?" She shook her head. "Why would you want me to strike you?"

"I need it." Those words had left his lips before he had even thought them, escaping him and rocking him to his core. He instantly released her and staggered backwards, his knees threatening to give out as sickness swept through him, disgust that he desired such a thing.

Rosalind's feelings mirrored his, her beautiful face twisted in lines of horror.

Now she had seen the true face of the monster he had become. A man who had had all softness and affection driven from him, replaced with something dark and sinister.

A man who took pleasure from killing.

A man who needed punishment, constantly hungered deep in his soul for the strike of a whip or the blow of a fist, so much so that he had attempted to force the most delicate and beautiful creature in the three realms to fight him.

Vail sank back against a tree trunk and stared at her, unable to tear his eyes away from her horrified expression or shut out the shock reeling through their bond.

He had no excuse, no reason to give her for his behaviour, and no way to make her believe she had misunderstood his intent, because he couldn't bring himself to lie to her.

He looked her right in the eye and said the only thing ringing around his head.

"Gods, I need it."

CHAPTER 23

Rosalind wasn't sure how to react to what Vail had said. She stood with her back against the tree opposite him, staring into his eyes, seeing in them and sensing in their link that he was telling the truth. He wanted her to strike him.

Glowing insects danced in the air between them and the light from the flowers of the trees cast a sickly blue hue across his pale skin.

He had shocked her, but he had shocked himself too.

"Why would you want such a thing?" she whispered.

He bowed his head and she had her answer.

Because it was what he was used to. He had grown accustomed to Kordula treating him poorly, punishing him both physically and emotionally, and he was struggling to cope in a world without what was now familiar to him.

He collapsed to his knees and she pushed away from the tree, but held herself back.

The sight of such a powerful, beautiful man looking so vulnerable and lost tore at her, and she hated it. She couldn't let him suffer alone. She wouldn't. She had to help him.

She crossed the trampled path to him and lifted her hand to touch his cheek.

He flinched away and hissed at her, baring long white daggers, and she had the terrible feeling that if she had struck him hard, he would have welcomed it, but he couldn't bear a gentle touch meant to soothe him.

Rosalind withdrew her hand. "You've given me no reason to hurt you, and if you think to provoke me so I will punish you, it won't work. I'm not going to raise a hand at you in retaliation. I'm not that sort of woman."

She knelt before him in the broken grass and wished he would lift his head and look at her.

"Vail?"

He didn't move. He kept staring at his hands between his knees, his shoulders hunched forwards and trembling.

Rosalind drew in a deep breath and risked it.

She reached out, firmly took hold of both of his hands, and clutched them as tightly as she could. He kept still, his eyes moving over her hands where they held his, and she let out her breath as her tension faded.

"Whatever happened to you, it's in your past now." She brushed her thumbs over the backs of his hands, the caress steady and slow, but with enough pressure that his skin paled in the lines she stroked. She wanted to touch him softly, but she also wanted to keep her head on her shoulders and her heart in her chest, so she kept up with the pressure, giving him a hard caress. "I know you can't simply overcome it and forget it, but I hope in time that you'll learn to come to terms with it, and I hope you'll learn to accept kindness again and learn to trust."

"Why?" That word came out quiet and she hated that he sounded as if he was on the verge of saying he didn't deserve kindness and reproaching her.

She sighed. "Because you deserve some good in your life to help wash away the bad. You deserve to be... loved."

He pulled back and she risked it and held on, refusing to let him go and distance himself.

"I've seen the good in you... a glimmer of the man you once were and somehow managed to retain despite the terrible things that have happened to you. You're a good man, Vail. A noble, loyal and deserving man."

"A man who has done terrible things," he snarled. "A man who has killed thousands and left a river of carnage in his wake."

"Under the orders and control of another." She wouldn't let him bring up the barriers between them again and shut her out, and she wouldn't let him force her away. No matter what he said or how sharp the barbs he threw at her were, she wouldn't give up and relinquish the progress she had made with him.

"I have killed... males... females... innocents... entire families. I have set realms at war with each other and watched them burn." His voice hitched and he tensed. His eyes gradually widened as his breathing accelerated. "I have... I have... pleasured that—"

Rosalind slapped a hand over his mouth to stop him. "I know. I know what that vile bitch did to you. You don't need to say it. You don't need to hurt yourself like this... you don't have to punish yourself and push me away."

He tore her hand from his mouth. "I am the vile one. I let her do those things to me. I did things with others while she watched... and I murdered innocents in front of her while she laughed in order to please her..."

Rosalind placed her hand over his mouth again. There was too much black in his beautiful purple irises and too much pain. When she felt certain he wouldn't continue, she shifted her hand to his left cheek and brought her other one up to cup his right, risking his wrath. She tipped his head up and made him look her in the eye.

"Kordula made you do those things, Vail. You had no free will. What she did to you was deserving of death... and if I had the power, I would heal your mind, would steal away those dark moments, every single one of them. But I cannot... I don't have that power. I wish that I did. The only power I have is in here." She took his left hand and brought it to her chest, settling it palm down over her heart, and held it there as she looked deep into his eyes. "All I can do is show you kindness and compassion, and be here for you when the darkness comes and your memories haunt you. All I can do is try to ease your pain and replace the terrible memories with better ones."

"How?" he croaked and his eyes searched hers, edged with desperation, as if his life depended on her telling him.

She stroked his cheek and squeezed the hand she held to her chest, the heart it hovered above melting as she saw the hope in his eyes and felt it flowing through him.

"I would show you that the things you have been forced to experience... they can be good. They can be different." She hesitated when his eyes began to darken again and tamped her magic down as it tried to rise to the fore to protect her, knowing it would push him over the edge and have him snarling that she was out to trick him and use him as Kordula had. "Like when you held me... remember how good that felt?"

His gaze bore into her, intense and focused, his pupils expanding to devour the purple of his irises. A hot shiver coursed through every inch of her in response to his heated gaze. He did remember it and it had felt good to him. Now she just had to make him see that other things could feel just as good.

Rosalind dropped her gaze to his mouth, taking in the firm sensual curve of his lips. His hand against her tensed.

She didn't want to push him too hard. She was aware of how close he was to her, and that his hand rested against her chest and he could easily call his armour to create his claws and hurt her, but she needed to show him that she meant what she had said and she would help him.

She would show him that it was possible to heal some of the pain in his past and learn to live again.

She leaned towards him, bringing her mouth close to his. His breath sawed from his lips, rough and hard, trembling as much as he was beneath her fingers.

Rosalind whispered, "Something shared between two people can be magical, Vail."

He pushed her back, his eyes darkening again, and she cursed herself for using that word. *Magical.*

He glared at her, his eyes narrowing into nothing more than thin slits. His hand against her tensed, his fingertips digging into her flesh and the heel of his palm pressing into her cleavage.

She waited for him to shove her away or turn on her.

He growled and swooped on her mouth, ripping a soft gasp from her throat and sending a million volts blazing through her. His lips pressed hard against hers and opened, and she was powerless to resist doing the same. He kissed her fiercely, devouring her with rough sweeps of his lips and strokes of his tongue that tantalised and teased her, driving her into submission.

Rosalind went willingly, lost in the arousal raging through her, burning up every inch of her as Vail dominated her mouth and mastered her body with only a kiss.

She tried to keep up with him, her lips clashing desperately with his, the temptation to wrap her arms around his neck and pin him to her becoming increasingly difficult to deny. If they kept going like this, both of them a slave to their passion and need, she was bound to make a monumental mistake with him.

Rosalind slowed her kiss, gradually convincing him to do the same, until his lips danced over hers and their tongues occasionally brushed. He softened it further, teasing her lips with his, a bare caress that drove her wild and brought her close to begging him to unleash his passion again. She ran her tongue across the seam of his lips and it brushed the tips of his fangs.

He growled into her mouth and shifted forwards, forcing her to lie back on the grass. He hovered over her as he kissed her, his hands braced on either side of her arms, caging her beneath him but holding him off her at the same time. He deepened the kiss, tangling tongues with her, flooding her with the taste of him and a need for more. Her body ached and hummed, hungry for more. Her breasts throbbed and it was hard to resist rubbing her thighs together to make the most of the pressure building between them.

He seemed content with only kissing, mastering her mouth and her heart, ruining her to all other men, but she ached for more even when she knew she shouldn't.

Vail didn't let up or give her a chance to draw breath as he kissed her, a constant low growl rumbling through his chest, a possessive sound that thrilled her and only made it harder to resist taking this to the next level.

It seemed Vail was on the same wavelength as her and wasn't as content with just kissing her as she had thought.

She gasped as he brought his body down into contact with hers, wedging himself between her thighs, and rolled his hips. The hard bulge in his armour rubbed her and she cried into his mouth as a thousand tiny sparks swept over her thighs and collided in her belly.

He growled into her mouth, the sexiest noise she had ever heard to accompany words that set her on fire.

"My female hungers... I will satisfy her."

CHAPTER 24

Vail's markings flared across his chest and arms, and over his hips, the sharp fiery feeling growing in intensity as it reached his groin beneath his armour. He grunted, balls drawing up as they tingled and his cock throbbed in response. Gods, he needed to be inside her again. He needed to spend himself in her hot body.

She lay beneath him, her golden hair cascading around her like a halo, her beauty arresting his breath and seizing it in his chest. Her rosy lips were darkened and swollen from his kiss. Kiss. His length jerked again, the sweet taste of her on his tongue and the thought of kissing her combining to send his arousal soaring.

He knew she had expected him to lash out at her, because he had expected that reaction in him too, but he had been transfixed by her lips and their invitation. He had been bewitched by the idea that he could kiss her, and she would let him, even after everything he had done.

The scent of her blood permeated the air, a potent reminder that he had hurt her, that he didn't deserve her, and he couldn't stop his eyes from darting to the sleeves of her black dress and the small holes where his claws had punctured the material and her flesh.

She was wrong. He didn't deserve her.

"Vail," she murmured softly, recapturing his attention and driving the darkness from his heart, filling it with light again.

She gently touched his cheek, bringing his gaze back to her, and he closed his eyes, shutting her out in the only way he could, unable to bear looking at her after what he had done and what he had revealed.

She sighed and stroked his cheek.

"I'm not mad at you," she whispered, her fingertips dancing along the line of his jaw, sending a tingling bolt of electricity down his spine. "I can feel you… remember? I know you regret what you did when the memories had you in their grip. You came back to me though. You didn't hurt me."

"This time." He turned his face away from her and she drew it back again.

"Open your eyes and look at me, Vail, please?" Those softly spoken words were a command he found impossible to resist.

He frowned and did as she asked, opening his eyes and looking down into hers. They were as soft as her tone had been, filled with the warmth and understanding that flowed into him through their bond, soothing his fears.

"I know a little more about you now and next time I'll know what to do. I won't let the darkness take you again like that. I promise."

Gods, he wished she had that power.

His eyebrows dipped lower. She had freed him from the grip of his memories several times now, driving back the darkness and bringing him back into the light. She had given him the strength to fight the beast within him too, and it had seized control of him less often since he had met her. The gaps between his episodes were growing longer. This forest wasn't the only thing healing him.

Little Wild Rose was too.

Perhaps she did have the power to help him through his madness and stop him from hurting her. It was all he wanted now. He wanted to be free of the darkness so he would never hurt her.

She brushed her fingers across his lower lip, making it tingle. "Kiss me again?"

He couldn't deny that request, felt humbled that she had asked it of him, and dropped his head to recapture her lips. The moment they came into contact, she moaned low in her throat and his markings flashed across his body in response. He grunted and nipped at her lower lip, catching it with his fang. She gasped and he swooped on the drop of blood that beaded on her lip, devouring it in another kiss. Gods, he needed more of her.

All of her.

He drew in a deep breath and settled his weight on his right elbow, and placed his left hand on her breast, a base need telling him to surrender to his desire and let his primal instincts take control. She groaned, the breathy sound encouraging him. His female liked this. She desired his touch. He squeezed her breast, feeling the soft flesh give beneath the pressure of his fingers, and she moaned again, tipping her head back and exposing her throat.

Vail snarled and devoured it with his lips as he touched her. Her pulse hammered against his lips and tongue, a tribal beat that called to him, and his fangs lengthened, the hunger of desire merging with a hunger for her blood.

She didn't resist him as he nicked her throat with one fang and wrapped his lips around the wound. She remained calm beneath him, giving her blood and her body to him, because he was in control. He was master now.

Her blood blossomed on his tongue, the sweet intoxicating taste tearing a moan from him, and he rocked his hips in response to the pleasure that trickled through him, heating every inch of his bones. She moaned and ghosted her hands over his shoulders, as if she wanted to touch him, but then raised them above her head, tangling her fingers in the grass instead.

The momentary ripple of fear that had swept through him faded and he lapped at the tiny cut, every drop of her blood exploding on his senses and making him bolder as it took him higher, sending his desire soaring. His female had said that she could make him see that pleasure could be a good thing.

He would show her that she was right, and she had never known pleasure like what he could give to her.

His hand shook as he lowered it to the hem of her black dress. It had fallen back to reveal her thighs and he looked down at them and his hips nestled between them. The sight of her pale thighs against his black armour was so erotic that he growled without thinking.

"Vail," she murmured, a desperate edge to his name, and he clutched her knee and slid his hand down her creamy thigh to the hem of her dress.

He shoved it up as he kissed the cut on her throat again, stealing another drop of her precious blood, and eased his hips back. He slipped his hand across the flat plane of her stomach, turned it, and placed it over her mound. Her black shorts were damp and warm with her need.

He unleashed a feral possessive growl. "My female needs."

She moaned in response, rocking her hips into his touch.

He growled for a different reason, grasped her hip and shoved it down. She strained against him but he held her firm, pushing his weight onto her hip as he rose off her, coming to kneel between her thighs. He hooked his fingers into both sides of her underwear and pulled them roughly down to her ankles. Her boots stopped his progress and he yanked them off, tossing them aside, and then pulled her black shorts off and cast them away too.

He paused, captivated by the sight of Rosalind laying before him, her knees bent and pressed together, her long legs completely on show, and her hands grasping the grass above her head, the position forcing her concealed breasts high into the air.

He growled again, the hunger and need he felt for her spiralling beyond his control. The scent of her arousal filled the air, a sweet heady aroma that called to him, urged him to take her and satisfy her, and spend himself within her.

His length jerked at the idea and he rose to his knees and hesitated only briefly before issuing the mental command to send his armour away. His heart pounded faster and he told himself this was necessary, fighting to control his fear and the seed of vulnerability that threatened to throw tendrils around his heart and squeeze it in his chest. Little Wild Rose would only look upon him with desire, not scorn or disgust. She wanted this and he wanted it too, needed it with a ferocity that drove back his fear, holding it in check.

The black scales of his armour peeled away from his body, racing up his legs, over his torso and down his arms to the twin bands around his wrists.

Rosalind's eyes tracked them and then roamed back to his chest, her pupils dilating as her gaze devoured him, the intensity of it scalding his flesh.

Her eyes slowly lowered, drifting over his chest at first and causing his markings to flare and a shiver to go through him, and then heading lower still. His heart raced and he fought the urge to call his armour back to him.

That urge died the moment her eyes fixed on his length, darkened to near black, and the scent of her desire grew heavier, the need he could feel in her more intense. It beckoned him, stoking his own hunger for her. The heat of her gaze on his cock, the way she looked at it as if she needed it more than anything in the world, stirred only fire and need within him when he had expected it to bring darker memories to the surface of his mind.

His own need for her, together with his instinct to please his mate and a new desire born of his growing feelings for her, kept them at bay. He wanted his female, his Little Wild Rose, to know pleasure from his touch and his body being within hers. He wanted her to feel every inch of him and know he desired her and no one else.

Needed her and no one else.

He placed his hands on her knees and eased them apart, his breath catching in his throat again as he revealed her plush glistening petals. His cock jerked, throbbed so hard it ached, and he couldn't hold back the feral growl that curled through him.

She wriggled, her desperation coming through their link, telling him of her need.

He lowered his left hand to her core and groaned as he dipped his fingers into her soft folds, and her hot moisture coated them. So hungry for him. Gods, he was as hungry for her.

He dropped himself over her again, grasped his cock and trailed the head down her. Her heat scalded him, tearing another groan from his throat that she echoed. One he drew out as he pushed inside her, inch by inch, forcing her to take as much of him as her body would allow. Her grip on the grass tightened, her body arching in response to the invasion, and her lips parted as she moaned until the head of him touched her deepest part.

Vail stilled, feeling her wet heat encasing him, her body gloving his, clenching him sweetly and tightly. Made for him. His mate. She would desire him and no other.

He leaned over her, settling his weight on his elbows and thrust forwards, pushing deeper, tearing a moan from her before he withdrew almost all of the way and plunged back in, ripping another from her lips. He lowered his head to her throat, nicked it again with his fangs, and drank as he pumped into her with long deep thrusts. He grunted and instinct seized control, hunger demanded he sate it.

He lowered his left hand to her thigh and grasped it, holding it against his hip as he thrust into her and stole drops of blood from the mark on her throat. She moaned and writhed, her breasts pressing against his chest, and he let her, loving the way she responded so beautifully to him.

When she placed one hand on his shoulders, he allowed it, welcomed the feel of her caressing his back as he made love with her, joining their bodies in a slow union that threatened to send him out of his mind with pleasure. Did she feel the same?

She moaned, as if she knew his thoughts and wanted him to know she felt the same, that bliss flowed through her with each thrust of his length into her, each meeting of their bodies.

"Vail," she breathed and he moaned against her throat, uttering her name in his mind as his balls drew up.

He grasped her harder and thrust deeper, shorter and quicker strokes that had his pelvis meeting hers. Each meeting tore another moan from her, a little noise of bliss that he used as a guide. His female was close.

She tensed and pressed her fingers into his shoulder. "More."

Vail could only comply with that command, felt driven to give his female what she desired, because he wanted to feel her climax on him, needed to hear her moan his name as she came with him in a blissful union, one that felt as if it was healing him.

He lost himself in her, in the feel of her clutching him and the sound of her moans, and the taste of her skin and her blood. She whimpered, the sound born of ultimate pleasure, and murmured his name, held him tighter as if she feared he would pull away at this critical moment.

Never.

He would never deny her anything.

Not anymore.

His Little Wild Rose had tamed him with her tenderness, had shown him that this act could be beautiful and everything opposite of what he had experienced before, and he was eternally grateful to her for it.

He withdrew and plunged deep into her again, and she cried out, the sound echoing around the forest. Her body exploded into a symphony of quivering and trembling, and her pleasure flooded the link between them, blasting through him as she climaxed.

He thrust again and grunted into her throat as seed boiled up his cock. He held her hip, clutching her to him, holding her immobile as he spilled inside her, his length throbbing with each burst of release. His entire body shook, trembling against hers, the pleasure stealing his strength as his mingled with hers, combining to leave him hazy.

He buried his face into her neck and held her to him, unwilling and unable to bring himself to release her. Not when emotions blasted through him that threatened to shake his world to its foundations.

Feelings he never thought he would experience.

He lay inside her as they crashed over him, gaining clarity at last, stealing his breath and shocking him.

Leaving him forever changed.

Little Wild Rose was his fated female.

And he was in love with her.

CHAPTER 25

Vail woke slowly to the calming smell of the woods around him and the unique scent of Rosalind. He focused on the forest, trying to calculate how far it was to the edge closest to the Third Realm. They had trekked for another four hours after resting and much of it had been uphill. Rosalind had quickly flagged, and he had set up a camp for her in a small clearing in the trees. He had hunted for her too, providing her with sustenance, and had cooked the meat over their fire. When he had offered it to her, she had told him to eat first.

Little Wild Rose knew much of the world but lacked knowledge about his kind.

Elves didn't partake of meat. He could eat fruits and vegetables for nourishment, but it was blood that kept him strong. She had been shocked to learn such a thing and had promptly offered her blood. Vail had refused. As much as he needed it, she needed it more. He couldn't risk her growing weaker.

After she had eaten, he had insisted that she rest. She had of course insisted that he rest too.

He had ended up laying under a tree beside her on his back, but during sleep, it appeared he had moved.

He now lay on his side with Rosalind nestled against him, her back pressing into his front.

He stared at the back of her head, watching the light from the tree's flowers dancing over the golden strands, waiting for the darkness to seize him and demand he push her away.

A wholly different reaction occurred within him.

He grew painfully hard in his black trousers.

Rather than pushing her away, he shuffled closer and pressed his aching erection against her backside. Gods, he wanted her again. He no longer feared the desire that overwhelmed him at times, how he would ache for her, a need that only she could satisfy. He no longer feared it because he knew she would let him be in control and she would welcome him. She would let him do as he pleased with her, trusting that he would be gentle and give her pleasure, and that humbled him.

That she trusted him when she was at her most vulnerable stole his breath and made him want to kiss her again.

He couldn't reach her lips though and his body seemed rather preoccupied with rubbing against her, an action he had little control over. He worked his hips against her backside, the friction both pleasuring him and maddening him. It wasn't enough.

She arched her bottom into his next thrust and he froze.

"Don't stop," she murmured, a sleepy quality to her soft voice. "Please."

He seized hold of her hip through her black dress and rubbed again, shuddering at the feel of her. He needed more too.

He grasped the soft black material of her dress and pulled it up. When it reached her hip, he slid his hand beneath it, exploring her stomach and edging ever higher, aiming for her breasts. He wanted to feel them.

She loosed a moan when he cupped her left breast beneath her dress and arched against him again, rubbing his cock with her backside. He groaned and thrust against her, the friction still not enough.

He fondled her breast, teasing the pert nipple between his fingers, eliciting another cry of pleasure from her. His female enjoyed this. He pressed kisses across her shoulder as he touched her, taking his time about it, learning every inch of her and divining what she enjoyed from her soft breathless gasps and the ripples of pleasure that flowed through their link.

His fingers quested lower again, over the plane of her stomach, and he slipped them into her underwear. She lifted her leg, opening to him, and he groaned against her skin as he felt her wetness and heat, the evidence of her desire for him.

"Vail," she whispered and the husky sound of his name falling from her lips aroused him further, making him painfully hard for her.

He gave a momentary thought to the fact that only days ago, he would have reacted negatively to her using his name and now he couldn't seem to hear it falling from her lips enough times to satisfy him.

She moaned and he growled when she rolled to face him, stealing her body away from his touch.

She looked up at him, her blue eyes sparkling and enchanting him. "Can I kiss your chest?"

He tensed.

The brightness in her eyes faded and he sensed a glimmer of the hurt his reaction caused in her.

"I don't have to," she said and he held his hand up, silencing her before she convinced him that she was right.

He mentally checked himself over. He didn't feel as if he would lose control if he allowed Rosalind to touch him and place her lips on him. He knew she was Rosalind and that she wouldn't hurt him, and her magic was at a low-level again, held back by her.

On top of that, he craved the feel of her hands on him, had enjoyed it when she had interacted with him the last time they had made love, participating in the moment they shared.

He nodded.

Rosalind leaned in and the first brush of her lips across his bare chest sent a ripple of heat through him. The second had his markings flaring in response, the fiery sensation unsettling him and cranking his arousal higher. She swept her lips over his pectoral, following the line of his markings. Her silky hair caressed his chest too, adding to the blissful feel of her touching him.

He felt each brush and sweep of her lips on his soul, every one of them speaking of tenderness, affection and desire, a combination that delighted him. When she reached his nipple, she swirled her tongue around it, and his markings flared again, chasing over his body and sending his hunger soaring, until he couldn't stop himself from rocking his hips, thrusting at the air and imagining being inside her.

He could smell her desire. He could feel it coating his fingers.

She kissed lower, following the valley between his pectorals, and he lifted his hand and stared at his fingers. He brought them to his mouth and licked them, tasting her honey. A shudder rocked him, leaving him aching with a need to taste more of her.

Vail was so lost in his hunger for her that he didn't even notice that she had moved him onto his back until she swirled her tongue around his navel. He groaned, the husky and hunger-laced sound startling him, and tensed.

"It's okay to express your pleasure, Vail," she whispered against his stomach, her lips brushing his skin with each word, and released a breathy moan of her own as she kissed lower.

His insides trembled. His heart hitched.

Her fingers skimmed the waist of his trousers and she looked up at him, her blue eyes dark with desire and intent. He didn't have the strength to stop her as she unlaced his trousers, her hands rubbing his length through the black material and her eyes on his the whole time. Her breasts hung in her dress, squashed together, enticing his gaze to fall there and his mind to race forwards to imagining kissing her breasts as she had kissed his chest.

She tugged his trousers open, the rough action sending a blissful shiver through him together with the cool air as it rushed over his straining erection.

She lowered her head. Her hot moist breath blew across the head of his shaft and it jerked, his balls squeezing tight. He grunted and clutched the grass, breathing hard as pleasure jolted him to his bones.

"Do you want me to place my mouth on you?"

Those low sultry words shocked him and he stared down the length of his body at her where she kneeled over him, her mouth dangerously close to his length and her blue eyes promising pleasure.

She was serious.

She would do such a thing?

Kordula had never done such a thing. She had taken her pleasure and given him none.

He frowned, his mood shattering and darkening as memories crowded his mind, visions of Kordula poised above him, pinning him down as she rode him.

"Come back to me, Vail." Rosalind's whispered words cut through the darkness like a shaft of light and she shimmered back into existence, a soft look in her eyes. "Focus on the woods and on me. You're here with me… and I want to kiss you. Will you allow it?"

He drew in a deep breath to calm himself, doing as Rosalind had instructed but shifting all of his focus to her rather than keeping part of it on the woods. He needed to feel her and know she was with him, that it was her lips and her touch that gave him pleasure. His Little Wild Rose. His eternal mate.

He nodded stiffly.

She smiled and lowered her gaze to his length. It jerked, bobbing towards her, as eager for her caress as the rest of him.

She skimmed her hands down over his hips and his markings flared again, the ones that curled over his hips and around his groin and buttocks illuminating her face with a rainbow of colours.

"They're so beautiful," she murmured and stroked them, tearing a groan from his throat and making his hips buck against his will. "You're so beautiful."

He went to frown at her but she ran her tongue over the head of his cock and he tipped his head back into the grass and moaned instead. He fisted the grass into his fingers, clutching it as she swirled her tongue around the sensitive head and stroked one hand down the shaft, revealing the crown. He squeezed his eyes shut and ground his teeth, unsure whether he would survive this. It felt too good.

No one had ever pleasured him like this.

She gently held him in one hand and wrapped her lips around the tip, and he swallowed hard as she took him into her mouth. Her moist wet heat enveloped him, instantly bringing to mind how she felt when he was inside her. He grunted and thrust into her mouth, unable to stop himself from shifting his hips and obeying the instinct to pump into her.

She moaned and her tongue vibrated against the head, sending a thousand tiny shivers racing down its length and through him.

"Rosalind," he murmured, lost in her and the moment.

She paused and he growled, could sense her surprise at him using her name and didn't want her to stop and take it in or mention it.

He placed his left hand on the top of her head, tangling his fingers in her silky hair, and guided her on him. She began moving her mouth on him again, every suck she made as she withdrew addling him and tearing another deep growling moan from his lips. He tried to keep still but it was impossible, the instinct to move too strong to deny.

He pumped into her with shallow thrusts as she sucked him, swirled her tongue around the sensitive head, and teased him with her fingers. She lowered them to his balls and rolled his sac and he grunted, jerking hard into her mouth in response, desperate for more. She moaned, the vibration of it through his cock almost his undoing, and brought her hand into play. She wrapped it around his length, holding it firmly, and began stroking in time with the movement of her hot mouth on him.

Vail was lost.

He tipped his head back into the grass and gave himself over to her, floating in a sea of pleasure where every inch of him felt alive and overly sensitive, the smallest caress of her hair on his stomach almost too much to bear.

Release coiled at the base of his length and he tried to hold it back, wanted to last longer and steal every drop of pleasure from this act. His balls drew up, tightening painfully, and he shuddered as she firmly stroked her hand down his length and sucked hard. A million stars exploded behind his closed eyes, fire and ice swept through him, and he snarled as his cock throbbed, shooting jets of seed into her mouth. She kept sucking him, her tongue teasing him, lapping at him and flickering over the sensitive head. He grunted, tensed, couldn't take it.

Bliss washed through him, melting his bones and turning his muscles to water.

He lay in the grass, his fingers still tangled in her long hair, holding her mouth to him.

He slowly opened his eyes and looked down at her as he released her and she raised her head, her gaze meeting his. The dark hunger in it called to him and awakened a glimmer of dissatisfaction in him that took the edge off his climax.

He had wanted to come inside her again.

He had wanted to give her pleasure too.

She rose onto her knees and his gaze fell to her thighs. The taste of her lingered on his tongue, sweet and tempting, stirring his desire back to life.

He would give his female pleasure.

He would taste her as she had tasted him.

CHAPTER 26

Vail rose to his knees, pushed Rosalind onto her back, and crawled up the length of her. Her heart began to race, the knot in her stomach growing tighter as her desire spiked, fuelled by the hungry look in his purple eyes. Mother earth, he could melt her with just a look and she lost her ability to think straight.

He dropped his hands to her knees and shoved her dress up to her stomach, and she trembled in response to the feel of his hands on her, pressing into her flesh and speaking of his strength.

They were moving too fast, but she couldn't bring herself to tell him that when he placed his left hand on her. Lightning whipped through her and she moaned and raised her hips into his touch, seeking a firmer one that would satisfy her. He growled and his eyes narrowed, but not in anger. No. There was only hunger in them, a fierce need that echoed within her, demanding release.

He pulled her knickers off and tossed them aside, and held her gaze, his hooded and dark with desire.

"I wish to taste you," he husked, each low-spoken word cranking her temperature higher and making her tremble with anticipation. "I want to devour you... will you allow it, sweet Rosalind?"

Mother earth, would she.

She nodded and couldn't stop herself as he pressed his hands to the insides of her thighs and eased them apart. He lowered himself, his fierce gaze dropping to her core, setting her on fire.

Bloody hell, he was really going to do it.

His hot breath flowed over her, making her flutter in response and her heart miss a beat. She tried to relax but it was impossible as he wedged her knees apart with his broad shoulders, his bare skin against hers.

He parted her and darted his tongue in to brush her most sensitive place.

She moaned at the same time as he did and his markings flashed over his shoulders and down his back.

He was still a moment in which she found it hard not to move and not to beg him to do it again, and then placed his mouth on her.

The universe exploded.

Rosalind collapsed against the grass and moaned as he flicked his tongue over her nub before swirling it in a circle, sending sparks of pleasure shooting through her body. She moaned and he grunted in response, his actions turning rougher.

"Gentle," she murmured, unsure whether he would appreciate the guidance or would turn on her.

He slowed and softened his approach, and mother earth, it had been worth the risk. Each swirl and stroke of his tongue, every soft puff of his breath across her sensitive flesh, sent her arousal soaring higher and drove her out of her mind. She clutched at the grass above her head, fighting the need to hold his head instead, pinning him in place until she had found her release.

He licked lower and lapped at her core. She moaned and rocked her hips against him. He stilled and she was about to berate him for it when he speared her with two fingers and she cried out her bliss.

He growled, the sound pure male satisfaction, arousing her further, and pumped her slowly with his fingers as he flicked his tongue over her nub.

She couldn't stop rocking her hips, writhing on his fingers as he stroked her inside. It wasn't enough. She needed more. She lowered her hands and fondled her breasts, pulling them free of her dress so she could pluck her nipples.

Vail stopped and lifted his head, his gaze boring into her hands.

She swallowed and looked down at him, refusing to stop what she was doing. She tweaked and rolled her nipples, moaning as pleasure skittered through her. His eyes darkened with desire that tore another groan from her and he growled. He thrust his two fingers into her and she cried out, clenching him inside her, wriggling and trying to make him thrust again. He refused her, his focus back on her breasts.

"Vail," she murmured, on the verge of begging him to keep going because she was close.

He growled, flashing extending fangs, and pulled his fingers from her. He was on her before she could protest at the loss of him inside her, his mouth swooping on her breasts as he filled her in one stroke with his cock. She cried out at the blissful invasion and moaned as he thrust harder into her, sucking on her nipple at the same time.

She couldn't stop herself from clutching his shoulders or raising her hips, pushing them higher so he could go deeper. He growled against her breast on his next thrust, evidently approving of her decision, and seized her hip with his left hand, holding her backside off the grass.

He pumped her hard and deep, long fast strokes that ripped moans from her as she clutched at him, scoring his back with her nails. He grunted in response and thrust harder, the wildness of it awakening that side of her, making her let go of her fears.

Rosalind dug her fingers into his hair and pulled him up to her. He swooped on her mouth and devoured her, his tongue tangling with hers. She grasped his hair as he slid one arm beneath her, wrapping it over her shoulder, and held her backside off the ground with his other hand.

"More." She pressed her free hand into the small of his back, pushing down each time he thrust into her, encouraging him to let go because she needed it harder. She needed to feel all of his strength used on her in a wild union.

He growled into her mouth and pumped her harder, his pelvis slamming into her with each fierce stroke. It wasn't enough. She needed more.

He gave it to her.

He sank his fangs into her throat and she cried out, a hot wave of bliss pouring through her from the point where his mouth fused with her flesh. He grunted and thrust deeper, keeping up his frenzied pace. The first pull on her blood sent her out of her head and all of her strength flowed out of her, replaced by a hazy feeling that gradually gained focus with each subsequent pull he made, until she had an inexplicable need for his blood.

She writhed beneath him as the hunger grew, slowly seizing control of her, making her needful and achy.

"Vail," she whispered, sure he could sense her need and would know how to satisfy it.

He licked her neck and lifted his head, and she flinched as his armour covered his fingers, turning them into claws, and he used one to nick his throat.

A tiny bead of blood broke the surface and trembled in time with each wild thrust of his body into hers. Another bead joined it and her gaze zeroed in on it.

Rosalind grabbed the back of his neck, dragged him down to her and latched onto his throat. She swept her tongue over the cut and shuddered as fire cascaded through her and the universe exploded again, glittering in a thousand colours. She moaned and wrapped her legs around him, sucking harder on the cut and swallowing his blood. Ambrosia.

He grunted with each pull she made, his actions turning jerky and rough, his bliss flowing into her and mingling with hers.

Mother earth.

She had never experienced anything like it.

And it only got better when he dropped his mouth back to her throat and sucked on his bite mark again, drawing her blood out of her as she drank his down.

He grasped her hip in a bruising grip and shoved into her, sending her over the edge. Pleasure detonated within her, her entire body quivering against his and turning liquid as fire flowed through her and sparks leaped along her nerve endings.

Vail thrust deeper and held her in place as his length pulsed within her, hot jets of seed marking her inside, increasing the bliss rippling through her. He shook against her, his grip on her hip unrelenting but his drinking slowing.

She released his neck and swept her lips over it one last time before licking away the final drop of blood.

He brushed his tongue over her throat, lifted his head, and pressed his forehead against hers.

"Mine now. Mine forever."

Those whispered words stole her heart and brought her both joy and pain.

She was his and he was hers.

But it could only be for now.

Not forever.
No matter how fiercely she wanted it to be.

CHAPTER 27

Vail led Rosalind through the forest, clearing the path for her and following his senses north, towards the Third Realm. They had walked for two days, taking regular breaks for his Little Wild Rose to rest, and had fallen into a sort of rhythm with each other.

She would set up the camp, gathering firewood and waiting for him to be at a distance hunting for her before she lit it using her magic. He always sensed it though. Not the magic. She kept that at a level low enough that he never felt it but just enough to make the spell work. He sensed the nerves in her through their link, her trepidation and fear, and knew she experienced those feelings because she had no desire to trigger an attack in him.

That touched him more than she could ever know.

The demons had bound her powers, had stolen them from her, and he knew that it had upset her, because having his abilities bound had upset him. He was beginning to understand her now, and it had only made his appreciation of her and how she held her magic in check around him grow.

Whenever he returned, she greeted him with a smile and asked him how his hunting had fared. He never returned empty handed. Little Wild Rose needed to eat and he would expend every drop of his power to ensure that she had the sustenance she required to keep her strong. No distance was too great. No creature too large. He would scour all of the Fifth Realm to find her something to eat.

If the portal pathways had been open to him, he would have scoured the entirety of Hell, and if that failed, he would have returned to a place he loathed but one he knew would easily supply him with food—the mortal realm.

After his ki'ara had eaten, she would tell him more about herself, speaking of her home in the mortal realm and the family she had left behind because she was a light witch, and they were darkness. She would press him to tell her about himself too and he would think back to better days to give her something pleasing to hear.

Each time he spoke of those days with his brother in the mortal world and in the elf kingdom, he felt lighter and the darkness seemed further away, slowly drifting into the distance.

And after they had spoken and his Little Wild Rose looked at him with sleep-filled eyes, they would settle against the same tree and he would hold her while she slept, watching over her to ensure her nightmares didn't return.

And not once had he felt the darkness push at him, commanding him to harm her because she was a witch.

Perhaps there was hope for him yet.

He glanced over his shoulder at her and found her staring at his backside.

Her eyes shot wide and darted up to his, and a deep scarlet blush coloured her fair cheeks.

"I... um... I," she stammered and her blush deepened. Her gaze leaped off to her left.

"Was staring at my backside?" he offered.

She scowled at him. "I think I liked you better when you didn't say much and mostly growled at me."

Liar. She liked this side of him that their long hours of talking and their growing closeness was bringing out in him. He confessed that he liked it too. He had lost himself somewhere along the line, but now he felt he had found himself again.

Loren hadn't been the only one who had laughed during their travels in the mortal realm as youths. Vail had always laughed harder and played harder too. He had always been the one to take risks and challenge the extent of their immortality, and it had always ended with his brother chastising him while tending to his wounds.

Vail drew in a deep breath and sighed it out as he looked around the forest, taking in the colourful bright flowers that illuminated the thick leafy canopy in this area, shades of pink, blue and yellow, and the black cragged mountains that rose through the gaps in the trees.

Loren would have loved this place.

Vail placed his bare palm against the thick rough trunk of the tree to his left, closed his eyes and focused on his link to nature and the one to his brother. He opened the barrier between them and his eyes too, and channelled the beauty of the forest through it to his brother, and that it was a place in Hell, far from the elf kingdom, but no doubt born of the power they had exerted there in order to create their verdant land.

Warmth travelled through the bond with Loren, a sense of happiness that wasn't born purely of what Vail had found and was sharing with him. He frowned, curious as to why his brother was so happy on this day.

"You okay?" Rosalind said, cocking her head at him, causing her ash blonde hair to sway across her breasts and distracting him.

He nodded.

"Spacing out?"

He frowned and shook his head. "Revealing this place to my brother."

She frowned now, her fair eyebrows dipping low above her azure eyes. "How?"

"We have a bond... a strong connection. I normally keep it closed to keep him from finding me, but I wanted to show him this place. He is happy today."

"Why?" She moved a step closer, brushed her hair over her shoulder, and canted her head the other way.

"I do not know why he is happy." Vail closed the link between them and removed his hand from the tree.

She smiled and shook her head. "No. Why do you keep it closed to stop him from finding you?"

Vail looked over her head into the distance, his eyes losing focus as he pondered how to answer that question. When he came up with no suitable answer, he lowered his eyes back to her.

"You know why," he said and her blue eyes grew solemn and she drew another step closer.

Little Wild Rose slipped her hand into his right one and brushed her thumb across his knuckles, her gaze fixed there. "Because you think he hates you... because you think every elf in your kingdom hates you."

"It is not my kingdom, Rosalind." Vail snatched his hand back from her and shoved his fingers through his hair. "You know that. I do not belong there... I am not welcome there... no matter how—"

He growled and cut himself off, but it didn't deter his brave little female.

"No matter how much you desire it," she finished for him and sighed, tiptoed and caught his right hand again, bringing it down to her chest and holding it there.

His gaze fell back to her and drank in the beautiful way she was looking at him as he absorbed every feeling flowing through their bond. Compassion. Tenderness. Love.

"Maybe one day things will be different, Vail. You never know. I hope you can go back there and be with your brother. I know you'll be happy there."

He hoped for that too, but he also hoped that Rosalind would be there with him. He could never be happy without her. She had become his entire universe. There was no happiness for him in this world without her. No good. No light. Without her, he would become the darkness again and he would embrace it to rid himself of the pain of living without her.

"You feel melancholy," she whispered with a frown and squeezed his hand. "Think happy thoughts."

He found that difficult when she spoke of him returning to the elf kingdom, and him being happy, with no mention of her.

"I am trying," he said to appease her and couldn't stop himself from clutching her hand and adding, "I hope we can go there and be with my brother and his ki'ara. I know we will be happy there."

The light inside her faded and her face fell, dark emotions swift to rise and travel through their link, speaking of sorrow and fear.

"Rosalind, what is it?" He drew her closer, wrapping one arm around her waist and palming the back of her head with the other, holding it to his chest. He pressed a kiss to the top of her head, breathed her in, and closed his eyes, savouring the feel of her against him and how she sought comfort from him.

Her arms looped around his waist and her hands pressed into his upper back, clutching at him, as if she feared he would let her go. Never.

They would be together forever.

She drew back, her hands trembling against him. The tears lining her eyes tore at his heart and he released her head and captured one with his fingertip. The diamond drop glittered at him.

"Little Wild Rose, speak to me," he whispered and she swallowed hard. Her eyebrows furrowed and her lips parted.

"Vail... there's something I have to tell you..."

A shudder went through the forest and through Vail.

He stilled, every muscle tensing and bone locking as a shadow swept over the land and nature receded.

The blossoms in the trees faded, their light dying, and the glowing insects stuttered and disappeared.

Rosalind looked around them as the forest plunged into darkness and pressed closer to him. "Vail, what's happening?"

Her magic rose, brushing over his skin, pushing at his control. He ground his teeth and held it together, refusing to succumb to the darkness and the despicable things it whispered to him. She was afraid, not out to harm him. Her power meant to protect her, not control him.

He meant to protect her too.

"We must move. Demons have entered the forest." He grabbed her hand and began running with her, crashing through the shrubs with her stumbling along behind him.

She found her stride and kept up with him, her magic rising still. She muttered beneath her breath and it grew stronger. A bright light burst into life off to his left, where she was, and he flinched away from it as it dampened his vision. The glowing blue orb shot ahead of them, lighting their path. Vail growled at the spell and forced himself to keep running in that direction as every instinct he possessed said to turn around and head the other way, away from the magic.

"It won't harm you. I won't harm you, Vail," Rosalind said, out of breath already. He could sense the strain in her as they sprinted, a reminder that she was close to a mortal in speed and stamina. "I don't want to upset you, but if those demons catch up, then I will use my magic to protect you. I'm not letting anything happen to you. Not on my watch."

He growled, swept her into his arms and teleported, landing just short of the blue orb that raced ahead of them, illuminating the way.

"Vail, no. You'll weaken yourself teleporting me with—"

He cut her off by teleporting again, reappearing further along the path. A tree loomed directly ahead and he barely managed to avoid it, teleporting again to a clearing. His knees wobbled on landing.

"Vail. Put me down. I can run... we can run. You need your strength." She pushed at his chest and he didn't have any choice but to comply with her demands because he didn't have the strength to keep hold of her.

His muscles ached, body trembling as it struggled to heal the effects of teleporting with her. He silently cursed her for being so powerful.

"Can you use a spell to transport yourself?" He fought to catch his breath. She nodded.

"Then do so."

Her eyes widened and she grabbed his shoulders. "No. You won't know where I've gone. We'll be separated. I'm not leaving you. We can fight together."

Stubborn, defiant, brave little ki'ara.

He shook his head and met her gaze, holding it and wishing he could agree to those demands.

"I will not let you fight." He reached out and brushed his knuckles across her cheek.

"I told you, I won't harm you with my magic. I swear, Vail." She clutched his hand and held it to her face, her blue eyes begging him to listen to her.

He smiled. "Your magic is not the reason I will not let you fight, Rosalind. I will not let you fight because I do not want you to go through that grief and guilt again. I want to spare you that pain... so I will fight for you."

A slight smile tugged at her rosy lips. "Thank you... but if it comes down to it, I will fight, whether you like it or not. At least let me help in the ways that I can."

She held both of her hands out in front of her and he felt her magic rising again, growing even stronger as it came to the fore. He nodded and she pressed her palms to his chest, her hands warming his black armour where they connected. Her magic crawled over him and he didn't fight it. He allowed it to seep into his flesh and down to his bones, healing him and gifting him with strength.

Rosalind whispered words he didn't understand and withdrew her hands. She took a few steps backwards, placing distance between them, and closed her eyes. Her blonde hair fluttered around her shoulders and her lips moved silently, forming words. She turned her hands palms upwards and lowered her head. Twin pinpricks of light glittered into existence above her palms and grew. They split into two and each of those into two again, and then two again, their brightness chasing back the darkness and stinging his eyes.

She lifted her head and opened her eyes, staring straight at him. Silver sparkled in the blue of her irises, illuminating them.

She mouthed another word.

The bright purple orbs shot off in all directions, three of them whizzing around him.

Darkness descended again.

Rosalind wavered on her feet and he caught her before she collapsed, tucking her against his side.

"What spell was that?" He slowly became aware of the fact that she had used high-level magic around him and he hadn't felt the darkness pushing at him. He had felt only awe at her power and the beauty of it.

"Trackers," she murmured and sagged against him. "Scanning the forest."

She felt weak in his arms, frail and vulnerable, and every male instinct he possessed demanded that he protect her and take her somewhere safe, where the demons would never find her.

"These trackers are linked to you?"

She nodded.

"Got to control them." She stiffened against him and then swiftly turned in his arms and clutched his shoulders, her sparkling blue-silver eyes locking with his and her fear shooting through him. "Too many demons, Vail. Coming from all directions. We must go. Now. I will slow them down."

"No!" he barked.

Bright purple light blazed in the distance, massive orbs of it exploding from the trees and shaking the earth.

Nature bared her fangs at Vail.

Rosalind cried out and he covered her mouth, silencing her scream of agony.

He growled. "Sever the spell, Rosalind, and do it now."

She slumped in his arms, out cold. Vail could smell the demon blood pervading the forest, could feel nature's wrath over the destruction of her beauty. Rosalind had failed to tell him the truth of her spell. The orbs had been more than trackers. They had been missiles.

He cursed her, lifted her into his arms and ran with her through the forest, his senses on high alert.

They were closing in on the edge of the forest. Once there, he could keep teleporting vast distances until they hit the edge of the Fifth Realm. Hopefully, they could walk through the border, but if they couldn't, Rosalind might be able to use her magic to reverse the spell. He looked down at her in his arms. If she woke.

He clutched her closer and broke out of the woods and onto the black plain stretching for miles around it, and skidded to a halt.

Demons.

They formed a line four warriors deep and one hundred warriors wide before him, blocking his path.

Too many for him to handle alone.

Too many for him to fight while Rosalind lay unconscious and vulnerable.

Bruan stepped forwards, his green helmet rising like a thorny crown atop his head, and sneered at him, flashing fangs. He hefted his broadsword onto his thickly-muscled bare shoulder and growled.

"Surrender, Prince Vail, and I will consider sparing the witch."

Vail hissed, baring his fangs, his pointed ears extending and flattening against the sides of his head. He mentally commanded his black armour to complete itself, forming his spiked helmet. The black scales thickened and smoothed as they crawled up his neck and across his head, coming to a point over his nose and flaring back into several dragon-like horns.

He clutched Rosalind to him with one arm and threw his other one forwards, sending a dozen demons flying through the air. The rest roared and broke rank, barrelling towards him and knocking their king in the process. Bruan's black leathery wings erupted from his back and he unleashed a furious snarl as he began to grow in size, his painted white horns curling around and flaring forwards beside his temples.

Vail teleported.

He landed in the middle of the glade near the lake and set Rosalind down against the gentle slope of a tree trunk.

"Wake up, Little Wild Rose," he whispered and she murmured. He gently caressed her cheek, his focus split between her and the woods around them, scouring it for a sign the demons were coming.

They were still in the forest. He could sense the disturbance in nature they caused and the trees still refused to bloom and light the woods.

Rosalind's eyelids fluttered and he breathed a sigh as she lifted them and looked up at him. The haze in them quickly evaporated, replaced by sharpness and a glimmer of horror.

"Breathe, Little Wild Rose." Vail rubbed her shoulders, monitoring her colliding emotions and her rocketing heartbeat. "You did what was necessary to protect us but now you will allow me to do what I feel is necessary… you will not fight. You will only use your power to protect yourself. Do you understand?"

She began to nod.

"How sweet." The deep male voice rumbled through the woods and Vail looked over his shoulder at Bruan where he stood flanked by four large warriors and growled. "Perhaps I will seize the witch and use her as I had intended… to control you and have you take the elf kingdom for me."

Vail shot to his feet, turning at the same time to face Bruan. "Never. I will never allow you to harm my people."

"*Your* people?" Bruan laughed. "You already harmed them more than I ever could, Mad Elf Prince."

Vail snarled at him and called his twin black blades into his hands.

"You are weak. I will defeat you here, seize your whore mate, and you will follow my orders if you want her to live. You will take your kingdom." Bruan twisted his broadsword, clutched it in both hands, and pointed it at Vail. "You will kill your brother."

Rosalind clambered to her feet behind him. "Don't listen to him, Vail. You're strong. We can defeat him and we will be free."

Free.

No one controlled him.

He was free.

He was master.

He would defeat this wretched demon and send him back to the Devil.

CHAPTER 28

Vail teleported and dropped out of the air behind King Bruan, landing silently on the soft short grass. He immediately kicked off, taking on the largest of the demon warriors escorting the king. The enormous dark-haired male snarled, his green eyes flashing fire, and swung his immense broadsword at Vail.

Light traced over Vail's body and he disappeared again, reappearing behind the male. He swept his twin black blades down the demon's back. The demon arched forwards, roaring as blood burst from the deep wounds and he stumbled into his comrade. Vail growled in satisfaction and attacked again, not giving the male a chance to recover. Their size and strength made them formidable foes at the best of times, and Vail was still weak from teleporting Rosalind a great distance. He couldn't afford to give them a chance to attack him.

He thrust forwards with one blade. The second demon struck it with his broadsword, knocking it upwards, the force of the blow ringing through Vail's sword and numbing his hand through his armour.

Vail lashed out with his other black blade, plunging it deep into the first male's back and straight out of his stomach. He yanked it sideways, splitting the male open, and teleported just as the second demon struck again.

Vail reappeared a short distance away in time to see the male's broadsword strike the grass where he had been standing, a blow that would have taken him down, giving the demons the opportunity to capture him. He snarled and the slats on his helmet came forwards, covering the lower half of his face.

His armour was strong against their weapons, but they could still knock him unconscious. He needed to be more careful.

For Rosalind's sake.

She stood with her back pressed against a tree, muttering a spell that formed a shimmering bubble around her, protecting her from the other two demons heading her way.

Vail growled, sent his blades away and rushed the one nearest him, tackling the male to the ground and teleporting with him. He reappeared high above the forest, pressed his feet to the demon's stomach, and used every ounce of his strength in a kick that propelled the male back to earth at a staggering speed. A portal formed beneath the demon but not soon enough. He crashed into a tree, sending leaves bursting into the air.

The world came rushing up towards Vail. He fell backwards through the air, his focus on Rosalind, and teleported at the last minute, appearing between her and the other demon. He kicked off and called his blades to his hands. The male blocked his first strike with the black leather and metal vambrace protecting his right forearm and launched a fist at him. Vail ducked beneath it and grunted when the male's unseen uppercut connected hard with his stomach, launching him into the air and knocking the wind from him.

"Vail!" Rosalind broke cover and shot a spell at the demon who had struck him, sending the male spinning through the air and into the trees.

Vail teleported and appeared in the male's path. He slashed with both blades as the demon reached him, slicing straight through his neck and sending his head toppling across the grass.

King Bruan roared.

Rosalind screamed.

Vail's heart stopped.

He snarled and teleported back to the glade. Rosalind fought hard, blasting spell after spell at the three demon males and clutching her side. Blood dripped from between her fingers.

Vail saw red.

He roared and launched himself at the three demons, taking them all on at once. Darkness welled up inside him and he welcomed it, goading the mad beast into rising, sure that he would retain control this time and not harm Rosalind, because every part of him wanted to protect her.

More demons appeared and he welcomed them too, relished the pain as they rained blows on him and the scent of blood as it filled the air. He took two out with ease, cutting them down at the same time with thrusts straight through their chests. Two more appeared to take their place and Vail killed them too, spinning on his heel to decapitate one before he had even finished teleporting and slashing the black wings of the other one, hobbling him before skewering him in the chest with both blades.

Pain erupted in his side and across the back of his skull, and Vail growled, the sound low and feral as his temper turned, the darkness within him rising to the fore. He teleported out of the centre of the fray and reappeared at the edge. His gaze darted to Rosalind and a momentary flicker of light illuminated his heart as he saw she was safe, nestled against the tree and protecting herself again, her wound no longer bleeding.

He stared into her wide eyes and then averted his when he saw the pain in them and knew she experienced it because of him. Not only because she could feel every blow he received, but because he was killing in front of her.

He didn't want her to see more death.

"I am sorry, Little Wild Rose. Close your eyes," he whispered and felt her gaze leave him. "This will all be over soon."

King Bruan laughed.

Vail fixed him with a deadly glare, narrowing his violet and black eyes on the demon male, and readied his weapons.

The wretched demon had five escorts now, but three were injured.

Vail bared his fangs and targeted them. He dropped his left blade and it buried itself point down in the grass just as he threw that hand forwards, scattering the demons with a telekinetic blast. One took the brunt of the blow and screamed in agony as a branch impaled him through the chest. Two more ended up sprawled out in the woods, battered and bruised from crashing through the trees. Nature turned her glare on Vail and he mentally apologised, vowing he would heal all that he harmed.

King Bruan teleported.

The other two demons followed his lead.

Vail pulled his second blade free of the earth and turned in the glade, his senses reaching in all directions, scouring the air for any trace of them. Darkness shimmered off to his right. He teleported there, appearing barely seconds after the demon began to emerge.

He slashed down the male's back between his wings. The demon battered him with them, each blow bruising him to his bones, and Vail backed off, gaining the space he needed. The second demon appeared right behind him and struck him hard across the back of his head. Vail teleported.

The demon grabbed him and went with him. Vail clawed at his hand, forcing the male to release him mid-teleport, and reappeared without him. The demon would live, but there was a high chance he would appear many miles from this place.

Something slammed into Vail's stomach, knocking him back several steps into a tree, and then struck his throat, pinning him to the trunk. Bruan. The demon king's claws pressed into Vail's neck as he clutched it, the scent of his own blood joining that of the demons' in the air.

King Bruan grinned and began to squeeze. Vail tried to teleport and failed. The last demon had drained his strength by forcing him to teleport with him. He growled and cursed the demon, and then cursed Bruan when he squeezed harder, the crushing force of his grip stealing Vail's breath and making his vision wobble.

"Let him go, you bloody bastard!" Bright red light filled the glade.

King Bruan slammed into him and they both growled. Bruan hauled him away from the tree by his throat and hurled him across the glade at Rosalind where she stood in the centre of it, twin dark purple orbs suspended above her palms. She ducked to avoid him and he hit the tree and slid down it, landing in a heap at its base.

"You fight him… then you have to fight me too." She threw her hands forwards, unleashing the spell.

King Bruan dodged both orbs but his comrades weren't as lucky. The two orbs split and struck them all, exploding on impact and filling the air with clouds of black ash and the stench of death.

Bruan looked over his shoulder at the places where his men had been and were now little more than dust, and then looked back at Rosalind, rage burning in his green eyes.

His painted horns curled around, flaring forwards, and his body began to expand, his muscles growing as he doubled in size. He flared his enormous black wings out, filling the glade with them, and swung his blade at Little Wild Rose.

Vail shoved to his feet. "Rosalind, run!"

She swept her hands forwards and a bright blue-white shimmering dome formed before her. Bruan's sword struck it and bounced off, but it didn't deter the demon. He drew up to his full height and swung again.

Vail grabbed Rosalind and teleported with her, moving her to the other side of the glade. He growled when she tried to get past him to fight, called his swords to him and turned on the demon king. His knees wobbled, his grip loosening as the effort of teleporting Rosalind took its toll on his remaining strength. He clenched his jaw and tightened his grip on his swords, forcing himself to stand tall and refusing to fall to Bruan's blade.

A slow smile spread across Bruan's face.

The wretch thought he had won.

Vail narrowed his eyes on the demon.

He would taste defeat this day.

The Fifth Realm would need a new king when this battle was through.

Vail's knees weakened again.

Bruan grinned and launched himself at Vail. The wretched demon had been waiting for him to show his weakness again, biding his time until Vail was at his most vulnerable.

He reached behind him to push Rosalind back and a chill bolted through him.

She wasn't there.

He turned took look over his shoulder at the place where she should have been and then swung his gaze back to Bruan and froze right down to his heart and marrow as she appeared between them, swinging her hands forwards to unleash the two black orbs she held.

"Rosalind!" Vail sent his blades away and reached for her but everything seemed to slow, his movements sluggish and his muscles stiff, refusing to respond as his heart burst into action, sprinting at a million miles per hour against his ribs and hurting with each beat.

Rosalind's spells flew and struck true, slamming straight into Bruan's broad bare chest and turning his skin black and strewn with bright orange cracks that glowed like fire.

Vail stretched and managed to grasp the back of her dress. He focused and light traced over his body as he pulled her back into his arms. She gasped and darkness swallowed them.

Together with pain.

Pain so fierce that it burned him to ashes inside, blazing like an inferno in the left side of his ribs but also in his right, duller there.

He reappeared on the other side of the glade and stared down at Rosalind.

She lay slumped in his arms, her blonde hair red with the blood that pumped from the deep wound in the left side of her chest. Crimson flowed over her skin, stark against its pale beauty.

Tears stung his eyes, burning as fiercely as his heart.

Darkness descended.

He laid Rosalind down and snarled as he turned on King Bruan. He didn't give the demon a chance to defend himself. He teleported above the demon, dropped onto his back with his legs around his waist, and twisted hard, sending the large male slamming into the ground. He bared his fangs and growled as he raked his black claws down the bases of the demon's wings, severing tendon and slicing through bones.

Bruan roared and bucked. Vail dug the claws of his left hand into the demon's wing and anchored himself. He grabbed the other wing with his right hand, pressed his feet into Bruan's back and pulled with all of his might until the wing snapped free. Bruan's pained cry was music to Vail's ears. He bared his fangs on a hiss and ripped the male's other wing away. Blood cascaded from the ragged wounds on the demon's back, staining all of him red.

Vail needed more.

Rosalind's heart laboured in his ears.

Her pain and fear flowed through him.

This demon would experience the same pain and the same fear.

He would die for what he had done to Vail's mate.

Vail growled and grasped the demon's horns. The male bucked again, almost throwing him this time. He pressed his knees into the demon's broken shoulders, pinning him down with his weight and pulled hard on the horns, yanking the male's head back. They refused to give.

He pressed one clawed hand against the back of Bruan's head and snarled as heat scalded him. The black caused by Rosalind's spells was spreading, creating fiery cracks in the male's skin. Incinerating him. The darkness within him purred in approval of her magic and commanded him to finish the male, to bathe in his blood and bask in his victory.

Vail grasped Bruan's head and bashed it against the ground, tugging on his right horn on the up and shoving it forwards on the down. Bruan struggled beneath him, writhing and trying to claw at him. His actions turned sluggish as Vail kept up his assault. The horn finally cracked and Vail grinned, satisfaction humming in his veins, and snapped it free. Bruan roared in agony.

Vail silenced him with his claws, running them deep across his throat, severing tendons and cutting through his vocal cords.

Blood drenched his hand and he still needed more. He needed to make the demon pay for what he had done to Rosalind. He would make the demon pay.

He grabbed Bruan's head and the male didn't resist.

Vail looked down at him, cocked his head to one side, and frowned.

Dead.

He growled and shoved to his feet, and scoured the glade for more demons. There would be more. He would kill them too.

There were no demons for him to fight.

He stood in the middle of the glade, darkness running through his veins, demanding satisfaction. There were more demons in the forest. He would hunt them and toy with them before killing them. They would all pay for trying to control him.

They would all pay for harming his Little Wild Rose.

Little Wild Rose.

He stilled, the darkness in him fading as he recalled why it had taken him, and turned slowly on the spot to face her.

Tears burned the back of his eyes and his strength left him, sending him to his knees.

She lay across the glade, the grass around her stained red with her blood, her skin ashen like starlight.

"Rosalind," he whispered and dragged himself to her, fighting back the tears as he reached out to her through their bond.

Her pain tore at him, cutting him to pieces inside.

Her heart stuttered.

"No," he murmured and shook his head, sending tears spilling down his cheeks. He pulled her into his arms and rocked her as she stared up at him with dull blue eyes.

Her fingers flexed and he took hold of her hand, clutched it to his lips and breathed in her comforting scent of wild blooms.

Her heart stuttered again.

She smiled weakly.

"No," he snarled as he sensed the link between them fading and pulled her closer, squeezing her to his chest. "Do not leave me, Little Wild Rose."

He drew back again and looked her over. She was immortal now, but the blade had pierced her heart. Even an immortal couldn't survive such a wound. She had magic though.

"You cannot leave me. I will not let you. You promised me forever." He kissed her hand again and then released it and pressed his palm to her chest, trying to remember how to slow bleeding so he could give her a chance to live. "You have magic. You can heal yourself."

She shook her head and tears streamed down her temples.

Her fear flowed over him and he took her hand again, sensing her need for him to comfort her.

"Do not leave me," he whispered and pressed his forehead against hers. "I cannot live without you. You promised me forever."

She slowly tipped her head back, brought her mouth to his and softly kissed him.

Goodbye.

He kissed her, pouring every ounce of his love for her into it, and then broke away from her. "I will not let you die. I will save you."

She smiled again, love shining in her dull eyes but no trace of hope. He wiped her tears away and then dealt with his own, scrubbing his bloodied hands across his face.

"It's alright, Vail," she murmured, her soft voice quiet and weak. "I knew this was coming. I could never promise to be with you forever... but I can promise I will love you forever."

It wasn't enough for him. He needed forever with her. Not forever with a memory of her.

Tears lined her blue eyes again.

Blood lined her lips.

"I wanted it so much," she whispered, her voice fading more with each word she spoke. "Even when I knew I could never have forever with you."

Her heart stopped.

Vail threw his head back and roared.

CHAPTER 29

Vail laid Rosalind down on the soft short grass in the centre of the glade she had loved so much, having removed the demon king's body from its boundaries, purifying it for her and returning it to how it had been when they had been here together.

The blossoms in the trees began to glow again, their faint light casting a pure white glow over Rosalind.

Little Wild Rose.

She would have that forever with him that she wanted and he would have forever with her.

His mate.

He kneeled beside her and held her hands, staring down at her beautiful face.

Vail drew in a deep breath, exhaled it, and closed his eyes. He focused on his connection to nature, mentally apologising to her for all the harm they had done to her beloved trees and plants as he fostered it, slowly pouring all of his strength into forging a strong link between them. It had to work.

Rosalind had asked him once if he could heal people as he healed nature.

Rosalind was nature.

She was one of her most beautiful creations.

It had to work.

He released her hands, laying them on her stomach, and pressed one palm to her chest and one to her forehead.

He channelled everything he could into her, doing exactly as he did when he healed wood and earth. The drain on his power was instantaneous, sapping his strength and scalding his bones until he trembled uncontrollably. Darkness crept into the corners of his mind and it began to spin and twirl, his grip on consciousness slipping as he gave everything to Rosalind. Crippling pain stabbed along his nerve endings, making them scream in agony, but he held on, his focus locked on Rosalind and saving her.

Bringing her back to him so they could have their forever.

After everything he had been through, countless centuries of pain and suffering that had driven him mad and killed all hope within his heart, he had finally broken the shackles of his past and had found something good. Something worth living for. He would not let death take that from him.

When darkness swallowed him for a second, it severed the connection between him and nature, halting his work. He had given everything he could and surely he would be rewarded for it. He opened his eyes, expecting to see Rosalind's smile as she came awake.

She lay still, her chest unmoving, their link still cold, forming an abyss within him that threatened to swallow him whole.

No.

Vail growled, moved both hands to her chest and pressed them against her sodden black dress. Fresh blood pooled around them and crept along the gaps between his fingers. He frowned and funnelled power into her again, using every last shred of it and drawing on all his reserves, giving everything to her until his muscles turned to liquid beneath his skin and his bones to ashes, fire seared his mind and blood poured from his nose.

She still didn't wake.

Tears flowed down his cheeks and he curled his hands into fists and collapsed over her, resting his head on her stomach, his shoulders shaking as he fought each sob that tried to escape him.

"Little Wild Rose," he whispered and looked at her face, imploring her to hear him and return to him.

A breeze stirred the trees and the blooms glowed brighter, nature mocking him with their light and how they danced, so alive and beautiful.

He wanted his mate alive and beautiful again.

He had failed her.

The darkness within him was too strong. It had tainted and destroyed his deepest connections to nature, so she would no longer grant him the power to save Rosalind.

But he couldn't give up on her.

She deserved to live.

She deserved forever in this world.

He didn't.

If he couldn't have forever with her, then she would have forever without him. She would live in his place because this world needed her more than it needed him. She was good and light. He was evil and darkness.

He rose off her and stared all around him at the trees. He dug his fingers into the grass and the earth, clutching it in his fists, feeling nature flowing around him.

Life flowing around him.

Rosalind deserved that life flowing through her.

"Please," he whispered, his lips trembling as tears blazed hot trails down his cheeks. "Hear me. Hear my wish… mother nature. Take my life in exchange for that of my ki'ara. She is more worthy of living in your world and she is connected to you just as I am. I willingly give my life for hers. Destroy me and save her. Please."

He looked down at Rosalind and blinked, clearing his eyes so he could see her.

"Please." It had to work. "She deserves life. My beautiful mate."

Cold swirled around him, chilling him to the bone, and the trees swayed, their light and life still mocking him. Nature was going to deny him, and he would die here anyway, with his mate where he belonged.

"Then take my life anyway, because I do not wish to live without her."

Heat rushed over him like a tender caress and he looked at the glade.

Plants burst from the grass, growing wildly, their colourful flowers blossoming and withering in the blink of an eye, only to be replaced by another wave of blooms.

Fine mist curled around him and sparkled like a rainbow in the bright glow from the trees that reached above him, their branches stretching towards each other, forming a canopy above him and Rosalind that shut out the darkness.

Vines crawled over his black armour and over Rosalind, twining through her hair. They caressed up his sides and over his shoulders, and tiny blossoms formed on their stems, the same pale blue flowers that grew on the castle in his kingdom. They glowed and their light traced over his body, increasing the heat rushing through him, filling him with strength.

He felt the power flow through him, the connection he had always possessed that had always been stronger than Loren's for some reason.

Flowers continued to burst into bloom only to die a second later, their fragile hold on life speaking to him as he placed his hands on Rosalind's chest and tried to give her back what had been taken from her.

He closed his eyes and funnelled all of the power flowing through him into her, using it to heal her damaged heart.

It stuttered back into life and he bit back a sob as it began to beat and she gasped her first breath.

Vail kept channelling everything into her, giving her all of his strength, determined to heal her fully before nature took its toll for the use of her power.

That power dwindled before he could finish his work, his connection with nature fading and the vines covering his shoulders and legs wilting away.

"No." He tried to grab them but they turned to ashes in his fingers.

Rosalind's heart beat weakly.

He wasn't sure how long it would hold on for before it gave out again. He wasn't sure why nature hadn't taken the life he had offered. He didn't have time to question either.

He pulled Rosalind into his arms and focused all of his remaining power on undoing the barrier surrounding the Fifth Realm and unlocking the portal to his rooms in the castle of the elf kingdom. Pain rippled through him, tearing at his muscles and lashing his bones, and he ground his teeth against it and held his focus, forcing his way through the walls that stood between him and where he needed to be in order to save Rosalind.

The barrier gave and it took most of his remaining strength to undo the locks he had placed on the portal to his rooms, sealing the elf kingdom to him. The moment it opened, he teleported, hoping he would have enough power to make it with Rosalind draining him.

He landed hard on his knees on the dark stone floor in a room now unfamiliar to him but painfully familiar at the same time.

Light streamed in through the tall arched windows to his right, where his large bed stood against the dark stone wall. He stumbled onto his feet and carried Rosalind there, setting her down on the dusty purple covers.

He brushed the tangled strands of her bloodied blonde hair from her face, pressed a kiss to her brow when she moaned, and whispered, "I will be right back, Little Wild Rose. I will bring you Olivia and she will heal you."

She reached for him and he took hold of her hands, pressed a kiss to both, and laid them on her stomach.

Stepping back from her was one of the hardest things he had ever had to do but he forced himself to place the necessary distance between them. Her life depended on his brother's female and Vail was weak right now, liable to stay here with Rosalind if he didn't push himself away from her and hold himself at a distance. It would be all too easy to surrender to his need to comfort her and she would slip away from him again. He refused to squander this second chance that nature had given him, this precious gift of his mate and a shot at forever with her.

He focused on the connection to his brother, wobbling on his feet. He had to find him fast, before anyone else discovered that he was in the castle. They would kill him without waiting to hear why he was here. Only Loren could stop that from happening.

And only Olivia could save Rosalind.

He sensed his brother in the great hall.

Vail teleported into the centre of it.

Right into the middle of a grand affair.

The ornately carved white wooden pews of the enormous hall were filled with females and males dressed elegantly in their finest attire, and some of them were not elves. Demons and mortals sat amidst the gathered, along with a few from shifter species.

Vail started down the long wide aisle between the towering black columns that supported the vaulted white ceiling. Light streamed in through the tall arched windows that lined both sides of the hall, illuminating the beautiful carvings of nature and life on the black columns, scenes that had fascinated him as a youth.

Each silent step pulled him back further into his past, to a time when he had walked this same path with his head held high and pride in his heart as all around him had turned to admire him and had whispered in awe.

A thousand pairs of eyes swung his way, a few startled gasps and fearful murmurs escaping their owners as they settled on him. None admired him now. All feared him. He couldn't blame them, not when he wore the blood of his enemies on his skin and his armour.

He flashed his fangs at them and looked for Olivia.

She stood at the head of the aisle, wearing a pale blue elven gown with silver metal curves and swirls forming a corset over her torso. Loren stood beside her, dressed in his finest black tunic with rich purple embroidery, trousers and his knee-high boots.

Behind Loren, Bleu growled and called his armour, replacing his formal attire with it. He drew his spear out of the air and ran at Vail.

Vail sensed several guards coming up fast behind him too but he couldn't move as he stared straight into Loren's wide purple eyes and felt surprise ripple through him too as he realised something dreadful.

He had just interrupted their wedding ceremony and Olivia's coronation.

Beside Olivia, the huntress he knew as Sable tossed her flowers, hitched her purple dress up and reached for her friend, and the demon king Thorne stood and reached for her. Intending to teleport both of them.

No. He would not allow them to take Olivia away.

Vail silently apologised to his brother for ruining what should have been a beautiful moment and teleported between Sable and Olivia. He knocked the huntress's hand away from Olivia, turned and grabbed the female before she could run to her mate. Olivia gasped as they disappeared.

Loren's bellow of fury echoed through the castle as they reappeared in Vail's apartments, his rage flowing through the bond between them. His brother would be coming for him.

He didn't have much time.

He set Olivia down and she shoved him in the chest, knocking him backwards. She swung at him and he barely dodged her fist, his movements sluggish as the last of his strength drained away.

"Listen to me," he snarled and she hit him this time, her fist connecting hard with his jaw and sending him stumbling towards the bed. He growled and shook his head to clear it, and held his hand up to Olivia. "Save Rosalind."

She froze mid-swing and her dark eyes darted to the bed and widened. She pulled the skirt of her pale blue dress up, rushed to the bed and checked Rosalind over from head to toe before pressing her fingers to her throat.

"Rosalind," she whispered and his mate's eyes fluttered open and slipped shut again. Olivia turned on him. "I need to know something important. Is she—"

Loren appeared with a roar, grasped Vail around the throat and teleported again. Vail didn't fight him. He let his brother slam him against the stone wall and pin him there, throttling him, and stared beyond him to Rosalind because she was all that mattered right now. His brother could kill him for all he cared, as long as his mate saved Little Wild Rose.

"Can you save her?" he croaked.

Loren looked over his shoulder at Olivia and his grip loosened as his gaze fell on Rosalind. "What is that damned sorceress doing here?"

Vail growled at him for speaking about his female in such a disrespectful manner and Loren turned wide eyes on him, the shock in them increasing.

"No," Loren whispered and shook his head.

"I need your help, Vail," Olivia said, speaking over her mate, and pressed a wad of material against Rosalind's chest.

"Anything." He stared at his Little Wild Rose, willing her to keep fighting. She was strong. Brave. Stubborn. She couldn't die.

"You have to answer my next question truthfully." Olivia looked at him and he nodded. "Is Rosalind your ki'ara?"

Vail stilled and felt Loren's fierce gaze on him, sensed his curiosity through their link.

He looked back at Rosalind. Brave Little Wild Rose. Beautiful Little Wild Rose.

His mate.

"Yes."

Olivia smiled. "Have you bonded with her?"

He stilled again and frowned at her. "Why must you know?"

Rosalind moaned in pain, the sound tearing at him, compelling him to shirk his brother's grip and go to her. He shoved Loren away, earning a growl from his brother, and was by her side a heartbeat later, kneeling on the bed and clasping her left hand.

"I am here, Little Wild Rose. You will be well again soon. I have brought you to Loren's female. She is a doctor, remember? Your friend. She can save you." He brushed his free fingers across her brow. It was damp and too warm, burning beneath his touch.

He looked across her at Olivia, silently imploring her to help Rosalind.

"You may have the power to do that yourself if you would answer my question," she said.

He frowned at her, trying to understand what she was saying. He had no such power. He had tried to heal her and he had failed. Only nature's power funnelled through him had given her a second chance, and that chance was slipping away while Olivia questioned him.

"Answer her," Loren growled.

He nodded. "We are bonded."

"Transfer her injuries to you." Loren strode across the room and Vail could only blink at him. He could do such a thing? Loren seemed to read that question in his eyes and nodded. "It is a power all mated males have. You can take some of her injuries."

"Not all of them," Olivia put in. "They're too severe. It might kill you. You just need to share the burden."

Vail nodded, more than willing to bear the pain to spare Rosalind and cursing himself for not having known that he could do such a thing. He could have helped her in the glade.

"Lay down next to her and change into something a little more comfortable while I take care of Rosalind." Olivia pointed to the bed and he did as instructed, laying on his back beside Rosalind and looking over at her.

Her chest rose and fell at a slow rhythm, her raspy breaths loud in his ears as her heart struggled.

He sent his armour away, replacing it with his trousers. Olivia tore Rosalind's dress down the middle, exposing her underwear, and Vail growled at Loren, warning him not to look at her.

"Mated… and was meant to be married by now," Loren bit out and took the ruined clothes from his female.

The door burst open and Bleu entered, his spear at the ready and his violet eyes flashing with a hunger for violence.

Loren held his hand up, halting the elf commander. "Bring medicine and blood."

Bleu cast him a frown and then looked back at Vail, and his eyes drifted to Rosalind and widened. Vail growled again, warning the unmated male to take his eyes off his female, her words about Bleu instantly filling his head. This male had looked upon her with an appreciative eye before, believing her skilled and as impressive as he knew her to be, and no doubt desiring her because of it.

"Rosalind." Bleu turned a black glare on Vail. "What did you do to her, you bastard?"

Loren grabbed the male's shoulders and shoved him back against the arched wooden door, slamming it shut.

"Rosalind is Vail's mate. We are trying to save her. You are slowing us down. Bring medicine and blood, Bleu. I will not ask again," Loren snarled and Bleu flicked his brother a glance, and then looked at him properly, disbelief in his eyes.

"I will not leave you alone with this fiend, My Prince." Bleu tossed a glare at Vail, and amidst the fury in it was pain that had Vail looking away.

He vividly remembered the night he had slaughtered most of the legion that he had been leading at the time he had met Kordula. Bleu had lost countless friends that one dark night and had come close to losing his life too, and the male couldn't forgive Vail for what he had done then, or through the centuries that had followed.

Vail couldn't blame him.

He regretted the night he had turned on his own men, killing many before they fled him, but it had been the only way of sparing the others, and sparing the kingdom the wrath and reign of Kordula.

He slipped his fingers into Rosalind's, clutched her hand and looked at her, focusing on her.

His brave little female.

She had fought for him. She had given her life for him. He would take her pain away. He would save her.

He closed his eyes and focused on their bond. Loren's presence grew stronger and his hand on Vail's shoulder was a welcomed comfort.

"Just think about taking away her pain and drawing it into you. Only take a little at a time. Do not try to take it all, Brother."

Brother.

He squeezed his eyes against the tears that rose into them on hearing that softly spoken word, laced with affection that touched him deeply.

Vail focused and did as his brother had instructed, the opposite to what he had attempted to do in the glade. Rather than trying to channel his power into her, he focused on drawing her into him through their bond.

He opened his eyes and stared at her profile, willing her to come back to him.

The link between them opened and he flowed into it, felt himself becoming part of her and marvelled at how he could pinpoint her injuries, feeling them echo on his body. He breathed slowly and sought the first one, coaxing it to him.

He flinched with the first stab of pain close to his heart and tried to distance himself from it and what was to come, focusing on Rosalind instead of his own body. He bore the pain in silence as his organs ruptured and bones shattered where the blade had pierced her.

His flesh split open and blood pumped from the wound and clogged his throat. He kept his eyes on Rosalind, aware of only her as Loren and Olivia raced around him, sewing wounds on both him and Rosalind and bandaging them.

"Drink." Loren offered a canister of blood.

Vail refused to take his eyes from Rosalind. He couldn't. He needed to see her as colour began to spread across her ashen skin again and her heart grew stronger. He was healing her.

Saving her.

Just as she had saved him.

Loren growled and the next thing shoved in front of Vail's face was a bloodied wrist. His brother pressed it to his mouth and Vail wrapped his lips around the puncture wounds and drank, drawing Loren's strength into him.

Rosalind writhed on the purple covers, the hand that clutched his turning cold and clammy. She moaned and her face screwed up as fresh pain tore at his chest. He could take more for her. All of it. He would take all her pain away. Every last drop.

"Vail, stop." Olivia's voice swam in his ears.

He ignored her.

He needed to save Little Wild Rose.

He tried to take more of her injuries and cried out as his heart clenched in his chest and stuttered. Loren's blood spilled down his cheek and onto the covers beneath him.

"Enough," Loren snapped and tore Vail's hand away from Rosalind's.

Vail wanted to protest, wanted to growl and attack his brother for stopping him, but he had already gone too far.

Darkness swallowed him, his gaze still fixed on Rosalind and his heart filled with hope that he had saved her.

Because he didn't want to live in a world without her.

CHAPTER 30

Every inch of her hurt. Rosalind grimaced and tried to recall what she had done to deserve so much pain. Her chest was on fire. Her mind swam, dark ripples chasing through it, her thoughts colliding and denying her. Whatever she had done, it had been stupid and dangerous, that much she was sure.

Something flexed against her left hand.

She focused there and the numbness infesting her body slowly gave way, allowing her to feel the press of fingers against the back of her hand.

Vail.

She knew that soft grip, that gentle tenderness, and that warmth that now chased up her arm and through her body, bringing it back to life and pushing the pain away.

She swallowed to wet her parched throat and tilted her head towards him, becoming aware of the softness beneath her and the silky feel of fine fabric against her skin.

Her very bare skin.

Why was she only wearing her underwear?

Rosalind opened her eyes, squinting at first to allow them to become accustomed to the light. It was too bright, stinging her eyes and making them water. Where were they? Not in the woods. This was somewhere else.

Voices drifted around her, quiet and soft. One male and one female.

One familiar female.

She fluttered her eyes open and gasped as she saw Vail.

Bloody gashes covered his bare shoulders and his face, dark and scabbed, but still red raw around the edges. His skin was too pale, drawn of colour and life, stark against his dishevelled blue-black hair. She tried to roll onto her side to face him so she could brush her fingers across his cheek without releasing his hand and pain tore through her left side.

"Whoa there!" Gentle hands grasped her right shoulder and pinned her back to the bed.

Bed.

She looked up at the woman.

Olivia.

Strands of her dark hair hung forwards as she leaned over Rosalind, slipped from a rather elaborate hairstyle that seemed out of place on the woman she knew to be very neat and plain.

"No moving," Olivia said with a slight smile. "You're lucky to be alive."

Rosalind tried to swallow again but couldn't shift the lump in her throat. Olivia's smile widened and she reached towards something beside Rosalind's head and came back with a delicate blue glass goblet.

"Drink." Olivia offered it to her with one hand and helped her into a sitting position with her other, supporting her back.

Rosalind opened her mouth and bit back a sigh as cool water poured into her mouth and down through her body, quenching the flames. She drank the entire glass and Olivia's smile only widened.

"You're a better patient than he is."

Rosalind looked down at Vail. "What happened?"

"Vail took your injuries into himself to save you." The deep male voice drew her gaze to the owner and she gasped.

Mother earth, he looked frighteningly like Vail. If she had risked peeking at Prince Loren when she had helped Thorne with his war, she would have instantly recognised Vail as a prince of elves on meeting him.

Loren strode silently across the room, his violet eyes locked on his younger brother, and ran a hand through his shorter black hair, pushing it back from the pointed tips of his ears as he sighed.

"I am afraid he overdid it. I warned him not to attempt to take all of your injuries, but he has always had a propensity to ignore my warnings."

Rosalind brushed her thumb across Vail's and stared down at him. Bandages covered his chest and stomach, and wrapped around his left thigh too. All places where she had been wounded. She could remember it now. She had done something terribly dangerous, but not stupid. She had wanted to protect Vail from the demon king.

She wrapped her right arm tighter around herself, wincing as her ribs ached. Vail had stopped before taking all of her injuries, and she was glad of it. She didn't want to lose him. She had been so afraid she was going to die and go into the afterlife without him by her side. She had been so afraid of being separated from him and leaving him behind when he needed her, just as she needed him.

"Here." Olivia draped a purple robe around her, covering her.

She appreciated the kindness, even though she didn't care that she was sitting in front of her mate's brother in only her underwear. She only cared about Vail. He had risked everything by bringing her to this place, to Olivia, because he hadn't wanted to lose her and now she feared she might still lose him.

"Will he be alright?" She looked to Loren for the answer, feeling he was the one most likely to know it.

He had a bond with Vail.

Her own bond with him said he was in incredible pain.

"I have given him blood and administered medicines. He will heal in time."

She dropped her gaze back to Vail, leaned over and brushed her fingers across his damp cold forehead. "I can help. I can heal."

"No." Loren moved a step closer and Olivia claimed her shoulder again.

She looked at both of them, seeing in their eyes they weren't going to allow her to use her magic on Vail, but for different reasons.

Rosalind fixed her focus on Loren, needing to allay his fears before Olivia's.

"I've healed him before. He can take it. When I use magic around him, it doesn't always trigger an episode. Please. Let me help him." She held Loren's gaze, wishing he didn't look so much like his brother when he looked so healthy and Vail looked close to death. It hurt too much to look at him, so she looked away, pinning her focus back on Vail.

She caressed his cheek and decided that she didn't care about gaining permission. Vail needed her help and she was going to give it to him. No one told her what to do where he was concerned. She would do whatever it took to make him better and bring him back to her.

Loren sighed. "Very well. But you must not hurt yourself. My brother would be upset if you did after everything he has done to help you."

She nodded. He was right about that and she didn't want the first thing Vail did on waking to be chastising her. She wanted him to wake and kiss her, and make her feel that everything was going to be alright.

They had escaped a nightmare and could be together.

Rosalind lowered her hand to Vail's chest and closed her eyes. She muttered the strongest healing spell at her disposal and channelled it into him, seeking out wounds that were draining his strength and giving his natural healing abilities a shove to speed them along. She wavered, her strength draining as she struggled to heal a deeper wound.

"Enough," Loren snapped and she nodded and withdrew.

The remnants of the spell would continue to heal what she couldn't.

"You need to rest now." Olivia took hold of her shoulders and Rosalind allowed her to guide her down onto the bed again.

She sank against it and stared across at Vail. She squeezed his hand and his eyelids fluttered. Her heart fluttered with them, nerves rising as she tried to shut out the two other occupants of the room and focus on him.

"If you don't fight, I'm going to have to come into the afterlife and kick your behind. So, fight… okay?" She glanced at Loren, found him staring at her, and then back at Vail. A blush coloured her cheeks. "I don't think your brother likes me very much."

Loren cleared his throat and scrubbed the back of his neck.

"Come along, you." Olivia grabbed Loren's arm. "I think we should give them some peace and quiet now. Doctor's orders."

Rosalind smiled her thanks at Olivia as she pulled Loren away. He remained facing the bed as he walked backwards, his eyes glued to Vail, and she could understand his reluctance to leave his brother.

"I'll call should he wake. I won't let him leave without speaking with you. I swear it," she said and he nodded, his eyes briefly meeting hers before going back to his brother.

"I will post someone outside the door, or I will be just across the hall in my rooms there if you need me."

She nodded and Olivia opened the arched wooden door and dragged her elf prince out of it, closing it softly behind them.

Rosalind sagged against the dark purple covers and turned her face towards Vail again.

She shuffled closer to him, wincing as her ribs protested, and caressed his cheek, studying his face. The wounds on it looked better already, the surrounding skin no longer angry red. She dropped her hand to his bandaged chest and focused there, calling on her magic.

"Olivia told you to rest." His deep gravelly voice shattering the silence tore a gasp from her and her heart leaped into her throat.

She didn't withdraw her hand. There was little point. He had caught her fair and square and she wasn't going to deny that she had intended to use more of her power to heal him.

She stroked her fingers over the bandages, her gaze following them.

"Thank you," she whispered, feeling ridiculously awkward. "For… you know… saving my life."

He sighed, the sound laced with the fatigue she could sense in their link. "I could have spared you so much pain and suffering had I known as much about bonds as Loren does. I could have healed you right away."

She frowned. "You did heal me once, but you were far away from me at the time… in that place you go when the darkness is too strong. You probably don't remember it. I'm glad you didn't heal me this time though."

She felt his eyes shift to her face and looked up at him, her heart aching from the thoughts spinning through her mind.

"You might have died without Loren and Olivia's help."

He gave a small nod and tightened his grip on her hand, lifted his other hand and placed it over hers on his chest.

"Rosalind," he whispered, the husky quality of his voice sending a shiver through her and heating her to her core, gaining her full attention. "What did you mean in the glade when you said you had known it was coming and you couldn't have forever with me?"

Her eyes darted away, back to his chest, and she tried to ignore the fierce ache in her heart and the fear that rose within her, threatening to ruin this quiet moment with him. A moment she wanted to cherish, without fear of her future death tainting it.

"I thought my prediction had come true."

"Prediction?" He canted his head and frowned at her, his violet gaze boring into the side of her face, demanding she look at him.

She drew in a deep, painful, breath and gave him what he wanted, lifting her gaze to his and not hiding anything from him. Perhaps he could help her find a way around her little problem if she confided in him and shared the burden, the weight on her shoulders that had been pressing down on her for most of her life, controlling how she lived it.

"I was told by my grandmother that one day I would meet an elf prince and shortly after that I would die. Back in the glade… I didn't care that my prediction was coming true. I would have gladly died to save you. Now I fear that destiny still awaits me and I will end up separated from you."

His black eyebrows dipped lower and pained filled his beautiful amethyst eyes. "You did die."

Her eyes shot wide. "I what?"

"Your heart stopped," he said in a matter of fact tone that made her frown at him. He answered it with a smile, released her hand and slipped his arm beneath her, curling his hand over her waist and drawing her closer to him. "I tried to heal you, but it did not work. When it failed, I offered my life to nature in exchange for yours. Rather I die than you… but nature allowed me to live."

Her heart broke for her elf prince as he stared up into her eyes, his violet ones overflowing with confusion. He didn't understand why nature had allowed him to live and she felt for him, because she knew he honestly believed that he deserved to die for what he had done throughout his life. She shook her head, and vowed that she would use this second chance she had been given by nature to show him that he deserved to live and he deserved happiness, with her.

"Rather no one dies," she whispered and pressed a soft kiss to his lips, careful not to hurt him.

He brushed his lips across hers, his breath warm against them, and his hand on her waist tightened, drawing her closer still.

Rosalind smiled and pushed back. "You need to rest."

He frowned and sighed. "Very well."

She stared down into his eyes, lost in them and how they shone at her, filled with love and a smile, so different from the dark eyes that had looked at her with a hunger for violence and hatred all those weeks ago. That time felt like an eternity ago now, a distant and dark memory, together with all of her fears and all of the days she had lived with a prediction hanging over her head.

She had met her elf prince.

She had died.

And he had brought her back to him.

He had moved Heaven, Hell and Earth to keep her with him, and she would be eternally grateful to him for it and the forever she could now have with him.

She stroked his chest, her fingers playing with the ridges of the bandages that bound his wounds, marvelling that he let her do this now and was so relaxed around her, comfortably holding her against him, allowing her to be close to him when her magic wasn't in check.

"Rest," she said and pressed another quick kiss to his lips.

"I will," he breathed against her lips and she withdrew to wait for the but she could feel coming. "If you promise me something."

Not a but, an if, but still a clause.

"Anything," she whispered.

His lips twitched into a slight smile. She took everything she had thought about him and Loren back. Vail was far better looking. Beautiful. Charming. Hers.

"You must rest too, and *not* use your powers to heal me." His smile held even as hers fell and she huffed. Damned elf. She had a feeling it was going to be impossible to do anything without him knowing exactly what she intended before she could do it. "I have had blood and medicine. I will heal soon enough. Already my body is healing and repairing itself, growing stronger. You need not worry, Sweet Ki'ara."

She wanted to deny that she was worried but knew he would see straight through that too and see the truth in her eyes.

"Come." He drew her closer again and she snuggled into his side, resting her head gently on his shoulder to make sure she didn't hurt him.

She closed her eyes.

A smile curved her lips.

She was free.

Free of a curse. Free of captivity.

Free to love Vail and be with him.

Forever.

And she had the feeling that forever with her elf prince was going to be an interesting journey with never a dull moment.

A journey she couldn't wait to begin.

CHAPTER 31

Vail stared down at Rosalind, gently brushing the strands of gold from her face, clearing them away so he could see her. She wrinkled her nose and burrowed into the pillow, her fair hair a beautiful contrast against the deep purple material.

A breeze blew through the arched doors onto the balcony at his back, carrying the scent of flowers, but their perfume couldn't contend with Rosalind's one of wild roses.

He sighed and brushed another strand away, studying her as she slept, smiling to himself at times when he thought about her and how they had come to be in this place, laying together surrounded by quiet and infused with calm, at one with each other.

That calm would shatter whenever he thought about where they were, replaced by a dark commanding urge to wrap his arms around her and shield her from this place and the danger it held.

The wooden door across from his bed opened and his brother stepped inside, wearing the same formal attire as the last time he had seen him, even though it must have been more than a day since Vail had crashed his wedding.

Vail barely tamped down the desire to call his armour to protect himself and pull Rosalind into his arms. He forced himself to remain seated beside her, his back resting against the intricately carved wooden headboard.

Rosalind murmured in her sleep and frowned. He swept his fingers over her temple and down her cheek.

"Shh, Little Wild Rose. I will not let anything happen to you," he whispered to her and she settled.

Her sleep had been fitful, waking him more than once, and when he had felt strong enough to watch over her, he had shifted into his current position and had done just that. Whenever her dreams troubled her, he repeated the same process, soothing her with the same words. She always sighed and settled back into a deeper healing sleep.

Loren eyed her with darkness in his gaze.

"I warn you to be kind to her, lest you rouse my temper." Vail flicked him a glance.

Loren sighed. "Do you know she is the reason I did not reach you that day on the battlefield? She was the sorceress who drove you away."

No. He hadn't known that.

He might have cared once, it might have roused the darkness within him and made him want to lash out at her, but not anymore.

"It was her magic, not her, that drove me away. Perhaps it had been for the best. Perhaps destiny had driven us apart so it could bring us together." He dropped his gaze back to her and smiled. She had spoken of destiny and so had he. They had both had predictions about the other.

They had been born for each other.

"You are changed." Loren drew closer, coming to the foot of the bed.

Vail lifted his eyes back to him and nodded. "For the better, I hope?"

Loren's smile answered that question for him.

"I am sorry I interrupted your ceremony." Vail settled one hand on Rosalind's shoulder and the other in his lap.

His brother rubbed the back of his neck and shrugged. "There is nothing to apologise for, Vail. You needed me and I am glad that you came to me. I am glad you are here."

Vail looked away from him, unsure how to respond to that. His brother might be glad that he was here, and his brother's mate might be too, but the rest of the castle was not so kind. The elf commander, Bleu, had made it clear that he wasn't welcome or wanted.

This place was no longer his home.

He closed his eyes as pain welled up in his heart.

"Brother." Loren moved around the bed to stand beside him.

The pale sheer blue curtains of the tall arched doorway that led onto the balcony fluttered a short distance behind him, dancing on the breeze sweeping into the room, bringing the calming scent of nature inside to swirl around him together with Rosalind's sweet fragrance. Her scent chased some of the agony away, but the one of his homeland brought it back again. It was a scent he had thought he would never smell again, the unique fragrance of the blue flowers that bloomed on the vines that spread across the balcony of his room.

Loren sighed and moved closer, recapturing his attention. "Do not think things that pain you. You have your mate now and you are free. This should be a happy time."

Vail shook his head. "They say that happiness is fleeting. I have my mate, but I have no home."

Loren slumped onto the bed, sitting side on to him, and leaned forwards, resting his elbows on his knees. He looked across his shoulder at Vail, the hurt in his eyes echoing through their bond.

"I am speaking with the council—"

"But they want my blood," Vail interjected. "And I cannot blame them."

Loren reached across with his left hand and settled it on Vail's knee, and it felt strange to him. Such tender contact with his brother was another thing he had never thought he would have again. It was another thing that pained him in a way, but soothed him too.

"I am speaking to them and I will make them understand what happened to you," Loren said. "I will make them see that you did what was necessary to spare the kingdom. You sacrificed few for the many. They will see that."

"As your commander sees it?" Vail turned his focus back to Rosalind, stroking her silky hair to soothe himself. "He despises me, as does the council. None want me here but you, Brother."

Loren squeezed his knee and Vail appreciated his support, and his belief that he could convince the council and the entire elf kingdom to welcome him back, but he had become something of a realist over his years as a slave.

He had lost the part of him who had been able to dream wild things and hope when there was none.

"Perhaps it is best that I leave," Vail whispered.

"No," Loren snapped and took hold of his shoulder, gripping it hard enough that it hurt. The strength of it and Loren's desire to keep him with him, to force him to stay, moved Vail and he closed his eyes against the tears that rose into them. "I will make them see."

"Perhaps you will... perhaps we will be family again in time." He raised his chin and looked into his brother's eyes, seeing the tears in his echoed in them, his pain reflected back at him.

"We were always family, Vail. We never stopped being brothers." Loren pulled him into an embrace before Vail could respond, squeezing him tightly. "I am sorry I tried to kill you. If you hadn't told Olivia you wanted to die... if you hadn't taken her... I might have lost you."

Vail rested his chin on his brother's shoulder and closed his eyes as he wrapped his free arm around him. He had thought he would never do such a thing again, would never feel the strength of Loren's embrace, an embrace that had always told him the infinite depth of his brother's love for him.

"And I am sorry I tried to kill you. But I am not sorry you tried to kill me. I wanted to die." Vail pulled back and Loren frowned at him.

"And now?" His brother searched his eyes.

Vail glanced down at Rosalind and stroked his fingers across her fair brow, a smile curling his lips.

"Now I am like my Little Wild Rose and I desire only to live."

Vail huffed as Loren tugged him back into a harder embrace, squeezing the air from him and sending pain jolting through his healing injuries.

"I don't want to interrupt your bromance... but owie." Rosalind pushed herself up onto her elbow beside him and rubbed her left side. "Easy on the ribs."

Loren instantly released him. "My apologies."

She grumbled. "This bond thing can be a bitch."

"Good morning to you too, Little Wild Rose." Vail dropped a kiss on her forehead.

She sighed and rubbed sleep from her eyes. "It doesn't feel good. I'm sore... and you're upset about something."

Her blue gaze slowly slid to his brother and fierce silver stars sparked to life in it.

"You had better not be upsetting him. He's meant to be resting."

Loren held his hands up in surrender. "He was awake before I entered his chambers."

She turned her glare on Vail. He attempted a shrug and grimaced at the same time as she did as his ribs ached.

"You promised you would rest." She slowly shifted into a sitting position beside him and covered herself with the long purple robe, closing it over her chest.

"I was resting, but you were wriggling."

A beautiful blush coloured her cheeks. "I was dreaming."

"A nightmare?" He frowned and reached for her, and her blush deepened, her gaze leaping away from his. Not a nightmare judging by her reaction and how her pupils dilated, gobbling up her irises.

Loren cleared his throat and looked away.

"Just a dream," she muttered.

Vail growled under his breath, hunger stirring deep inside him. A dream he would fulfil as soon as he was able. His female needed, dreamed wicked things, and he would satisfy her.

"So what were you both talking about so loudly that you woke me when I was meant to be resting?" Her smile teased him and her words turned Loren uncomfortable.

"I did not mean to disturb you," his brother said and Vail held his hand up.

"Little Wild Rose has been awake longer than I had suspected." He caught her chin between his finger and thumb and made her look at him. "How long?"

She didn't attempt to look away. She stared deep into his eyes, her blue ones filled with understanding and love, and a touch of sorrow for him.

"Long enough." She took hold of his hand and brought it to her lips, pressing a kiss to it. "Until you feel this place is your home again, you have a home with me. Although… it's quite small and you might bang your head a lot because the ceilings are pretty low and the beams are very solid… and I will have to practice magic because a girl still needs her profession even when she's mated to a prince… but it has a nice garden and it's in the countryside, and—"

Vail pressed his finger to her lips, squashing them together to silence her. "It sounds wonderful."

She seized his hand, pulled it away from her mouth, and arched an eyebrow at him. "You're a terrible liar."

It had been worth a go, but she was right. He had never been very good at lying.

"It's the magic thing, isn't it?"

He shook his head, twisted his hand from her grip and caught her wrist, and pulled her to him for a kiss. Her magic bothered him at times, but he was growing accustomed to it and how it differed from dark magic.

She broke away from him. "What is it then?"

He tipped his head back, resting it on the headboard, and sighed. "I hate the mortal world."

"Well... you hated me once too." She said it with such sincerity in her eyes that the words lashed at him, cutting him deep.

Foolish little witch.

Vail slipped his arm around her waist and drew her closer again. "I never hated you, Little Wild Rose. I always loved you."

She smiled and pressed her hand to his chest, stopping him from drawing her in for another kiss.

"And I love you... and you'll love my little corner of the mortal realm. I promise."

He still wasn't sure about that, but he was willing to try to live in it, because he wanted to be wherever she was and she needed to be in that world, helping others and using her power for good. Perhaps he could find peace there as he had in the forest, surrounded by nature, slowly restoring his connection to it and purging the darkness from his soul, with Rosalind at his side.

His home was with her.

He dipped his head to kiss her.

Loren cleared his throat.

"I am still here," he said, his deep voice laced with a biting edge.

Rosalind blushed again, her cheeks blazing in a way that drew a smile from Vail.

"It is settled then," Loren said to Rosalind and she nodded, and Vail nodded too. "You will take care of my brother while I deal with the council... you *will* take care of him?"

She smiled and touched Loren's hand. "I will. I would never let anything happen to him. You can visit anytime you want... but alone... or with Olivia. Bleu isn't allowed to come."

Loren dipped his chin. "Agreed."

Vail's heart filled with light as he looked at his mate, his fair Rosalind, his Little Wild Rose, and saw the stunning depth of her love for him in her eyes and realised that his home truly was wherever she went. He would never part from her. They would always be together.

Just as destiny had desired.

Loren stood and squeezed his shoulder. "And when you marry, I shall crash your wedding."

Vail chuckled, the sound so alien that it startled him, and apparently startled his brother too.

"You cannot crash what you will be invited to attend, Brother," Vail said, brushing off how both Rosalind and Loren stared at him as if he had grown two heads, all because he had found his laugh again.

Rosalind had given it back to him.

His Little Wild Rose had given everything back to him.

His smile.

His laugh.

His heart.

She had filled his soul with light that held back the darkness and gave him the strength to keep fighting the beast within him.

She had shown him how to love again and how to live again.

She had given him everything.

She was his now, and he was hers.

And they would finally have their forever.

"Who says we're getting married?" Rosalind said in a flat tone, the link between them calm and devoid of her emotions and her face a picture of seriousness. "I don't recall you asking me to marry you."

Vail growled, dragged her against him and kissed her hard to silence her.

Loren sighed and teleported from the room, leaving him alone with his mischievous witch.

She moaned into his mouth, wrapped her arms around his neck and pulled him down on top of her, the ferocity of her kiss matching his passion. She nipped at his lower lip and he growled again, and pulled back before he gave in to the temptation to do the same to her, with his fangs.

Her blue eyes only held more temptation, the wide chasms of her pupils speaking of the desire he could feel in her now, flowing through their bond, demanding he kiss her again and satisfy her every need.

He lowered his head to do just that and she pushed a palm against his chest, stopping him. He growled at her.

"I thought you had something to ask me?"

Vail pressed his forehead to hers, his heart beating wildly in his chest, dark thoughts crowding the back of his mind. He squashed them and erased them, shoved them out of his head. This was no trick. This was no ploy to lure him into lowering his guard so she could hurt him. This was a reach for him and for reassurance, and he would give that to her and mean every word that he said so she could feel it in him and know he spoke from his heart.

"Little Wild Rose... fair Rosalind... I love you... my perfect, brave, strong and beautiful ki'ara. Be mine forever."

She wrinkled her nose. "Forever. I like the sound of that."

"It is ours, Ki'ara." He pressed a kiss to the tip of her nose and she smiled up at him, her blue eyes sparkling with stars.

She tunnelled her fingers into his hair, brushing the points of his ears and sending a hot shiver down his spine, and slowly drew him back down to her, a playful smile teasing her lips.

"I will be yours, Vail, because I love you... my perfect, courageous, powerful and handsome elf prince." She pulled him closer still, until their lips brushed as she spoke in a low whisper, tormenting him and making him ache to kiss her. "What was it you said before, back in the woods after we shared blood? Mine now."

He growled and finished it for her before seizing her lips in a kiss that relayed every drop of his love for her.

A love that would never die.

"Mine forever."

The End

ABOUT THE AUTHOR

Felicity Heaton is a New York Times and USA Today best-selling author who writes passionate paranormal romance books. In her books she creates detailed worlds, twisting plots, mind-blowing action, intense emotion and heart-stopping romances with leading men that vary from dark deadly vampires to sexy shape-shifters and wicked werewolves, to sinful angels and hot demons!

If you're a fan of paranormal romance authors Lara Adrian, J R Ward, Sherrilyn Kenyon, Gena Showalter, Larissa Ione and Christine Feehan then you will enjoy her books too.

If you love your angels a little dark and wicked, the best-selling Her Angel series is for you. If you like strong, powerful, and dark vampires then try the Vampires Realm series or any of her stand-alone vampire romance books. If you're looking for vampire romances that are sinful, passionate and erotic then try the best-selling Vampire Erotic Theatre series. Or if you prefer huge detailed worlds filled with hot-blooded alpha males in every species, from elves to demons to dragons to shifters and angels, then take a look at the new Eternal Mates series.

If you have enjoyed this story, please take a moment to contact the author at **author@felicityheaton.co.uk** or to post a review of the book online

Connect with Felicity:
Website – http://www.felicityheaton.co.uk
Blog – http://www.felicityheaton.co.uk/blog/
Twitter – http://twitter.com/felicityheaton
Facebook – http://www.facebook.com/felicityheaton
Goodreads – http://www.goodreads.com/felicityheaton
Mailing List – http://www.felicityheaton.co.uk/newsletter.php

FIND OUT MORE ABOUT HER BOOKS AT:
http://www.felicityheaton.co.uk

42156491R00156

Made in the USA
Lexington, KY
10 June 2015